DIAMONDS IN DANBY WALK

If Ralph Jackson had not been selfishly intent on an afternoon's stolen pleasure with his East End mistress Clara that day in 1900, a great many lives would have been different—most notably that of Amy Atkins, Clara's skinny young niece. Her hard-working but penniless father George wants a better start for her than the mean streets of Bethnal Green, and if he has to resort to a spot of blackmail to get it, so be it. For fear of his philandering ways coming to the notice of his rapier-tongued wife, Ralph Jackson offers Amy a job at his smart West London jewellers. Later, Ralph's handsome son Clifford secretly begins to pay court to her. But when one thing inevitably leads to another, weak-willed Clifford is quite happy to leave Amy holding the baby. He has, however, reckoned without the powerful influence that George Atkins still exerts over Ralph. An amazed Amy finds herself Mrs Clifford Jackson, but even love and gratitude do not blind her to her husband's weaknesses, and when tragedy strikes she is faced with some difficult choices...

DIAMONDS IN DANBY WALK

Pamela Evans

CHIVERS PRESS
BATH

First Published 1992
by
Headline Book Publishing plc
This Large Print edition published by
Chivers Press
by arrangement with
Headline Book Publishing Limited
1996

ISBN 0 7451 7962 2

British Library Cataloguing in Publication Data available

F
415167

Photoset, printed and bound in Great Britain by
REDWOOD BOOKS, Trowbridge, Wiltshire

To Camilla with love

DIAMONDS IN DANBY WALK

CHAPTER ONE

Had Ralph Jackson known of the serious, long-term consequences of his determination to commit adultery on that bitter winter's day in 1900, he would undoubtedly have accepted the fact that he was in no fit state to go gallivanting across London, and curled up in bed with a hot-water bottle.

But he was a man of commercial talent rather than prophecy, with a thriving business to his credit, and he was damned if he was going to let a few aches and pains interfere with his love life. The current influenza epidemic might well be creating a boom for undertakers, but it suited him this morning to believe that what ailed him was nothing more serious than the beginnings of a common cold.

Breakfast was progressing ordinarily enough in the Jackson household. Ralph and his wife Florence were seated at the table in the maple-floored dining-room of their fine suburban home. The room was well-appointed, with reproduction Jacobean furniture in dark polished wood and heavily patterned wallpaper, most of which was covered with pictures and family photographs. A fire crackled cosily in the hearth which was surrounded by an ornate, wood-carved mantel littered with expensive ornaments and vases, boldly displayed to show the family's wealth and good taste.

Florence, whose ample proportions were rigidly confined by boned and laced corsets beneath her high-necked day dress, observed her husband with mild curiosity as she daintily stirred her coffee. 'Are you feeling quite well this morning, Ralph dear?' she asked, her brown eyes lingering on him quizzically. 'You look a bit peaky. I do hope you're not about to go down with this dreadful influenza that so many people are catching.'

'I'm perfectly all right, thank you, my dear,' he lied smoothly, struggling not to wince with the pain of swallowing. Even Ralph, who was not normally sensitive to life's ironies, could see fate mocking him on this occasion. For it was not in his nature to suffer in silence, and had he had less interesting 'business' to attend to, he would have welcomed the opportunity to retire to bed, to be pampered and plied with hot milk lavishly laced with whisky. But today was earmarked for clandestine pleasure with a woman as different to his wife as beef broth was to vanilla soufflé. The fiction continued to flow from his lips with practised ease. 'And it's just as well I am, as I have important business to attend to in Hatton Garden today. I will leave the shop around mid-morning and travel into the city by train, so Marshall and the carriage will be at your disposal for the rest of the day.'

'Thank you, dear.' Satisfied that her husband was, after all, in good health, Florence sipped her coffee and mulled over her choice of apparel for today's social events. Perhaps the blue velvet dress for her luncheon engagement at the riverside home of a friend in Chiswick, she thought, and the lilac with the embroidered bodice to entertain guests for tea this afternoon here at Floral House. In her mid-forties, Florence was a plain-featured woman who wore her greyish-brown hair piled high on top of her round face which was habitually set in an expression somewhere between complacency and hauteur. 'It will be cold and draughty for you on the train,

2

though, on such a chilly morning.'

'I don't doubt it,' he said, his deepset grey eyes lack-lustre, plump cheeks stained with a feverish flush. The sandy-coloured hair on the crown of his head had thinned more noticeably than his bushy side whiskers, giving his face an egg-shaped look. 'But it's simpler to take the train. The traffic in central London is something appalling these days with more of these new-fangled motor cars coming on to the roads. Damned things should be banned, the way they upset the horses with their noise and poisonous fumes.'

'Quite so,' she agreed to appease him, though that particular invention had not affected her unduly, for motor cars were still rare on the roads of Ealing. 'Shall I send Marshall to the station to meet you with the carriage this evening?'

'No, I'll walk or take a cab to save him the trouble,' he said, sipping some coffee to try to ease his sore throat, 'I'm not sure which train I shall catch.'

'As you wish,' she said, glad that she had such a considerate husband.

In fact, Ralph was being artful rather than altruistic. He didn't want his afternoon ruined by clockwatching. Nor did he want his coachman to get a hint of what he was up to, which was why he always took the train when he made his illicit trips to the East End.

To a man like Ralph, who had firmly established his place in the middle classes through his jewellery business, and whose happiness was measured solely in terms of material wealth and social standing, a mistress was a symbol of success, like having servants and his own carriage, albeit she could not be flaunted in the same way. It did not diminish the importance

3

of his marriage in the least. Florence, who was his age, was a most suitable wife. The daughter of a small-time grocer, she shared her husband's enjoyment of a higher social status, and had refined her manners to match their position as it had ascended over the years. She was respectable, faithful and practical. She ran their home with maximum efficiency and did not concern herself with his life outside their front door. She had never been a warm or passionate woman, but since he had made other arrangements in that department, he wasn't unduly bothered.

He saw his liaison as the spice to brighten the boredom of everyday life. The blatant beauty and bold personality of his mistress created a balance with Florence's staid matronliness. It made him feel young and dashing and assured him that he was still attractive to the opposite sex. And, with discretion, he saw no reason why the affair should not continue indefinitely. Discretion being the operative word, in the interests of domestic harmony.

'Why are the children not at the table?' he asked accusingly, as though their absence was entirely his wife's fault.

'They'll be down in a minute, I expect,' she said with the bland indifference of habit.

'It's time Clifford was up and about if he wants anything to eat before we leave for the shop.' He sipped his coffee, his free hand pulling his fob-watch from his waistcoat pocket. He consulted it, frowning. Breakfast was the only meal of the day at which he allowed a modicum of flexibility, and that was only because he had heard that the aristocracy adopted a lax attitude towards it. 'And where's Gwen? She'll be late for school. Have they been called?'

4

'Yes, of course they have. Violet took their hot water up to them some time ago.' Floral House, which was named from the first three letters of both their names, was one of the few properties around benefiting from a built-in bathroom and wash basins in the bedrooms. But, in common with many other dwellings, it lacked a hot water system which meant that the servants had to carry it up from the kitchen in cans and jugs. 'Do stop fussing, dear, and eat your breakfast. They'll be down at any moment.'

And a few minutes later the door opened and seventeen-year-old Clifford swept in, followed by his sister Gwen who was three years younger.

'Good morning Father. Good morning Mother,' said Clifford exuberantly, throwing a dutiful glance in his father's direction and brushing his mother's cheek with a kiss before strolling to the sideboard and helping himself to a hearty portion of bacon, kidneys, tomatoes and eggs from the silver tureens. Though only in the incipient stages of manhood, he was noticeably handsome with a fine straight nose and fair hair worn fashionably short with a middle parting. Thick lashes of a length to inspire envy in any woman fringed his hazel eyes, and his mouth was well shaped and attractive despite a tendency to weakness. Like his father he was dressed in a formal business suit with waistcoat and high stiff collar and tie. In keeping with the fashion for a young man-about-town, he was clean-shaven. 'Mushrooms! Good-o, I'm starving.'

Gwen, a weighty adolescent with docile brown eyes, greeted her parents with less ebullience, for she never had so much to say for herself as her gregarious brother. She followed him to the sideboard, her puppy fat emphasised by the shapeless brown frock

5

which was customary attire for the pupils of the Mary Miller School for Girls, an elite establishment to which the crème de la crème of West London sent their daughters.

When his offspring had settled themselves on the high-backed carved chairs, Ralph said, 'I won't be in the shop this afternoon, Clifford, so I shall expect you to keep an eye on things. Mr Rawlings is the senior assistant, it's true, but you are family and therefore above him. You must make sure the staff keep their place, what with the dratted trade unions giving them ideas above their station. Damned socialists! All this talk about having a Labour group in Parliament only unsettles the working classes into thinking they are entitled to more than they actually are. It's them and us, Clifford, and they must not be allowed to forget it when I'm not around to remind them.'

'You can rely on me, Father,' said Clifford absently, for his social life by far outweighed business interests and he was still thinking about the colour and glamour of a musical comedy he'd seen the night before in the West End. It was useful being able to hop on a train to town without involving Marshall, but one was subject to railway timetables and Clifford had a mind to improve matters in that direction.

'Percy Grover's father has bought a motor car,' he announced, deliberately sowing the seeds of discontent in his pater. 'A real beauty, a Rover twelve horse-power.'

'Has he indeed?' This snippet of gossip about the family who lived in an impressive house at the far end of Orchard Avenue annoyed Ralph intensely because he couldn't bear to be outdone by his neighbours. I

6

mean, what was Edward Grover anyway but a glorified draper, even if his store was the largest in Ealing and had various departments. Who did he do business with but the hoi-polloi of the town who went to him for dishcloths and bedsocks? He had none of the prestige of a jeweller, patronised only by those in the very highest echelons of society.

'It might be a good idea for us to get one before very long, eh, Father?' suggested Clifford hopefully.

'Dreadful things, motor cars,' barked Ralph, whose opposition to the machine stemmed from the fact that it was fashionable to dislike motorists because of the noise and pollution they caused. The prestige of car ownership was desirable indeed, but not if it was going to harm his reputation as a respectable and considerate citizen. 'All they do is break down and belch out horrible smoke. Personally, I wouldn't be seen dead in one.'

'Mr Grover is enjoying his, I think.'

'Humph. He won't be popular with the neighbours, I can tell you.'

'Some people say we shall have to get used to motor cars because they will eventually replace the horse altogether,' said Clifford, tucking into his food with gusto.

'Nonsense,' snapped Ralph, who didn't like the way the day was progressing at all. First of all nature had conspired against him to make him feel ill when he needed to feel well, and now some upstart of a neighbour had upstaged him by becoming the first car owner in the avenue. That was the trouble with new inventions—one had to acquire them or be made to feel inferior by one's peers. 'You shouldn't listen to the fools who talk such rot.'

7

'I don't think it's rot,' said Clifford, who even as a small boy had turned convention on its head by making himself very much heard as well as seen. 'It makes sense, when you think about it. I mean, look at all the changes that have come about in Queen Victoria's reign. The railways, for instance, and the telephone, and when you think that we even have electric street lighting in Ealing Broadway now instead of gas...'

Ralph's brow furrowed. Education was all right up to a point, but it gave children the idea they were smarter than their parents. 'You're talking rubbish, my boy,' he blustered. 'The horse will never be replaced.'

'Motor cars are very expensive, of course,' continued Clifford, aiming at his father's most vulnerable spot, 'but I suppose the Grovers can afford it.'

'I hope you are not suggesting that a man who sells drapery for a living is better off than me,' Ralph snorted.

'Of course not, Father,' said Clifford artfully. 'But he can't be badly off to have bought a car, can he? And that's not all. Percy was saying that his father is thinking of having a telephone installed in his shop quite soon.'

That was definitely the last straw. Ralph needed to leave this house before anything else happened to threaten his self-esteem. Thank God he was due for a boost to his ego later on. Being with someone of a socially inferior class meant never having to try to go one better. It was wonderfully relaxing. 'Hurry up and finish your breakfast, both of you,' he boomed at son and daughter.

'Yes, Father,' said Gwen obediently.

8

Clifford simply got on with his food without comment.

*   *   *

The rooftops and privet hedges were white with frost as Ralph and his children rolled along Orchard Avenue in the carriage towards Gwen's school in Hanger Lane. Ralph surveyed the scene through the window with satisfaction, his customary feeling of pride diminished only by the debilitating symptoms of his ailment. Hard work and good judgement had bought him a house in this salubrious avenue in the very best part of Ealing.

For many years he'd been in partnership with Harold Cox, and had no doubt whatever that teaming up had been the wisest move he had ever made. Ralph was the son of a pawnbroker from Shepherds Bush. Harold's father had been a watchmaker in the same area. The two boys had been schoolfriends. When Ralph had inherited the family business from his father over twenty years ago, he had sought a change of course, having seen the commercial viability of jewellery retailing from his experience in the pawnshop. When Harold's father had died, leaving him with a run-down watchmaking business, Harold had seized the opportunity to join forces with Ralph because he lacked the other man's confidence and needed a partner to lean on. They had changed the dismal watchmaker's premises into a stylish jeweller's shop and it wasn't long before they were doing well enough to open another branch.

Prosperous Ealing had been the obvious choice of district, with its growing population drawn from the middle classes whose wallets were bulging with

9

money they were only too eager to spend. The less adventurous Harold hadn't wanted a change of area, but Ralph had jumped at the chance of a move to the Queen of the Suburbs. He and his family had lived in a modest house at first, moving to one of the more impressive homes in Orchard Avenue as soon as they could afford it.

The partnership continued to work well to this day. Harold looked after their interests in Shepherd's Bush, with the help of his son, Ned, while Ralph ran things in Ealing's prestigious Danby Walk, with Clifford who was learning the business. Both Ralph and Harold had agreed to take their sons into the business legally at twenty-five by means of each partner transferring a proportion of his shares to his own offspring.

Ralph turned his attention back to the scene through the window. Situated to the north of the town, Orchard Avenue was lined with horse chestnut trees on wide grass verges. Built some fifteen years ago on land that had hitherto been the country estates of the aristocracy, the 'high class villas' were all detached with good-sized grounds and stabling facilities, for most of the residents kept their own carriages.

Errand boys with bicycles and carts were out in force this morning for the owners of these houses were a shopkeeper's dream, living lavishly as they did. Large quantities of bread, milk, greengroceries and meat were being deposited into the safe keeping of cooks and servant girls in well-organised kitchens, out of sight of their employers. The street reverberated to the clip-clop of horses' hooves, the rumble of carriage wheels and the chirpy whistling of the delivery boys.

Turning into Hanger Lane the ambience became quieter and more rural, the bare trees arching overhead beneath heavy grey skies, the gaps in the hedges showing fields suffused with white. Depositing Gwen at the gates of her school, a one-time country mansion standing in large grounds, Marshall turned the carriage back towards Ealing Broadway.

Approaching the District Railway Station, plastered with posters advertising 'reduced fares to the city', Ralph's poor aching head was buffeted by an increase in street noise as the pace of life quickened. Here the pavements were thronged with people. Men in dark city suits poured into the station; shoppers hurried towards the stores, heads down against the cold, the women's coats brushing the ground. The newsboy's placard bore the announcement of a new chief for the army in the Boer War. A row of horse-drawn cabs were lined up opposite the station under the leafless trees that edged Haven Green.

Coming into the Broadway with its smart stores and elaborate buildings, they turned left and drew up outside Jackson & Cox in a promenade of high-class shops lined with plane trees. The main road was crowded with horsedrawn carts, carriages and cabs. A horse bus rolled by, boldly extolling the virtues of Nestlé's Milk. The faces beneath the top hats and bowlers on the open upper deck were screwed up with the cold, and the driver's legs were wrapped in a blanket.

Ralph had just alighted from the carriage when his mood was depressed further by the grinding roar of a motor car passing by. A figure whom Ralph assumed to be Edward Grover, though he was barely

11

recognisable in goggles, tied-on hat, heavy coat and leather gloves, waved triumphantly from the driver's seat. Ralph raised a reluctant hand and forced a smile. 'You'd think he'd do the job properly and have a chauffeur, wouldn't you?' he grumbled to Clifford, as they walked towards the shop.

'I expect he's enjoying driving himself,' said his son. 'They say it's awfully good fun.'

Clifford walked on, smiling, a striking figure in his dark overcoat and Homburg hat. He was confident that he would be at the wheel of the family car at sometime in the near future. Father wouldn't be able to resist getting one when a few more of the neighbours began to travel in style. Clifford also knew that when they did get a car it would be the smartest, most expensive one around. What a dash he would cut with the girls then! Ah, but it was good to be young and rich at the dawn of the new century.

Walking towards the shop, Ralph was shivering uncontrollably, his limbs throbbing with a persistent ache. Thank goodness he was taking most of the day off. He'd do only what was absolutely necessary at the shop, then make his way round the corner to the station as quickly as possible. Once he was with Clara, he would forget all about this wretched cold of his.

*   *   *

Dusk was falling in Bethnal Green. The yellow glow of an oil-lamp lit the second-hand stall outside the butcher's shop in Green Street where young Amy Atkins was working. Market barrows lined the pavement for as far as the eye could see. Fruit; flowers; vegetables; sweets; fish; cakes; old clothes;

pets, were all on offer here, the stall-lanterns creating a cheerful radiance in the sooty air. Crowds coughed and chatted and haggled with traders. Horse traffic rattled by on the muddy road, the spray of dirt and horse dung lessened by the fact that it was frozen hard in places.

The penetrating cold coupled with an empty stomach was making Amy feel sick and faint. She breathed in the smell of pease pudding and saveloys from the butcher's shop as though this might somehow give her sustenance. Feeling ill with cold and hunger was nothing new to her. In fact she usually felt like this when she was working at the stall, which was every day after school for a couple of hours while the stallholder, Mabel, took a break. Saturdays Amy was here all day working alongside Mabel. For this she was paid twopence a session and sixpence on Saturdays which her mother relied on to help feed the family of four children.

'How much is that bird, love?' asked a man with straggly ginger hair and a battered trilby hat, pointing to a hideous stuffed owl with sad staring eyes that made Amy want to weep with pity every time she looked at it.

'Sixpence,' she said, managing a friendly smile despite her personal discomfort. Her painfully thin frame was wrapped in a black shawl which she wore over a grey flannel frock, holey woollen stockings and boots with the toes worn through.

'It ain't worth that much,' he said, a bargaining gleam in his eye.

'That's the price, mister,' she said cheerfully. 'And I won't take anything less.'

'Daylight robbery.'

'No, it ain't! It's a good quality bird,' she told him,

13

accepting his remark without offence since it was all part of the job. 'I bet yer it won't be 'ere tomorrow. So if you wannit, you'd better snap it up quick.'

'I'll give yer threepence for it,' he said.

'Fivepence,' she countered.

'Fourpence.'

'Fourpence-ha' penny.'

'Fourpence-farthing, and that's me last offer.'

'All right, mister, you've twisted me arm,' she said, grinning and handing the poor deceased creature to him in its glass case. 'You'd be doing it a kindness if you buried it rather than putting it on show, I reckon. The poor thing looks as miserable as sin stuck on that perch. When things is dead, they want putting to rest.'

The man laughed. 'I want it for the missus. She thinks this sort of thing looks classy in the parlour. All the nobs 'ave em.'

'Oh, well, what can you expect from that lot?' laughed Amy.

'You waited till I said I'd 'ave it before telling me you don't like it, I notice.'

'Course I did,' she grinned. 'I ain't daft.'

'You've got some cheek for a little un.'

'You need it when you work in a market.'

He handed her his money with a grin, for he found her chirpy frankness rather endearing. 'Mmm, I daresay you do.'

The soot-filled air had darkened her skin as well as the naturally fair hair that poked from beneath her smutty straw hat. But she had a sparkle about her for all that, her perky little face dominated by round blue eyes that still managed to shine despite the fact that she was underweight, undernourished and dirty. Poverty had made her defensive; an active mind had

14

tempered that with defiance. She knew a system that allowed people to starve while others made gluttons of themselves couldn't be right, even if it was the accepted way of things. She listened to what adults said, she noticed what went on around her. She might not have travelled far from the East End but she'd been up West a few times. She'd seen how the other half lived.

'Whoever runs this stall has got a treasure in you,' he said.

'I only 'elp out after school.'

'Still at school, eh?'

She nodded. 'I'm leaving soon though.'

'Will you work here all the time then?'

'No, Mabel can't afford a full-time assistant.'

'Oh, well, you'll find something, a bright gel like you,' he said. 'Tata, ducks.'

'Tata, mister.'

A flurry of business occupied her thoughts for a while. She sold a chipped vase, a tarnished pocket watch, a woman's coat and a pair of men's shoes. She turned a blind eye to a street urchin stealing an apple from the fruit barrow next to hers. The poor soul looked as though he needed it.

Two rough-looking boys of about her own age swaggered up to her stall. 'I fancy that picture, don't you, Tommy?' said one of them, pushing his greasy checked cap back from his brow jauntily and pointing towards a framed landscape at the back of the stall.

'Yeah, that's a bit of all right, I reckon.'

''ow much is it?' asked Greasy Cap.

'Sevenpence,' said Amy.

'It'll look nice on the wall in your 'ouse,' said Tommy, as though Amy hadn't spoken.

15

'Sevenpence,' she repeated, her stomach churning as she sensed trouble.

Greasy Cap, who was a thin, spotty individual with dark sullen eyes and matted hair sticking out from under his cap, gave Amy a lazy smile. 'Talk sense, gel, where would we get that sort of dosh?'

'I dunno,' she said, guessing that a spot of friendly haggling wasn't what these two had in mind. 'But without it you don't get the picture.'

He took a furtive look to either side of him. 'Oh, yeah, and who's gonna stop us from taking it?'

'I am,' she stated categorically. One cry from her and any number of traders would rush to her side, but she'd only call for help as a last resort. These toe-rags needed to know she wasn't afraid of them or they'd come back again and again to torment her whenever she was here alone. They certainly wouldn't dare while the awesome Mabel was around.

'Did yer 'ear that, Tommy?' sneered Greasy Cap. 'She's gonna stop us. Ain't that a scream?'

'Funniest thing I've 'eard all day,' said Tommy.

As Greasy Cap's grimy hand snaked across the goods towards the picture, Amy reached under the stall. In a matter of seconds the riding whip that was kept there for just such emergencies came down across his fingers with such a swipe he moved back, yelping and clutching his hand to his chest.

'Why, you little bitch!' he rasped, through gritted teeth, his eyes narrowed on her venomously.

'Like I said, the picture is sevenpence,' she said. 'So clear off unless you're gonna pay it.'

After hurling some strong abuse at her, the boys moved away into the crowd. She was used to dealing with bullies like them. You had to stand up for yourself on the streets of Bethnal Green or louts like that terrorised you.

A stout, toothless old woman in a dirty grey coat and a black straw hat with a feather in it appeared, smoking a pipe. 'Everythin' all right, ducks?' asked Mabel, back from her break.

'Yeah, everything's fine,' said Amy, giving her employer a brief account of what had happened while she'd been away, including the incident with the boys.

'Little buggers,' growled Mabel, in a voice made husky by too much strong tobacco. 'Still, it sounds as though you sorted them out good and proper.'

'I sold that horrible stuffed owl an' all,' said Amy.

'Thank Gawd for that,' said Mabel with a raucous laugh. 'They say there's one born every minute.'

Amy shivered and hugged her shawl around her.

'You'd better get off 'ome for your tea,' said Mabel, handing the girl the two pennies she'd earned.

'Ta, Mabel.'

'See you tomorrow, ducks.'

'Yeah. Tata, Mabel.'

The young girl jostled her way through the crowds, feeling the warmth and vigour of street life throbbing around her, for a strong, recalcitrant spirit prevailed among the local people despite their crippling poverty. She passed barrows and buskers, tramps and rogues, and ordinary housewives out buying something cheap for tea. She passed the pie shop, the faggot shop, the Jew's shop, the pawn shop, and stood gazing wistfully for a few moments at the glass jars in the sweet-shop window. Her hand closed over the two pennies in her frock pocket, her mouth watering at the thought of a ha'porth of acid drops. But her money was all accounted for. Her mother would be waiting for her to get home with it to send

17

her out for some bread and marge for tea.

At the corner of the street a horse-drawn tram rattled by and there was a log jam of other traffic. As she waited to cross the road, the conversation she had had with the stuffed-owl buyer came back into her mind. Amy was not given to despair, she saw no point in it, but she did find herself anxious at the thought of the changes imminent in her life. In three months' time, at Easter, she would leave school and go into full-time employment. This saddened her because she enjoyed lessons and the teachers said she was quick to learn. She was good at sums and everyone said she was the best in the class at drawing.

But it was no use wishing for the impossible. Girls like her couldn't stay on; their parents needed them to be earning. Most of her friends were planning to go into domestic service, but she didn't fancy that. She was hoping to get a job in a shop. In the big stores the staff lived in, she'd heard. You got regular meals, too, by all accounts. If she did manage to get herself fixed up, at least it would be one less mouth for her parents to feed, which would help them considerably since she would expect to hand over part of her wages to them whether she lived at home or not.

Whether it was because she was cold, hungry and tired, she didn't know, but for a split second she was overwhelmed with a feeling of panic. It was as though she didn't feel ready to go out into the world alone to earn a living yet, which was really quite ridiculous considering the fact that her thirteenth birthday was almost upon her. The traffic cleared and she hurried on her way, admonishing herself for having such childish doubts which wasn't like her at all.

Making her way home through the narrow cobbled backstreets, the gaslit streetlamps shone eerily on dark, dirty buildings with broken windows and open doors exuding repulsive smells, which rose above the ever present stench of horse dung, bad drainage and inadequate sanitation. The sounds of screaming babies and quarrelling adults filled the air. Even in the freezing weather women stood at their doors gossiping, with babies at the breast or squirming against their shoulders. Children kicked and shuffled at their games, the boys scrapping and squabbling, the girls giggling and squealing.

Passing the burial ground near the workhouse, it was quieter and full of black, shadowy corners out of the range of the streetlights. Deep in thought, she hurried on, her shawl drawn tightly around her, her toes and fingers aching with the cold. She was startled when two figures stepped out of the shadows and blocked her path.

'What do yer want?' she asked, her heart racing with fear as she recognised Greasy Cap and his mate.

'Yer didn't really think you'd seen the last of us, did yer?' said one of them.

'Get out of my way,' said Amy, trying to push past them.

'Not until we're good and ready,' said Tommy.

'We don't like being made to look stupid,' said Greasy Cap.

'You shouldn't act stupid then, should you?' riposted Amy, determined not to let them see how unnerved she was. But it was one thing confronting them in a busy market street with a whip in her hand, and quite another meeting them unarmed in a deserted corner like this. 'Now get out of my way!'

'We've been thinkin',' said Greasy Cap, grabbing her arm roughly.

'Blimey, you'll give yourselves an 'eadache,' said

19

Amy, retaining a bold front.

'We've been thinkin',' he repeated, ignoring her gibe, 'that if yer goes to work, yer gets paid, so come on, let's have yer wages.'

'I don't get paid till the end of the week,' she lied desperately, for there would be terrible ructions at home if she arrived without her precious twopence.

'Don't give us that,' said Tommy. 'Casual labour is always paid cash in 'and.'

'Well, I ain't bin paid and that's that,' bluffed Amy.

'Come on, 'and it over,' said Greasy Cap. And as he grabbed her by both arms, Tommy went for her pocket, speedily removing the two pennies.

'Give it back,' she screamed, kicking him on the shins and causing him to drop the coins.

'Why, you little cow . . .'

'It's all right, Tommy, I've got it,' said his friend, gleefully picking up the money and tormenting her by holding it close to her face.

'Give it back,' Amy gasped again, wriggling and writhing to free herself as Tommy grabbed her, bruising her upper arms.

'You 'eard what she said,' said a sudden voice, and a newcomer appeared on the scene, a dark-haired boy of Amy's age dressed in ragged clothes. 'So give it back to 'er, sharpish.'

'Bernie,' gasped Amy, relieved to see one of her best friends.

The louts were startled by the new arrival into letting her go. And that gave Amy the chance to lay into Tommy while Bernie grabbed the boy with the money and forced him against a wall until he let the pennies drop.

'Clear off out of it,' Bernie ordered, his dark eyes

flashing. 'And don't you come near 'er again.'

And despite the fact that they were two boys against one, Tommy and Greasy Cap scuttled away, because Bernie Banks had learned at a very early age how to defend himself on the streets of the East End. His confidence by far outweighed his physical strength because he was no bigger or fitter than them, but by creating an impression of brawn by sheer bravado, he was already a powerful force among the youth of the area.

'Thanks, Bernie,' said Amy, as he handed her the pennies.

'Are you all right?' he asked.

'Yeah, I'm all right,' she said, rubbing her arm. 'A bit sore where 'e grabbed me, but as long as I've got me money back, I ain't worried. There would have bin hell to pay at home if I'd arrived without it.'

'I know what yer mean,' he said. 'You should have 'eard my old man the other day when I lost a threepenny bit through an 'ole in me pocket.'

'I did 'ear him.'

He laughed because he and Amy lived in the same tenement house which didn't have very thick walls. One family's quarrels provided entertainment for all the others. 'I suppose you would have done.'

'Lucky you came along just now.'

'Yeah, I'm just on me way 'ome.'

'You bin working?' she asked.

'Yeah, bin doin' a round for the carbolic man.'

Bernie did a number of jobs outside school hours, delivering and selling round the houses for local traders, including the baker, the milkman, and the cat's meat man. Amy had heard her father say that Bernie was up to all sorts of fiddles on his rounds, and there were rumours that he watered the carbolic down and pocketed the extra takings. She wouldn't be surprised if it was true for it was common knowledge that his slovenly parents relied on Bernie's earnings. His unemployed father never searched too hard for work and the younger children looked to their elder brother for their daily bread.

Amy had known him all her life and there was only a matter of a few weeks' difference in their ages. Even before the two families had come to live in the same house, they had resided in the same street. Families like the Atkins and the Banks, who fell behind with the rent, moved around a lot but rarely out of the area. People said that you had to watch your pockets when Bernie was about. Maybe they were right. But he looked after his own and that included friends as well as family. Whatever his faults, Amy regarded him as a true pal and knew he would never do anything to hurt her.

They began walking home, chatting companionably. 'I've bin thinking about what I'm gonna do when I leave school,' she said.

'Have yer? And did yer come up with any ideas?'

'I think I'll try to get a job in a shop.'

'Good idea,' he said. 'Better than skivvying.'

'What are you going to do when you leave, Bernie?'

'I'm gonna make money,' he stated categorically.

'Doing what?'

'Oh, a bit of this and a bit of that. Business, yer know.'

'Perhaps you might be able to get a regular job,' she suggested wisely.

'No thanks,' he said. 'I wouldn't want one even if there were any.'

'Why not, if it pays steady money?'

22

'Not excitin' enough for me,' he declared. 'Anyway, there ain't enough dough in steady work. I ain't gonna be like me dad, skint every day of me life.'

'But that's only because he doesn't have steady work,' she pointed out.

'Yeah, I s'pose so,' he agreed. 'But it ain't what I want. I don't wanna be shut up in some factory all day to earn a crust.'

'It's better than starvin'.'

'I'll never starve, Amy,' he said with a gleam in his eye. 'Not while I've got a brain in me 'ead.'

'Mmm, I can believe that.'

'But I wanna do more than just have enough to eat,' he said. 'Money is power. If you're rich, nothing can hurt yer.'

'But how can someone like you get rich?' she asked. 'It's as much as most of the people round 'ere can do to live from day to day.'

'There are ways, if you've got your 'ead screwed on.' They turned into Tucker Street, a narrow road with broken paving stones and dingy buildings closing in from either side. Damaged front doors opened directly on to the street. The bitter smell of the nearby canal hung damply in the air. Children played around the gaslamps and sat in the kerb. 'I ain't gonna spend the rest of me life in a dump like this, I know that much.'

'Money ain't everything,' she reminded him.

'Oh, but it *is*, Amy. It *is*.'

'You be careful, Bernie,' she said, bothered by his attitude.

'Don't worry about me,' he said, as they reached the front door of number twenty-three and turned to go in, 'I'm a survivor.'

'I know that,' she said. 'It's the way you plan to

survive that bothers me.'

He gave her a wicked grin. 'I'll get by.'

And she didn't doubt it. She just hoped he didn't get into too much trouble along the way.

CHAPTER TWO

Amy's mother Gladys was her usual harassed self when Amy entered the living room. One-year-old Bobby was yelling in his mother's arms; two-year-old Pete had gashed his leg on a broken chair and was snivelling for attention against her skirts; and if that cacophony was not enough, ten-year-old Alfie was being stridently rebuked for coming home from school with a black eye.

'Thank Gawd you're 'ome, Amy,' said Gladys. 'These kids are drivin' me mad.'

'Never mind, Mum, I'm 'ere now to 'elp out,' she said brightly, pleased to be home for all its chaos. She hung her shawl on a hook on the door and grinned at the children. 'And they'll be good now, won't yer, kids?'

'It's just bin one of those days,' Gladys continued wearily. 'The baby's got the belly ache, Billy's leg is pourin' with blood, and Alfie's bin fightin' again.'

A fairly average day then, Amy thought wryly, but said sympathetically, 'Oh dear.'

'I've told Alfie till I'm blue in the face that he's gotta stop all this fightin',' said Gladys. 'I mean, it ain't right for 'im to go about punchin' every poor kid who upsets 'im, is it, Amy? You tell 'im, 'e might listen to you.'

Her mother's comments were not without

24

exaggeration, for Alfie didn't use muscle on *everyone* who annoyed him, but it was true to say that he was partial to a regular spot of fisticuffs.

'I couldn't 'elp it, sis,' protested Alfie, a round-faced urchin with the same fair hair and laughing blue eyes as his sister. 'This big boy in the playground was tormenting a little kid who ain't all there and can't stick up for himself. I had to thump that bully to stop him at it, didn't I?'

Amy put her hard-earned twopence into an empty jam-jar on the mantelpiece and turned to her mother. 'If he was defendin' someone else, maybe we shouldn't be too 'ard on 'im, eh, Mum?' she suggested, winking at Alfie whom she loved for his charitable fearlessness which got him into so many scrapes.

'He shouldn't be so quick with his fists, whatever the reason.' Gladys turned her attention to the limpet attached to her skirt. 'See to Pete's leg, will yer, Amy, while I try and find a clean nappy for the baby. The poor little mite 'as got the runs.'

The girl scooped up her soggy little brother who seemed to be leaking from every possible source. His nose was running, his cheeks soaked with tears and his trousers suspiciously moist. She sat him on the wooden table and wiped his face. Then she went to get some cold water from the bucket in the corner, pouring some into an enamel bowl which the family used for washing a variety of items including themselves. There was one water tap in the backyard to serve the three families resident in the house, and a shared outside lavatory. The dilapidated terraced property comprised three floors with two rooms on each. The Dobbs lived downstairs, the Banks upstairs and the Atkins in the middle. They had this

25

room, a bedroom adjoining, and the use of a washing copper and mangle in a lean-to scullery in the backyard.

'You got anythin' I can use as a bandage for Pete's leg, Mum?' asked Amy, having cleaned the cut as best she could with icy cold water and a well-used face flannel. 'He'll need somethin' on it to soak up the blood.'

Gladys went into the bedroom, returning with a strip of old bedsheet which she handed to Amy. She disappeared into the bedroom again for a few minutes, and re-emerged without the baby but carrying the soiled napkin which she scraped on to the fire which could barely be seen for the steaming washing hanging around it on the fireguard. She dropped the soiled article into a separate bucket to soak. 'It won't hurt the baby to stay in his cot for a minute. He's worn me out today with 'is bloomin' 'ollering. It sets my nerves all on edge.'

Having bandaged Pete's leg, Amy gave him a comforting hug and lifted him down on to the bare floorboards. 'Got anything to eat, Mum?' she asked, without any real hope. 'I ain't 'alf 'ungry.'

'Afraid not, love, not until you go down to the shops to get somethin',' Gladys said predictably. 'I've got a bit o' tea, though, so we can have a cuppa before you go, if yer like.' She frowned and drew in her breath tensely as the woeful sounds from the other room persisted. 'Put the kettle on, will yer? I'll have to try and do somethin' about that poor child. He's got the gripes good and proper.'

Amy filled the kettle from the bucket and put it on the hob in the fireplace to boil, moving the fireguard back so that they could see the coals while they drank their tea. She set chipped mugs out for them all on the

26

table, her glance moving around the room which was damp and smoky with mouldy black patches staining the walls. The unwholesome tang of an earlier day's mutton stew lingered in the air. A palace it certainly was not, but at least her mother tried to make it into a home with a plethora of brightly coloured nick-nacks which always seemed to be covered with a layer of soot despite her regular dusting. The furniture was basic and broken: a few hard chairs, a table, an old sideboard. The mantelshelf was draped with a brown plush cloth with tasselled edging, upon which stood a miscellany of market-stall pots and vases.

She made the tea and called to her mother, who came back into the room with the baby and sank on to a chair by the fire with him on her lap. Alfie and Pete sat on the floor at her feet and Amy perched on a hard chair next to her mother. While they were drinking their tea, the baby's screams subsided at last.

'So 'ow did you get on today, Amy?' her mother asked at last, because she was not uncaring of her daughter, just preoccupied with the more pressing demands of the younger ones.

'All right, thanks.'

'Yer dad's working a few extra hours this week so we'll be able to have a bit o' meat on Sunday,' said Gladys, a fair-haired, cadaverous woman whose good looks had been crushed by hardship and lack of nourishment. At thirty she looked old, with sunken cheeks, bent shoulders and hands rough and chapped. Her blue eyes were red-rimmed and her lips dry and pale. 'He's managed to get some extra work at the pie shop as well as his usual bits and pieces, so if we're very lucky we might even be able to 'ave faggots or saveloys for supper on Saturday, too.'

27

'Whoopee!' cried Amy, for the scarcity of food gave it standing of hallowed proportions to her and her brothers.

Amy's father was an unskilled labourer who did any work he could find. The fact that he was known and trusted on the streets of the East End kept him supplied with odd jobs from market traders and shop owners, lifting and carrying, cleaning, or helping out on the stalls. Several part-time jobs often made up a full day's work for him, but it was irregular and the pay abysmal. Out of male pride he refused to allow his wife to join the band of women who slaved at home for a pittance, making matchboxes or cardboard cartons. Amy had once asked her mother why he didn't object to his daughter earning money, as he always made such an issue about the family being his sole responsibility. Her mother had muttered something about his masculine status not being threatened by a child of the family, but Amy wasn't really old enough to understand such complexities.

'Will you pop round to your Aunt Clara's on your way back from the shops, Amy?' asked Gladys. 'Ask her if she can lend us some sugar till I get me 'ousekeeping money at the end of the week. The little bit of cash I've got won't run to that and yer dad likes a spot of sugar in 'is tea.'

'Course I will,' said Amy cheerfully, accepting it as her duty to run the family errands. Alfie got all the heavy jobs like fetching coal from the backyard and carrying potatoes home from the market.

'You're a good girl, Amy.' Her tone was softer. She was more relaxed now that the baby was quiet. She got up and took some coins from the jar on the mantelpiece and handed them to her daughter. 'Get a

28

pickled herrin' from the Jew's shop for yer dad, will yer, ducks?' She was thoughtful for a moment. 'And brewis will be a change from bread and marge for us,' she said, referring to bread and salted dripping broken into boiling water. 'So get a loaf, and some dripping from the butcher's.'

'Yeah, all right, Mum,' said Amy, collecting a basin for the dripping from a shelf near the fire and taking the brown leatherette shopping bag from a hook on the wall.

She had just taken her shawl from the peg on the door and was about to leave when her father swept in—a thickset man of thirty-four with warm brown eyes and a ready smile, a layer of grime covering his city pallor. Roughly dressed in a shabby cap and torn grey coat over dark trousers and scuffed boots, he nevertheless filled the room with his presence for he was the dominant force in the family. His word was law around here, and no one dared to argue because they had all been taught to respect the fact that he knew best.

'Where are yer off to then, Amy?' he asked.

'To the shops for Mum, then to Aunt Clara's,' she said.

'When you get back you can take the jug down the Rose and Crown to get me some ale,' he said.

'All right, Dad, I won't be long.'

'Make sure you're not.'

'I will. Tata.'

Closing the door behind her, Amy screwed her face and closed her eyes at the sound of her father's ear-splitting roar. 'Bloody 'ell, just look at that boy's eye. You've bin fightin' again, young Alfie. Now what 'ave I told you about that?'

'But, Dad...'

29

'None of yer cheek, yer little bugger. Now come 'ere.'

'Don't 'it him, George!'

'He's gotta learn, Gladys.'

'No, Dad, no,' wailed Alfie, 'No ... no ... Ooh ... ow ... ouch!'

Amy was still smarting from her brother's screams as she clattered down the wooden stairs and out into the street. She was glad to get out of the house for it made her tremble inside when Dad took his belt to Alfie. Boys needed discipline, her father said, or they got out of hand. But surely there must be another way?

She made her purchases and hurried on towards Folly Road near Victoria Park where her Aunt Clara lived in a flat. A posh one, too, on account of the fact that a rich gentleman paid her rent. It was all supposed to be hush-hush but it was hard for parents to have secrets from their children when they lived in such close proximity and shared the same bedroom. Amy heard all sorts of things she shouldn't, especially if she was still awake after Mum and Dad went to bed.

Visiting her father's younger sister was a source of great enjoyment to Amy, for it was like entering another world. Aunt Clara was a singer on the halls. The warm personality that drew the crowds was also manifest in her private life, and she was always very kind to Amy. The young girl thought her aunt beautiful and was quite dazzled by her pretty clothes. She had a whole flat to herself, with lino on the floor, lace curtains at the windows, and a small kitchen with a sink and a water tap all of her own.

There were fewer people on the streets as Amy turned into Folly Road. These were bigger, smarter

30

houses, mostly converted into flats. They were neat and well kept, and there were no filthy children or tramps littering the pavements. Her heart lightened at the sight of clean windows and whitened front door steps. Just being here reminded her that there was something better than life in Tucker Street. She hurried on her way, eager for as much time as possible in her aunt's smart abode, wishing she didn't have to hurry home with the errands.

*   *   *

'Well, you've really bin taken poorly, ain't yer, Ralphie?' said Clara Atkins to the sick man residing in her bed. The greenish-brown, almond-shaped eyes that attracted so much male attention were full of concern. ''Ere, 'ave a nice cuppa tea, love. Remember what the doctor said. You've gotta have plenty of fluids, and you're to stay in bed and keep warm until your fever's gone down.'

Brashly dressed in a scarlet day dress which swept the floor in elegant folds, shapely figure laced tightly beneath it, bosom forward, bottom out, she set a tea tray down on the bedside table and leaned over to help him sit up. His skin burned beneath her touch, the noxious odour of sickness emanating from him.

She fiddled anxiously with one of the blonde curls that framed her face, for she was very worried about him. He'd given her quite a turn earlier when he'd arrived at her door in a state of near collapse. People were dying like flies of the influenza, which was why she'd called the doctor in. It wasn't as though Ralphie couldn't afford proper medical attention.

He wasn't able to keep the tea down and threw up in the bowl beside the bed, retching and wheezing and

31

looking like death. Gawd Almighty, what was she going to do? She was supposed to be working tonight, singing at three different halls. What if she came home to find him dead in her bed? Quite apart from the grief, there was the scandal. Not that he would know anything about it, poor love, and it would take more than a bit of gossip to hurt Clara. But it would blow the lid off their affair and be a terrible shock to his wife to discover that her husband had been keeping a mistress in comfort for some years.

'Water,' he requested feebly, lying back on the pillow, his skin soaked with sweat.

'I'll get yer some, love.' She went to the kitchen, making a decision as she filled the glass. She couldn't leave him alone. Not while he was as ill as this. The punters would just have to do without her for one night. She'd get a message to the manager of the Paragon at Mile End and he would get word to the other hall managers with whom she was booked for tonight. She'd wait till Ralph was sleeping, then slip down there in a cab. She'd only be gone half an hour.

Clara had no illusions about her stage career. She knew she would never be in the same league as Marie Lloyd or Florrie Forde. Clara's singing voice was pleasant but mediocre. It was her looks and personality that kept her working, and she prayed she wouldn't lose them yet awhile for it was the only occupation she was any good at.

He managed to swallow the water and clung to her hand feebly, appealing to her. 'My wife,' he groaned. 'She'll wonder where I am if I don't get home tonight.'

'Mm, she will an' all,' Clara agreed, for Ralph never complicated matters at home by staying here

32

overnight. He was a happily married man who enjoyed a bit of loving on the side. This was another area in which Clara did not delude herself.

'Oh dear,' he muttered weakly. 'What am I going to do about it?'

'Well, there ain't a lot yer can do about it, is there, Ralphie boy?' she said, shovelling some more coal on to the bedroom fire. 'You can't go 'ome in this state, not unless yer wanna make yer wife a widow.'

She went to the kitchen and returned with a cool flannel which she laid gently on his fevered brow, inwardly mulling over their relationship. Ralph had come to her dressing room one night about five years ago when she'd been singing at a music hall in the West End. He'd taken her out to supper, and that was all there had been to it the first few times. When he'd wanted more and offered to set her up in a decent place of her own, she had seen no reason why not, even though he was twenty years her senior. After all, she liked him well enough and her own wages didn't run to a place like this. That was how casually it had started, but over the years she had grown fond of him and had stopped seeing other men.

Of course she wasn't proud of sleeping with another woman's husband, but if it hadn't been her it would have been someone else. He was that sort of a man. And chances to improve her circumstances weren't exactly thick on the ground for a third-rate singer like herself. She had to think of the future when her voice and sex appeal would no longer earn her a living. With Ralph contributing substantially to her income, she could put a bit by for later on. She knew all about poverty; her parents hadn't lived to see old age because of it.

Sure, she would have liked a more normal way of

life with a husband and children. But she'd never attracted the marrying kind. Men chose homely shop girls and housemaids as wives, women who would shine on the domestic front, not someone who was out every night treading the boards. If she was really honest with herself she had to admit that she had come to want more from Ralph. But since he had made it clear from the start that he would never leave his wife, she made the most of what she did have and didn't hanker for the impossible. Ralph was selfish and arrogant and wanted the best of both worlds. But people were all just human beings, after all, and if you expected too much of anyone you were doomed to disappointment.

Ralph's eyes shot open and rested on her worriedly. 'She'll think I've had an accident,' he croaked.

'Course she won't,' said Clara, hoping to soothe him.

'She might,' he persisted, his fears exacerbated by his current helpnessness. 'And what if she calls in the police to look for me? I mustn't be found here.'

'Calm down,' said Clara gently. 'You're lettin' yer imagination run away with yer. Anyway, they'd never find you 'ere. How could they, when none of your people even know that I exist?'

'The police have their ways of tracking people down,' he said. 'And if I'm not well enough to go home for a few days, it will give them more time.'

'So what, if they do find you 'ere,' she said to calm his fevered imagination, 'you'll just 'ave to ask 'em not to tell yer wife where they found yer, won't yer?'

'You can't tell the police what to do.' He tried to sit up but fell back against the pillow, holding his head. 'Anyway, even if I'm not found, how do I explain

34

where I've been to Florence when I do get back?'

'I'm sure you'll think of something.'

He struggled into a sitting position. 'I must get a message to her,' he croaked.

Given the parlous state of his health, Clara was surprised he had the strength to worry about such practicalities, which just went to prove the value he put on his homelife. She pondered the dilemma. A letter would take days to get there, and he didn't have one of those newfangled telephones in his house or shop. A personal messenger was the only answer. 'All right, Ralph. In the morning, we'll see about it.'

'Tomorrow will be too late.'

'Stop being so dramatic, Ralphie,' she urged. 'Where are we gonna get someone to go all the way to Ealing tonight? It's right the other side of London.'

'I don't care how much I pay to get a message delivered tonight.'

'Oh.' That put a very different light on the matter. 'I see.'

A knock at the front door interrupted the conversation and Clara went to see who it was, closing the bedroom door behind her.

''Ello, Amy,' she said, smiling and ushering her niece inside. 'You're just the person I wanna see. I want you to give yer dad a message.'

'Mum said can we borrow some sugar till the end of the week.'

'Course you can, ducks,' she said in a speedy, preoccupied manner. 'Sit down for a minute while I get some from the kitchen.'

Amy sat in an armchair enjoying the softness of the upholstery, her eyes running over the polished sideboard, the pink three-piece suite and the untarnished mirror hanging over the fireplace. Her

35

aunt had seemed in a strange mood, she thought, guessing that she had her gentleman friend here and wanted Amy out of the way as soon as possible. Amy had seen him once or twice and had been disappointed. Someone as glamorous as Clara should have a handsome young man, not a balding old boy like him.

'Here yer are,' said Clara, returning from the kitchen with some sugar in a paper bag, 'Mind you don't spill it on the way 'ome.'

'Thanks Aunt Clara.' Amy took the sugar and stood up, guessing that she was not going to be asked to stay for a cup of tea and a chat as sometimes happened. She made her way to the door. 'I've gotta hurry back. My dad wants me to go down to the pub for him to get some beer. What's the message?'

'Tell 'im to come round here right away. Tell 'im I've got a job for him that will be well worth his while.'

'Yeah, I'll tell him,' said Amy.

'Ta, ducks.'

* * *

Ealing was new territory for George Atkins and he decided to have a quick look at the town before getting the train back to the East End, having delivered a pack of lies to Mrs Florence Jackson as instructed by her husband. The fairy tale had gone along the lines that Ralph Jackson had been taken ill with influenza while doing business in Hatton Garden and was staying with a business acquaintance until he was well enough to travel home. To add authenticity to the tale George, dressed in Sunday best, had pretended to be the odd

36

job man of the business acquaintance, sent to Ealing to put her mind at rest by a 'considerate' husband who didn't want her to be worried.

Ralph was certainly going to a lot of trouble to cover his tracks, presumably so that he could continue his affair with Clara unhampered by a suspicious wife. Typical of a toff, thought George, they were a devious bunch. Still, he had paid George well for his efforts, so he wasn't complaining.

He drew his scarf more tightly around his throat against the cold and walked through the Broadway, past Ealing Theatre with its ornate front. He liked what he'd seen of the area so far. It was a cut above Bethnal Green and no mistake, he thought, noticing the wide pavements flooded with electric light, the shiny shop windows, the hat shops and high-class grocery stores. Plenty of carriages about, too, and even the occasional motor car.

It was turned nine o'clock but some of the shops were still open and there were quite a few people around as he walked on in search of a certain jeweller's shop, the name of which he had got from Clara.

And suddenly there it was, a large shop occupying the place of two, in a tree-lined mall. So this was what paid for his fine house and lavish life style. This and another shop, too, according to Clara. Diamond rings and brooches; tie pins and cuff links; necklaces and pendants; pocket watches and a wealth of other costly items sparkled in beds of rich red satin in the window. A prosperous business indeed. The stock alone must be worth a fortune. A fine place to work. And Ealing looked to him like a good healthy place in which to live.

Walking back towards the station, George

seriously considered the idea that had begun to form in his mind when he had noticed how eager Ralph Jackson had been to pay for his trip to Ealing to remove a threat to his marriage and reputation.

In all honesty George considered himself to be a man of integrity. He worked hard to keep his family who meant everything to him, even if he did use a firm hand to discipline them. He didn't cheat employers or friends, and he had never strayed from the marital bed. Over the years of impoverishment, sheer desperation might have forced him to appropriate the occasional item of food from a market stall, bruised fruit, bread, potatoes and so on, but only when there had been no other way.

But it was also true to say that the harshness of his life had taught George to recognise an opportunity when he saw it, and here was one staring him in the face right now. Ralph Jackson had everything a man could want in the way of material comfort, yet he was greedy enough to want more: George's sister to be precise. He was using Clara. When it suited him he would disappear from her life, and so would her nice little home and all that went with it. What chance would she have to find a husband then, a music hall singer who'd been a kept woman?

Life was a matter of give and take. Ralph had done more than his fair share of taking, now it was time to give something back to the lower classes from whom he plucked his pleasures so easily. Clara had made her bed and she must lie on it, but that particular bed might just benefit another member of the family...

As he walked into the station, the acid smell of steam smarting in the back of his throat, George went over the details of his plan.

*　　*　　*

'But that's blackmail!' exclaimed Ralph, a few evenings later in Clara's sitting room, having listened to George's proposal.

The two men were alone, sitting either side of the fire. Clara was out working. Ralph was recovering and planning to return home soon. George had chosen his time carefully for this was men's business and he didn't want Clara to interfere.

'I prefer to call it business,' he said, 'buyin' and sellin'. I'm sellin' my silence about your affair with my sister and you're gonna pay for it with a job for my daughter as an assistant in your posh jeweller's shop in Ealing. And since she'll need somewhere to live, you'll also provide 'er with accommodation.'

'Like hell I will,' Ralph growled. 'Why, you're nothing more than a cheap crook.'

'I'm no more of a crook than you are, mate,' he argued, 'I'm simply using your deceit to give my eldest kid a decent start in life, something your sort take for granted. People like me 'ave to make the most of their chances since there ain't too many of 'em about. You've bin doin' all right for yourself for years with my sister. Now you must do something in return for one of 'er family. Seems fair enough to me.'

'I'll go to the police.'

'Do so, by all means, mate. It depends 'ow much yer value yer marriage.'

'What if I tell Clara how you're using the situation?' threatened Ralph.

'Go ahead,' invited George. 'She'll not be pleased but she'll not stop me. She's family, yer see. She'll understand that I 'ave to do what I can for me kids, by whatever means I can find. Anyway, she's

39

very fond of Amy, she'll not want to spoil a chance for her.'

Ralph stood up with his back to the fire, immersed in thought. He was still feeling weak from his illness but was hoping to be well enough to travel home in a day or two, thank God, for he was missing the luxury of his own home comforts. Clara's little place was all right for short visits, but not for any length of time, even with the inducement of her invigorating company. Clara excited him in a way that no other woman ever had and he had grown quite fond of her. Her common ways and general earthiness pleased him and he couldn't even consider the idea of giving her up. But at this moment he wished he'd never set eyes on her, for the thought of one of her relatives encroaching upon his other, respectable life filled him with dread.

'How about if I give you some money?' he suggested. 'Then you can do what you like with it. Have a few treats, get some new clothes for yourself and the family. Surely that would be a more sensible idea than my having your daughter come to work for me?'

He had made the mistake of equating George's values with his own. 'No thanks, mate. Money is just money. I'll always manage to get enough of that to live on somehow. A decent start in life is much harder to come by. Besides, if I were to take money from yer it really would be blackmail, and I want nothing for nothing from you. My Amy will work 'ard for 'er money and she's a bright girl, so you'll get a good return on the wages you pay her.'

'So you'd rather have a job for your daughter than money for yourself?' Ralph said in amazement.

'That's right. I've just told yer me terms, ain't I?'

'But I don't need an extra assistant at the moment,' said Ralph.

'I'm sure another pair of 'ands would be useful,' George suggested. 'Everyone knows how you shop-keepers overwork your staff.'

'But I don't have facilities for live-in shop staff like the big stores,' protested Ralph. 'I employ all local people.'

'This'll be the first time then, won't it?' said George firmly.

'But where would she live?' asked Ralph, scratching his head worriedly. 'The rooms above the shop are all used for offices and stock, and the workshop takes up all the space at the back.'

'You got room in yer house, ain't yer?' suggested George. 'In the servants' quarters?'

'She can't live at my house!' said Ralph, aghast. 'It would never do to mix shop staff with domestic servants.'

'Why not? They're all employed by you, ain't they?'

'Yes, of course, but the servants work as a team,' Ralph explained irritably. 'Your daughter would be an annoyance to them, an unsettling influence. Questions might be asked as to why I've employed a girl who needs to live in when I don't have the proper facilities.'

'That's easily solved,' said George. 'As far as anyone in Ealing is concerned, Amy is the daughter of the odd job man of a business acquaintance of yours, and you've taken her on as a favour to him. No one will query it, surely?'

'I suppose not,' muttered Ralph.

'There yer are then,' said George brightly. 'No one need ever know any different.'

41

Ralph was thanking God that Florence took no interest in his professional life whatsoever. Apart from Harold Cox, who was a family friend, one business acquaintance was much the same as another to her because she rarely met any of them. Maybe it would be possible for this scheme to work without any real complications.

'Anyway,' continued George, rising with his cap in hand, his brown curly hair sticking up untidily around his rugged face, 'I'm sure you'll get something sorted out by the time my daughter is ready for the job, which will be after Easter when she's thirteen and old enough to go into full-time employment. She won't need anythin' special in the way of accommodation, but I want 'er made comfortable and paid the proper rate for the job.'

Ralph chewed his lip anxiously, his normally plump face emaciated from his illness, his skin paper pale. The damned influenza had really sapped his strength and he didn't feel up to coping with this sort of dilemma. Oh, if only he'd stayed at home when he'd first felt ill, this would never have happened! George Atkins would not have been given an insight into his private life which had inspired his miserable plan. 'But what about your daughter, how do I know that she won't say anything to my wife or my staff?' he asked. 'She must know about Clara and me. She's seen me here.'

'She'll not say a word,' said George, 'I can promise you that. She'll be fully primed before she starts work. And my kids are brought up to do what I tell 'em. They all know how to behave themselves.'

The mention of behaviour depressed Ralph even further, for there was no place for rough manners in his shop. Although his sales staff were all from the

42

lower classes, they were the carefully selected sons and daughters of clerks and shop workers. There was a vast difference between someone from the respectable Ealing working classes and the daughter of a rough, casual labourer from the East End who didn't even have what could be called regular employment. Lord knows what the wretched girl's demeanour would be like. She would have to be thoroughly groomed before he could let her anywhere near the customers.

'And the first time I have cause to reprimand her, I suppose she'll go running to tell you and I shall have you on my back complaining?' said Ralph.

'I'm not an unreasonable man,' said George. 'You must treat 'er the same as anyone else on your staff. You be fair with 'er and you'll 'ear nothing from me. A deal is a deal as far as I'm concerned.' George gave him an enquiring look. 'Well, what do you say?'

'I'll think about it.'

'Oh no, that ain't good enough for me, mate,' boomed George. 'I want this thing settled 'ere and now, or I might start fancying a breath of clean air out Ealing way. A good respectable woman, your missus . . .'

Ralph's teeth were clenched with frustration. He wasn't used to being at the mercy of someone from the lower classes and he didn't like it one bit. 'All right,' he sighed wearily, 'when it gets nearer the time, your daughter had better make an appointment to see me at the Ealing shop. I'll interview her in the normal way for the sake of appearances, but she'll get the job. Three shillings a week to start, plus board and lodging.'

George's craggy face creased into a lop-sided grin. 'I thought you'd probably decide to be sensible in the end.' He was thoughtful for a moment. 'There's just one more thing.'

'Yes?' sighed Ralph. 'What is it now?'

'Will she 'ave to wear a uniform?'

'No, we're not big enough for that sort of thing. The staff wear their own clothes which must be plain and smart. A blouse and dark skirt will be quite suitable.'

'You'll have to supply the money for 'em then, 'cos I ain't got it.'

Ralph tutted. 'Yes, all right,' he agreed, taking a purse from his pocket.

*   *   *

'Ealing?' said Bernie in a tone of baffled surprise one Sunday afternoon in the spring. 'Where the 'ell is that?'

'Out West London way,' Amy informed him. 'It's ever so posh. Big 'ouses and people in nice clothes and that.'

'Blimey!' said Bernie, his dark brows rising. 'A bit different to Tucker Street, eh?'

'I'll say.'

'Do you wanna go and live there?'

'You bet,' said Amy, who would never be disloyal to her father by admitting to anyone that she would have preferred to choose her own employment rather than have someone else arrange it for her. She'd guessed from the elegance of the shop, when she'd been for the interview, that a common girl like her would not have been considered suitable without some sort of influence being exerted. Judging by the pretences she was being asked to make, and the fact that Aunt Clara's gentleman friend owned the

44

business, the nature of that influence was obvious. Even at this tender age, her independent spirit shrank from the idea of receiving such a dubious favour. But she was in too much awe of her father to oppose him, and planned to prove herself worthy of the favour once she was actually working. 'I'll miss everyone round 'ere, o' course, but it's a good chance for me. And I'll be able to come 'ome visitin' sometimes on Sundays when I can afford the train fare.'

'It'll seem funny, you not bein' around,' said Bernie sadly. 'I'll miss yer.'

'I'll miss you an' all,' she said wistfully. 'But we're growin' up, Bern, it's time to spread our wings.'

'Yeah, course it is,' he agreed. 'So, when are you off?'

'Tomorrow.'

'Cor, as soon as that.'

'Mmm. I'll have to be going 'ome in a minute an' all,' she said. 'Mum is making a special tea as it's my last day at 'ome.'

They were sitting on a bench in Victoria Park near the boating lake. The spring sunshine had brought out the crowds in their hundreds. Courting couples strolled the footpaths in their Sunday best, and young women paraded up and down in their smart hats, coyly eyeing the young men who were also casting a selective eye.

The lake was crowded with rowing boats creaking and splashing around the island in the centre, the screams and laughter from the occupants only barely audible against the many other sounds. Distantly they could hear the band in the bandstand enclosure; a religious group was singing hymns somewhere in the trees; children squealed at their games, dogs barked, birds twittered in the trees and bushes. Pet

45

linnets and finches, deprived of light and liberty in small cages covered in black cloth, sang for all they were worth at old men's feet as they dozed on the benches in the sunshine.

'I'll walk 'ome with you, if yer like,' said Bernie.

'That'll be nice.'

'And I'll treat yer to an ha'porth of toffee from the toffee man at the park gate as a going away present.'

She gulped back the tears. As much as she was looking forward to her new life, she was going to miss the old one terribly. Bernie had always been there for her when she'd needed a friend. 'Ta, Bernie, that's good of yer,' she said, rising and straightening her straw hat and smoothing her grey woollen dress.

The toffee was deliciously sticky and sweet, almost pulling their teeth out as they walked slowly back to Tucker Street, chewing happily. 'So, now that you've left school, Bernie, are you gonna start on your plan to make your fortune?' she asked.

'Yep,' he said, with complete confidence. 'I'm taking on more rounds. In a few years you won't know me because I'll be all dressed up like a toff, you just wait and see.'

'Will yer still be sellin' stuff round the 'ouses?' she asked.

'For a start, yeah,' he said with a wicked laugh.

Amy didn't ask him to elaborate because she wasn't sure she wanted to know.

At the door to their house he said, 'I ain't goin' in yet, I'm gonna see some mates down Stepney way.'

'Oh.' She felt choked with emotion.

'Good luck with the job. See you around when you come 'ome visitin'.'

'Yeah. Tata Bernie.'

'Tata, Amy. Mind 'ow yer go.'

46

As he swaggered off down the road, his boots kicking up the dust, the sound of a bell heralded the arrival of the muffin man on one of his last visits of the season, ringing his handbell and carrying his wares in a wooden tray balanced on his head and covered with a white cloth.

The front door burst open and Alfie appeared with a plate in his hand, grinning fit to bust. 'We're havin' muffins for tea 'cos it's yer last day, and there's winkles and shrimps an' all to go with our bread and marge.' He paused and gave her an uncertain look. 'You'll be back visiting quite a lot, won't you, sis?'

'Course I will.'

'That's all right then,' he said, smiling again and darting into the street to join the crowd who had gathered around the hawker.

Amy couldn't help but smile. Alfie would miss her, of course, but she could go away again and again if it meant having something special for tea. She was assailed by a plethora of emotions. Deep affection for her family who would have to go without tomorrow to pay for today's extras in her honour; sadness at the thought of leaving home and ending an era.

But predominant was a feeling of excitement for the future. Her father had made this chance possible for her by the only means at his disposal, and she considered it her bounden duty to make good from it.

CHAPTER THREE

When Amy crawled into bed the following Saturday night after an exhausting week, she was ready to pack her bags and go back to Bethnal Green. She didn't mind the long hours, it was being a misfit she found so hard to take. She didn't belong here, and it was a very lonely feeling. Never before had she been made to feel so painfully aware of her humble background. Having previously only mixed with her own sort, the people here seemed like foreigners. In comparison with Amy, even the shop staff were uppercrust with their modulated accents and cultivated manners.

Jackson & Cox's prestigious showrooms were situated on two floors of the three-storey premises. The jewellery department, including clocks, watches and barometers, was on the ground floor; silverware upstairs. Both floors had a central cash desk connected to the assistants' positions at the counters by stretched overhead wires, along which ran small wooden containers to transport money to and fro when a handle was pulled to release a spring. On the ground floor behind the showrooms was a busy workshop. The administration was conducted from offices at the top of the building.

The stock was not the only thing that gleamed in this establishment. So did the polished floors, the ebony and glass showcases, the mahogany counters, and the wide wooden staircase that curved impressively to the upper floors from the jewellery department.

Confined within this elite atmosphere, Amy felt gauche and childish. The rest of the staff were efficient, well spoken, and slavishly subservient towards the rich patrons who made purchases for sums of money Amy had never even heard spoken, yet alone seen change hands. The fact that all the other shop assistants were a lot older than her added to her sense of isolation.

Mercifully, Mr Jackson Senior, whom she found

particularly loathsome on account of his blatant condescension and constant criticism of her general deportment, seemed to spend most of his time upstairs in his office or out on business, leaving the senior assistant, Mr Rawlings, in charge. The latter was a middle-aged man with a supercilious manner and the build of a broom handle. His sparse dark hair was worn flat to his pointed head and parted in the middle, a small neat moustache adorning his thin lips.

About the only other person around under thirty was the boss's son, Clifford, known respectfully as Mr Clifford to the staff. He was training to be the manager, apparently, and seemed to wander around all day in a rather preoccupied way. Since he was the only one with any sort of warmth or humour about him, Amy took an instant liking to him. He sometimes asked her how she was getting along and gave her the occasional reassuring smile as she continuously dusted stock, polished shelves and showcases, made tea, ran errands to the bank, the post office, and the tobacconist for cigars for Mr Jackson Senior. Clifford was like a ray of sunlight in the sombre atmosphere and could often be heard humming popular tunes under his breath, 'Goodbye Dolly Gray' seeming to be a particular favourite. Amy's tender years, coupled to his good looks and fine physique, led her to see him as something of a hero.

Her monotonous daily routine continued for several months, which disappointed her for she knew she had more to offer than the re-positioning of dust for so much of the day. Naturally she hadn't expected to be dealing with customers right away, but she had hoped to be doing something more interesting than the work of a cleaner-cum-errand girl by now.

Having been raised to stand up for herself in the big outside world, she felt compelled to remind the senior assistant that she had actually been employed as a shop assistant.

Mr Rawlings wasn't used to such outspokenness from one of his customarily obedient staff, whose opinions about anything were discouraged. 'It isn't your place to question the tasks you are given, Miss Atkins,' he snapped when she approached him in the manager's office at the back of the jewellery department, 'but to earn your wages by getting on with them.'

'Surely I've a right know what me prospects are,' she said. 'If I'd wanted to dust and polish all day, I'd 'ave gone into domestic service.'

This stunned him into silence for a few moments. Such nerve from a thirteen year old! Prospects indeed. Since when did shopgirls have those? 'Mr Jackson has asked me not to put you on the counter until you are quite ready, and you are certainly not ready yet,' he informed her brusquely at last. 'So you will carry on as you are until I say otherwise, and stop wasting time by querying the matter.'

'But 'ow can I ever be ready if I ain't given a chance to get some experience?' she said impatiently, 'I'm good at figures. I told Mr Jackson that at the interview.'

Mr Rawlings winced as though her rough speech caused him physical pain. 'You still have a great deal to learn,' he said. 'You need to be thoroughly familiar with stock, for one thing.'

'I know a lot already,' she insisted exuberantly, 'I keep me eyes open and I'm a quick learner. Me teachers at school were always sayin' so.'

50

He gave an impatient sigh. 'There's much more to serving customers than being good at figures and knowing the difference between gold and platinum.' His lips twitched with annoyance. 'You have to know how to deal with people. The customer must be made to feel special. You should study the technique of the other assistants. And you simply *must* learn to speak properly.'

Amy was in no doubt as to her place in the social structure, and really didn't need to have it drummed into her day after day. 'Surely it's what I say that matters, rather than the way I say it?' she ventured boldly.

His look of scorn suggested she had just told him that pearls were things that grew in flowerbeds. 'Of course it isn't,' he said. 'You'll be taught what to say. How you speak is of the utmost importance in this trade. You're not working on some market stall, you know.'

'More's the pity.'

'What was that?'

'I said it's a bit nippy,' she lied quickly, remembering the promise she made to herself to succeed in this 'golden' opportunity.

'Good, I'm glad that's all you said,' he told her, narrowing his eyes shrewdly. 'Because I don't want to have to report you to Mr Jackson for insolence when you have been with us such a short time. Please remember that you are a junior assistant here and as such will do whatever I or the other senior members of staff tell you, cheerfully and without question. Is that clear?'

'Quite clear,' she said, meeting his glare unwaveringly, and mentally throttling him.

And if things at the shop were bad, the situation at

51

home was even worse. Not that she could call the attic room she shared with Violet, the Jacksons' housemaid, 'home' since the obvious resentment of her room-mate made her feel about as welcome as chilblains. And it was a pity because having a bed to herself, with clean sheets, was luxury indeed.

Violet was a few months older than Amy, a thin, plain girl with sullen brown eyes and enormous teeth that protruded like overhanging roof tiles. Having shown Amy her bed on her first day she studiously avoided any conversation thereafter, creating an unbearable atmosphere whenever the two girls were in at the same time, which wasn't often because Violet worked even longer hours than Amy. The latter's attempts at friendship only seemed to provoke even more rancour in the other girl.

'Look, I'm sorry you're upset at 'aving to share your room with me,' Amy said, though having slept in a bedroom with five other people she couldn't see the problem, 'but it ain't my doin'. You'd better take it up with the mistress if you ain't 'appy about it.'

'Don't matter to me, one way or the other,' mumbled Violet, her colour rising, 'I ain't in the room long enough to notice.'

The implication being that Amy had an abundance of spare time, which wasn't true at all. She did, however, have the whole of Sunday off and finished work at eight o'clock every night except Fridays and Saturdays when they stayed open until nine. Whereas Violet's day sometimes stretched until eleven at night, with only the afternoon off on a Sunday.

Then there was Mrs Wilks, the cook, a formidable widow woman who ruled her kitchen with a rod of iron—and God help anyone who didn't conform to her rules or her mealtimes. And this was where part of Amy's problem lay. Being out at the shop every day except Sunday meant she couldn't have her meals at the same time as Mrs Wilks, Violet, and Marshall the coachman, which meant Mrs Wilks had to keep something hot for her. And as if that was not aggravation enough, the cook was expected to provide Amy with some bread and dripping to take to work for her lunch.

'I don't know what things are coming to, I'm sure,' she could often be heard to mutter, 'with shopgirls living in with domestic staff. That's the trouble with working in a small household—they've no class. They don't do things proper.'

Hungry for the warmth of home, Amy lived for the one Sunday a month when she could afford the train fare to Bethnal Green. Yet, strangely enough, although she counted the minutes until she got there and throbbed with excitement all the way, she began to feel like an outsider there too. In fact, she no longer seemed to belong anywhere.

One Sunday supper-time in the late autumn, when she had been at Floral House for about seven months, matters between her and the servants came to a head. Mrs Wilks and Marshall were discussing the return of the first troops from the Boer War, expected to arrive in London the following day.

'There's gonna be a procession from Paddington Station to St Paul's for a thanksgiving service, according to the paper,' said Marshall, a dapper bachelor in his thirties. 'I wish I could be there to give the soldiers a cheer.'

'There'll be some crowds up West tomorrow all right,' said Mrs Wilks, slicing herself more bread and cutting a hunk of cheese. 'There's nothing quite like a procession to draw people out.'

'I think processions are ever so exciting,' said Amy, forcing herself into the conversation. On the one day a week that she did eat her meals with the servants, she did her utmost to break down the barriers and be friends with them. 'Why don't you go and take a look, Marshall?'

'Mr Marshall to you,' snapped Mrs Wilks, her grey eyes hard and cold. 'How many more times do I have to tell you to watch yer manners, girl?'

'Sorry,' said Amy, refusing to be goaded, and turning her attention back to the coachman 'Well, why don't you, eh, Mr Marshall?'

''Ow can I?' he asked, 'I won't be able to get the time orf.'

'Why not ask? You never know your luck,' suggested Amy brightly. Of the three servants, Marshall was the least intimidating. 'It is a special occasion, after all.'

'And what business is it of yours whether he goes or not, young woman?' rasped Mrs Wilks, through gritted teeth.

The fierce and unnecessary spite in the older woman's tone finally tried Amy's patience too far. 'None at all,' she rasped, forcefully pushing her chair back from the table with a loud scraping sound as she stood up. 'I was just trying to be friendly—something that seems to be beyond the capabilities of you lot.'

Completely enraged, she stood with her hands on her hips staring furiously into the plump, shiny face of Mrs Wilks whose colour had risen at this unexpected rebellion. 'What have I done to deserve this sort of treatment from you, eh?'

Remaining silent, the cook lowered her eyes.

'Come on, let's have it out in the open,' persisted Amy, glaring from one to the other of them. 'You've

54

all gone out of your way to be horrible to me since the day I arrived here, and I think it's about time I was told why.'

An abrasive silence filled the room, broken only by the scraping of Violet's chair against the tiled floor as she wriggled uncomfortably in her seat. Three pairs of eyes studiously avoided Amy's.

'Surely I deserve to know why my life has been made such a misery?' she insisted.

Mrs Wilks gave an embarrassed cough. 'You ain't done nothin' in particular,' she said uncertainly, lifting her gaze to meet Amy's.

'I'm glad to hear you admit it. So why then...'

'You're out of place living 'ere because you're not one of us,' the cook explained hotly. 'You ought to be living out.'

'On the wages they pay me!' Amy fumed. 'You must be joking. Board and lodging is part of the terms of me job. I can't help it if they chose to put me in with you.'

'Airs and graces...' mumbled Mrs Wilks. 'I dunno who you think you are, putting on a posh voice.'

'Oh, so that's it,' roared Amy. 'I'm in trouble with you if I try to talk properly, and in trouble at the shop if I don't. I can't win either way.' She wrung her hands, angry tears threatening. 'Don't you realise how humiliating it is for me to be picked up every single time I drop an "h" or say ain't? Wouldn't you try to improve the way you spoke if your job depended on it?'

'I hadn't really thought...' began Mrs Wilks sheepishly.

'Obviously,' bellowed Amy, beside herself with rage. 'For two pins I'd pack the job in. You're snobs, every last one of you, the Jacksons and all their staff.

55

Though Gawd knows what *you've* got to be snooty about since we're all just slaves to the family.' She paused for breath as all three of them stared wide-eyed at her. Violet struggled to restrain an attack of nervous giggles by clamping her hand over her mouth. 'Well, you might as well get used to having me around, 'cos I'm gonna stick it out however miserable you make things for me. I don't see why I should be driven away by the likes of you.'

Marshall coughed, Violet shook silently on the brink of hysteria, and Mrs Wilks took refuge in her cocoa, holding the cup to her lips with an unsteady hand.

As a final shot, Amy said, 'I've every bit as much right to be here as you, and I'm stayin' whether you like it or not.'

And with that she pulled open the sliding wooden door next to the pantry, which covered the servants' stairs, and rushed up them to the attic. Inside her room she threw herself on her bed and sobbed.

The nights were cold as winter drew near and it was freezing in the unheated room. She began to shiver as the fury that had swept her along downstairs drained away, leaving her deflated and disillusioned. So much for the bright new future, she thought miserably. I'll be out on the street once that old cow Wilks says her piece to the Jacksons. Shopgirls are ten a penny, but good cooks are hard to come by these days, with factories and shops offering women an alternative to domestic employment.

For all that she had felt wretched these last few months, she was sad at the thought of losing her job. Not only because it would mean she had let her father down but because she was actually beginning to enjoy the work. True, she was still just a dogsbody

56

and didn't work at the counter yet. But she was beginning to learn something about the trade. She knew that diamonds, rubies, emeralds, sapphires and pearls were generally regarded as 'precious' stones, while amethyst, aquamarine, topaz and others demanding a lower price were known as 'semi-precious'. She knew the importance of making showcases containing silver nearly airtight to prevent tarnishing, and that a little gum camphor placed with gold jewellery stored in a safe avoided deterioration from the foul air.

Oh, yes, she was getting to be a positive mine of information. This was mostly due to the informative Mr Burridge who was in charge of the workshop where she lingered whenever she had cause to go in there, usually with the men's tea or materials she was sent out to collect from the other shop.

Absorbed in her thoughts, she didn't hear the door open and was startled at the sound of a voice.

'I brought yer supper up,' said Violet, standing uncertainly inside the door holding a tray.

'Oh,' said Amy in surprise, 'ta very much.'

'You'll be starvin' 'ungry later if you miss yer grub. And you know how Mrs Wilks goes on at yer if yer ask for anything outside of mealtimes.'

'Don't I just.' She sat up, her face blotchy from tears. She stared quizzically at Violet who had set the tray down on the chest of drawers and was hovering awkwardly by the door. 'You've changed your attitude all of a sudden. Why's that?'

Violet stared silently at the floor.

'Come on, tell me what happened to bring you up here with my supper,' persisted Amy. 'Did Mrs Wilks send you up with it so that I can't say I've not been properly fed when the Jacksons give me the sack.'

57

'No, she didn't,' denied Violet, looking up sharply. 'It was my idea.'

'I'll fight Mrs Wilks, you know,' said Amy defensively. 'I'm not gonna let them dismiss me just because you lot downstairs don't want me here.'

'It's true that Mrs Wilks didn't send me up with your supper,' repeated Violet in a quivering voice, 'but she didn't try to stop me either.' She gave a wary smile. 'I think you really took the wind out of her sails just now. You shook us all.'

'Good job, an' all,' said Amy, rising and going over to the tray on which there was some bread and cheese and fruit cake, and a mug of cocoa, a feast indeed for a girl for whom supper had once been just a drink of water. 'Seems to me you all need taking down a peg or two. I mean to say, I expected snobbery from the bosses, but not from the workers too. Talk about class! Why, there's more layers of it round here than there is in a cabbage. It makes me sick.'

'I don't think Mrs Wilks means to be so rough on yer,' said Violet, her top lip getting caught on her ill-fitting teeth as she spoke. 'I think it's just that she doesn't know how to cope with having someone like you around. Not part of the set-up below stairs yet living with us, yer know.'

'Mmm, I suppose you're right,' said Amy, sitting on the edge of the bed chewing a piece of bread and cheese, her dark-stockinged feet swinging above the linoleum floor. 'But why the big freeze from you, Violet? I'd have thought you'd welcome company of your own age with all these old codgers around.'

Violet came right inside the room and closed the door. 'I do,' she said earnestly. 'I've bin stupid, I'm sorry I've bin so rotten to yer.'

'That's all right,' said Amy, far too pleased to

58

hear a friendly word to bear a grudge. 'But why did you do it?'

'I suppose I was jealous,' she admitted, her starched pinafore rustling as she sat down on the edge of her own bed, 'I followed Mrs Wilks' lead, and once I'd started bein' nasty I couldn't seem to stop.'

'What have you got to be jealous of me about?' asked Amy.

'You're so bright and confident,' said Violet. 'And you have more freedom.'

'That's easily rectified,' said Amy. 'You could work in a shop. That would give you more confidence and a little more free time.'

'No, I ain't got it up 'ere,' she said, pointing to her head. 'Domestic work is all I'm fit for.'

'Your parents put you into service, I suppose?'

'Ain't got parents,' she explained. 'I'm illegitimate. Me mum died when I was little. I was brought up in a children's 'ome.'

'Oh dear,' sympathised Amy. 'I am sorry.'

'No cause for you to be sorry,' said Violet, the prickliness returning to her tone. 'I ain't bothered.'

Sensing how very much she was 'bothered', Amy changed the subject. 'I hope you and me can be friends, now that the ice is broken.'

'Yeah, me an' all,' said Violet.

The sound of Mrs Wilks calling Violet from below echoed up the back stairs. 'I must go. I've got to collect the supper things from the dining room.'

'You'd think they'd do it themselves on a Sunday so that you could have the evening off, wouldn't you?' said Amy.

'In really big houses where they've got a lot of servants, you do get a Sunday afternoon and evening off now and then,' Violet explained, 'but with a small staff like ours, there's too much to do. Them having nothing cooked after Sunday lunch 'elps though, at least we get the afternoon off. And there's not so many dishes to wash after supper so we get finished early.'

Amy stifled the urge to offer to help Violet finish her work, guessing such a gesture would be seen as gross breach of domestic protocol by Mrs Wilks.

'I'd better go,' said Violet, whose gaunt face softened quite prettily when she smiled. 'And when I've finished downstairs, if you're still awake perhaps we can 'ave a chat.'

'I'll try to stay awake until you come up then,' said Amy.

The events of that evening proved to be a watershed in Amy's life. Much to her surprise, news of her eruption did not reach the ears of her employers, and instead of dismissal, she found a friendlier atmosphere towards her below stairs at Floral House. Her monthly trips home seemed to come around quicker now that she was happier and didn't await them with such urgency. With a friend of her own age to talk to, all things were tolerable, even Mr Jackson Senior who made her skin crawl. Painfully humiliating incidents in the working day didn't hurt so much when they could be discussed with Violet afterwards. Gales of laughter echoed from the girls' room as they exchanged stories about the idiosyncrasies of their seniors. The agonising uncertainties of growing up were chewed over and made bearable too. Some nights they whispered and giggled into the small hours, other times they were both too tired to say a word.

By no stretch of the imagination could Mrs Wilks' post-rebellion attitude towards Amy have been

60

called friendly. The woman's tongue could still slice sharper than any carving knife, and it was obvious she wasn't sure how to deal with the cuckoo in the nest. But she no longer excluded Amy from meal-time chatter, or picked on her unnecessarily.

And so the huge kitchen, which had once seemed so cold and unwelcoming to Amy, now radiated a warmth quite other than that emitted from the temperamental, coal-eating kitchen range on which delicious concoctions boiled and simmered.

As winter softened into spring and then summer Amy began to feel more at home in the town, too. On Sunday afternoons she and Violet would put on their best clothes and take a stroll in the park to listen to the band. Or take a horse-bus to the village of Hanwell and sit on the banks of the River Brent, which gently wound through the park and meadowland surrounding the bustling shopping area. Sometimes they would take a walk in the country at Hanger Lane, past a grand array of brightly painted milk carts lined up outside one of the farms. They could never stray too far, though, because Violet had to be back to help with the supper, an arrangement that infuriated Amy.

When the electric tramway opened in Ealing, offering fast new travel, their horizons were widened to the extent that they could take a tram to Shepherds Bush and still be back in time for tea. Amy thought the new transport a real triumph of technology, and her regular trips between the two shops with messages during the working week took on a whole new meaning with the opportunity of a ride. She enjoyed these outings enormously, even if it did mean seeing the arrogant Ned Cox with his brusque manner and probing eyes which always seemed to be accusing her of something. He was a real sobersides, that one, and she was very glad he didn't work at the Ealing branch. The sons of the two partners couldn't be more different, she often thought. Clifford was so lively and full of fun while Ned was as serious and forbidding as an old man, and him only a year older than Clifford.

Gradually the ties to home became less strong. She still missed her family and the warmth of the people in the East End. Bethnal Green would always be her true home, of course, but when it was time to leave after her monthly visit, she no longer felt such a wrench. It had taken a while to adjust but she was at last beginning to feel comfortable living the other side of London.

*   *   *

'It's a beautiful piece of jewellery, Madam,' said Amy dutifully one spring Saturday afternoon as she cast a critical eye over an ornate gold pendant set with diamonds and sapphires, lying against the fleshy throat of a lady customer of advanced middle age. Her dumpy form was squeezed incongruously into a pale blue dress with a mass of buttons and bows and frills sweeping from the bodice. Her enormous hat was elaborately trimmed with white ribbons.

'Mmm, I'm not quite sure,' said the woman, studying her reflection in the mirror. 'I fancy it might be a little too plain.'

Too plain! thought Amy incredulously. Why, she already looks like an overdressed pantomime dame. Personally, Amy considered the piece, with its abundance of carved leaves and elaborate patterns, to be quite wrong for this multi-chinned customer, but during her five years in the trade she had learned that the primary role of jewellery was to display a person's wealth and position in society. The customer's opinion was influenced by the obviousness of a piece's financial value rather than its aesthetic merit. Amy's more imaginative eye favoured a plainer piece for this particular lady.

'I think anything fancier might be a little too much,' she suggested warily.

'Oh, do you really?' said the woman, with a note of surprise in her voice, for it was unusual for an assistant to disagree with someone of her purchasing potential. She turned to her husband who was sitting on a chair at the counter. 'What do you think of this pendant, Henry?'

'It looks well on you, but you have to wear it, my dear,' he said patiently, but without a great deal of interest.

'I'm not quite sure if this is the one for me,' said his wife doubtfully.

'We do have a similar piece that might interest you,' said Amy, moving from behind the counter and going to one of the central showcases. She took a plain gold pendant, set with diamonds and pearls, from its black satin bed and spread it on the counter for the customer to see. 'Perhaps you might prefer this? It's a little plainer than the other one, but extremely beautiful, don't you think, with the pearls dropping from the diamond cluster in the centre?'

'You *really* think this is more impressive?' said the woman, studying the piece.

'I think it's lovely,' said Amy, with unveiled admiration. As she had become more experienced in her work, she had grown to see jewellery as more than just a commodity for sale. The designs interested her.

63

She had taken the trouble to learn about the various metals and techniques used in jewellery making, and had occasionally made sketches of brooches and buckles and showed them to Mr Burridge. He had been enthusiastic about a few of them and had even suggested to Mr Jackson that he make some of them up and put them on display in the window. But Ralph Jackson had frowned upon the idea of using the ideas of a shopgirl, and had said they would continue to limit their own productions to modified copies of the popular mass-produced pieces they bought in from wholesale jewellers. Amy carefully fastened the pendant around the woman's neck. 'There, isn't that gorgeous?'

'Mmm, it is nice.'

'It really suits you,' said Amy.

Observing herself in the mirror, the woman fingered the piece, looking at it from a variety of angles. 'Well, Henry?' she said, turning to him.

'It's your birthday present, my dear,' he said. 'You must choose.'

Still undecided, the customer continued to consult the mirror, while Amy went back to her place at the counter and waited in silence for the choice to be made.

Turning to Amy, the woman said, 'Do you *honestly* think this one suits me better than the other one.'

'Yes, I do,' said Amy. 'But it is only a personal opinion.'

Madam thought about this for a few more moments. 'We'll take it,' she said at last, her smile indicating her pleasure in Amy's advice.

The item was carefully placed in a bed of black satin in a red case embossed with the Jackson & Cox

64

name.

'That will be thirty guineas please, sir,' said Amy, delighted with the transaction for she was confident in her judgement.

*   *   *

Soon after the couple had left, Amy was summoned to Mr Rawlings' office where he was sitting at his desk, pale with anger. 'I have just watched you sell a pendant for thirty guineas,' he said.

'Have you?' She was so used to his vigilant presence in the shop as to be almost oblivious of it.

'Yes, I have. And since you could have sold one for forty guineas, I am not best pleased.'

'The more expensive one didn't suit the customer.'

'And that is your considered opinion, is it?' he snapped sarcastically.

'Yes, it is. She's far too short-necked for anything so fancy. The plainer one looked much better on her.'

'Oh, I see.' He sneered at her across the desk. 'So now you're an expert on what style of jewellery people should wear, are you?'

'No, not at all,' she said with determined calm, 'but I've been here long enough to know a little bit about what looks right.'

'It is not your place to offer an opinion,' he growled.

She threw him a cynical look. 'It would have been perfectly in order for me to offer my opinion had I persuaded her to buy something *more* expensive, though, wouldn't it?' She was aware that she was overstepping the mark, but was too angry to care.

He ignored that. 'You are here to sell jewellery, not to comment on it. If a customer wants an opinion you

65

should call a senior member of staff. They all have far more experience than you.'

'But it was *my* opinion she wanted,' Amy pointed out firmly.

'Both pieces were of the finest quality, well worth the price,' he rasped. 'You should have steered her towards the more expensive one. It makes good business sense.'

Clifford entered the office, but both Amy and Mr Rawlings were far too involved in their conflict to pay any attention.

'Sharp practice, more like,' she snapped. 'Customers won't come back once they realise the advice they've been given is in our best interests, not theirs.'

'The more expensive piece looked better on her,' insisted Mr Rawlings. 'I wouldn't suggest you should have sold it to her otherwise.'

Amy glared at him, her cheeks flaming. 'That's a matter of opinion,' she said. 'I realise it's in your interests to get the shop turnover as high as possible because of your bonus, but I don't see why I should have to lie to the customers because of it.'

'Don't you *dare* speak to me like that,' he shouted, springing from his seat and glowering down at her.

'Don't expect me to tell lies then.'

'Hey, steady on, both of you,' intervened Clifford, rather hesitantly, for he was not partial to quarrels or scenes.

'I'm sorry, Mr Clifford,' said Amy hotly, 'but we must sort this out once and for all.' She turned back to Mr Rawlings. 'If the way I do my work doesn't suit you, perhaps I should leave?'

'Oh, no,' said Clifford impulsively. 'I'm sure there's no need for anything so drastic.'

66

Mr Rawlings was taken aback by Amy's suggestion. It was coming to something when a common shopgirl thought she could resign, when she should be living in fear of dismissal. People should know their place within the framework of society. Damned socialist propaganda! It did nothing but unsettle the lower orders and cause problems for their superiors.

He met the unnerving stare of his underling as she waited for his reply. His mind was racing. Miss Atkins had her faults. She had far too much to say for herself for one thing, and a mind of her own which wasn't expected in someone of her status. That wretched Pankhurst woman and her suffragettes had a lot to answer for, giving females ideas above their station. But, loath as he was to admit it, the girl was very good at her work. More sales went through her invoice book than any of the other sales staff's. It was a rare thing for one of her customers to leave without making a purchase, even if they spent less than they could afford.

For some peculiar reason the customers seemed to like the damned girl. The women responded to what some might see as a sunny disposition, and some men just couldn't resist a pretty face. It hardly seemed possible that such an uncouth scrap of a girl, with no idea of how to conduct herself, could have developed into such an elegant, well-spoken young woman. How old was she now? She must be about eighteen. But for all her adult demeanour, she still had a great deal to learn. And if she thought she could undermine his authority, she must think again. He didn't want to lose her but if she stayed it must be on his terms.

'Unless I have an immediate apology, then I think I had better suggest to Mr Jackson Senior that you look for another position, Miss Atkins.'

CHAPTER FOUR

Amy's knees were trembling. What on earth had possessed her to give him the opportunity to get rid of her? She liked her job here. The jewellery trade interested her. She didn't want to work in some dreary draper's store, or grocery shop slicing bacon and cheese all day. But, on the other hand, she'd rather not stay on if it meant losing her integrity. 'I'm sorry I was rude to you, Mr Rawlings,' she said at last. 'But if working here means I can't be honest in my dealings with the customers, then there's no point in my staying.'

'Come, come, Miss Atkins,' interjected Clifford anxiously. 'Surely there's no need to resign over a small difference of opinion?'

She turned her attention to him, her head held high, small round face flushed against the white starched blouse she wore with a long black skirt. 'There is if I'm not to be allowed to conduct myself in the way that I think is right.'

'I'm sure Mr Rawlings isn't suggesting you do anything that is against your principles.' He turned to his male colleague. 'Are you, Mr Rawlings?'

'Of course not,' said Mr Rawlings, changing his tune since it was obvious where Clifford's sympathies lay. The older man was under no illusions as to the power of Clifford's position in the firm as a member of the Jackson family, despite the fact that he was about as much use to the company as a prongless toasting fork. Edmund Rawlings had been with the

68

firm since it started in Shepherds Bush and, strictly speaking, was senior to Clifford in rank. But that counted for nothing against Jackson blood when it came to this sort of conflict. Amy Atkins' sales record would not have gone unnoticed by the directors either. 'I was merely pointing out some business tactics, that's all. If Miss Atkins genuinely thought the less expensive item was right for the customer, then so be it.'

Clifford looked from one to the other doubtfully. 'Well, Miss Atkins, are you happy with that?'

Guessing the senior assistant's volte-face was for Clifford's benefit, she was uncertain. But on considering the meagre employment alternatives open to her, said, 'Well, yes, I suppose so.'

'Good. I suggest you get back to work now then,' said Mr Rawlings briskly, looking through the office window into the shop. 'There are people out there waiting for attention.'

'Yes, Mr Rawlings,' she said, reverting to her usual respectful manner and leaving the room, her skirts sweeping the floor as she walked.

Mr Rawlings turned to Clifford, who was watching Amy through the window as she returned to her place. 'Did you want to see me about anything in particular, Clifford?' he asked.

'Oh, yes,' he said absently. 'Mr Burridge wants to know when the brooch pins are expected from the supplier. He needs them urgently for the copies he is making of the butterfly design that proved so popular.'

'Yes, I know the ones.' Mr Rawlings ran a worried hand over his brow. 'The order was sent to the suppliers several weeks ago. I'll check with the office upstairs as to the delivery date.' He scratched his head. 'I suppose I'd better send Miss Atkins to the other shop to get some pins to tide us over until they come in.'

'Good idea,' said Clifford, a gleam coming into his eye.

*   *   *

Amy walked briskly to the tram stop, glad of a respite from the shop after the altercation with Mr Rawlings. It was a fine sunny afternoon, just the sort of weather for a ride on the upper deck of the tram. Being a Saturday afternoon, the Broadway was heaving with shoppers. Well-dressed women with pretty hats and parasols poured into shops or gazed into the windows, while long-suffering husbands hovered nearby. Across the road a crowd had gathered. Eager to know what was going on, she peered this way and that, until the head of a big brown bear with a muzzled mouth came into view. It was bobbing and swaying above the heads of the audience as it danced on its hind legs, the trainer holding the end of its lead in one hand and a heavy pole in the other. The dusty road was crammed with carriages and carts; bicycles; horsebuses; and a procession of trams going the other way.

Feeling a tap on her shoulder, she turned to see Clifford. 'Hello,' he said, beaming at her.

'Hello,' she said without surprise, for he was often to be seen strolling in the Broadway during working hours. Such was the privilege of family.

'Nice day.'

'A treat to be out.' She wasn't quite sure what to say. 'You out on business?'

'Something like that,' he said, flashing her a wicked

70

smile.

She grinned. 'Swinging the lead, eh? Well, I can't say as I blame you on an afternoon like this. I was glad of the excuse to get out of the shop myself. A tram ride makes a nice change from the counter.'

'I probably shouldn't be saying this,' he said, leaning towards her confidentially, 'but I thought you were awfully good just now, the way you stood up to Mr Rawlings. He's a nice enough fellow, but set in his ways.'

'You're right, you shouldn't be saying it,' she said. 'You being on the same side of the fence as him.'

'I meant what I said, though,' he told her earnestly. 'I admire you enormously.'

What was she supposed to do when the boss's son paid her such attention? She could hardly be rude to him. And naturally she was flattered. Clifford Jackson was one of the most handsome young men in the area. She grinned up at him, noticing the warm eyes, the smiling mouth, the straw boater side-tilted rakishly.

'Thanks very much,' she said, blushing and tucking a stray lock of hair into her black straw hat. To alleviate the sudden awkwardness, she turned away and looked along the road, shading her eyes from the sun. 'Ah, good, here comes my tram at last.'

'I was wondering if you might like to come out with me sometime soon,' he blurted out.

She stared at him in astonishment. A little harmless flirting was one thing; an invitation out quite another.

'Me, go out with you?'

'That's right,' he said. 'Why not?'

'I should have thought that was obvious,' she said in her usual down-to-earth manner.

'With me being who I am, you mean?' he said breezily.

'Of course.'

'Oh, I don't bother about things like that,' he assured her lightly.

'If you're not worried, then neither am I,' she said lightheartedly.

The tram clanked and rattled to a halt. 'Can we fix it up then?' he asked quickly.

'When did you have in mind?' she asked, though there was not much choice, given her limited free time.

'How about tomorrow afternoon?' he suggested.

Relieved that it wasn't her Sunday for Bethnal Green, she said, 'Suits me.'

'I'll meet you outside the station at two-thirty. Is that all right?'

'That's fine.'

Clasping her hat to her head, she hopped on to the tram and clambered up the curved staircase to find a seat on top. Well, well, she thought excitedly as the breeze from the movement of the tram nearly took her hat, little ole me walking out with Clifford Jackson on a Sunday afternoon. Isn't that the most amazing thing?

* * *

Clifford Jackson was in high spirits as he strolled back to the shop. He hadn't been so excited about a girl in ages. Amy Atkins was a corker and no mistake, even if he had been a bit slow to realise it. The familiarity of working alongside her every day had blinded him to the fact that she was growing up. But a few weeks ago while walking in the Broadway he'd

72

been shocked to realise that the blonde attracting the attention of passing males was none other than little Amy, the shop's most junior assistant. Since then he'd watched her about her work with increasing fascination. In the office just now he had thought her magnificent. So full of spirit and dignity. Much more alluring than the well-bred ladies he usually escorted on outings.

One did occasionally have a fancy for those from the lower orders. He remembered once having a crush on the housemaid at the home of a friend he'd been staying with. There had been a few furtive embraces in his room, he recalled, but one drew the line at actually escorting such a girl in public. That would be *too* embarrassing.

So why had he committed himself to doing just that with Amy? Perhaps because she worked with him at the shop, the gulf seemed less than it might had she been a housemaid. One might even stretch a point and call her a colleague, he thought, with determined self-deception. And frankly all other considerations were swept aside by his attraction towards her. There would be a row at home if the parents got wind of it, of course. Mother would have a fit at the idea of him being seen in broad daylight with one of the staff. But he'd cross that bridge if he came to it.

*   *   *

The moment the words were out, Amy realised her mistake in mentioning the exciting change in her fortune in the presence of Mrs Wilks.

'No good'll come of it,' said the cook gloomily over supper that night. 'You should have declined his invitation.'

73

'I don't see why,' grinned Amy. 'It'll be fun. Mr Clifford is a good sort. He was kind to me when I first started work at the shop.'

'That's as may be, but what do yer think the master and mistress are gonna say if they find out?' she warned, glaring at Amy over the rim of her cocoa cup.

'What I do in my spare time is none of their business.' Amy was no fool. She knew her place in the scheme of things even if she wasn't so obedient to it as some. But if Clifford Jackson was prepared to break the rules for an afternoon, so was she.

'It is when you're walking out with their son,' said Mrs Wilks. 'They ain't gonna like it one little bit.'

'I think it's dead romantic,' said Violet dreamily. 'I'd go if Mr Clifford asked me out. I think he's lovely.'

'Stupid girl,' tutted Mrs Wilks. 'Many a housemaid has had her head turned by the son of the house. And it's landed every last one of 'em in the street, often with an extra mouth to feed.'

'But I'm not a housemaid,' Amy pointed out.

'Housemaid, shopgirl, it makes no difference when it comes to class. Ask yourself why, when you both live in the same house, he's asked you to meet him at a place outside of it?'

'Such a fuss. All I'm doing is going out with him for a few hours,' Amy declared hotly, 'I'm not planning on marrying him.'

'I should think not,' roared Mrs Wilks. 'You'll be disappointed if you are. It's them and us, and you'd be wise not to forget it.' She tutted again and looked at Amy with concern, her tone softening. 'Mr Clifford really ought to know better. You just be careful, my girl.'

Amy laughed. 'Don't you worry about me, Mrs Wilks,' she said amiably for she knew the older woman only had her welfare at heart. 'I was brought up in the East End, remember. I was working in the market when I was ten. If I managed to cope with the villains around there, I'm quite sure I can cope with the likes of Clifford Jackson.'

'I do hope so, for your sake,' said Mrs Wilks, shaking her head in a doom-laden way.

*　　　*　　　*

Having been a secret admirer of Clifford's for years, Amy found it hard to believe that he was actually waiting for her when she turned the corner into Haven Green and saw him standing outside the station in the sunshine, looking a real gent in his blazer, cream-coloured flannels and straw boater. She was overly conscious of the fact that her pink frock and matching hat had been purchased from a stall in a street market one Sunday recently when she'd been home for the day. But her doubts were soon diminished by the warmth of his greeting.

'Hello there,' he said, beaming and handing her a box of chocolate creams.

'For me?' she said with surprise and delight, since she had never before received such a gift.

'Yes, of course they're for you,' he said with a chuckle, her pleasure in what to him was a mere trifle boosting his self-esteem.

'Thank you. Thank you very much,' she said, a touch embarrassed. 'Isn't it a lovely afternoon?'

'It is indeed.' He looked across the road to the cab rank. 'I thought we night take a cab to the river at Richmond.'

'What a lovely idea.'

'We could take a boat out, perhaps? Would you like that?'

'I'd love it. I've never been to Richmond.'

With his hand on her arm they crossed the road and climbed into a taxi, dark and musty in contrast to the bright sunlight. Into the quiet of the Sunday afternoon came the cries of children playing on Haven Green. Glancing out of the cab window as they rolled away, Amy saw some sailor-suited boys and little girls with their dolls in basket prams. Nannies in dark uniforms diligently trudged behind gleaming baby carriages.

The waterfront at Richmond was a blaze of colour. Young men and women in fine clothes strolled beside the glinting river which was crowded with a varied assortment of crafts. There were punts, skiffs, rowing boats. Sails flapped in the breeze, and brightly coloured parasols shaded the female passengers from the sun. Ice cream vendors and flower sellers peddled their wares on the lawns and promenades of the waterside.

Clifford hired a small rowing boat and steered them out of the busy stretch of river, with its party atmosphere and palatial houses, into a quieter, more rural ambience. The boat creaked and drifted past grassy banks with lush overhanging foliage and willows trailing into the water.

'Shall I take the oars for a while?' Amy offered as he became breathless.

'Certainly not,' he told her, smiling. 'Rowing is man's work.'

'If you're sure.'

'I am,' he assured her. 'I'll pull into the bank at a suitable spot upriver and we'll sit on the grass for a while.'

They found a shady bank under some trees and settled down on the grass. Amy sat with her legs tucked to the side of her, her dress covering her completely. Clifford half-lay, leaning to one side on an elbow. Stifling a childish urge to keep her gift intact until later to show Violet, she opened the box and offered him a chocolate.

'I want you to have them,' he said.

'I'd like to share them with you.'

'You've talked me into it,' he smiled, 'I'm a glutton for chocolate creams.'

Having made themselves thirsty by working their way through the box, he said, 'We'll quench our thirst with some tea when we get back to the town.'

'Why did you ask me out, Mr Clifford?' she asked.

'Do drop the "mister", please,' he said, adding quickly, 'Keep that for the shop.'

'As you wish,' she said, refusing to ruin her day by letting his last comment upset her. 'But I would like to know why you chose me as a companion.'

Looking into her challenging blue eyes, he realised that she was not simply fishing for compliments. The vivid shade of her eyes and her pink, determined mouth made a stunning combination with her pale skin and fair hair, yet she seemed completely without vanity.

'Isn't it obvious?' he said. 'You are a very pretty girl.'

'Thanks for the compliment,' she said, blushing, 'but you can have your pick of the most beautiful girls around to take out. Why choose a member of staff?'

'Because you are lovely and I am very attracted to you,' he told her candidly.

'I'm flattered,' she said. 'But won't your parents disapprove?'

He averted his eyes. He had deliberately taken her out of Ealing for their date to lessen the possibility of being seen with her by anyone who might relate the incident to his parents. He didn't court trouble with them because they were useful to him in that they provided him with a comfortable home and a good salary for minimum effort on his part. Amy was a bright girl, she must know how the system worked. 'Well, you know how it is with these things...'

'You mean you won't tell them,' she said frankly.

Avoiding the question, he said, 'I didn't bring you here to talk about my parents. I want to get to know you better. You've grown up so suddenly.'

She grinned. 'The process took the usual amount of time.'

He took her hand, smiling into her eyes. 'I imagine it did, but I didn't notice it until a few weeks ago. I must have been going about with my eyes shut.'

'Or too busy noticing other girls,' she said, hoping her voice didn't betray the frisson caused by the touch of his hand.

'Is my reputation that bad?'

'Well ... you're known to have an eye for a pretty girl.'

'Surely there would be something wrong with me if I didn't?' he said. 'Don't tell me you ladies don't look at us chaps with the same sort of eye.'

'Of course we do.'

'Well then.'

'You men have the best of it, though, because you can choose who you go out with, whereas a decent girl has to wait to be asked.'

'That's true.'

78

'I think it's a bit unfair.'

He shrugged. 'I suppose it is really, I've never given it a thought.'

'I doubt if I would if I was a man, either,' she said lightly.

'Anyway, I'm very glad you agreed to come out with me.'

'I'm pleased you asked.'

At the beginning of their outing, Amy had been unsure of her ability to sustain such a long period alone with someone from a different world. Now, she felt confident and deliciously happy to be with him.

After tea in a riverside tea-shop, they caught a cab back to Ealing. On the way, he slipped his arm around her shoulders and she snuggled contentedly against him.

'I'd like us to go out together again,' he said softly.

'Me too.'

'How about one evening next week?'

'Fine.'

'We could go to a show, if you like.'

'That would be lovely,' she said. 'But I finish too late on a Friday and Saturday to make a theatre.'

'How about Wednesday then?'

'Fine.'

'What sort of show do you fancy?'

'What about a music hall?'

'Good idea. We'll go up West,' he suggested enthusiastically, 'I've heard they have a very good show at the London Pavilion.'

'I don't mind which one.'

'And Amy...'

'Yes?'

'Just to avoid any trouble at home, can it be our secret for the time being?'

79

'Not ashamed of me, are you?' she joked, refusing to let doubts spoil the joy of the moment.

'Of course not,' he declared. 'But I think it would be wise to keep our meetings to ourselves for the moment. People will only try to spoil things.'

How right he was, she thought, imagining what Mrs Wilks' reaction would be to her seeing him again. 'I'll not say a word,' she assured him.

CHAPTER FIVE

'Wasn't she wonderful?' exclaimed Amy, as thunderous applause arose for bosomy blonde singer Lily Larkwood ending her act at the London Pavilion. Dressed to the nines in a riot of blue frills and flounces, she had given her all, armed with a lilting voice and a lively personality which swung from the boldly suggestive to the touchingly sweet. The audience had been held spellbound throughout a selection of favourites, concluding with a robust rendering of 'Oh, Mr Porter', during which the assembled company had been invited to join her in the final chorus.

'She was, indeed,' agreed Clifford, who was enjoying himself immensely. Amy was delightful company, and it was a real treat to be able to bring a girl to a lively show like this. Music hall entertainment was a little too lusty for the taste of most other females of his acquaintance, even these days with its more respectable image appealing to a wider clientele than previously.

Nowadays drinks were prohibited in the main auditorium and meals no longer served, the idea

80

being for people to come primarily to watch the show, not to drink. Even a sprinkling of the uppercrust could be seen in the luxurious foyers and lavishly appointed auditoria of West End halls like this one, which proudly boasted the innovation of tip up seats to replace the old-style tables and chairs of the tawdry establishments of the past.

'These peppermint bullseyes taste good, Clifford,' said Amy, sucking enthusiastically on a confection from the bag he had bought for her in the foyer on the way in. 'Would you like another?'

'*Rather!*' He dipped his hand into the paper bag, his cheeks glowing with the heat, the jovial atmosphere and a couple of gins in the bar before the show. Amy's zest for life was exhilarating, indeed, especially in comparison to the fastidious dispositions of the more refined young ladies he was used to escorting. He was really quite smitten by the novelty of her unrestrained vitality. She looked stunning this evening, too, in a lavender dress and a straw hat trimmed with matching chiffon. Her hair was swept up under it with honey coloured curls spilling saucily on to her brow.

'It's a rope walker next,' she said excitedly, consulting her programme then fanning her face with it, her glance moving around the crowded auditorium from her seat in the front of the stalls. A pall of smoke rose to the balconies and galleries where glowing faces shone beneath elaborate millinery, adornments of fruit, flowers, ribbons and feathers bobbing and swaying brightly among the dark caps and bowlers.

There was an expectant hubbub as they waited for the next act to come on. The vibrant atmosphere enveloped Amy in a warm, comforting tide. She was

81

having a marvellous time. Clifford was great fun to be with and very attentive to her. He seemed an awfully decent type. A real gent, in fact. They were in the best seats at the finest show in town. What more could a girl ask?

The chairman, a well-groomed man in full evening dress, puffing on a cigar, requested silence with a rap of his hammer then introduced the next act: a bald-headed, wiry little fellow in a red and gold jacket and white tights who pranced about on a high rope, pretending to lose his balance to loud 'oohs' and 'aahs' from the audience. He was followed by a troupe of trapeze artists, some performing dogs, and a line of heavily rouged chorus girls in short candy-pink dresses who clattered across the stage high kicking and smiling as though their lives depended on it. Top of the bill was a famous male comedian who recited a few monologues, told some jokes, and ended the show with community singing to 'My Old Man Said Follow the Van'.

Amy was still feeling uplifted from the effects of the entertainment when she and Clifford emerged from the station at Ealing.

He apparently felt the same. 'I haven't enjoyed myself so much in ages,' he confessed as they headed in the direction of Orchard Avenue.

'Nor me.'

'We *must* go out together again soon, eh, Amy?' he said eagerly.

'If you like.'

'Are you doing anything on Sunday afternoon?'

'Nothing special,' she said, once again relieved that it was not her Sunday for visiting her folks.

'Would you like to go to Hyde Park if it's a nice day?'

82

'That would be lovely.'

'I'll meet you at the station at two o'clock then.'

'Very well.'

As they turned the corner into Orchard Avenue, he stopped and turned to her. 'Perhaps we'd better go separately from here,' he suggested rather sheepishly, 'just in case we're seen together.'

'If you wish.'

That Sunday she spent another glorious afternoon with him, sitting in the sunshine by the Serpentine, eating ice cream and talking. They had tea out, then travelled home on the train thoroughly content. Their first kiss came from a mutual impulse as they turned into Orchard Avenue and prepared to part and finish the journey separately. Amy was quite breathless with the pleasure of it.

One evening during the following week, she met him after work and they went to a bioscope show in a public hall in Acton. They sat enthralled through a one-and-a-half-hour programme comprising several short films that flickered and wobbled on a screen that seemed to have continuous rain pouring down over it. Outside they laughed because a fine rain was actually falling.

As spring turned to summer and their affair intensified, they spent most of their spare time together. They went to theatres, music halls, bioscope shows, took boat trips on the river, and sometimes they just walked, anywhere, simply to be alone. Always their meetings took place away from Ealing, though they once threw caution to the winds and went to a musical comedy at Ealing Theatre. It became increasingly difficult to pretend there was nothing special between them when they were together at the shop. Somehow they managed,

83

though furtive embraces were stolen in all sorts of incongruous corners—the stock room, the backyard, the offices upstairs if they could find one that was empty.

Ealing Broadway Railway Station became their special meeting place, and shadowy corners beneath the trees on Haven Green became their own romantic retreat. Swept along by the strength of her passion for him, Amy existed only for their next meeting, deliberately blinding herself to the doubtful future of this clandestine affair.

Violet was her only confidante. Amy's happiness had simply been too great to bear alone, though Mrs Wilks rested easy in the belief that that first outing with Clifford had been the only one.

One Sunday evening when Amy emerged from the station, having paid her duty visit to Bethnal Green, she was pleasantly surprised to find Clifford waiting for her.

'I've missed you,' he said, impulsively sweeping her into his arms and kissing her. 'I've had a perfectly beastly Sunday without you.'

'Me too,' she said, for she felt like death without him. 'But I have to go and see my folks once a month.'

Occasionally reality penetrated her romantic cocoon, and she was hurt that he never showed any interest in her family or any aspect of her life that didn't include him. But doubts were soon overruled by the strength of her feelings for him.

'I can't bear to say goodnight yet,' he said.

'Nor me.'

'Let's go somewhere.'

'Where?'

'Anywhere,' he whispered. 'Let's just walk. I don't

care where we go as long as I'm with you.'

The evenings were long and it was still light as they walked away from the station, oblivious to all else but each other.

*   *   *

'Are you warm enough, Florence?' asked Ralph from the wheel of the Rover as he and his wife proceeded along the Broadway, turning at The Feathers in a homeward direction. Marshall's night off was no anathema to Ralph since he had become a motorist, because it gave him a chance to play with his new toy.

'Yes, thank you, dear,' replied Florence happily, for she had enjoyed her visit to friends in Kew and was in good humour. 'It's quite a pleasant evening.'

In common with other motorists proudly disporting themselves in their open-topped vehicles, she was well protected against the dust and fresh air. Despite the time of year, she had a blanket wrapped around her legs, and was wearing a motoring hat with a thick veil across her face, and goggles.

'Quite a few people about, aren't there?' he remarked idly as they approached the station area.

'Mmm. It's the fine weather that brings them out of an evening.'

A train had just come in and there was a rush of people flooding out of the station and hurrying across the road to the cab rank. They slowed down by the cabs so as not to frighten the horses. Florence glanced absently towards the station, feeling wonderfully superior to the pedestrians. In fact, her general feeling of well-being was derived from the fact that the people they had just visited did not yet have a car. Their envy was nectar to Florence.

85

Suddenly her attention was caught by a young woman in a straw hat coming out of the station. 'Oh, look, Ralph, isn't that Amy Atkins?' she said, familiar with a member of the shop staff only because she was resident at Floral House.

'So it is,' he said, removing his attention from the road for long enough to take a quick glance.

Then his eyes widened and his hands tightened on the wheel. They both watched in horror as their only son strolled towards the creature, flung his arms around her and kissed her, right there in public, before walking away with her hand on his arm.

* * *

'I love you, Amy,' declared Clifford ardently as they strolled beside a hedgerow in Hanger Lane. The country lane was silent and deserted as dusk began to fall.

'Do you really, Clifford?' she asked, thrilled by this declaration.

'Yes, *really*,' he said, the words flowing impulsively with his affectionate mood. They came to a stile into a field and climbed over, giggling and touching. On the other side they fell into each other's arms, hidden from the road by the tall hedges. 'I want us to be together all the time. I can't bear another Sunday away from you.'

'Nor I from you.'

'I'm lost without you.'

'Does this mean you're going to bring things out into the open?'

'We certainly can't go on like this,' he said, kissing her passionately as she leaned against the trunk of an oak tree.

86

'You'll tell your parents then?'

'Yes.'

'You really mean it?'

'Of course.'

'It'll be lovely to be together openly. Not to have to hide the way we feel, especially at the shop.'

'Mmm.'

'We'll be a proper couple.'

'So we will.'

'Clifford ... no! Don't do that.'

'Why not?'

'You know why.'

'But I love you,' he proclaimed earnestly, completely caught up in the passion of the moment.

'Yes, but...'

'Do you love me?'

'You know I do.'

'If you really did, you'd want to.'

'It isn't that I don't...'

'Well then, stop being silly and show me how much you care,' he persuaded urgently, cursing her manproof layers of undergarments.

'Are you really going to tell your parents?' she asked, more to slow things down than for reassurance.

'Yes, yes, tonight when I get home, if they are still up,' he murmured, feverishly wrestling with a maze of whalebone and laces. 'If not, I'll tell them tomorrow.'

Amy's sexual education was very limited. She knew all about the evil of sin and the glory of virtue. In vague embarrassed mutterings, her mother had warned her that the 'dreadful deed' must be avoided at all costs until after marriage because of the dire consequences for a girl who found herself in trouble.

87

But Amy had always had the impression that sex was pleasurable only to men. No one had ever told her about the power of instinct that made the whole thing irresistible to the female of the species too.

The grass beneath her was damp with nocturnal dew. Somewhere in the distance a dog barked, a train rumbled. Overhead a light summer breeze rustled through the branches of the oak tree.

* * *

'You'll have to dismiss her, Ralph,' pronounced Florence, having regained her powers of speech after the shock of seeing Clifford disgracing himself in public with that *dreadful* girl. Florence and her husband were in the drawing room and she was speaking in a low tone for fear of being overheard by the servants. Looking very pale, she lolled weakly in her high-backed, leather chair. 'Just think of the scandal this will cause. Our son walking out with one of your shopgirls. If we've seen them out together, so will other people if we don't put a stop to it.'

'Yes, dear.'

'We'll be a laughing stock among our friends,' she ranted. 'The sooner she's gone the better. Clifford will soon forget her when she's not around him all day.'

He didn't reply, fearing such drastic action might wreak havoc for him personally. George Atkins was a sharp operator. He might well choose to say that Ralph had renegued on their deal if his daughter was dismissed, even though she had been with the firm for five years. Damn Clifford! Ralph didn't mind him having a fling with a girl like that, but to allow himself to be seen ... had the boy taken leave of his senses?

88

'Ralph,' said Florence, when his answer was not forthcoming, 'you *will* dismiss her at once, won't you? As soon as she comes home you must send for her and tell her she is not to go into the shop again and we want her out of this house first thing tomorrow morning.'

'Do you think that's wise, dear?' he suggested warily, searching his mind for a viable excuse to offer Florence.

'Whatever do you mean?' she asked tearfully.

'Well ... don't you think such a dramatic action might only serve to increase Clifford's interest in her?' he said. 'Might it not be wiser to let the thing run its course? It's obviously not serious, just a flirtation.'

She ran a weary hand across her brow. 'No, no, we can't do that. It must be stopped before it becomes a topic for every gossip in town.' She sniffed into her lace-edged handkerchief. 'I can see what you mean about dismissing her, though. It might make him feel he has to defend her. Perhaps it would be better to point out the foolishness of his behaviour, and tell him to end his relationship with her. Once he knows he has been found out, I think he'll do what we want because it isn't in his interests to go against us. The girl will probably leave of her own accord then.'

'I still think we should leave Clifford to lose interest in his own time,' he said, instinctively wary of any action that might come to the attention of the mischief-making George Atkins. 'He'll finish it with no regrets then.'

'No, it must end now,' she insisted. 'We'll wait up for him and talk to him as soon as he gets in.'

'Very well, my dear.'

*   *   *

89

'Have you taken leave of your senses, my boy?' barked Ralph an hour or so later. 'Disgracing yourself in broad daylight with one of the staff.'

'Oh dear,' said Clifford sheepishly. 'You saw us.'

'Saw you?' roared Ralph, his anger increased by the problems this could cause him personally as well as the risk to the family reputation. 'I should think the whole of Ealing saw you, canoodling in a public place like that.'

'Disgusting behaviour for a young man of your background,' said Florence, dabbing her brow with a handkerchief. 'I'm disappointed in you, Clifford, I really am.'

'You've made your mother feel quite ill,' barked Ralph.

'The shock has given me palpitations,' said Florence, clasping her chest theatrically.

'I'm sorry, Mother,' said Clifford, chewing his lip anxiously.

'I should think so too,' she said, cheered a little by his apology. At least he had acknowledged the fact that he had done wrong. She'd been afraid he might have gone out of his mind altogether and imagined himself to be fond of the creature. 'So, can we take it that you will end this ridiculous affair at once?'

'Oh!' Despite what he had said to Amy, Clifford had had no intention of bringing their affair into the open. But neither had he planned to give her up. This unexpected development had thrown him into confusion and he needed time to gather his wits.

'Well,' said his father, 'what do you have to say?'

'Er . . .'

'Come on, my boy,' urged Ralph. 'I mean, we assume that this association is nothing more than a mild flirtation.'

'Of course,' said Clifford.

'Good. So please end it at the earliest opportunity,' he ordered briskly. 'As the heir to my estate, you have to be very careful of the company you keep. You mustn't make yourself vulnerable to every damned gold digger.'

'Now that isn't fair,' said Clifford impetuously. 'Amy isn't a gold digger.'

'Of course she is,' said Ralph. 'And it's perfectly understandable that she should be. After all, what chance has she of better things in life, but by marrying someone like you?'

Clifford knew his father was wrong. Amy wanted him for himself not for his money, he'd stake his life on it. But Clifford was to courage what King Henry VIII had been to self-denial, and he was particularly weak against his parents for through them all good things came. As much as he felt drawn to Amy, he wasn't prepared to put his comfortable lifestyle at risk for her. 'Yes, I suppose you're right,' he agreed, looking from one parent to the other.

'Can we have your word that you'll stop seeing her then?' said Ralph.

'Certainly you can.'

'Thank goodness for that,' said Florence.

'As that's settled, I'm going to bed,' said Clifford, giving his mother a dutiful peck on the cheek. 'I'm sorry to have upset you. Good night.'

'Good night, son.'

Upstairs in his room, he flopped on to the bed fully dressed, staring at the ceiling and thinking of Amy and what had happened between them earlier. Just the memory made him groan with pleasure. Her warmth and vibrant femininity drove him crazy. He simply could not bear to stop seeing her, not for the

91

moment anyway. It was out of the question. And since he couldn't afford to upset the parents either, he would just have to continue to meet her in secret and make sure they weren't seen together.

*　　*　　*

'Anyway, Amy, my mother wasn't feeling too well when I got home last night, so I didn't get the chance to speak to my parents about us,' lied Clifford, as he lay beside her on the grass beneath that same oak tree the following evening.

'Oh, that's a shame,' she said lazily, breathing in the scent of hay from nearby fields. 'But you will tell them soon?'

'Of course I will,' he said, leaning over to kiss her. 'But there's plenty of time.'

'Mmm, that's true.' Whether or not his parents, or anyone else for that matter, recognised them as a couple seemed unimportant in the joy of being with him here like this.

*　　*　　*

'Is everything all right at work?' asked Amy's mother one Sunday tea-time in the autumn.

'Yes, of course it is,' snapped Amy. 'Is there any reason why it shouldn't be?'

'Pardon me for breathing, I'm sure,' retorted Gladys, 'I was only makin' conversation.'

'Sorry, Mum.'

'What's the matter with you today, Amy?' asked her father. 'You got a right mood on yer.'

'No, I haven't,' she lied, 'I'm a bit tired that's all.'

'The Jacksons are treating yer right, I 'ope?' said

George.

'I've no complaints.'

'Have some more winkles, love,' said Gladys.

'No thanks, I'm not all that hungry.'

'Don't you want your muffin?' asked Alfie hopefully.

'No, you can have it.'

'Ooh, ta, sis.'

'You're welcome,' she said, managing a smile for her fifteen-year-old brother who was now a strong, muscular youth who worked in a soap factory.

She glanced at the table which was rather more generously spread than when she had lived at home: winkles; bread and marge; tinned meat; muffins. And all set out on a checked tablecloth too. Things were easier for her parents now that both she and Alfie were earning. The room was still overcrowded and untidy, but at least smelly nappies were no longer a feature now that Bobby and Pete were bigger. It was still a poor home, though, and no place to bring Clifford Jackson, she thought gloomily. It wasn't a question of being ashamed of her family. It was a matter of facing the fact that a visit from Clifford would embarrass them all. Class was class, whichever way you looked at it. And that was why Clifford still hadn't told his parents about their affair, however much he made excuses and pretended that he just hadn't had the opportunity.

'Young Bernie Banks is doin' well for 'imself,' said Amy's father chattily. 'Goes around dressed like a real toff these days. Works in the bar at the Empire Music Hall, amongst other things.'

'Other things?' she asked.

'Sells stuff cheap. Watches, cigarettes, and that. He makes a lot of business contacts through working in a

93

bar, I expect,' George explained. 'No questions asked as to how he comes by the stuff. You know Bernie, 'e always was a right little villain, even as a kid. 'E'd sell 'is grannie if he could get a good enough price for 'er.'

'He said he'd be rich one day,' said Amy, forcing an interest, though her mind was dominated by a far more important matter.

The conversation drifted on to other topics. 'Did Alfie tell yer he's been asked to fight in a boxing booth at a fair down Southend way?' asked her mother.

'No, he didn't,' she said, frowning.

'He'll get paid for it,' said George. 'All above board.'

'You be careful, Alfie,' she warned. 'Knocking someone about is no way to earn money.'

'Better than workin' in a factory any day o' the week,' he said cheerfully.

'Maybe, but you could end up not being able to think straight,' she warned.

'Don't fuss, sis,' he said. 'It's only a one-off thing.'

The visit was not a success and Amy left earlier than usual, feeling thoroughly depressed. Sitting on the sooty train as it rattled across London, she made a decision. She wouldn't keep her problem to herself any longer.

* * *

'You're pregnant?' Clifford's look of horror was clearly discernible in the moonlight. 'You mean, you're having a baby?'

'Yes, a child does result from pregnancy, so I'm told,' she said waggishly, trying somehow to lessen the drama of the moment.

94

Clifford closed his eyes and leaned weakly against their favourite oak tree, the moonlight shining on his troubled face. 'Oh God,' he muttered. 'Oh God.'

Crushed by disappointment, for she had been unable to stifle the hope that he might be pleased, she said, 'Is that all you have to say?'

He opened his eyes and looked at her. 'It's such a shock.'

'I felt like that too when I first realised why my period hadn't come,' she said. 'But it shouldn't be a surprise to either of us, should it? Not when you consider how we've been spending our time this last few months.'

'How far gone are you?'

'About two months, I think.'

'Not too late to do something about it then,' he said with relief. 'I've heard there are these women you can go to...'

'No.'

'I'll give you the money.'

'I'm not going to do that, Clifford. I've made up my mind,' she said, plunged into misery at his heartless attitude. Why had she thought this was something that happened only to other girls? How could she have been so stupid as to think Clifford was different, and would want to marry her?

'So you're going to have it then?' he said in dismay.

'Yes.'

'Oh dear.'

'Do you have nothing more helpful to say than that?' she asked coldly.

Clifford searched for coherent thought. Amy was a terrific girl. He liked her a lot. Even loved her, in his way. But marriage was the last thing he had in mind. In fact he'd not planned anything beyond seeing her for as long as he could without his parents finding out. Now, faced with this awesome responsibility, he wanted to put as much distance between her and himself as possible. He wasn't one of the Ned Coxes of this world, boringly reliable and honourable. Clifford was a self-confessed hedonist. The dreary ties of marriage were not for him.

'I don't know what to suggest,' he said, as though he had played no part in her problem. 'I'm blowed if I do. I can help you with money, but...' He shifted uneasily from foot to foot. 'More than that is out of the question, I'm afraid. My parents would disown me if I were to marry you so I'd have no income and no home. I don't have a legal share in the business yet, you see.'

'Surely a man with your experience could get another job,' she pointed out hopefully. 'And we could rent a couple of rooms till we get on our feet.'

Clifford could imagine nothing more hellish and it showed on his face. 'Well, I wasn't actually planning to get married at the moment, to tell the truth.'

Now Amy was angry as well as hurt. 'So I am to bear the burden alone, am I?' she said coldly.

'Not entirely. I've told you, I'll see you're all right for money.'

'Money is the easy way out for you, isn't it?' she snapped. 'Well, I'll tell you this much, Clifford Jackson, a little cash from you isn't going to solve my problems. The workhouse will be my only option. Is that what you want for the mother of your child?'

'Now you're being melodramatic,' he said irritably. 'You can go back to live with your family.'

She gave a cynical laugh. 'You don't seriously imagine they'll have me back to bring shame on them, do you?'

96

'Perhaps they'll surprise you,' he suggested hopefully.

'I doubt if I'll live to have the child once my father finds out.'

'I'm sure you're exaggerating,' he said, biting his lip anxiously. She looked so small and vulnerable with her hat removed to reveal silky golden hair falling untidily around her face. He felt an unexpected moment of compassion for her. It was a pity this had happened because he still wanted her and was going to miss their meetings terribly. 'Anyway there's no need to tell anyone yet. We've got time to work something out.'

'Don't you worry about me,' she said, her head held high. 'I'll manage somehow.' She turned and marched towards the stile.

'Amy, wait for me.'

'I'd rather walk back alone, thank you,' she said haughtily.

He caught her up and helped her over the stile. 'Don't go like this.'

'You are weak, Clifford Jackson, and no use to me,' she said furiously, shrugging off his hand on her arm.

'Hey, steady on,' he said.

'It's better if I walk home alone, just in case anyone sees us together,' she spat, driven to sarcasm by her pain. 'At least you won't have to worry about that anymore because I won't be seeing you again, outside of working hours.'

And she walked away up Hanger Hill with tears streaming down her face. She had never felt more desperate, but she was damned if she would demean herself by showing it.

Watching the small, proud figure in the glow from a solitary street light shining among the trees, Clifford felt a powerful urge to go after her. But he was neither strong enough of character to shoulder his responsibility and stand by her, nor perceptive enough to recognise his weakness. So he merely cursed the fates for conspiring to threaten his comfortable lifestyle, and waited until she was out of sight before starting to walk home.

*   *   *

Violet was unlacing her corsets ready for bed when Amy entered the room. 'Wotcha, Ame,' she said chirpily. 'You 'ad a good time?'

'Yes, thanks,' said Amy, forcing a smile. 'How about you?'

'Lovely, ta,' said Violet, with a sparkle in her eye. 'Joe took me to Hampton Court. We were ages findin' our way out o' the maze. It was ever such a lark.'

'I'll bet,' said Amy, removing her hat and bolero jacket and putting them away in the wardrobe she shared with Violet.

Liberated from the torturous undergarment, Violet scratched herself, sighing blissfully, before slipping into a winceyette nightdress with long sleeves and a high neck. At the washstand she poured some cold water from the jug into the bowl and dipped the flannel into it before soaping it and washing her face.

Violet's life had been transformed by a greengrocer's assistant called Joe Butler, whom she

98

had met when he was delivering vegetables to Floral House. She had been 'walking out' with him all summer in what little spare time she had. Mrs Wilks thoroughly disapproved. According to her he was a wrong 'un with far too much to say for himself. But Amy was pleased to see her friend looking so happy.

'Whassa matter, Ame?' asked Violet, as she climbed into bed and peered at Amy over the sheet. 'You look a bit down.'

Amy took off her skirt and stood in her full-length cotton petticoat. 'I'm all right,' she insisted.

'Well, you don't look it,' said Violet.

The sight of Violet's sympathetic brown eyes proved too much for Amy. 'I'm pregnant,' she said.

'Oh, my Gawd!' said Violet, her hand flying to her mouth. 'That's torn it.'

'I know.'

'What yer gonna do?'

'I've absolutely no idea,' admitted Amy.

*   *   *

Life was unbearable for Amy the following week with Clifford avoiding her, and her having to hide her queasiness from all and sundry.

When she awoke on Sunday morning, the thought of the long hours without him was more than she could bear. The small room was damp and cold with autumn chill, condensation covering the window and forming little lakes on the sill. Violet was already downstairs at work and the emptiness around Amy intensified the void in her heart. Feeling tired and nauseous, her first impulse was to bury herself beneath the covers for the entire day and hide from the world, but such behaviour would only arouse

99

Mrs Wilks' suspicions.

There was nothing else for it: she would go home to Bethnal Green for the day. At least there if she seemed out of sorts, everyone would just assume she was in a bad mood.

It was drizzling as she walked to Tucker Street from the station, around midday. The pavements were squelchy with mud from the road and the sooty buildings looked dingier than ever in the rain. The smell of bad drains and horse dung rose from the streets in an overpowering miasma.

Bernie Banks was coming out of the house as she went in. 'Wotcha, Amy. How yer goin', love?'

'Mustn't grumble, Bernie,' she said, noticing his smart navy suit which he wore with a rather dashing checked cap. His boyish features were firming into manhood, his jaw squaring up, his nose becoming almost aquiline. He had the same sharp eyes, though, always on the lookout for the chance to make a fast quid. His dark looks made him look rather striking, she thought. 'You look well.'

'Never better,' he said. 'Got a place of me own now just off the Roman Road. I've just bin payin' the folks a visit.'

'I heard you're doing fine.'

He pulled a pocket watch from his waistcoat and consulted it. 'Well, it's good to see yer, love, but I must be off,' he said, putting up his umbrella. 'I've gotta meet a man in a pub about a spot o' business.' He looked more closely into her face, and frowned. 'You sure you're all right, you look a bit peaky.'

'I'm fine,' she said emphatically.

'Oh.' He still looked doubtful. 'Oh, well, as long as yer sure?'

'I am.'

'See yer around then.'

'Yeah, sure.'

Although she and Bernie had gone their separate ways, she knew, without him saying a word, that he was still her friend and would always be there for her if she needed him. But he couldn't help her now. This was strictly her problem.

She paused in the hallway of the house, wanting to heave as an amalgam of foul smells engulfed her. Boiled cabbage; damp; urine; mouse droppings. At one time she had been so used to it as to be unaffected. Now she thought she would choke. Forcing back the threatening bile, she made her way upstairs holding her breath. Once she was inside her parents' rooms, it would be better.

'Blimey!' said Alfie as she entered the room. 'You 'ere again, sis? You came last Sunday.'

'Good to see yer, ducks,' said her mother in surprise as she turned from the stove where she was preparing Sunday dinner. 'We weren't expecting you this week.' She had a knife in her hand with which she had been prodding some potatoes boiling in a saucepan. 'We're 'avin' mutton and roast potatoes. I'll put a couple more spuds in for you. I'm just bringin' 'em to the boil before they go in the oven.'

'Smells nice,' lied Amy, for the greasy fumes were making her glands feel watery. 'But don't worry about doing extra for me. I'm not all that hungry.'

'Don't be so daft, it's no trouble,' said Gladys. She threw Amy a shrewd glance as her daughter took off her hat and coat and hung them on the hook on the door. 'So, what brings you 'ome again so soon?'

'No particular reason, I just fancied coming over.'

'Boyfriend chucked yer, 'as he?' teased Alfie.

'Amy's boyfriend's chucked 'er,' chaffed Bobby in

101

a sing-songy voice, erupting into fits of laughter along with his brother Pete.

The family had jokingly speculated all summer about Amy's boyfriend. She had admitted only to there being someone. She was so used to their harmless ribbing as to be immune to it as a rule, but today their childish comments pushed her to the brink of tears.

'Take no notice of 'em,' said Gladys, observing her daughter's flushed cheeks and overbright eyes. 'Go on, yer little horrors, clear off out of it and stop tormenting yer sister.'

The two little boys moved away from the cooking area and began tumbling and wrestling on the floor.

'Shall I give you a hand with the dinner, Mum?' offered Amy, managing to recover her composure.

'You can make the gravy later on,' said Gladys. 'But yer dad won't be back from the pub for ages so we won't be 'avin' it yet.'

Her mother opened the oven door and removed a baking dish containing a small joint of fatty meat which she basted before replacing it. It was too much for Amy. The sight of all that fat, along with the pungent cooking steam, finally destroyed her resistance. She felt the blood drain from her face, and her whole body was cold with sweat. Gagging, she rushed from the room and tore downstairs to the lavatory in the backyard.

When she came back into the room, weak but feeling better, her mother was sitting at the table in an empty room. 'Right, my girl, I've sent the little 'uns to play downstairs in the 'all, and Alfie to the Jew's shop for some gravy browning that I don't need. So now we've got the place to ourselves, let's 'ave it out in the open.'

102

'I don't know what you mean.'

'Come off it, ducks,' said Gladys, her thin face creased with worry, 'I wasn't born yesterday. I know pregnancy when I see it. How far gone are yer?'

The relief of having her mother know was overwhelming. 'A couple of months, I think,' she said softly.

'Who did it to yer?'

'Clifford Jackson.'

Gladys' eyes widened. 'The boss's son?'

'I'm afraid so.'

'Oh, Amy, you little fool,' gasped her mother. 'Why the 'ell didn't you stick to yer own class?'

'Because I fell in love with Clifford,' said Amy simply. 'And his class didn't seem to matter.'

'What price love now, eh, my girl?' said Gladys. 'If you'd gone with a boy of yer own sort, at least there might have been a chance of marriage, with a little persuasion from yer father. No 'ope of that now. The upper classes couldn't give a toss about the likes of us.'

'All right Mum, don't go on about it, please,' begged Amy. 'What's done is done. I'll manage somehow. And don't worry, I don't intend to bring my trouble home.'

'Where else would you go?' asked Gladys. 'Do yer think yer dad and me would let you walk the streets?'

'Dad'll kill me,' said Amy miserably.

'He'll do his nut and that's a fact,' said Gladys. 'But you'd better leave 'im to me. I'll tell 'im when you're not around. Give him time to cool off before you 'ave to face 'im.'

'I'm not afraid to tell him,' said Amy, 'I don't expect you to fight my battles for me.'

'It'll be better for all of us if I break it to him,' said

103

Gladys.

'Well ... if you're sure.'

'I'm sure.'

'Thanks for being so good about it,' said Amy, going to her mother and hugging her.

'Who else can yer turn to when you're in trouble but your own?' said Gladys. 'No one else'll wanna know, that's for sure.' She was thoughtful for a moment. 'At least you can stay on at Jackson's until you start to show. That'll give us time to sort ourselves out.'

'That's true.'

'Now, 'ow about us 'avin' a nice quiet cuppa tea before we let those little hooligans back in?'

Amy was moved almost to tears by her mother's warmth and understanding, but she knew that she could not come back here to live with her baby. Firstly, because it wouldn't be fair to inflict her shame on the family. And secondly because she had grown out of the parental umbrella. She must stand on her own two feet, however difficult that might be in a society that treated unmarried mothers like lepers.

*   *   *

'What's all this about?' asked Ralph Jackson, as he stood with George Atkins at the bar of The Feathers a week or so later. 'You didn't make it clear in your note why you wanted to see me.'

George took the head off a pint of brown ale, looking along the bar counter which was crowded with men, many of them coachmen. The smoky atmosphere resounded with loud chatter and raucous laughter. 'Let's go and sit somewhere a bit

104

more private and I'll tell yer.' They moved across the bar room and sat down at a corner table underneath the gas mantle.

'Well?' said Ralph, sipping his whisky. Although he was going to pains not to show it, he was inwardly quaking because it was obvious that this was no social occasion. George Atkins' request for a meeting spelled trouble. The damned man had more power over him than any other person alive.

Taking a swig of his beer before setting his glass down on the stained wooden table, George said, 'That son o' yours has put my daughter in the family way and I wanna know what you're gonna do about it.'

Ralph turned pale. It was a few moments before he could collect his thoughts sufficiently to speak. 'Your daughter may well have got herself into trouble,' he said, at last, 'but it has nothing to do with my son.'

Observing him coolly, George said, 'My daughter ain't a liar.'

'She is if she's blaming Clifford for her plight,' blustered Ralph. He didn't have the slightest doubt that the blame for the girl's trouble lay at Clifford's door but he wasn't fool enough to admit it.

George lit a cigarette. 'I don't see 'ow yer can be so certain.'

'Because my son would not get involved with a member of staff,' he lied.

Drawing lazily on his cigarette, George said, 'Seems to me he's inherited his father's liking for a bit o' rough.'

The whisky was downed in one swallow. 'What exactly are you getting at?' Ralph demanded, cheeks feverishly bright.

'Just this, mate,' said George, his eyes ice hard as

they rested on Ralph's face. 'You see to it that your boy does right by my daughter, or your missus will get to know about you and Clara.'

'You're going back on your word?' rasped Ralph, glancing furtively around to make sure they were not overheard. 'Our deal was for me to give your daughter a job and a roof over her head, which I've done for over five years. You promised there would be no further demands.'

'And there ain't been,' said George. 'But this is a different issue. Your son's taken advantage of my daughter. And unless her child is born in wedlock, her whole life will be ruined and my grandchild branded a bastard.' He drew on his cigarette and exhaled the smoke through his nose. 'I can't let that 'appen, now can I?'

Ralph's beady eyes narrowed. 'You're not seriously suggesting that Clifford marry her?' he exclaimed, almost as though George had asked him to sign over his entire fortune to Amy.

'Too right I am,' said George. 'My Amy won't stand a chance in life unless he does. No other man will want 'er once she's got a kid on 'er 'ands.'

'But even you must realise that such a thing isn't possible.'

'Don't talk wet,' said George. 'O' course it's possible. No law that I know of says rich can't marry poor.'

'But it wouldn't work, can't you see that?' protested Ralph, 'Amy wouldn't be happy as a member of our family. She wouldn't fit in.'

'You'll have to try 'ard to make sure she does then, won't yer?' said George. 'In the same way as yer gonna have to make your boy pretend to want to marry her. My daughter's got her pride. She'd sooner

106

starve than 'ave someone marry her against their will. She 'asn't said as much to her mother, but I get the idea he's made it clear 'e doesn't wanna know about 'er now she's in trouble. He'll have to change his tune sharpish before 'er condition gets obvious. He'll tell her that now he's thought it over he's realised he loves her and wants to marry her after all, or something like that. I don't want her to know that I had anythin' to do with it, is that understood?'

'I'm damned if I'll do what you say,' said Ralph.

George shrugged. 'It's up to you, mate. But if my girl ain't full o' the joys o' spring with a date for the registry office fixed, by a week from today, I'll be payin' your missus a visit. If I had any other choice I'd take it, but I don't. My girl only has one chance in life now and that's through your boy.' He stood up. 'I'm orf now. I've a train to catch.'

And he walked out of the pub, leaving Ralph staring helplessly after him.

*   *   *

Clifford could hardly believe his ears the next day when his father took him into his office and told him that he must marry Amy. And even more incredible was the reason why. His father and a music hall singer! Who would have thought the old boy had it in him?

'You and Amy's aunt?' he gasped incredulously.

'That's right, son,' said Ralph with a note of pride in his voice. Since Clifford was obviously a chip off the old block, Ralph had decided to adopt a man to man attitude for this difficult interview. For, in order to make Clifford realise the gravity of the situation, he had had no option but to tell him the whole

107

complicated story.

'All these years and Mother still doesn't suspect anything.'

'That's right. You can see the power George Atkins has over us.' He leaned back in his chair, his manner distinctly chummy. 'I mean, you and me, son, we're men, these things are a natural part of our make-up. But women are different. They don't understand a man's hunter instincts. And it would break your mother's heart if she found out about Clara. That's why you're going to have to do what I ask and marry Amy.'

The younger man was far too concerned about how all this would affect him personally to be troubled by any great sense of loyalty towards his mother. All he could think of at the moment was the trouble he would be in with her when she learned about Amy's condition. 'But Mother will be furious if I marry Amy.'

'Of course she will at first. But it's the lesser of two evils as far as she's concerned,' said Ralph. 'She'll get over it, especially when you explain to her that you want to do the right thing by the girl. Women like that sort of thing, honour and duty and all that. It will make her proud of you once she gets used to the idea. She'll think you are the victim of a female plot and eventually see you as a hero. It might take a while but she'll come round. Whereas discovering that I have a mistress could destroy her.'

'Mmm, I can see that,' said Clifford thoughtfully. 'But even so, Father, I'm not sure I want to get married at the moment.'

'Let me put it another way, son,' said Ralph smoothly, leaning across the desk towards him confidentially. 'Unless you do as I say, there will be no future for you in the family business. Since you don't become a director until you're twenty-five, I can terminate your employment whenever I like.'

Clifford gulped. 'You wouldn't do a thing like that to your own son. Mother wouldn't hear of it.'

'You know as well as I do that when it comes to the business, she doesn't have a say,' Ralph reminded him. 'So, if you decide not to co-operate you'll suffer along with your mother and me.'

'I didn't realise you could be so hard,' said Clifford.

'With my marriage at stake, I've got to be.'

The whole thing was ludicrously ironic, thought Clifford. Having originally stood to lose everything if he married Amy, now he would lose it all if he didn't. And on giving the matter more thought, he wasn't altogether displeased at the way things had turned out. He dreaded the scene with his mother, of course, but the prospect of marriage didn't seem nearly so damnable now it was to be his saving grace. After all, he hadn't wanted to give Amy up. She was dashed pretty, entertaining company, and wonderfully passionate. Once she'd mastered middle-class ways, things should work out very well.

'All right, Father, I'll do as you ask.'

CHAPTER SIX

'We're going now, Amy,' said Gladys Atkins, about to make an early departure from her grandson Victor's christening party. 'You put on a lovely spread, ducks, and I'm proud of yer, but the Jacksons ain't our sort, so I think it's best if we slip off before

109

one of us loses our temper.'

Having watched her family suffer at the mercy of Florence Jackson's superior attitude all afternoon, Amy wasn't about to argue. She wished now she hadn't persuaded her parents, much against their better judgement, to come. But why should they be excluded from such occasions in Victor's life? He was as much their grandchild as he was the Jacksons', and this was her home not Florence's despite that woman's proprietary manner whenever she set foot inside the door. 'I can ask Marshall to take you to the station in Ralph's car, if you like,' she said, holding her three-month-old son in her arms, 'He's outside with the car waiting to take Clifford's parents home later.'

'No, don't trouble yerself, love,' said Gladys with a touch of inverted snobbery. 'Shanks' pony has always bin good enough for us, and we ain't about to change our ways just because you've married into money.'

'Your mother's right,' agreed George, closely united with his wife on their own side of the class divide which had been so painfully evident here today.

'It's no trouble,' said Amy. 'But if you really would rather walk...'

'We would, ta.' Gladys and her husband and two younger sons, all spruced up in new clothes purchased from Amy's allowance with the idea of making them feel more equal to the occasion, were gathered in the hallway of Amy's Ealing house. Although modest compared to the senior Jackson's residence, it was palatial by Atkins standards by the mere fact that it was detached with a bathroom. Gladys glanced towards the floor where Bobby and

110

Pete were sparring noisily. 'Pack that up, you little bleeders, and let's get out of 'ere.' She looked towards the main body of the house and emitted a shrill cry which rose above the sedate conversational hubbub with the same sort of impact as a barrel organ suddenly springing into action during a church sermon. 'A-l-fie!'

Her son appeared almost instantly from the sitting room. 'We're gonna make tracks then, are we?' he said gleefully.

'Wait a minute while I tell Clifford you're leaving,' said Amy, valiantly trying to ease the situation by adhering to the normal social graces as though this had been a happy occasion for her parents. She found her husband in the crowded sitting room, standing by the open french doors talking to his sister Gwen and Ned Cox. 'My folks are off now so will you come and say goodbye?'

'Oh, yes, righto,' he said blearily, for he had been making significant inroads into the celebratory wine all afternoon. He followed her dutifully out to the hall whereupon he bade his in-laws a polite farewell and returned to the guests in the other room amongst whom he felt more comfortable.

Amy kissed her mother at the door. 'Thanks for coming, Mum.'

''S all right, love,' she said. 'Let's 'ope there ain't too many of these sort of occasions, though. Once every twenty years is more than enough for us to get together with your in-laws.'

Closing the door behind them, Amy leaned against it, closing her eyes with a sigh of relief. What an ordeal this christening party had been, and the same with the wedding. It was difficult enough coping with Florence Jackson's blatant disapproval of herself; a

111

thousand times worse trying to defend her family from it. And it wasn't only the Jacksons' snobbery that made her parents ill at ease here. It was the rich trappings to which their daughter was inevitably becoming accustomed. The comfortable home, the tree-lined street, the fine furnishings—things Amy wanted to share with them, not put between them.

'You look exhausted. Are Clifford's people getting you down?' Opening her eyes Amy found herself looking into the friendly face of Ned Cox's fiancée, Molly Johnson.

Surprised to hear implied criticism of the Jacksons from someone of their circle, Amy was unsure how to reply, so just gave a non-committal smile.

'Here, let me take the baby for a few minutes to give you a break,' said Molly, coming closer.

'Well . . .' began Amy, intending to pretend that she was unperturbed by the constant battle which raged between herself and Clifford's mother. But the friendliness in Molly's warm brown eyes swept caution aside and she handed over little Victor who was elaborately swathed in a lace-trimmed christening gown and shawl. 'Yes, I must admit to feeling a little harassed by Florence's presence. And carrying His Nibs around is beginning to make my arm ache.'

'He's beautiful,' said Molly, moving aside his shawl and gazing down into his face.

Although no great beauty, twenty-one-year-old Molly had a pleasant appearance with shiny chestnut hair and a round, homely face which reflected the warmth of her personality. Amy had met her several times since becoming part of the Jackson clan for the Coxes were close friends and both families appeared at the same social functions. Although Molly's

112

parents were comfortably off, being the proprietors of a large and prestigious draper's store in Shepherds Bush, she seemed to lack the pretentiousness of many of Clifford's other friends.

'I think so,' said Amy, beaming proudly and feeling more cheerful than she had all day. 'But then I would, wouldn't I?'

'You'd be a bit odd if you didn't,' agreed Molly, grinning. 'I'm very fond of children. I do hope Ned and I have a big family.'

'When is the wedding?'

'January,' she said. 'And the six months until then can't pass quickly enough for me.'

'I can imagine.' Amy found herself hoping that this genuinely nice young woman was not disappointed in her marriage to Ned, for she had noticed how friendly he was with Gwen Jackson. They had been brought up in close proximity, apparently, but neither were children any more and they did seem very pally . . .

'I must say I think you stand up to Clifford's mother awfully well,' said Molly unexpectedly. 'You don't let her talk down to you, do you?'

'Not if I can help it,' said Amy, pleased to have found an ally. 'I suppose it isn't in my nature to sit back and let her treat me like dirt. She and I don't like each other. We just have to try not to make it too embarrassingly obvious when Clifford is around, for his sake.'

'She doesn't seem to try very hard, from what I've seen when the two of you are together.'

'That's a fact,' laughed Amy.

'Quite a cross to bear, having the Jacksons as in-laws,' remarked Molly companionably. 'Clifford and Gwen are all right, but their parents are the most

113

frightful snobs. I only tolerate them because of Ned. The two families have always been very friendly, apparently. Ned was raised almost like a cousin to Clifford and Gwen.'

'Yes, I've noticed how close they all are.'

'Mmm, especially Ned and Gwen,' remarked Molly casually. 'Those two are great friends.'

Amy was relieved to hear her say it. If Molly knew and accepted it, it must be purely platonic. But somehow a germ of unease remained. There was something about the two of them together she couldn't quite put her finger on. Not intimacy exactly ... 'Yes, I've noticed how well they get on.'

'Gwen's a strange girl, though, don't you think?' remarked Molly. 'Always seems to be in a world of her own, somehow.'

'Yes, I've noticed that, but at least she's not inherited her parents' arrogance,' said Amy. 'In fact, she seems to have quite a social conscience. She's interested in the women's movement, I believe. She was saying something about it the other day.'

'Oh dear, Florence won't like it if she becomes a suffragette,' laughed Molly. 'That really would tarnish the respectable Jackson image, with Emmeline Pankhurst and her supporters having such bad reputations.'

'It would too,' grinned Amy. This friendly interlude had lifted her spirits enormously, for hers was a difficult marriage. Her love for Clifford was not in question, and she had been overjoyed when he had proposed marriage to her most romantically one momentous day last autumn. They had walked among the fallen leaves on Ealing Common and he had said that he'd discovered he couldn't live without her after all, and wanted to marry her however much his parents disapproved. She had been far too relieved and happy to bear a grudge over his earlier attitude towards her pregnancy, and had resolved to make their life together her raison d'être.

But being Clifford's wife was not an easy role. For in the sobering light of everyday living, his immaturity and lack of backbone had soon become obvious. In fact, she sometimes wondered how he had found the courage to defy his parents by marrying her at all, when he was still so much under their influence. She was hurt by his lack of support for her against his mother. And it irritated her to find that his way of dealing with anything unpleasant was to ignore it altogether.

Knowing that she herself was far from perfect, however, she accepted his faults and worked at making their marriage good. He wanted an easy life without scenes or quarrels and she respected that. After all, he did have some redeeming features. He was kind and affectionate; he gave her a free hand in the house, and was not ungenerous with money. And they still pleased each other in bed, and enjoyed each other's company.

'It'll be interesting being on the sidelines watching the sparks fly,' remarked Molly lightly.

'If Gwen were to become a suffragette, it would probably send Florence into a complete decline,' said Amy. 'After having her son marry a common shopgirl from the East End who promptly provides her with a suspiciously *premature* grandchild.'

An awkward silence fell. Molly was uncertain how to respond to Amy's frankness. 'It can happen to the best of us,' she said at last. 'And he's certainly a beauty.' She looked into the snoozing Victor's face. 'Aren't you, darling?'

'Anyway,' said Amy, relieving the other woman of the child, 'I must put this little fellow down for a nap and see how things are coming along in the kitchen.'

She hurried upstairs and settled Victor in his crib in the nursery, leaving the door open so she could hear if he cried, then went into the kitchen where Violet, who was on loan from Florence for the day, was battling with a pile of dishes at the sink.

'How's it going?' Amy asked.

'Not so dusty,' she replied wearily. 'Do you think anyone will want more sandwiches?'

'No, they're well into the sweet stuff,' said Amy. 'Just finish this load and you can go. I'll do the rest of the dishes later.'

'Ta, Amy.'

'I hope Florence isn't expecting you to work when you get back to Orchard Avenue?' she said.

'No, she said I can have the evening off as I've worked all afternoon.'

'I should think so too.'

One of the biggest bones of contention between Amy and Florence was the fact that Amy refused to have domestic staff to run her house for her. She was not being awkward; she genuinely didn't feel justified in employing someone while she idled her time away, just to keep up appearances. And, as she frequently pointed out, it wasn't as though the house was on the same grand lines as Floral House with proper facilities to accommodate staff.

But Florence claimed that only the poor did their own housework and Amy was damaging the Jackson reputation in the eyes of their peers. Amy had made a special concession for today by allowing Violet to help with the christening party. But she was determined that if she ever did decide to employ help,

116

it would be because she considered it necessary, and not just to feed Florence's snobbery.

'Are you meeting Joe later on?' asked Amy chattily.

'No,' said Violet dully, taking a pan of hot water off the stove and emptying it into the deep square sink, clouds of steam filling the kitchen.

'Oh,' said Amy in surprise, making a start on the drying up and stacking the crockery on the scrubbed wooden table. 'I thought you spent all your spare time together.'

'It's all off between Joe and me,' Violet said sadly.

'Oh, Vi, I'm so sorry,' Amy exclaimed. 'What happened? Did you have a tiff?'

'Somethin' like that,' she said in an overly bright tone. 'Oh well, that's life, I s'pose. It was good while it lasted.'

Seeing the dark shadows under her friend's eyes, emphasised by an unusual pallor, Amy recognised some inner turmoil beneath the chirpy front and cursed herself for not noticing it before. 'I'd no idea things weren't going well,' she said. 'But I don't see so much of you now that I'm married, and I've been so busy with the baby and everything.'

'That's all right. I don't expect you to bother with the likes of me now that you're a Jackson,' said Violet sharply.

Amy almost dropped the pot she was drying in her haste to divest herself of it. 'Oh, Vi,' she said, taking hold of the other girl's arm urgently and looking into her face, 'you know me better than that. Of course I still care about you.'

'It ain't the same any more,' she said. ''Ow can it be?'

'I haven't changed,' said Amy, 'I'm still the same

117

old me. Still your friend.'

'You can't deny the fact that you're on the other side of the fence now, though?'

'Technically, I suppose I am,' Amy admitted. 'But I still value my friends.'

'They'll soon alter that.'

'No one can stop me being myself.' Looking into her friend's eyes, she saw a very troubled woman. 'Come and see me when you get some time off and we'll have a chat. I'd like that, Vi. I miss you, you know.'

'And what's Mr Clifford gonna say about his mother's housemaid paying a social call on his wife?' she asked with an edge to her voice.

'Don't you worry about Clifford,' Amy said. 'I can handle him.'

Which was perfectly true. Clifford's lack of moral fibre and hatred of scenes meant he rarely made a stand about anything, even in the unchallenging environment of his own home. Whereas Amy, being constantly on the defensive, tended to stand her ground, making her the more dominant of the two. Basically, Clifford would go along with the opinion of whoever he was with at the time simply because it was easier that way.

'Maybe I will pop round then,' said Violet.

'I'll look forward to it.'

Amy did a little more drying up, then went back into the sitting room to join her guests who were mostly ageing relatives and friends of the Jacksons. The younger element to whom Clifford was paying court had been joined by Molly and were still gathered by the french doors, through which a soft breeze drifted into the room, stirring the chintz curtains and sweetening the smoky cigar fumes with

118

the scent of roses from the garden.

'Where's the baby?' demanded Florence, ostentatiously dressed in blue with two enormous black feathers sprouting like antennae from her hat.

'He's asleep in his cot upstairs.'

'On his own?' Florence exclaimed, her loud accusing tone changing the sociable hubbub around them into a hushed, listening silence.

Realising that the other woman's query stemmed from a desire to belittle her daughter-in-law in front of her guests, rather than genuine concern for her grandson's welfare, Amy threw her a withering look and said, 'Yes, of course. Do you expect me to employ an army of nursemaids to sit watching him sleep?'

A communal gasp rippled through the room.

'He shouldn't be left alone up there,' proclaimed Florence

'Nonsense! He'll come to no harm for a few minutes,' said Amy. 'As soon as he cries I'll go to him.'

'The child needs a nanny,' Florence stated categorically, rising enthusiastically to her favourite theme. 'Lord knows what sort of a misfit he'll grow up to be without one.'

'As his mother, I think I'm the best judge of that. If I find looking after him too much for me, I'll employ someone,' said Amy cuttingly. 'In the meantime, I am enjoying doing the job myself, thank you very much.' She paused and moistened her nervously dry lips, aware that the entire company was being entertained by this contretemps. Despite her outward show of confidence, she felt emotionally drained by every one of these all too frequent altercations with Florence. Never before had she felt so deeply disliked, and it was a miserable experience for someone of such a warm and sociable nature. Funnily enough, though, Ralph, whilst never actually friendly towards her, was noticeably less hostile than his wife. 'Now, Florence, can I get you anything? Another piece of cake or a drink, perhaps?'

'No, thank you,' she snapped.

'How about you, Ralph?' asked Amy with determined charm. 'Would you like anything?'

'Yes, I'll have a glass of port if I may.'

'Certainly,' she said, and moved to Clifford who was standing looking dumbstruck beside Ned, Gwen and Molly. Her tone to her husband was firm. 'Clifford dear, will you get your father a drink, please, and see if anyone else would like one?'

'I say, that was a bit strong, wasn't it?' he hissed, courage boosted by liberal helpings of sherry. 'Mother is only trying to be helpful, you know.'

Resisting the urge to ease his head into the fruit trifle, Amy said brightly, 'Don't embarrass our guests any more than they have been already, dear. Now will you *please* do your bit as host and fix some drinks?'

'Oh, yes, righto,' he said woozily, vaguely aware through the alcoholic mists that he had upset her, and hoping he hadn't spoiled things for later, as he was feeling quite amorous.

As he swayed off into the company to play host, Amy turned to the trio and said lightly, 'Sorry about the tension, folks. Most embarrassing for you.'

'Don't worry about us,' said Molly.

'You're right not to be forced into having a nanny for Victor if you'd rather not,' said Gwen in her soft manner, her round face flushed by this uncharacteristic display of outspokenness. 'If all

120

women stood up for themselves as you do to my mother, our cause would be helped tremendously.'

'Goodness me, do we have a budding suffragette in our midst?' said Ned, his shandy-coloured eyes resting on Gwen affectionately.

'I believe in their ideas, if that's what you mean,' she said, brown eyes flashing, 'but what modern, intelligent woman doesn't want a right to the vote?' She had grown into a woman of moderate beauty. She still tended towards plumpness, though her excess flesh was tailored into submission by her corsets, bosom fashionably forced forward, exaggerating its fullness.

'Don't say you are going to become one of these strident females who interrupt political meetings and heckle speakers?' said Ned. 'I read in the paper recently that Herbert Asquith was completely howled down by women campaigning for the vote.'

'I'm not sure if I'd go that far,' she said, 'but I'm not saying I wouldn't if the situation arose.'

'Your parents would have a fit.'

'I know.'

'It seems our Gwen has hidden depths,' said Ned, smiling affectionately at her.

'Good for you, Gwen,' said Molly.

'Hear hear,' said Amy. If the Women's Movement had done nothing else, it had united women from all backgrounds. 'Now, if you'll excuse me, I think I can hear my son demanding attention from upstairs.'

*   *   *

Gwen watched Amy go with a certain amount of admiration, her shapely form complementing a lemon outfit with lime green trimmings in the new

121

straighter line that was becoming popular with young women. Even from the back her steely resolve was detectable. Clifford had certainly met his match in her. And so had Mother. It was about time someone stood up to her. Gwen herself had never dared, even though she knew her mother was not all she pretended to be. In fact Gwen was still reeling from the firm stand she herself had just taken about women's rights. She, Gwen, who was known for her reserve.

Her interest in the battle for suffrage was quite new. Only last month she had been persuaded by an old schoolfriend to go and hear Emmeline Pankhurst speak at a rally in Trafalgar Square. With nothing much else to do, she had gone along more from curiosity than desire to change things for womankind. Having been raised with her mother's Victorian views, that decreed women should not have a say in anything at all outside the home, it was only natural she should grow up with the idea that the female of the species was second-rate.

Fortunately, the school to which she had been sent for the sake of appearances had brought to light her aptitude for mathematics, making her useful to her father's accounts office, and rescuing her from an empty life of socialising with well-to-do ladies of the town who had eligible sons.

She tensed at the thought of her lack of success with men, for without the status of marriage she would become increasingly more of a misfit in society as her spinsterhood lengthened. She wondered if the passion Emmeline Pankhurst had aroused in her with her ardent proclamation: 'We have been patient too long. We will be patient no longer', had been a transference of the ardour she could not feel for a man. She decided not; she would feel as strongly on this issue if she was happily married with a couple of babies into the bargain.

Gwen knew she was not unattractive to the opposite sex. Her problem lay in the fact that she had not yet met a man to whom she felt sufficiently drawn in the physical sense. In fact, just the touch of a man filled her with such fear and loathing as almost to paralyse her. Naturally, when this became apparent to suitors, they withdrew, leaving her relieved of the prospect of having to suffer the intimate side of marriage but tormented by a profound and painful sense of failure. The latter was intensified by her mother, who made no secret of the fact that she regarded an unmarried daughter as something of a stigma.

The young woman had enough common sense to suspect that the blame for this difficulty lay in the past. To her mother's excessive preaching of morality in her formative years, and a day in her early teens when a drama had occurred that changed her life. Only one other person knew about that incident. Dear Ned. What would she do without him?

* * *

Ned, formally dressed in a dark frock-coat and highstanding white collar, also watched Amy cross the room with feelings of high regard. She had such spirit and vitality. Clifford had certainly taken on more than he could handle when he got Amy into trouble. No one in the Jacksons' circle believed that young Victor was premature, though courtesy dictated that they go along with the Jacksons' official explanation of the child's early arrival after the wedding. What had surprised Ned was the fact that Clifford had actually done the decent thing. Knowing him as he did, he'd have expected him to deny all responsibility. Which just went to show how smitten he must be with her. Money could not have been an incentive since the girl didn't have a bean.

In fact the general opinion was that Amy had deliberately trapped him into marriage to better herself. It was rather pleasing to know that Clifford, who had always treated the affections of girlfriends as casually as morning coffee, had finally got his come-uppance. Not that Ned could imagine marriage to Amy carrying any sort of hardship. On the contrary, her charms were obvious for all to see.

But then Clifford had always aimed his attentions towards beautiful women, usually empty-headed daughters of wealthy businessmen. At least this time he had chosen someone with a little grey matter too. Oh, Amy might not be educated, or have a decent pedigree, but she was as sharp as a barber's blade. That had been obvious to Ned years ago when she had first come to work for the firm. She'd appeared in his office one day to deliver some watch parts, full of cockney confidence and indicating to all and sundry that she would not be easily belittled. He'd always been too taken aback by her unnerving self-assurance, or preoccupied with other things, to say much to her. But then, Ned never said much to anyone, let alone young girls with too much to say for themselves.

The fact that he was rather taciturn by nature was often mistaken for arrogance. He knew that, but was unable to change his brusque attitude. His mother had died giving birth to him, and being raised by a series of brusque nannies and a father who used

124

business as a crutch for the grief he was unable to dismiss had taught Ned never to show his feelings or to burden other people with his problems. His aloof manner was a kind of defence mechanism he felt neither comfortable with nor able to shed.

It had caused problems for him with the opposite sex when he was growing up. Girlfriends had been put off by his coolness, usually assuming that there was something lacking in them. But fortunately now, at twenty-four, he had a settled courtship with Molly who seemed happy with his quiet, undemonstrative nature. She was the perfect partner for him, being gentle and undemanding, and she meant a lot to him. They might not have the most passionate love affair in London, but at least they were well suited and from a similar family background, which was more than could be said for Clifford and Amy.

But on considering the other couple, he had to admit to sensing a certain excitement about the volatile chemistry of that relationship. One could feel it in the air when they were present. It had sent a kind of electricity crackling through the room just now after Amy had put Florence firmly in her place and reminded Clifford of his duties as host. Ned experienced an unexpected moment of envy towards Clifford for the thrill of Amy's challenging personality and uncontrived sex appeal.

Recalled to the present, he observed that Gwen and Molly were discussing the recent bill in parliament, banning women from dangerous sports, following the death of a woman parachutist.

'Surely we should have the right to choose whether or not we wish to kill ourselves, the same as men?' said Gwen.

The odd choice of words she had used to try to

125

make her point produced a roar of laughter. 'In your present mood, perhaps this bill isn't such a bad thing,' teased Ned, 'or we might lose you to mountain climbing or hot air ballooning.'

'Not at all,' she said, 'bicycling is quite strenuous enough for me. I just think women should have the same right to flirt with danger as men, if they wish.'

Ned studied the two very different women who both meant so much to him. Warm, uncomplicated Molly, with whom he would soon share his life. And complex Gwen, burdened with a punishing load of psychological luggage. As much as he cared for Molly, she could never be part of what he shared with dear, dear Gwen.

*   *   *

'I think I'd better give you a hand to get him upstairs to bed,' said Ned later, referring to Clifford who was much the worse for drink and singing a tuneless version of 'Waiting at the Church' whilst leaning heavily on Amy in the hallway en route for the stairs. All the guests had left except Ned and Molly, who was ready to leave and waiting for Ned in the sitting room.

'Don't worry, I can manage,' said Amy, partly because it was so embarrassing to have to enlist the help of a guest to get the host to bed, and partly because she always felt uncomfortable in Ned's company and was eager for him to leave. But just then Clifford began giggling and swaying to the point where she almost lost her balance, her slight build no match for his masculine weight. 'Shush, Clifford, you'll wake the baby.'

'Oh dear ... I th ... th ... think I'm a lickle bit

tiddly,' he stuttered, clapping his hand over his mouth with feigned remorse and erupting into a fit of drunken laughter. 'But if a ch . . . chap can't get t . . . tight at his son's chris . . . chriss-ning party, when can he, eh, Ned? You tell me that.'

'Come on, old boy,' intervened Ned, taking his friend's weight by wrapping Clifford's arm around his own shoulders. 'You need to get to bed to sleep it off.'

'Not unless my wife comes too,' said Clifford, with a silly laugh. 'Isn't she lovely, my wife, eh, Ned?'

'Yes, she's lovely,' agreed Ned, humouring him, half-dragging him towards the stairs.

'I'm so sorry about this,' said Amy, as though Clifford wasn't there. 'He's let the side down good and proper today, I'm afraid.'

'Don't worry about me, I'm used to Clifford's excesses,' said Ned. 'He never knows when to stop at a party.'

Together they hauled him up the wide staircase into the bedroom and lifted him on to the double bed where he fell into an immediate stupor.

'I've not seen him in such a bad state before,' she said apologetically, a little unnerved as always by the depth of Ned's eyes. He was not a man who could be called handsome, his nose being rather too broad, his mouth too wide and eyebrows too bushy, but she couldn't deny a certain appeal in that square, aggressive face, even if it did usually wear a chilly expression.

'Well, you've not known him as long as I have,' he said conversationally, and, intending only to put her at her ease, added, 'But there's no harm done and you married him for better or worse, I suppose.'

Knowing that her marriage to Clifford was seen by

some as a deliberate plan on her part to better herself, she assumed that this was his implication. 'Oh, yes, there is no pleasure without pain,' she said sarcastically. 'If I want the better things like a nice house and a comfortable life, I have to pay for them with the worse bits like this.'

Ned was astonished at her prickliness. 'I wasn't suggesting...'

'It doesn't matter,' she interrupted haughtily, 'I'm used to it. I know what people are saying.'

'Naturally some people will draw their own conclusions about your marriage,' he said, unsure as to why he felt quite so angry with her for misunderstanding him. 'But I don't happen to be one of them. Clifford can marry whoever he damned well likes as far as I'm concerned. I couldn't care less.'

'You surprise me. I thought you were supposed to be friends.'

'We are, but Clifford is quite capable of choosing his own wife.'

'Meaning that he should know better than to let himself be conned by a gold digger like me?' she said, her eyes dark with rage against her flushed cheeks.

'Your words, not mine,' he said, disturbed by this sudden and unexpected conflict, but unable, somehow, to put matters right.

Clifford stirred and called her name.

'I'll leave him to you then,' said Ned sharply. 'Molly and I can see ourselves out.'

'If you're sure you don't mind?' said Amy curtly.

'We don't. You'd better quieten him down before he wakes the baby.'

'Yes, I know.'

'Goodnight then.'

'Goodnight. And thank you for helping me

128

upstairs with him.'

'No trouble at all,' he said with icy politeness, and turned and left the room.

Her eyes were smarting with tears as she watched him go. Arrogant swine, she thought, before turning her attention to her husband.

*   *   *

'Come on darling,' urged Clifford blearily. 'Get into bed with me. I want to make love to you.'

She awarded him full marks for optimism, considering his condition, but said, 'Not yet, I have to see to the baby first. I won't be long.'

He pulled her playfully down on the bed beside him and nuzzled her ear. 'Whoops, I'm feeling a bit dizzy,' he said.

'I should think you are,' she said. 'The amount of booze you've put away.'

'It was a good party though, wassen it?' he said, hiccuping. 'Do you think everyone enjoyed themselves?'

'Umm, I expect so.' She yawned, longing to divest herself of her corsets. 'The baby was good, he hardly cried at all.'

'He's good like his mother,' he said, his fair hair ruffled over his brow youthfully. 'Not a bad boy like his daddy.'

'You've certainly excelled yourself today,' Amy said, without any real malice for there were far worse crimes in her book than having one too many to drink at a party. 'But I forgive you.'

'I love you, Amy,' he said sleepily.

'And I you,' she said fondly. Nothing else mattered to her when they were together like this. Not his weak

129

character, his mother, what people said about her, or Ned Cox's insinuations.

'I'm pleased I married you,' he drawled, his eyes closed.

'I should think so too,' she smiled, smoothing his hair from his brow fondly.

'I was scared stiff when my father first came out with it, though, I must admit,' he mumbled almost incoherently as he hovered on the brink of slumber. 'Seems silly now.'

'Mmm,' she said rather absently, until a moment later when his muddled utterance registered properly. 'What do you mean, when your father first came out with it?'

'You know, darling,' he muttered, yawning heavily. 'All that damned business about your father spilling the beans to my mother about my father and your aunt if I didn't . . .' His voice faded away as his lids dropped.

Her blood ran cold. 'Clifford!' she said, shaking him. 'If you didn't what?'

'Mmm? Whassamatta?'

'Wake up, it's important.'

'In the morning . . . tired . . . so tired now.'

'If you didn't marry me,' she said, her whole body leaden with humiliation. 'Is that what you were going to say?'

'Whassat?' he muttered, without opening his eyes.

'What did you mean just now? I must know. It's urgent.'

'What did I say?' he mumbled. 'I dunno.' And he fell into such a deep sleep Amy knew she must leave him for the moment.

She lay awake beside him until the dawn, thrashing about in the sheets, trying to make herself believe that

130

her suspicions were unfounded. After giving the baby his morning feed she woke Clifford for work with a cup of tea. 'You and I need to talk,' she said.

'Not now, Amy,' he said, wincing. 'I've a head like a bucket.'

'It has to be now, Clifford,' she persisted, 'it simply cannot wait.'

He peered at her from red raw half-closed eyes. 'Oh, go on then, say what you have to, but don't expect sensible answers.'

'You said something last night that worried me,' she said gravely.

'Did I? Well, whatever it was I don't remember,' he said. 'In fact, I don't remember anything much after we cut the christening cake.'

'Did you change your mind about marrying me because your father forced you into it?' she asked.

He looked up sharply, holding his head, his eyes screwed up with pain. 'Oh Lord,' he said. 'Did I tell you about that?'

'So it *is* true?' she said miserably.

'I was drunk last night,' he said evasively. 'I didn't know what I was saying.'

'Maybe not, but what you did say was true, wasn't it?'

Chewing his lip anxiously, he avoided her eyes.

'I think you'd better tell me the whole story.'

He sat up and looked at her with his fingers pressed to his temples. 'My father will kill me,' he said. 'Part of the deal was that you were never to know the truth.'

'So, I'll be a widow,' she said. 'But I want the truth.'

He told her, concluding with, 'But I'm glad they forced my hand, really I am, Amy. Because I love

131

you, and I enjoy being married to you.'

'But you'd not have married me if it hadn't been for the pressure?'

'Well, probably not,' he admitted. 'But I'd have regretted it, honestly. I'm really glad the way things worked out.'

The fact that she believed him did nothing to assuage the total loss of self-esteem this revelation inflicted on her. 'The reason you gave me for changing your mind was just a lot of romantic claptrap so that I wouldn't suspect anything, then?'

Clifford retained a thoughtful silence. Whatever he said was going to be misunderstood. 'Your father did insist that you were to think it was all my idea, yes,' he said at last. 'But I meant what I said just now, Amy. Maybe I did need prodding at that time because I didn't feel ready for marriage, but once I got used to the idea I was pleased, and that's the truth.'

'I don't disbelieve you,' she said dully.

'Why so sorrowful then?'

'Because the whole thing has made me feel so cheap,' she said. 'I'd sooner have managed alone than have someone marry me because they were forced to.'

'Don't be silly.'

'I can't help the way I feel.'

'What does it matter how we came to be married?' he said, taking her hand and squeezing it sympathetically. 'As long as I did the right thing in the end and we are happy together now.'

'It matters very much to me,' she said, pulling away from him. 'My whole future was decided by other people without my knowledge, as though I was five years old.'

'So what? It was all for your own good.'

132

'My father had no right to go behind my back, arranging things, threatening people,' she said. 'Can't you see how degrading it is for me?'

'He was only doing what he thought was best for you.'

'How dare he interfere?' she rasped vehemently. 'None of you had the right to choose what was best for me without telling me about it.'

'I had no choice but to go along with my father, I've told you that. Anyway, I don't know why you're making such a fuss,' he said, becoming impatient with her. 'You have a good life with me, don't you? I don't beat you or keep you short of money.'

'No, of course not.'

'Well then, what are you complaining about?' he snapped. 'You came off a damned sight better than if you'd been left to raise Victor alone.'

'Materially, yes, but there is more to life than that.'

'It's enough to please most women.'

She sighed. 'Yes, I realise that and I'm very grateful. But what I feel inside right now is something you will never understand if you live to be a hundred, Clifford.'

And as she made her way downstairs to the kitchen to make breakfast, smarting with mortification, she knew there was something she must do.

CHAPTER SEVEN

Bethnal Green that afternoon was hot and sticky, the bright July sunshine making the buildings shabbier, the streets dustier, and the smells nauseously overpowering. Weary from her sleepless night, and

133

breathless from carrying the baby, Amy took a cab from the station to Tucker Street.

She had planned to arrive in the late-afternoon, knowing that she was sure to find her father at home then, that being the period between his finishing work and departing to the pub for a pint with his mates.

After greetings from the family, surprised at seeing her again so soon, she asked her mother to send the boys out, settled the sleeping Victor in the bedroom, and came straight to the point.

'How *could* you humiliate me by having Clifford forced into marrying me?' she fumed to her father, who had his sleeves rolled up and was pouring water from the jug into the bowl on the table ready to wash. 'Using devious methods to get me a job is one thing, interfering in my personal life quite another.'

'So, those lousy rotten Jacksons have told yer,' he said, swinging round to face her, his sweaty cheeks streaked with grime from a coal-heaving job. 'Ralph Jackson's broken 'is word, the bastard.' His eyes glinted with fury. 'I'll soon show 'im what Eastenders think of people who welsh on a deal.'

'No, don't do that, please,' she said coldly.

'Why not?'

'Because I don't want you to,' she declared emphatically. 'Clifford let it slip last night, quite unintentionally. He'd had a few too many to drink and didn't know what he was saying.'

'You just wait till I get my 'ands on 'im.'

'No! No! No!' she cried vehemently. 'You are not to touch him, nor are you to make trouble for him by telling his father.'

'Oh, ain't I?' riposted George with equal passion. 'And since when did I take orders from my daughter?'

134

'Since now.'

He put the jug down on the table with such force, the water slopped over the top. 'Oh, yeah?' he said with a scornful smile. 'And do you really think I'm soft enough to let a child o' mine tell *me* what to do?'

'Surely you can see that you shouldn't have interfered in something so personal?'

'Someone 'ad to,' he retorted. 'You'd 'ave been in real trouble now if I 'adn't.'

'But you had no right to go behind my back,' she said.

'No right!' he boomed, pop-eyed with fury. 'No right! Since when did a man not have the right to do what he thinks best for his daughter?'

'When she grows up,' she said. 'As I have.'

'Think you know it all, don't you, yer little madam?' he said, bitterly hurt to be criticised for carrying out his paternal duties as he saw fit. *And* by a child who had let the family down so shamefully. 'Well, if you're so clever, 'ow come you were daft enough to get yourself up the spout?'

'There's no need to be vulgar,' she snapped.

'Don't yer come yer high and mighty ways with me, my girl,' he roared. 'What would 'ave happened to yer if Clifford 'adn't married yer? Just tell me that.'

'I don't know, but that isn't the point,' she said, swept along by a profound sense of worthlessness. 'I'd have managed somehow, and I'd sooner have gone to the workhouse than have someone marry me because they were forced to.'

'Easy to say that now you're safely settled with a fine 'ouse and plenty of money, ain't it?' barked George. 'It would 'ave bin a different story if you 'ad gone to the workhouse, I can tell yer that much.'

'How do you think I feel, living with a man who

135

married me because he was blackmailed into it?' she pleaded.

'You ain't the first and you won't be the last. A lot of men need a shove in the right direction when their chickens come 'ome to roost.' This was the first time his power within the family had been challenged and it frightened him. If he let Amy successfully oppose him, the others would soon follow suit and he'd lose all control over the boys.

'And that's supposed to make me feel better, is it?' she said.

'It's up to you 'ow you feel about it,' he barked. 'I'm just statin' the facts as I see 'em. It's an 'ard old world we live in. Anyway, what are yer moaning about? You've fallen on yer feet, ain't yer? You've got a bloomin' great 'ouse, nice clothes, and a damned sight more money than me and yer mum will ever 'ave. And you've got the cheek to come 'ere complainin'! You wanna think yourself lucky I bothered to help yer out at all. Many a father would have washed his hands of yer.'

She reeled from the impact of his words. 'Perhaps it would have been better if you'd done that,' she said, tears smarting. Why could no one understand how demoralised she felt at being part of such a shabby deal? 'At least then I'd have had my self-respect.'

'Self-respect!' he bellowed, eyes bulging in his dust-encrusted countenance. 'You lost your right to that the day you said yes to Clifford Jackson, you little slut!'

'Dad!' gasped Amy, shocked into realising that the argument had gone too far. She'd been raised with vulgar talk, but her father had never spoken to her like this before. It cut deep. Made her feel cheap and dirty.

136

'There's no call for that sort of talk, George,' reproached Gladys, albeit rather timidly.

'She started it,' shouted her husband, his rage now blind and uncontrollable, the words pouring out from anger and pain. Amy had insulted him by undermining his authority, the ungrateful little bitch. He'd loved that girl. Always done his best for her. Never once laid a finger on her. And this was how she repaid him. 'Coming round 'ere criticising me, when she's the one who's done wrong.' He stared at Amy, smarting with the pain of his own words but unable to stop the flow. 'Go on, clear orf out of it. Get back to yer big 'ouse and yer fancy ways. We don't wanna see you back 'ere again, ever. Do yer understand? Not ever.'

She trembled with the gravity of his words, anger turning to fear. Humiliated by what she had discovered, she had come here on impulse, intending only to admonish him for interfering in her life. The last thing she had wanted was to sever relations with him altogether. Faced with that terrible possibility, she deeply regretted what she'd said. Why hadn't she respected the fact that he had acted in her best interests and left her own scruples unspoken? 'You don't mean that, Dad,' she said cautiously.

'Course he doesn't,' said Gladys shakily.

'I do, yer know,' he declared.

'But this is my home.'

'No, it ain't, not any more,' he pointed out. 'You live in Ealin' now, in a fine 'ouse you wouldn't 'ave at all if it wasn't for me.'

'All right, Dad,' she said desperately. 'I'm sorry for the things I've said. If only you'd told me what you were planning to do, I could have made the decision—at least had a hand in my own future.'

137

He took a rasping breath. 'I didn't tell yer because I wanted you to be 'appy, and I knew you wouldn't be unless yer thought the wedding was all Clifford's idea.'

Her dominating emotion now was terror at the sense of valediction in the air. 'All right, Dad, so you acted in my best interest, I'll accept that. Can we forget all about it?'

His rage had changed to an icy calm. 'No, we bloody well can't. What's said is said.'

'But, Dad . . .'

'Get out, Amy. I don't want you visiting us again, upsetting me and yer mum. We don't want you 'ere. Is that clear?'

'You don't really mean that.'

'Oh, yes, I do. And you needn't worry. I shan't make trouble for yer husband by telling his father that he can't keep 'is mouth shut.' He gave a trembling sigh. 'All I want now is to be shot of the lot of yer. I never wanna see yer again.'

Devastated, she turned to Gladys for support.

'You'd better do as yer father says, love,' her mother said.

'But . . . I'm your daughter.'

'And he's my 'usband,' she said sadly. 'As you've just said, you're grown up now. You've your own life to lead. Go and live it and leave us to get on with ours.'

The strength of their unity was a palpable force in the room, making Amy feel excluded and alone. To quarrel with one was to quarrel with the other, it was as simple as that. Her mother would not be persuaded to see her again because in her eyes it would be disloyalty to her husband.

She fed and changed the baby in the bedroom, the

138

strong maternal bond she felt with Victor of little comfort to her at this time. Guessing that any attempt to put things right would only make matters worse, she left quietly with a terrible void in her heart. Maybe her parents had never been able to give her much in the way of home comforts, but she had grown up secure in their love, unsentimental though it had been. Even after leaving home there had always been the comfort of knowing they were there for her if she needed them. But not any more.

At the end of the street she met Bernie, looking smart in a bold pinstriped suit and Homburg hat. 'Wotcha, Amy,' he said breezily. 'How are things with you, love?'

'Not so bad, thanks.'

'So this is the nipper,' he said, squinting at Victor. 'I 'eard you'd had a kid.'

'Yes, this is Victor.'

'A fine-looking boy,' he said, tickling the baby under his chin. 'A real credit to yer.'

At that point Amy burst into tears.

*   *   *

They went to Victoria Park and sat on a bench near the lake, as they had so many times in the past. Bernie bought them both an ice cream from an Italian seller at the gate, but Amy was too upset to finish hers. Bernie was the only person alive to whom she felt inclined to bare her soul on this issue, and out came the whole story in tearful bursts.

'Don't worry too much, love,' he said kindly. 'Yer old man'll come round, in time.'

'I'm not so sure, I've never seen him as angry as that before.'

139

'Well, I suppose he thought he was doin' the right thing for yer,' said Bernie thoughtfully. 'An' 'e's 'urt that you don't see it that way.'

'I shouldn't have blasted off at him,' she said. 'But what he did made me feel so cheap.'

'Don't be daft,' he said, grinning at her, ''ow can a diamond be cheap?'

She gave him a grateful smile. 'You're a good friend.'

'I should think so too, after all these years.'

'You're not shocked by my getting myself into trouble then?'

'Course not.'

'I thought I'd be branded as no-good in the eyes of all men.'

'Do leave orf,' he said. 'You know me better than that.'

'I do love Clifford, you know,' she said defensively. 'He's the only man I've . . .'

'You don't 'ave to explain to me,' he interrupted quickly. 'I'm yer mate, remember?'

'Yeah, I know. Thanks.'

They sat in thoughtful silence for a while. Then she said, 'All this about me. What about your love life? Have you got a steady girlfriend?'

'Give over,' he said scornfully. 'When a girl starts to get serious, I back orf. I don't wanna get tied down.'

'Confirmed bachelor, eh?'

'Too true. Marriage wouldn't suit me at all,' he explained. 'I like to come and go as I please.'

'It always strikes me as odd that a man can stay single without shame, whereas a spinster is treated like a second-class citizen.'

'There's nothing odd about it,' he said. 'It's a

140

woman's place to get married and 'ave babies.'

'Doesn't seem fair to put a stigma on single women though, does it?'

In the absence of a plausible argument, he just said, 'Oh, well, you can't change 'uman nature, can yer?'

Her own problems flooded back. 'So, what do you think I should do about Dad and Clifford ... and everything?'

'Go home to Clifford and give yer marriage all you've got,' he advised. 'You can't change the reason he married yer, so forget all about it and enjoy your posh new life. And as for yer dad ... well, give 'im time to cool down, then try to patch things up. If it doesn't work first time, try again and again until it does.'

'You make it all seem so simple.'

'It is simple,' he said. 'You take life too seriously.'

'It's all a game to you.'

'I ain't denying it,' he said. 'We're all a long time dead.'

There were a lot of children in the park, for the schools were closed for the summer holidays. A crowd of them were clustered around the drinking fountain, pushing and fighting for one of the metal cups that were chained to the edge. 'It doesn't seem long since we were doing that,' she said.

'Exactly. You'll be old before yer can look round, so you may as well make the most of life while you're young.'

Amy settled the baby against her shoulder and stood up. 'Well, I'd better be going. Clifford will be home from the shop and waiting for his meal.'

'Yeah, I must be on me way an' all. I'm seein' a man about some business before I go to work at the music hall.'

'Thanks for listening, Bernie,' she said, 'I feel a lot better now.'

'No need to thank me,' he grinned. 'What are friends for?'

She smacked a kiss on his cheek and made her way to the station.

* * *

'There you are at last,' said Clifford crossly when she finally arrived home, feeling dirty and dishevelled from the journey. 'I wondered where the devil you'd got to.'

'I left a note explaining where I was,' she reminded him.

'Yes,' he said, scowling at her. 'But I didn't expect you to be back so late. I don't like coming home to an empty house and no meal ready.'

'Sorry, Clifford, but there was something I had to do,' she said.

'Obviously,' he said, coming to the real reason for his pique. 'And I must say I'm disappointed in you, Amy. I expected you to have more consideration for me than to go running to your father with tales. I'll be in terrible trouble with Dad when he finds out that I've told you.'

'Don't worry,' she assured him, 'you're quite safe. My father will not breathe a word to yours.'

'Thank the Lord for that!'

The fact that Clifford viewed the problem solely from a personal angle, with no thought as to how she might be feeling, did not escape her notice. This, added to the fact that her parents had just turned their backs on her, imbued her with a deep sense of loneliness. But it also produced a defiance which

142

strengthened her and gave her the confidence to carry on. Maybe the course of her life had been decided by others, but what she made of it was up to her.

'You know you were saying how pleased you are that we got married?' she said.

'Yes,' he said uncertainly, wary of her in this mood.

'Well, I'm very glad about it too,' she said, laying Victor on the rug, and slipping her arms around her husband. 'And I hope we'll both stay that way for many years to come.'

* * *

When Violet came to see her one evening about a week later, Amy realised just how lucky she was.

Clifford had gone to meet some of his pals at his club so the two women were quite alone. Amy laid a tray with coffee and garibaldi biscuits and they settled down for a chat in the sitting room, which Amy had had daringly appointed in Art Nouveau style, with wallpaper and armchairs in the new flowing patterns, and hand-made occasional tables in light wood.

'So, what's on your mind?' she asked, pouring the coffee from a fine china pot.

'I'm pregnant.'

'Oh, Vi!' exclaimed Amy. 'Joe?'

'Yeah, o' course. Scarpered as soon as I told 'im,' she said. 'Disappeared into thin air.'

'Oh dear.'

'The rotten bugger,' said Vi. 'I really trusted 'im too.'

'So, you and I both fell at the same fence?' said Amy.

143

'Yeah, but I'm well and truly in the cart,' she said, 'cos I'll lose me job and me 'ome as soon as the mistress finds out.'

Amy nodded in agreement, because it was obvious that Florence wouldn't lower the tone of her household by having an unmarried pregnant woman within a mile of the place. 'What can I do to help?' she asked.

'I was wondering if you could lend me some money to get it seen to,' said Violet miserably. 'The same thing 'appened to the housemaid next door and she went to some woman in the backstreets of Paddington.'

'Is that what you want?' asked Amy.

'No, but I ain't got a choice, 'ave I?' she said tearfully. 'With nowhere to live and no job, I ain't got nothing to offer a kid.'

Amy lapsed into a thoughtful silence.

'I'll pay you back as soon as I can, honest,' said Violet.

'Leave it with me overnight,' said Amy cryptically. 'Come and see me tomorrow afternoon, if you can get away. I might have a more satisfactory solution to the problem to offer you by then.'

*　　　*　　　*

'Violet is pregnant,' announced Amy to Clifford at breakfast the next morning.

'Is she?' he muttered absently from behind his newspaper in which he was reading about Charles Rolls' and Henry Royce's latest automobile, the elegant Silver Ghost.

She repeated the statement in a louder tone.

'Mother's housemaid, you mean?' he said,

144

dragging his attention from the paper. 'Crikey, Mother will have a fit.'

'She'll do more than that,' said Amy. 'She'll dismiss her.'

'Boyfriend deserted her, I suppose?'

'Yes, that's right.'

'Oh, well, I expect the parish will look after her,' he said disinterestedly, for this sort of thing was all too common among the lower classes.

'I want her to come and live here with us and work as a housemaid,' said Amy.

'Wh-a-a-at!'

'She'd be a maid-of-all-work.'

'Wh-a-a-at!'

'You heard.'

'An unmarried mother living here?' he gasped incredulously.

'That's right.'

'Come on, Amy. Be reasonable.'

'I am being.'

'You must admit it isn't the thing.'

'Maybe it will raise a few eyebrows among the neighbours,' she admitted. 'But from our point of view, and Violet's, it's the obvious solution. She gets a roof over her head and a steady wage, and we get help in the house. Since we'd be giving her a much needed job, I could live with my conscience about it.'

'But how can she look after the house properly if she has a baby to look after too?' he asked.

'Same way as I do,' said Amy. 'I have a baby, remember? Anyway, she'll only be helping, not running things.'

He was still doubtful. 'No, Amy,' he insisted firmly, 'it just isn't on. We'd be objects of gossip among our friends.'

145

She sipped her coffee, observing him with a shrewd eye. 'The thing is, dear,' she said gravely, 'I don't want to have to go and tell your father what you told me the other night when you were drunk, but if there is no other way to make you change your mind...'

'Oh Amy, you wouldn't!'

Actually, he was right, she wouldn't, but it served her purpose for him to think otherwise, for she saw it as her bounden duty to offer Violet some practical help. 'I will if I have to,' she said. 'Violet is a dear friend. I can't just stand by and do nothing when she's in trouble.'

'But consider your position, darling,' he persisted. 'It just isn't proper for you to have a servant as a friend now that you're a Jackson. You must put your past behind you.'

'You know I could never do that,' she said emphatically, 'I wouldn't want to turn my back on people I care about.'

'Have you considered my feelings in all this?'

'Yes, and you only stand to benefit from such an arrangement,' she pointed out, 'because Violet is an excellent worker. And you've complained often enough about our standing with the neighbours being affected by our lack of domestic help.'

'Mmm, there is that,' he admitted. 'But ... an unmarried mother. No, it really isn't on.'

'I see,' she said calmly. 'Now, I wonder when would be the best time for me to see your father tomorrow? Would he be free in the morning? I could walk round to the shop with Victor in the pram...'

'Amy,' he warned.

'Yes, Clifford?' she said innocently.

'You're serious about this?'

'Deadly serious.'

Clifford quaked at the thought of the ghastly scene there would be with his father if she were to tell. And as he still had another two years to wait until he was given a legal share in the business, his father could even go so far as to dismiss him from the firm. A further weakening of his defences was the fact that he was no real match for Amy in this mood. The provocative way she was looking at him, those vivid blue eyes gleaming determinedly against her pale skin, simply melted him.

'I don't stand a chance against you,' he said, catching her hand and squeezing it for a second as she went to butter some toast.

'Stand with me, then,' she urged him with a grin.

'Oh, all right then,' he conceded. 'I suppose it will be good to have help in the house, like normal civilised people.'

'Thank you, Clifford,' she said, leaving her seat and hugging him. For, despite the rather devious tactics she had been forced to employ in this matter, she did feel genuinely tender towards him. 'I promise you won't regret it.'

*　　*　　*

'I'm sorry to call on you without letting you know first, Florence,' said Amy, the following afternoon as a worried Violet ushered her into the drawing room at Floral House, 'but I have something rather important to tell you.'

'I hope it won't take too long,' said her mother-in-law, showily clad in a lavender day dress with masses of chiffon and lace. 'Only I have guests coming for tea in about half an hour.' She paused, frowning at her daughter-in-law. 'Since you're here, though, you'd better sit down.'

Amy perched tensely on the edge of an armchair. 'Don't worry, I'll be gone long before your guests arrive,' she said. More plainly dressed than Florence, Amy was wearing a patterned silk blouse with a cream flannel skirt. Although she wouldn't dare to wear them herself, she was a great admirer of the less restrictive clothes with skirts that cleared the ground, that were beginning to be worn by some women who took an active part in sport.

Florence waited silently to hear what Amy had to say. Normally the two women only met when forced into it by some family occasion, which meant they were not used to being alone together. All attempts at friendship by Amy had been curtly rejected. It seemed a pity that two people who found themselves related couldn't be friends, she thought. It was a shame for Victor, too, for the only interest Florence took in him was as a means of finding fault with his mother. Having expected this meeting to be difficult, she had left him in the care of Mrs Wilks downstairs in the kitchen. The atmosphere now was charged with the icy undertones of mutual dislike. Unfortunately, Amy's mission here today was unlikely to improve matters.

She cleared her throat nervously, then told Florence about Violet's plight and what she and Clifford planned to do about it. 'She was rather nervous about telling you herself,' she explained in conclusion. 'And since she is about to become our employee, I offered to do it for her.'

The older woman's face twisted with rage, the plump cheeks brightly suffused. This would bring shame on the whole Jackson family. They would be the talk of the avenue. 'And my son has agreed to ruin

148

our family reputation by having this ... this whore living in his house?'

'She's not a whore,' denied Amy, struggling to keep calm. 'She's just been unlucky, that's all.'

'Unlucky?' rasped Florence, her gargantuan bosom heaving against the bodice of her dress. 'What utter rubbish! The girl has behaved like a slut, so she should be treated like one. You must not have her to live in your house. I forbid it.'

'With respect, Florence,' said Amy, managing to keep her temper, 'you have no right to tell me who I can have living in my house.'

'I shall order Clifford not to allow it then,' she said.

'He's already agreed, I doubt if he'll change his mind. It may have escaped your notice but Clifford is a grown man now, old enough to make his own decisions.'

'What's the matter with my son?' shouted Florence, all dignity gone as she hauled herself out of the chair rather clumsily and began to pace up and down. 'Does he have some sort of perverse ambition to fill his life with fallen women or something? First you, now Violet. God knows what people will think.'

Realising that the woman was genuinely upset, Amy stifled her own annoyance and tried to soothe her. 'Can't you take comfort in the fact that at least Violet will have somewhere to go?' she said more gently. 'She'll be off your hands. But for the grace of God, and all that.'

A peculiar look came into Florence's eyes, and she turned pale. 'What do you mean?'

'Exactly what I said.' Amy shrugged. 'That sort of trouble can happen to any one of us. We're all women, after all. Surely we should support each other at times like this?'

'Oh.' Florence looked relieved. 'I see.'

Amy realised that she had touched on a raw nerve, but found it hard to imagine the highly respectable Florence having any sort of murky secret. She was one of those people who never seemed to have been young, and definitely never reckless.

'Anyway,' said Amy, rising, 'I must go. Obviously, Violet will work out her notice here.'

'Tell her to pack her bags and go at once,' screeched Florence. 'I want her out of my house this minute.'

'All right, Florence,' said Amy, frowning. 'But don't take on so. I'm sure it can't be good for your health.'

The older woman's face hardened even more as she stood with her back to the bay windows which overlooked the garden, currently awash with summer flowers. 'You and I can never be friends, so stop insulting my intelligence by pretending to be kind.'

'Why do you hate me so much?' asked Amy.

Florence stared at her, lips pressed firmly together.

'All right, so I was already pregnant when Clifford married me,' Amy persisted. 'But I love him and I do try to be a good wife to him.'

'You don't love him,' the other woman rasped. 'He was merely the means for you to have a better life.'

'You're wrong,' argued Amy.

'Of course I'm not wrong. It's obvious to anyone with half a brain,' said Florence. 'You came to Ealing to escape the poverty of the East End with the idea of finding a rich husband as soon as you were old enough. You set your cap at Clifford because you knew he was weak and could never resist a pretty face. You'd have done the same whoever he was as long as the money was there. Your type are all the

150

same. You've only one chance of making good and that's through your looks. And by God you make the most of them.'

Amy was too deeply hurt to be angry. 'You really are quite wrong, you know,' she said.

'Don't take me for a fool,' roared Florence. 'Just get out and take your wretched friend with you. I'm well rid of her.'

Amy left with Florence's cruel words ringing in her ears. Coming so soon after the punishing dialogue with her father, they were very hard to bear, however much she pretended otherwise.

CHAPTER EIGHT

'Gwen seems to have found herself a man,' remarked Clifford to Amy, as they waltzed around the dance-floor at the wedding reception of Ned Cox and Molly Johnson the following January. 'She's been dancing with that chap John Bates all evening.'

'So I've noticed,' said Amy. 'And I'm very pleased for her.'

'A friend of the Johnsons', I believe.'

'Yes.'

'His family are jewellers, apparently. They have a couple of shops over South London way somewhere.'

'Mmm.'

'My parents will be delighted,' said Clifford. 'I think they're beginning to despair of Gwen ever finding a suitable husband.'

'She's only twenty-one, Clifford,' Amy pointed out. 'Hardly cause for alarm.'

151

'Not alarm, perhaps, but of some concern to the parents, I should imagine,' he said. 'After all, most of her contemporaries are either married or engaged. All the eligible men are being snapped up and she never manages to keep any damned one of them. I can't imagine what's the matter with her. She's not bad-looking when all is said and done.'

'Perhaps it's something the matter with *them*,' suggested Amy. 'Men aren't the only ones who need pleasing.'

'You've obviously been listening to my sister's crazy ideas,' he said, drawing back and smiling down at her. 'I hope she's got the sense not to hammer on about women's rights to John, or the romance won't even get started.'

'Some men support the cause.'

'And many more do not,' he riposted. 'The demonstrations and arrests are enough to put anyone off. No man wants to marry a woman who might end up in jail. It just isn't feminine. A woman's place is in the home, and that's all there is to it. They should keep out of politics.'

'Surely you can't deny that we have a right to vote?'

'Yes, yes, if you say so, my darling,' he said impatiently, reluctant as ever to be drawn into an argument, and obviously bored with the subject.

Amy bit back further comment, knowing it would be wasted on Clifford who had neither the interest nor the patience to give the matter any serious thought. By the very fact that she was an intelligent female, Amy could not fail to see the value of the suffragettes' work. In fact she had been to a couple of the more peaceful meetings herself with Gwen and Violet, though she'd deemed it wise not to mention it to Clifford. Although she admired the courage of those women who went to prison for the cause, she was not prepared to take the risk of arrest herself, having Victor to care for and another baby due in the summer.

'I'm sure Gwen will find her Mr Right eventually,' said Amy, changing the subject.

'Let's hope so.'

'Ned and Molly certainly seemed happy when they went away on honeymoon, didn't they?' she said conversationally.

'Oh, yes, a couple of dull old birds together,' he laughed.

'Now, that's unkind,' she reproached mildly. 'Just because Molly and Ned like a quiet life.'

It had been a splendid white wedding with bridesmaids and pageboys. Molly had looked radiant, Ned proud and happy. This grand reception was in the banqueting suite of one of West London's classiest hotels. The wedding breakfast had been delicious: turtle soup followed by turbot with lobster sauce, rib of beef with horseradish, and a deliciously fruity macedoine jelly.

Now as the event drew into the final stages they were in the ballroom, lavishly appointed with maroon and gold wallpaper and gilt-edged chairs set around marble-topped tables surrounding the dance floor. Fresh cut flowers filled a multitude of vases and bowls, and red velvet curtains draped the windows. The dark formal suits of the men looked well against the brightly coloured satins and silks of the women's long dresses.

Amy was wearing a cornflower blue dress with long sleeves and needlepoint from the collar to just below the waist. But she didn't feel at her best

153

because her waist was already beginning to thicken and her corsets were squeezing horribly. What with that and heartburn from her condition, she was most uncomfortable.

'Talking of dull old birds,' she said, 'I'm about to be one by suggesting that we go home soon. I know the cab isn't due to collect us until midnight but I'm very tired. Would you mind awfully if we took an earlier cab?'

'Oh, all right,' said Clifford, with unveiled regret, for he hated to leave a party before the end.

'You stay for a while, if you like,' said Amy, who accepted his gregarious nature without resentment. 'I'll go on my own, and you can follow later when you're ready.'

'Well...' He looked sheepish.

'Go on,' she smiled. 'You know you want to.'

'If you're sure you don't mind?'

'I'm sure.'

'I'll come and find you a cab then,' he said, beaming. 'And I'll come home a bit later on.'

*　　　*　　　*

During the Veleta, Gwen's partner said, 'I'm enjoying myself enormously, thanks to you.'

She smiled graciously. 'Thank you. I'm having a good time too.'

'In fact, we seem to get along so well I was wondering if you might allow me to escort you to the theatre one evening?'

Stepping back in accordance with the dance, Gwen took the opportunity to study John Bates briefly before making a reply. He was a tall, lean man with black hair side-parted and worn close to his head.

Neither handsome nor bad-looking, he was thin-faced with deep-set eyes, a hawkish nose and a small neat moustache. He was older than her, about thirty, she thought, and had the admirable quality of firm, dry hands. Having often partnered men with paws like cold egg custard, this was a considerable attribute.

Obviously this alone didn't make her any more at ease with him than any of the other men of her acquaintance. But adapting her vision to see him through her parents' eyes, a habit which had become almost second nature, her findings were favourable. He was presentable, rich and single. Potentially, he could liberate her from spinsterhood and all its parental pressures. She made a decision. She would do everything in her power to marry John Bates; however much the physical side distressed her. As someone's wife, at least she could hold her head up in society.

'Yes, I would like that very much,' she said, smiling her warmest smile.

*   *   *

The inside of the cab was cold, damp and musty and Amy hugged herself, shivering, as it rattled across London through the chaotic, Saturday night traffic. The din was deafening as noisy motor buses snorted along the highways in bold competition with cars and horse-drawn vehicles to find an opening to turn left or right.

To add to her discomfort, Amy's feet began to ache with the cold and she felt a little nauseous from the richness of the wedding breakfast. Home was a blissful thought indeed, her anticipation sharpened

155

by the certain knowledge that Violet would have kept the fire going in Amy's bedroom and remembered to put a stone hot water bottle in her bed. Such things were second nature to her.

Dear Violet, she had proved to be such an asset to their household. Even Clifford had to admit to the success of the arrangement because his home ran like clockwork around him, Violet being housemaid, occasional babysitter and companion to his wife. Rather than have their relationship operate on an employer—servant footing, Amy kept things informal between them, she herself taking the larger share of the workload at present as Violet's pregnancy reached its final stages. Judging by the capable and caring way she handled Victor, who was with her now, Amy guessed Violet would make a wonderful mother when her time came. Amy was looking forward to it almost as much as her friend.

In the interests of everyone's privacy, Amy had had the larger of the attic rooms done up for Violet, and made sure she had a reasonable amount of time to herself. Violet helped fill the void left by Amy's parents, whom she still missed dreadfully. She'd written to them several times begging for a reconciliation but they had never replied. Family news came to her through Alfie whom she met at Aunt Clara's, who still welcomed Amy into her home. Care was taken, however, to avoid her visits coinciding with those of her parents or father-in-law which would be all too embarrassing.

Approaching Ealing Broadway, the street lamps spread a yellow light over the wide pavements, the windows of the public houses glowing cheerily among the closed shops. Crowds were pouring out of the Hippodrome in a slow, chattering stream. Amy

156

wondered if amateurs had been used to keep the show going, for many music hall artistes were on strike because of a raw deal from hall managers. Some performers were doing twenty performances a week for no more pay than they would get for twelve, apparently. Aunt Clara had pulled out of several shows in sympathy.

To Amy's surprise, her front door opened as she made her way up the path.

'Thank Gawd yer back,' said Mrs Wilks. 'Violet's gone into labour.'

'But she's not due for a few weeks yet,' exclaimed Amy worriedly.

'The baby doesn't seem to know that,' pointed out the older woman, her waggishness designed to lighten the rather dramatic atmosphere.

'Lucky you're around,' said Amy. 'Is Victor all right?'

'Fast asleep. Vi put 'im to bed before this 'appened,' explained Mrs Wilks. 'I popped round for a chat, seeing as there was no dinner wanted at Orchard Avenue with them being out at the wedding, and found Violet in a right flap because 'er waters had broken. The pains are coming quite strong now. I was thinking I ought to go and get the midwife but didn't want to leave 'er alone. And she's in no fit state to be left in charge of young Victor.'

'I'd never have gone out if I'd thought this was going to happen,' said Amy, filled with remorse. 'If you could be a dear and run round to get the midwife, I'll take over indoors.'

*　　　*　　　*

A tormented shriek greeted Amy as she entered
157

Violet's room, and she found her friend clinging to the iron bedstead, head thrown back, hair soaked with sweat around her agonised face.

'All right, Vi,' she said, offering her her hand. 'Hang on to me.'

'Oh, Amy,' she cried, crushing Amy's fingers in her pain, 'Why didn't yer tell me it would be like this?'

'Easy now,' Amy soothed. 'That's it ... good ... you're doing fine.'

When the midwife arrived Amy was banished to the kitchen where she and Mrs Wilks drank vast amounts of tea. Clifford arrived home, and on being told of the situation, made a hasty retreat to his bed. Amy and Mrs Wilks sat listening to Violet's screams, wincing with empathy and waiting for that one cry that would tell them all was well.

But all fell ominously silent. And eventually the midwife appeared in the doorway, ashen and distraught. 'There was nothing I could do, I'm afraid,' she explained shakily. 'The baby was born dead, strangled by the umbilical cord. A lovely little girl, too.'

*   *   *

Ralph Jackson didn't value Clara for her physical qualities alone. She was also useful to him as a sounding board for his business worries. He couldn't discuss such things with Florence because she saw the shop as his sole responsibility and didn't think he should burden her with such tedious matters as a drop in sales figures or falling profits. She ran the home with perfect precision without bothering him, and expected him to do the same with their livelihood.

158

Anyway, such problems confided to Florence would only invite criticism. Whereas Clara, whose lifestyle was not threatened to any real extent by a slight lowering of profits at Jackson & Cox, could be relied upon to give him a sympathetic hearing without fault-finding. Her unshakable optimism was a great comfort to him at times like this. 'Things'll pick up, love,' she'd say or: 'A man like you 'ull soon have things fine and dandy again.'

It was a disappointment to him, therefore, to find her noticeably preoccupied when he visited her one afternoon in February, intent on unburdening himself to her...

They were seated by the fire in her sitting room with its soft pink furniture and frilly lace curtains. He said, 'Business is very slack at the moment.'

'Mmm.'

'It seems to be pretty general in the trade and no particular fault of ours,' he continued, 'but then, our goods and services are the best in the area.'

'Mmm.'

'The jewellery trade is very competitive, that's one of the problems,' he said.

'Yeah?'

'I'm trying to think of some way in which we can perk things up.'

'Oh.'

'But I don't know what. I mean, it isn't as though we don't already carry a wide variety of stock. Some original pieces too,' he said. 'I have my chaps in the workroom copy the top-selling pieces, with minor alterations.'

'Mmm.'

'We've a fine selection of silverware.'

Silence.

159

'Clara, what *is* the matter with you? You haven't heard a word I've said.'

She came out of her thoughts with a start, and gave him her full attention. 'You're right, Ralph, I ain't bin listening.'

'Oh, that's nice, that is,' he said, looking very peeved.

'I have other things on my mind.'

'Obviously,' he snorted.

'There's something I need to talk to you about.'

'It'll have to wait till later,' he said dismissively, 'I'm trying to clear my mind on matters of *real* importance.'

'What I have to say is important.'

'Now don't be tedious, Clara dear,' he said, patronisingly. 'Perhaps we should do some advertising or have some sort of special promotion?'

Realising that shock tactics were the only way to gain his attention, she said, 'I'm pregnant, Ralph.'

'What sort of promotion? That's the question,' he said, as though she hadn't spoken. 'A high-class jewellery firm cannot flaunt its wares like a market trader. Anything too brash could cheapen the reputation it's taken years to build.'

'Did you 'ear what I said, Ralph?' she shouted.

'Mmm ... what's that, Clara?' he said, still full of his own problems.

'I'm havin' your baby.'

He stared at her in bewilderment, his mind still on stock and sales figures. What she had said seemed unreal, unrelated to him. *A baby! Him!* Why, that was ridiculous. He was far too old for that sort of aggravation. He had little enough patience with young people of any age, and small children were quite beyond the pale. A baby, what a ghastly

160

prospect!

'A baby,' he muttered at last. 'Mine.'

'Of course it's yours. I hope you ain't suggestin' there is any other man in my life,' she snapped, for this development meant serious problems for her and she was very worried. Her living depended on her having a good figure. She'd be booed off the stage if she staggered on looking like a teapot. Then there was afterwards. How was she going to look after a baby when she had to go out working? Ralph contributed to her income it was true, but he didn't fully support her. His financial contribution meant she had been able to save a bit over the years, but how long would that last with a child to keep? The public would soon forget her if she disappeared for a while, and it might prove impossible to get work when she returned.

She was thirty-two years old. It was getting harder all the time to beat the competition, with fresh young talent coming on to the halls every week. Especially with her looks and personality carrying her voice to such an extent. She was in a mess and no mistake. It wasn't as though she hadn't been careful. She always made him withdraw well before the crucial moment, and it had worked for all these years, until now. Her timing had gone wrong somewhere along the line, that was for sure.

'Oh God,' he said at last, his small grey eyes clouded with worry.

In moments of fantasy she had imagined him being pleased, eager to leave his wife to make a new start with her and their child. In reality she had known it would be like this. But it still hurt. Oh, yes, for all her cheery brashness, Clara wanted to be loved and looked after, the same as anyone else.

161

'My sentiments exactly,' she said. 'This has landed me in the soup, good and proper.'

'You'll have to get rid of it,' he said, struck with panic.

As desperate with worry as she was, that was something she would not consider, because, problems aside, she did actually want the child.

'No, I won't do that,' she declared in an uncompromising tone.

Ralph was infuriated by this turn of events. His retreat from the worries of business and the irritations of homelife had now become a source of worry in itself. Was there no escape? He looked at Clara, with her glorious eyes and painted face, her evocative perfume and wonderfully sinful aura. And he saw in her place a homely woman smelling of baby's milk, her breasts no longer merely objects of pleasure for him but practical means of nourishment for the child. His first instinct was to deny all responsibility. But as selfish as Ralph was, even *he* couldn't bring himself to be that callous, for she had been a part of his life for a very long time and he had grown fond of her. If only she could be persuaded to have the problem removed, life could go on as before with nothing required from him except one cash payment. But he knew from her tone of voice that she would not change her mind.

He tensed further as another potential problem reared its head. What pressure would her brother bring to bear if Ralph didn't make provision for Clara and the baby? Ralph had no way of knowing that he was quite safe from George Atkins who had vowed never to intervene in the affairs of his relatives again, after Amy's ingratitude.

Biting back his irritation, Ralph said briskly, 'In

that case, we'll have to come to some sort of a practical arrangement. Obviously you will have to raise the child alone. I told you from the very start that I would never leave my wife.'

'I know that,' said Clara coolly.

'But I will see to it that you are not short of money.'

Clara would have liked to have been in a position to refuse his help, and not be beholden to him. But she couldn't afford to be heroic. And, anyway, why should he get off scot free? If all he had to offer was money, she would take it for the sake of the child which was as much his responsibility as hers. 'Thank you,' she said, with unfamiliar formality.

Already their relationship had changed, he thought. How quickly passion evaporated when responsibility reared its head. He thought again of her brother and what a meal he would make of this, given the opportunity. 'I shall make sure that you have enough money to live decently and either not work or pay someone to look after the child while you do, if that is what you would prefer. You will not find me ungenerous.'

'I'm sure.'

'So, this sort of arrangement will be acceptable to you, will it?' he said, eager for her agreement with the threat of her brother still in mind.

'Yeah, sure, it's fine by me,' she said in a businesslike tone. Those two words 'I'm pregnant' that should have brought them closer together, had turned them into strangers.

'And I think it would be best for all of us,' he continued solemnly, 'if the child doesn't know that I'm its father, as it grows up.'

The rejection of her child hurt far more than any personal insult, and she couldn't trust herself to answer immediately. 'All right, Ralph,' she said at last, with icy politeness. 'If that's what yer want, I'll make sure that's 'ow it is.'

She admonished herself for feeling so deeply upset. After all, she'd known what she was getting into when she embarked upon an affair with a married man. Self-pity wasn't going to help anyone. She'd just have to get on with it as best as she could. And at least he was going to ease his conscience in a practical way, so the child wouldn't starve.

But for all that, the future without him seemed bleak. It was over between them, he didn't need to spell it out for her.

CHAPTER NINE

Drastic action was needed to counteract Jackson & Cox's ailing sales figures, in Amy's opinion. 'Why not look further afield for new business, rather than just sit back and wait for things to pick up?' she suggested.

'If only it were that easy,' said Clifford, who took a dim view of having to apply his mind to business matters outside shop hours, and was only doing so from necessity. 'But how the devil can we find new customers from outside our own area?'

'Why not try mail order?' she suggested, 'I was reading an article about it in one of the trade magazines the other day. It can be very profitable, apparently.'

He made a face. 'A bit tasteless though. All right for selling cornplasters to the masses, perhaps, but jewellery is in a different league.'

164

'This is no time for snobbery,' she declared. 'If you want to put your business back on top you must open your mind to new ideas and to hell with the old-fashioned traditions that dominate the jewellery trade.'

'But you can't deny that jewellery is a commodity of the rich?'

'In the main, yes.'

'And the rich demand personal service.'

'Most of them do, yes,' she agreed, 'and those sort would never buy through mail order. But there is another section of the public, those who only buy jewellery occasionally. They might enjoy the convenience of shopping by post. Remember, this will only be an expansion of the business, to give people a choice and bring custom from further away. Obviously local people will still come to the shop to make their purchases.'

'Mmm, put like that I suppose it does have possibilities,' he said thoughtfully. 'But how would we actually get something like that underway?'

'You'd have a catalogue produced containing your complete stock range,' said Amy, speaking partly from common sense and partly from what she'd read on the subject. 'Then place advertisements in various provincial newspapers with sketches of a few selected items from the catalogue, possibly in the less expensive range to appeal to the people who are not regular jewellery buyers. Watches, a selection of wedding and engagement rings, and cuff links, for instance.'

'Would people order directly from the advertisement, do you think?' he asked.

'Some will, I suppose,' she said, her interest growing as the idea began to take shape. 'But mostly

165

I should think they'd send for the catalogue and choose from that. You'd have to stipulate that payment is enclosed with the order to avoid bad debts.'

'Yes, I can see the logic in that.'

'You could even have a credit scheme.'

'Mmm.'

It was a blustery Sunday afternoon in March and they were having tea by the fire in the parlour. Shafts of watery sunshine filtered through the lace curtains and dappled across the framed photographs on top of the piano. Violet had taken Victor for a walk in the park, so the house was silent but for the wind rattling the windows and the gentle pop and crackle of the fire.

'But whereas *I* can see that mail order might be the answer,' continued Clifford, 'I doubt if my father or Harold Cox will agree to give it a chance. They're very set in their ways, and they'll probably see the scheme as a lowering of standards.'

'They'll have to be more adaptable if they want to save the business,' said Amy firmly.

'I know.'

'As well as mail order, you need something unique to Jackson & Cox,' she went on thoughtfully. 'Like a reputation for original pieces. Continue to do the copies of the mass-produced jewellery, of course, but have something completely different every now and then, too.'

'Your designs, for instance?' surmised Clifford.

'Why not?' she grinned.

'But you know how Father is about using anything new.'

'Especially if it's been designed by me.'

'Well...' he said, looking sheepish. 'I suppose

166

there's no point my pretending otherwise.'

'You'll have to try and persuade him to do something to boost trade, though.'

'I know. The trouble is, I've no say in company policy until I get my directorship next year.'

'Ned Cox has though, hasn't he?' she pointed out.

'Yes, he became a director last month when he was twenty-five.'

'Why not mention my thoughts on the subject to him, see if you can get his support?' she suggested. 'Being of a younger generation, he might have more of an open mind. If he likes my ideas, get him to suggest them at the next directors' meeting. If you put them to your father yourself, he may not even bother to mention them to the others. But if they are raised by someone else at a meeting...'

'Good idea,' agreed Clifford enthusiastically. 'I'll talk to Ned about it tomorrow.'

*　　*　　*

'The purpose of this meeting is to discuss what can be done about our drop in turnover,' announced Ralph to his two co-directors at an emergency meeting in his office a few days later. 'So, has anyone any suggestions?'

'Amy has come up with a couple of good ideas,' said Ned, who was far too honest to claim the credit for himself even though it might have been more expedient in the light of Ralph's well-known dislike of his daughter-in-law.

'Oh, has she?' said Ralph dismissively.

'Let's hear them then,' urged Harold.

Ned gave them a full account.

'Mere feminine fancies,' said Ralph predictably.

167

'Amy knows nothing about business.'

'I disagree,' said Ned. 'These ideas are well worth considering.'

'I second that,' said Harold, a lean-faced man with white hair. He tended to be much less assertive than Ralph who had assumed the dominant role throughout their partnership. But with their livelihood at stake, Harold was determined to have a say.

'But mail order of all things,' sneered Ralph, feeling threatened by such strong opposition. 'What are we, high-class jewellers or market traders? And as for having Burridge make up some of Amy's designs...'

'Do you have anything better to suggest?' asked Ned candidly.

'Well, no, not at the moment,' he was forced to admit, 'but I'm sure we'll think of something more suitable if the three of us put our heads together.'

'I doubt if we'll come up with anything better,' said Ned. 'I think we should at least give it a try.'

'Hear, hear,' said Harold.

'You realise that setting up a mail order operation will entail a lot of costly administration?' grumbled Ralph, whose instinct to block Amy's ideas was largely due to the wrath he knew it would incur when Florence discovered that her daughter-in-law's suggestions had been given credibility. Something big like this was bound to come out, despite Florence's lack of interest in the business.

'Perhaps Amy would be willing to get the project underway?' suggested Ned.

'That's an idea,' said his father.

'Especially as we'd run it from the Ealing shop, since you have more office space here than we have at

Shepherds Bush,' said Ned.

Ralph tutted. 'How can Amy get involved in business, with a child to look after and another one on the way?'

'Mmm, I can see that it might be difficult for her,' agreed Ned. 'Obviously she couldn't work on a permanent basis. I was thinking more in terms of employing her part-time for a brief period, just to set the scheme up. When it's in place, we can re-shuffle the other office staff to maintain the system. It would be better if we didn't strain our wages bill at the moment by taking on extra staff permanently, until it begins to pay its way.'

'No,' protested Ralph hotly. 'It simply wouldn't work.'

'Perhaps Amy has someone who would look after the child for a few hours a day while she comes into the office?' suggested Harold.

'I'm sure something can be arranged,' said Ned.

'That's as may be,' snapped Ralph. 'But there's still the matter of her pregnancy which is not invisible. Customers don't want to see that sort of thing when they come into the shop to do business.'

'She'd be upstairs in the office,' Ned reminded him. 'No one in the shop would see her.'

'That's true,' said Harold.

'It still isn't right,' barked Ralph. 'A pregnant woman should be at home and out of sight.'

'I suggest we take a vote on it,' said Ned.

'Since it's obvious that you will both oppose me, there's no point,' said Ralph furiously. As if he didn't have enough problems with Clara managing to get herself pregnant, now he was going to have Florence bending his ear about Amy. Oh, how he wished he'd never heard the name of Atkins.

169

Having lost her own child so tragically, Violet channelled all her maternal love into Victor, and was delighted to have him to herself in the afternoons while Amy went in to the office.

Happy in the knowledge that he was being well cared for, Amy applied herself to the project whole-heartedly. Having planned a catalogue which a local printer produced, she devised a tasteful advertisement, a different code in each newspaper added to their own address to enable them to assess the number of replies they received from each paper, for future reference.

To add a little spice to the showroom's side of the business, she designed a striking, diamond-shaped pendant in gold with filigree edging and set with pearls and rubies in the centre. Having discussed the proposed piece with Mr Burridge, who assured her it would be possible for him to produce, she then put the idea to Clifford, who in turn spoke to the directors, who agreed to have one made and display it in the window.

And so, having completed her task, she returned to her role as housewife to await results. They were disappointing. In fact, the plan was a consummate failure. The few enquiries they did receive in response to the advertisements failed to develop into sales, and no interest was shown in the pendant whatsoever. They tried the advertisements in some other newspapers, all with the same negative result.

'Don't worry about it,' sympathised Clifford as Amy tortured herself. 'It was a good idea, and it didn't work. These things happen. At least you came up with something, which is more than can be said for

170

the rest of us.'

'But what about all that money we wasted on advertising and printing?'

'Water under the bridge,' said Clifford. 'Forget about it, and we'll try to think of something else.'

But Amy couldn't accept defeat. The idea was sound so the fault must lie in the way she had handled it. After several sleepless nights, light began to dawn.

'It's the tone of the advertisement,' she said to Clifford. 'It wasn't bold enough. In trying to keep the Jackson & Cox image refined, I've failed to attract the sort of people who are most likely to become mail order customers. Those who probably only go into a jeweller's shop once or twice in a lifetime, perhaps to buy an engagement or wedding ring. We need to be blatantly eye-catching, to demand attention. If just a fraction of the occasional purchasers buy from us, we'll be laughing all the way to the bank.'

'Surely a couple buying an engagement ring would prefer to go into a shop and choose it,' he said. 'It's all part of the excitement.'

'That isn't true of everybody,' she said sagely. 'Many working-class people feel daunted by the grandness of a jeweller's shop where they are approached immediately they walk in. They might prefer to browse through the catalogue and choose something in private in their own time.'

'You really think so?'

'Yes, I do.'

'So what do we do now?'

'I'd like to work on another advertisement, with one particular item at a reasonable price to draw attention. You know the sort of thing ... keyless watches, only five pounds, or something.'

'I doubt if the directors will want to pay for more

171

advertising.'

'Persuade Ned and you're halfway there,' she said, 'because I'm positive I've got it right this time.'

'I'll do my best,' said Clifford, his interest held by the threat to his comfortable lifestyle if the company wasn't steered back on course.

Fortunately, the directors were equally as concerned and agreed to give the idea another chance in the absence of a plausible alternative. It proved a wise decision because there was a substantial increase in the amount of requests for the catalogue, a good percentage of which were converted into sales. After a bad start, the Jackson & Cox Mail Order Division was on its way.

The lack of interest in the pendant was disheartening. Someone would buy it eventually, Amy guessed, but it was obviously not going to set the world on fire.

In fact, her second son, Dickie, had made an appearance before it was finally sold. She cheered herself with the thought that at least she had not made a loss for the firm. But her brief spell as a businesswoman was over. She had thoroughly enjoyed it and felt she had much more to contribute. But right now she had a family to look after.

* * *

'She's beautiful, Aunt Clara,' said Amy one day in August as she gazed into the crib at Clara's little daughter, a pink scrap of a thing with a downy thatch of sandy-coloured hair.

'I won't disagree with that,' said Clara, lying back against the pillows contentedly. ''Cos I'm nuts about 'er.'

Amy had left her own children with Violet while she made this visit, rather than drag them across London. 'Who wouldn't be?' she said.

'Seems funny, dunnit, me bein' a mum?' remarked Clara. 'I ain't never bin the domesticated type.' She paused, her eyes moistening. 'But honestly, Ame, she's the best thing that's ever 'appened to me.'

'I'm so pleased for you, Auntie,' said Amy, squeezing her hand. 'What are you going to call her?'

'Connie,' said Clara.

'That's nice,' said Amy. 'Connie Atkins. They go well together.'

'Yeah, she'll take my name.' She gave a wry smile. 'It would really put the cat among the pigeons if I gave her her father's, now wouldn't it?'

Although Amy had always been good friends with her aunt, Clara was of a senior generation which had deterred Amy from raising the delicate subject of the child's paternity, as obvious as it was. It was rather an uncomfortable feeling to know that your husband's father was also the father of your cousin. But since her aunt now seemed to want the matter discussed openly, Amy said, 'Ralph Jackson?'

'Yeah, o' course,' said Clara.

'I guessed so.'

'And while we're on the subject, Amy,' Clara said, lowering her tone confidentially as though they were not alone in the flat, 'I shall bring Connie up to think that 'er father was a merchant sailor who was drowned at sea while I was carrying 'er. I shall tell 'er he was the love of me life who intended to marry me when he got back 'ome. It'll be better for 'er to think her ole man ain't around 'cos he died, rather than because he disowned 'er. I don't want 'er to grow up feeling rejected. I think it's best if all the family know

173

my intentions right away so we can get used to it from the start. I've already told yer mum and dad.'

'I see,' said Amy.

'It will be less complicated for everybody this way,' she continued. 'After all, we don't want Connie turnin' up on Ralph's doorstep upsettin' his family when she's grown up, do we? Yer do 'ear about such things.'

'What does Ralph think of her?' asked Amy.

'He ain't seen her,' Clara said sadly. 'It was all over between us when I told 'im I was pregnant, and I ain't seen 'im since.'

'Just like that, he ended it?' said Amy in astonishment.

'Yeah, that's right. He doesn't want any contact with the baby at all, I suppose in case she puts two and two together as she grows up and causes trouble for 'im at 'ome. He sends me money regular, though,' she explained, 'he's been doin' that since he knew I was pregnant.'

'That's something, I suppose.'

'Oh, yeah. Credit where it's due, he never misses and he ain't a bit stingy. Once a month I get a payment in the post, so I ain't complaining. Conscience money, o' course, but at least I can live decently.'

Fear of what her brother George might do if she wasn't looked after, more like, thought Amy, but said nothing.

'So, how are you managing to stay in bed?' asked Amy. 'Being that you're on your own.'

'I can afford to 'ave a nurse come in every day to see to the baby while I'm layin' in, thanks to Ralph,' she explained. 'And yer mum pops round every day to make me meals and clean up.'

174

'I only wish I lived near enough to help,' said Amy.

'Don't you worry about me, love,' said Clara cheerfully. 'I'm one of life's natural survivors.'

'Do you hate Ralph for dropping you?'

'You know me, love, I don't 'ate anybody. I knew from the start that I was just his bit on the side, so there's no point in wasting energy feelin' bad about it. I've got to get on with the job of bringin' Connie up. All right, so I ain't got the security of marriage, but I've a damned sight more than I deserve. I've got Connie.'

A knock at the front door sent Amy's heart pounding with a mixture of hope and fear at the thought that it might be her parents. But it was Alfie, carrying a pudding basin wrapped in a tea-towel.

'Wotcha, sis,' he said breezily, his bruiser's face broadening into a smile as she opened the door. 'How yer going, love?'

'Mustn't grumble,' she said.

'Mum sent me round with a meat puddin' for Aunt Clara,' he explained.

Amy hugged him enthusiastically, smacking a kiss on his cheek. She still missed her parents dreadfully and seeing him made her feel closer to them.

''Ere, watch out, Ame,' he said, for demonstrations of affection embarrassed him. 'I'll drop this puddin' in a minute if you carry on like that.'

The basin was safely deposited in the kitchen and they adjourned into the bedroom where they jointly extolled the virtues of their new cousin before turning to general conversation.

'I can't stay long,' said Alfie. 'I'm boxing tonight at West Ham and I need to get me 'ead down for a couple of hours to make sure I'm on top form.'

'Is there a fair on over that way, then?' Amy asked.

'No, I'm fighting in an 'all,' he explained, his eyes bright with enthusiasm. 'A promoter saw me boxing round the fairgrounds and started arranging proper bouts for me. Decent money they pay me, an' all.'

Amy frowned disapprovingly. 'Surely you don't enjoy fighting for a living?'

'Givin' someone a good hidin' ain't no trouble to me,' he said. 'You know me, sis, I've bin in scraps all me life.'

'Yes, but that was just kids' stuff, usually for someone else's benefit,' she said. 'Beating someone senseless just to provide entertainment is something else altogether.'

'It's a good clean sport,' he defended hotly. 'All right, maybe I don't always feel like knocking someone about. But it's what I'm good at and it brings in a damned sight more dough than workin' in a factory all day. If I do well, I'll be able to get me own place and give Mum and Dad more space.'

'You be careful,' she warned.

'Don't you worry about me,' he said. 'I'm a big boy now.'

*　　　*　　　*

In the spring of 1908 a development of ornate white buildings outlined in electric lights, and Venetian-style waterways set in fantastical gardens, appeared on an area of common land at Shepherds Bush. Known as The White City, this two-hundred-acre wonderland was the setting for the Franco-British exhibition, and was opened in driving rain by the Prince and Princess of Wales one Thursday in May. The two new railway stations that were built with the

176

exhibition site in mind proved to be justified as crowds of visitors amounting to some 120,000 arrived on the first day alone, sheltering beneath umbrellas and turning the newly planted grass into mud.

One Saturday a week or so later Amy and Clifford made a foursome with Ned and Molly Cox to pay the exhibition a visit, the two men having taken the afternoon off, and Amy having left the children with Violet because of the crowds.

'It's very impressive, isn't it?' said Amy as they stood by the elaborate white railings edging the lagoon known as The Court of Honour. At the head of this lake was a semi-circular waterfall shining in myriad hues as the water cascaded over a series of multi-coloured glass steps.

'Stunning,' agreed Molly, watching the sunlight shimmer on the undulating waters and spread across the intricate domes of the palaces and pavilions.

'Well, they've certainly spared no effort to strengthen Anglo-French ties,' said Ned, soberly dressed in a grey suit and bowler hat.

'Quite splendid,' agreed Clifford, stylishly attired in a checked suit with highly polished shoes, buttoned cloth spats and a straw boater.

Londoners and visitors from far and wide were here in their thousands. A sea of summer boaters and parasols bobbed and weaved along the walkways and clustered around the lagoon. There were gentlemen in top hats, and young dandies like Clifford in spats. The women's summer pastels made a fine display, their hats decorated with flowers, fruit and ribbons. People were exuberant and noisy. An excited hubbub drifted pleasantly around Amy and her friends as the weekend crowds poured in.

177

Amy looked fresh and pretty in a pale lemon dress with cream trimmings, in the new looser style, and artificial yellow roses on her matching hat. 'I'm glad I didn't bring the kids,' she confided to Molly with whom she had become increasingly friendly. 'They're too small to drag around in a crush like this. Violet and I will bring them on a weekday when it isn't quite so busy.'

'Good idea,' said Molly wistfully.

Knowing how disappointed Molly was not to have started a family after almost a year and a half of marriage, Amy tried to share the pleasure of her own children with her. 'Why don't you come too?' she said warmly.

'I'd love to,' she said, shading herself beneath the lavender parasol that matched her dress.

'Come on, girls,' Clifford was saying. 'Let's move on, there's plenty to see.'

And that was an understatement. They wandered in and out of the many exhibition halls which housed fine displays of everything from British shipbuilding to French cuisine. They saw the fine arts of India, shown in a dignified white building of Saracen design. There were exhibits from Algeria and the West African colonies, and a good range of furs from Canada. They strolled through a reproduction of an Irish village, and marvelled at the new 70,000 capacity sports stadium.

'This is where the Olympic games will be held in July, then,' said Amy, as they took a tour of the arena, gazing with awe at the long swimming pool. She was very impressed by this joint achievement of the two countries which was quite unprecedented in her eyes.

'That's right,' said Ned. 'Isn't it something? The

178

biggest of its kind in the world, they say. And come July it will be filled to overflowing.'

Weary from sightseeing, they decided to take a break and have tea in the sunshine at tea-rooms overlooking the lagoon. Having discussed the exhibition thoroughly, Clifford changed the subject to something that was very dear to his heart: motor cars. In particular the one his father was going to buy for him to celebrate his twenty-fifth birthday in the autumn, when he was also to be given some of his father's shares in the business.

'What do you think of the Silent Sunbeam, Ned?' he asked.

'I can't say I know much about it,' said Ned, who was one of the many people not altogether in favour of the motor car. 'I suppose it will be much the same as the others—dirty, noisy, and frightening for horses.'

'The motor car is here to stay, old boy,' said Clifford, nibbling a slice of seed cake. 'So you may as well get used to it. Especially when Ford's Model T comes on to the market in this country. Their mass-produced cars will be quite cheap, I reckon.'

'God help us all,' said Ned.

'You're so dashed old-fashioned for a young man, Ned,' reproached Clifford. 'Even my father is more up to date than you.'

'Only because he feels compelled to be the first to get something new,' said Ned.

'They've already got a nickname for the new Ford,' said Amy, sipping her tea. 'The Tin Lizzy, they're calling it. I read about it in the paper.'

'Seems quite appropriate. I suppose it'll sound like a dozen sets of saucepans clanking round the streets,' Ned said, producing a roar of laughter.

179

'You've no sense of adventure, that's your trouble,' teased Clifford lightheartedly. 'I know it seems hard to believe but one day horse transport will be a thing of the past.' He finished the seed cake and helped himself to a pastry from the cakestand on the table. 'You can see it coming already with the number of motor vehicles on the streets.'

'Don't remind me,' said Ned. 'You can't cross the road near our shop without almost being mowed down by one.'

'You can't stop progress, Ned,' said Amy, helping herself to an iced bun. 'But at least there are strict laws now about the amount of noise motor buses are allowed to make on the streets.'

'Thank God for small mercies,' he said.

Amy's attention wandered as the discussion continued in similar vein. She perceived the colourful scene around her with pleasure; the carnival atmosphere among the crowds, the elaborately ornamented buildings, the scenic railway etched against the sky near the stadium. It was good to see everyone looking so relaxed and happy. Her glance settled idly on an attractive young woman in a candy pink outfit passing by on the arm of a man. As the woman looked up at him, he bent over and kissed her. It was when Amy's observations extended to the man that her eyes widened. My God, it was Gwen's husband, John Bates!

Instinctively protective towards Gwen, Amy glanced at Clifford and was relieved to see him engrossed in conversation with Molly, and unaware of his erring brother-in-law's proximity. The fewer people who knew about this the better, for the sake of Gwen's pride. Unfortunately, Amy was not the only one to witness the incident. Glancing across the table, she perceived that Ned had noticed the transgression too and was obviously upset by it. In fact he looked furious, staring at John with eyes dark and murderous.

Amy was concerned. It was worrying enough to witness a blatant betrayal of Gwen; even worse to see that Ned Cox was so strongly affected by it. It was understandable that he would feel sympathetic towards Gwen, for they were lifelong friends. But this was something more than that. The man was positively distraught. She couldn't help but wonder if she ought to be feeling sorry for Molly too.

As the couple disappeared into the crowds, Amy's glance met Ned's. A moment of understanding passed between them. Neither wanted what they had seen to go further. It was the first time Amy had ever felt any kind of rapport with Ned. For some unaccountable reason she enjoyed the feeling, even though she neither liked nor trusted him.

'How about a ride on the scenic railway when we've finished tea?' she suggested brightly, forcing her attention back to the rest of the company. 'It might take your mind off motor cars for a few minutes, Clifford.'

There was a general cry of approval, so they finished their tea and moved on into the crowds. But Amy's thoughts were elsewhere. More dominant in her mind than Gwen's problems was the question that had puzzled her for so long. Why was a man who seemed so happily married and devoted to his wife, so overly concerned about another woman?

*　　　*　　　*

One Sunday in June, Gwen stood in the crowd in

181

Hyde Park at a gathering of a different sort, a Votes for Women rally organised on a colossal scale. Women from every corner of Britain and abroad had come here today to join the Women's Social and Political Union in a demonstration intended to show the Prime Minister that the movement in favour of women being given the vote had the support of the majority of females in the country.

Many had come in processions, rich and poor united for the cause, the few females who had managed to gain a place in the professions walking with factory girls and housemaids. There were bands playing, bugles blowing, and banners with their slogans boldly flying: 'Who would be free themselves must strike the blow' and 'Not chivalry but justice'.

Now, with everyone assembled, the crowds were packed so tightly around Gwen she felt starved of air, her shoulders pressed close to those on either side, her chest jammed to the woman in front. A pantechnicon centred a formation of wagons which were being used as platforms for the speakers.

Through the densely packed mass, Gwen could just see Christobel Pankhurst on the platform nearest to her, wearing a sash in the campaign colours of purple, green and white. With passion and vigour this courageous lady told the crowds that this demonstration would convince the government that they had public opinion on their side. Despite a gang of ruffians, bent on opposing her and almost overturning her platform, she continued to hold forth for an hour and a half.

'Wonderful, ain't she?' said the woman next to Gwen.

'Yes, she is,' agreed Gwen, having to shout above the noise of the crowd.

'Plucky lot, the suffragettes.'

'I'll say.'

Distantly they could hear the sounds of trouble. Scuffles; shouts; thuds; police whistles. Someone fainted nearby and there was pandemonium as they tried to get her through the crowds into the fresh air. 'I'm orf if there's any trouble near 'ere,' said Gwen's companion. 'I daren't get arrested. My old man would 'ave a fit if he knew I was 'ere. He thinks I'm at me mother's. How about yours, luv?'

'He doesn't mind me being here,' she said.

'A supporter, eh?'

'Sort of,' lied Gwen because it was easier than explaining that her husband didn't mind her being here because he had no interest in what she did. It was less painful than admitting that her marriage had been a complete failure because of her incurable frigidity, and her husband was probably at this very moment finding happiness in the arms of another woman.

'You're lucky, mate,' said the other woman, who was a common sort with bad teeth and a dusty assortment of wax fruit adorning her hat.

She wouldn't say that if she knew the truth, thought Gwen, that John is hardly ever home and it's probably only a matter of time before he leaves altogether. And despite all the gossip and criticism from Mother, I'll be *glad* to see the back of him, which must make me some kind of a freak.

The speeches eventually concluded and the rally came to an end to loud cheers and a universal waving of handkerchiefs and hats. Optimism and high spirits abounded as the gathering began to disperse, stranger bidding farewell to stranger as emotionally as old friends.

Gwen said goodbye to her companion and left the park feeling at one with womankind and convinced that some day soon their fight for justice would be won. If only she could be as positive about her personal life, she thought dismally, as she made her way to the station to catch the train home to an empty house.

CHAPTER TEN

As Clifford's twenty-fifth birthday was also the day he was to become a legal partner in the firm, Amy decided to make a really special occasion of it. By way of a gift to him, she designed a tie-pin and matching cuff links in gold with diamond chips, which Mr Burridge produced with his usual expertise. In terms of financial value, it couldn't compete with the offering Clifford was to receive from his parents, of course, but she was confident it would satisfy his enjoyment of fine things.

Since his birthday was to fall on a Sunday this year, she decided to organise a surprise celebratory luncheon for him, including his parents on the guest list. It was rather a fruitless hope but she still wanted to be accepted by her in-laws, more for the sake of the children and Clifford than herself. Maybe she and the Jacksons could never be friends, but surely some sort of compromise could be reached with a little effort on both sides? With this in mind, she vowed to be extra nice to them at the party and not to be goaded into losing her temper with Florence, whatever the provocation.

Carefully planning the festivities for her party-

184

loving husband, Amy saw this as a way of showing her appreciation to him for three years of marriage. He wasn't a model husband by any means. In fact, even now his attitudes were more those of a bachelor-about-town than a family man. Stylish clothes and motor cars were of far more interest to him than his home or the simple pleasures Amy drew from the development of their children. But having learned to live with his immature ways, she was still very much in love with him.

Now, as Saturday afternoon advanced and the big day approached, she checked her list of pre-party jobs. Menu prepared and food ordered, yes; birthday cards written and presents wrapped in fancy paper, yes; champagne; flowers for the table, place names, all in order. Satisfied that everything was under control, she began to feel quite excited. It was all going to be such fun. Clifford would be thrilled. Tomorrow couldn't come quickly enough.

*   *   *

Clifford enjoyed the atmosphere of the West End. He liked the sophistication of the shops, the cosmopolitan mix of people on the streets and the tantalising suspicion that something exciting was in progress behind every closed door. Even the humid weather and the ubiquitous flies buzzing around his face didn't lower his spirits. It was one of those oppressive September afternoons with heavy sunshine and a suffocating sense of airlessness. Fat bluebottles flew around the horse dung in clouds, crawled over the ripe fruit on the street barrows and settled in swarms on the horses as they waited patiently in their shafts to get through the traffic,

185

shaking their heads and swishing their tails with pathetic ineffectiveness to remove these purveyors of torture.

He was always glad of an excuse to come here, and had taken a slight detour after attending to some business for his father in Hatton Garden. This afternoon he was feeling particularly pleased with himself at having escaped from the shop because it gave him a chance to indulge in blissful anticipation of the birthday gift he was to receive from his father tomorrow.

Passing the Oxford Music Hall, at the corner of Oxford Street and Tottenham Court Road, he noticed on the board outside that one of his favourites, Florrie Forde, was on the bill. He enjoyed her cheery songs enormously, especially 'Down at the Old Bull and Bush'. Maybe he'd bring Amy one evening next week. She liked a good rousing show. But more importantly, it would be somewhere to go to show off his new motor car.

Excitement set him tingling at the mere thought of the car. It meant far more to him than the other acquisition his father was about to bestow on him. As far as Clifford was concerned, becoming a director of the firm had distinct disadvantages. Certainly, he'd have more money and more power over what went on at the shop, but were these privileges worth the added burden of responsibility they carried with them? Did he want to spend precious time and energy on business matters? Frankly, the thought of having to attend directors' meetings in his own time simply appalled him.

But Clifford had similar habits to those of the ostrich when it came to potential problems. And as he strolled nonchalantly along Oxford Street towards Marble Arch, he found it easy to convince himself that somehow his directorship could be made palatable, and there was no earthly point in spoiling the fun of having his first car by dwelling on troublesome thoughts beyond that.

He glanced idly towards the road which was a chaotic mass of traffic and noise as cars and motor buses fought with horse-drawn buses, carts, traps and countless other vehicles for space on the highway. Making his way towards Marble Arch station, he passed the building construction of the new store that was being erected for an American called Gordon Selfridge. Progress was good, he observed, noticing the wide apertures in the shell which would eventually be the shop windows. He'd already had a look at the drawing of the finished store, which was on show to the public outside the building works, and it looked as though it was going to be grander than anything Oxford Street had seen before.

Marble Arch was teeming with people, most of whom seemed to be hurrying towards Hyde Park. 'There's a lot of people about,' remarked Clifford to a newspaper seller. 'Is there something special going on in the park?'

'Yus, mate,' said the man. 'The crowds are arrivin' ready for the demonstration tomorrow.'

'What demonstration is that?' queried Clifford.

'They're gonna be protestin' against the Licensing Bill,' explained the man. 'It'll be a big turnout, I reckon. I dunno what the government thinks it's playin' at, threatening to restrict openin' hours? That's interfin' with a workin' man's freedom, that is.'

'You're quite right,' said Clifford dutifully.

187

Confident that any such laws designed to moderate drinking habits for frequenters of public houses would not manage to penetrate the hallowed portals of his gentleman's club, Clifford could not bring himself to feel passionately on this issue. But being partial to any kind of social gathering, he felt irresistibly compelled to join in the fun. Taking his watch from his waistcoat pocket, he observed that it was three o'clock. The shop would be busy at this time on a Saturday afternoon, so he ought to go straight back. But on the other hand, what difference would another half an hour or so make? He simply *had* to take a look at the proceedings in the park.

Delighted with the decision to prolong his outing, he moved with the crowds to the kerb, stepped into the road and began to fight his way across, a slow hazardous process as the traffic roared and rattled around him. Suddenly the atmosphere changed and the movement of the crowd became frenzied. People began to make a dash for the safety of the pavement as warning cries of, 'Get out the way. Quick, quick!' rose above the alarming sound of thudding hooves. Panic welled to near hysteria among the masses and they scattered in all directions, screaming and shouting.

Clifford was paralysed with fear as a black and white bolting horse came into view, galloping towards him, its coach clattering and swaying behind it, the coachman clinging to the reins, pale with fright. Shrieks filled the air; people fell to the ground in their haste to get clear. Finding his legs at last, Clifford stumbled out of the way of the horse and right into the path of a motor-bus coming the other way and veering towards the middle of the road. Much to Clifford's relief, the driver saw him and

188

changed course.

Completely out of control, the horse thundered onwards, rearing and snorting, its eyes mad with terror as the engine of the bus suddenly backfired. Surrounded by confusion, the bewildered bus driver acted on impulse, swerving to avoid the poor demented creature and losing control of his vehicle.

Frozen with terror, Clifford watched the bus hurtle towards him, its front lamps mesmerising him like huge, staring eyes. The choking smell of petrol fumes and sweating horseflesh filled his nostrils until the heavy wheels crushed him and pain racked his body, killing all other sensations. Sharp, unbearable agony that seemed to scramble his mind. Then, at last, oblivion.

*   *   *

Amy was putting the children to bed when she learned that she was a widow. Two kindly policemen came to the house and wrecked her life, having traced her through some papers in Clifford's wallet. Numb with shock, and far too desolate for tears, she settled the children in their beds, left Violet in charge and set off for Orchard Avenue.

*   *   *

'You should have telephoned to let us know you were coming,' said Florence Jackson sharply, as she swept into the drawing room where Amy was waiting, having been shown there by Rosie the maid. 'That's the whole idea of having the instrument put in. You really must get accustomed to using it.'

'Florence, I...'

'Ralph and I have guests for dinner this evening,' she interrupted, completely insensitive to the fact that all was not well with her daughter-in-law, 'and I really don't have time to receive other visitors.'

'I, er ... I have something to tell you,' Amy said, ashen-faced and weak-kneed. All her energy had drained away, leaving her so very tired. 'And I think Ralph should be here with you.'

'If it's about the arrangements for Clifford's birthday tomorrow,' she snapped, 'we are quite familiar with what is happening. Ralph will bring the car round to him when we come for lunch and...'

'Please stop, Florence,' begged Amy, feeling nauseous and faint with delayed reaction, perspiration suffusing her skin.

'I won't be told what to do in my own house!'

'Get Ralph, please,' she entreated, sinking weakly into an armchair.

'He's busy getting dressed for dinner,' said Florence impatiently, continuing to ignore Amy's obvious distress. 'Just get on and say what you came to say.'

'But, Florence, I really think Ralph...'

'Get on with it, do.'

'Very well.' She took a deep breath. 'I'm sorry to have to tell you that Clifford was run over and killed by a motor-bus this afternoon.'

Florence didn't move but stared at Amy accusingly, crimson blotches staining her throat and face. 'Don't you dare come round here trying to hurt us with such a wicked tale,' she said at last. 'If anything had happened to our son, his father and I would have been the first to know about it.'

Amy shook her head sadly. 'No, Florence, not now that I am his next-of-kin.'

'It's a vicious lie,' Florence spat, her voice trembling as the awful truth began to penetrate.

'I wish it was,' sighed Amy wearily, 'I really do. But it's true, I'm afraid. The police came to the house to tell me about half an hour ago.'

'No, no, no!' screamed Florence. 'I don't believe you. Get out of my house.'

As unkind as Florence had been to Amy, the young woman was filled with compassion for her, for being a snob didn't make her invulnerable to grief. 'Florence, my dear,' she said kindly, going to the older woman and slipping a sympathetic arm around her, 'I don't know how to bear it either. Let me try to help you, please. We need each other now.'

A forceful shove sent Amy staggering across the room. 'I don't want you anywhere near me,' Florence yelled, on the verge of hysteria, her voice resounding through the house. 'Nothing has been right in our family since you forced your way into it.'

'But, Florence...'

'Whatever's going on?' asked Ralph, appearing at the door with his collar unfastened, having heard the commotion from upstairs.

Florence fled into his arms and gave him a tearful account of the facts. Seeing how genuinely distraught she was, Amy tried not to be hurt by her rejection at this traumatic time. But being badly in need of comfort herself, it was hard to understand why the enormity of this tragedy didn't dispel prejudice and bring them together.

'Shall I ask the maid to bring up some tea?' she suggested hopefully, as a pale, trembling Ralph tried to comfort his wife.

'The best thing you can do is to leave our house,' he said coldly. 'We wish to be alone with our grief.'

Their grief. 'But it's *our* grief, mine and yours,' she cried emotionally. 'Don't shut me out. We all loved Clifford. Surely this is a time to forget all past differences and help each other?'

Sobbing loudly while her husband administered brandy, Florence spluttered, 'Get out, get out!'

'Yes, please go,' echoed Ralph, ashen-faced and bewildered.

'Very well,' she said icily, 'I'll go home to my children, *Clifford's* children. *Your* grandchildren. Your own flesh and blood.'

Neither of them reacted. They didn't even look up as she left, but clung to each other, Florence weeping, Ralph on the verge of tears.

During the next twenty-four hours, after she had identified the body and the fact that Clifford was never coming home again registered with Amy, she longed to see one person above all others. But since her mother's comforting presence was no longer a luxury available to her, it was Violet's shoulder that took the brunt of her grief.

* * *

With two small children to look after, Amy's personal feelings had to be kept under control, for both boys were too young to understand anything much beyond their own needs. Victor, who was two, was told that his daddy had gone to another place, but Dickie was still too much of a baby even to notice that his father was not around. At least the fact that Clifford had never been an indulgent parent meant that neither of his sons really missed him.

As it seemed to mean so much to Clifford's parents, Amy allowed them to take care of the

192

funeral which was a large, showy affair crammed with the Jacksons' friends. Florence, as the stricken mother, completely overshadowed Clifford's widow and Amy was made to feel incongruous and unwelcome by everyone except Ned and Molly Cox, who were kind and supportive to her. Gwen was not cold towards Amy exactly, but preoccupied. Amy could see that the poor woman had enough problems of her own with grieving parents and the noticeable absence of her husband to contend with.

Feeling completely excluded from the Jackson family, it would have been all too easy for Amy to begin to feel as though she had never been a part of Clifford's life at all. Without his presence to warrant any show of manners from them, his parents made no secret of their dislike of her. For herself she could take it, but what hurt so much was the fact that Florence and Ralph behaved as though Victor and Dickie didn't exist.

But with the funeral behind her, such grievances were overshadowed by practicalities. Her income had gone along with Clifford and she had two growing boys to raise alone. The Jacksons had made it obvious that they felt no responsibility for her or the welfare of their grandchildren whatsoever. Which left her in rather a mess.

'At least the house is legally mine,' she confided to Violet a few weeks after the funeral, 'so the children and I will have a roof over our heads.'

'Yer won't be able to afford to keep me on, that's for sure,' said her friend.

'I won't be able to afford not to,' said Amy. 'I'll need you to look after the boys while I go out to work to feed them.'

'That's a bit drastic, ain't it?' said Violet. 'Workin'

193

in a shop or factory'll come hard after bein' married to the boss's son.'

'I don't care about that,' said Amy. 'Anyway, what else can I do? I could sell the house and rent a place, I suppose. But I want the children to grow up in the secure environment that I never had. It's what Clifford would want too.'

'Didn't 'e make any provision for yer at all?' asked Violet.

Amy shook her head. 'No, I doubt if he'd got round to thinking of anything like that. Death seems a long way off when you're only twenty-five.' She paused thoughtfully. 'The irony of it is, had he died just a few hours later, the share of the business he was due to inherit would have come to me automatically, as his widow.' She shrugged. 'But he died having no legal share in the business at all.'

'Ain't there nothing you can do about that?' asked Violet. 'Because it don't seem right, you bein' poverty-stricken because of a technicality while the Jacksons are rollin' in money. The boys are Jacksons, after all. Clifford would 'ave wanted the best for 'em. He'll be turnin' in 'is grave at the way 'is folks are treatin' yer.'

'You're quite right, Vi,' said Amy, her mind clearing suddenly. The shock of Clifford's death had left her feeling muddle-headed. Now, the answer to her impecuniosity seemed obvious.

*　　　*　　　*

'I don't think we should stay enemies,' said Amy to Florence and Ralph Jackson the following evening as she confronted them in their drawing room. The nights were shortening and the heavy maroon

194

curtains were closed across the windows, the gaslight flickering over the cumbersome furnishings. Ralph and Florence were seated either side of a roaring fire by the tiger skin rug. 'After all, we are related.'

'No, we are not,' denied Florence. 'Not any more, thank goodness.'

'But my sons are your grandsons, they have your blood in their veins,' Amy pointed out. 'Surely you care what happens to them?'

'Your brats are no concern of ours,' said Florence, her face ashen against her dark mourning clothes, her hair drawn back in a bun. 'They are simply the manifestation of Clifford's weakness in allowing you to manipulate him. Something we do not wish to be reminded of. Isn't that so, Ralph?'

Her husband got up and stood beside his wife's chair supportively, taking the hand she reached out to him. 'Yes, that's quite right, my dear,' he said, after only a brief hesitation. He felt so much less vulnerable to that damned Atkins family now that his affair with Clara was over. It was annoying to find that he still missed her so dreadfully, though. Only the fear of becoming involved with the child stopped him from rushing over to Bethnal Green this very minute. At this time of great personal sadness he needed Clara more than ever. He yearned for her warmth, her cheerfulness, her uninhibited loving, to ease his suffering and give him some respite from the strain of helping Florence to cope. It was as though the bright side of his life had gone forever, leaving only pain and darkness.

Amy shook her head in disbelief. 'How anyone can not care about their own grandchildren is quite beyond me,' she said. 'Thank goodness Clifford didn't inherit your cruel streak.'

'How dare you...' interrupted Florence.

'Don't you dare...' said Ralph.

'Clifford was not a man of strong character, as you have said,' she resumed, ignoring their attempts to interrupt her, 'but at least he was neither cold-hearted nor cruel. And I shall do everything I can to make sure his sons are raised with the proper priorities in life. With the right guidance, hopefully they will not grow up with the appalling attitudes of their grandparents.'

'Leave this house at once,' ordered Ralph.

'No, not just yet,' said Amy, looking elegant in a plain black dress and wide-brimmed hat. She was perched on the edge of an armchair near the piano, her confidence boosted by her disgust and fury at their treatment of her. 'Not until I've finished my business here.'

'You've finished as far as we're concerned,' said Florence. 'Show her out please, Ralph.'

'*No*, I am *not* leaving.' The command in her tone was so powerful, it surprised even Amy herself. 'I insist that you hear me out.'

'Oh, very well, but don't be long,' said Florence irritably.

'Had Clifford lived a few hours longer, until his birthday, a percentage of shares in the business would have been his, and would have come to me as his widow,' she said. 'Is that correct?'

Ralph's small eyes narrowed suspiciously. 'I suppose so, yes. Why?'

'I think the share Clifford would have had is morally mine and should come to me anyway,' she stated in an even tone.

A shocked silence filled the room.

'Why, you scheming bitch!' spat Florence at last.

196

'You would try to profit from our son's death?' She observed Amy with venom before resorting to calumny. 'If he hadn't had the accident, how long would it have been before you pushed him under a bus just to get your hands on our family business?' She rose and lunged towards Amy, intent on physical attack, but was restrained by Ralph who was nevertheless not able to still her tongue. 'My God, I always knew you were a bad lot but I didn't think you'd stoop so low as to capitalise on your own husband's death. A man you claim to have loved.'

The words hurt Amy deeply, but they were no more than she had expected from these unreasonable people. 'I did love Clifford very much,' she said coolly, carried along by the courage of her convictions. For herself, she wouldn't have come within a mile of this hateful couple. But the future of two young boys was at stake. 'And I also love his sons, which is why I am asking for what is rightly mine and will be theirs in the future—their father's share of the business. It is what Clifford would have wanted for us.'

'What you are demanding is scandalous,' said Florence, dabbing her face with a lace-edged handkerchief.

'It's unforgivable of you to make such demands on us at such a time,' said Ralph.

'Unforgivable!' exploded Amy, leaping from her seat and glaring at them, her face flushed with fury. 'You have the audacity to call my behaviour unforgivable when you are prepared to cheat two innocent young boys out of their birthright just because their mother doesn't happen to meet your snobbish requirements. Two children who are part of you.' She paused for breath. 'Well, they may not have

197

your love or support, but they certainly have mine and I shall fight for what's theirs until they are old enough to do so for themselves.'

'You're insane,' muttered Florence, flopping into her armchair in a state of semi-collapse.

'On the contrary,' said Amy, 'my brain has never served me better.'

'You're asking for something that even I don't have,' said Florence

'Only because Ralph is alive and well,' said Amy.

'I wouldn't want his shares if he wasn't,' Florence declared. 'Business is best left to the men. Any decent woman should be at home with her family.'

'Oh, it's easy for you to say that. You want for nothing.' Amy turned to Ralph who was hovering by Florence's chair. 'In any case, the firm can only benefit from my being a part of it. It was me who saved it from ruin not so long ago, remember?'

It didn't suit him to recollect so he just said, 'Nonsense.'

'You know I'm right,' insisted Amy. 'I could do wonders for the company.'

'So now you're claiming that you can help us,' said Florence, 'when all you're doing is begging for a handout.'

'No, I'm not. I'm asking for the regular income that is rightfully mine as Clifford's widow, and which I shall earn,' said Amy. 'Surely you don't want your grandchildren brought up in poverty?'

Neither of them replied.

'Oh, I could go out cleaning or work in a shop or a factory,' she continued, 'but why should I slave long hours for a pittance on which to feed my sons, when part of a jewellery business is mine, and in turn theirs?'

'Your circumstances are not our problem,' said Florence.

'Nothing to do with us at all,' echoed Ralph.

'You *really* believe that?' she said, looking from one to the other in astonishment.

'Yes, of course, we wouldn't say it otherwise,' said Florence.

Amy crossed the room, turning at the door. 'There's nothing more to say then, for the moment, so I'll go,' she said in disgust. 'Don't bother to ring for the maid to see me out. I'm quite capable of leaving the premises unaided.'

And as Ralph reached for the brandy, she walked out.

*　　　*　　　*

'She's a real baggage and no mistake,' said Florence shakily, as the front door closed behind their son's widow.

'Here, drink this, dear, it will calm your nerves,' said Ralph, handing her a glass of brandy.

'I do believe she's made me feel quite ill.'

'I'm not surprised,' he sympathised. 'I've never heard the like.'

'At least Clifford's death means we can rid our family of her for good and all,' said Florence.

'Mmm.'

'Thank goodness we shan't have to suffer her common ways ever again,' she said, sipping the liquid and shuddering at its strength. 'I don't know how Clifford stood it, the poor lamb. When you think of the things she did to him. Humiliating him by refusing to have domestic staff, then forcing him to have a pregnant servant living in the house. It must

199

have been quite mortifying for him.'

'Yes, dear.'

'It will take us a while to get our reputation back to what it was before she came on the scene,' said Florence, 'but people will soon forget once she's no longer associated with the family.'

'Quite so.'

'Ralph...'

'Yes?'

'Are you sure there's no legal way that she can possibly make you give her shares in the business?'

'Positive,' Ralph assured her. 'As the legal transfer to Clifford was not due to take place until his birthday, it is now null and void. Amy Atkins simply doesn't have a case.'

'Amy Atkins,' echoed Florence, listening to the sound of the words with satisfaction. 'That sounds better than Amy Jackson. I wonder if there's any way we can force her to revert to her maiden name.'

'I doubt it.'

Florence finished her drink, becoming calmer but melancholy. 'Poor Clifford. He was too young to die,' she said emotionally.

'He certainly was.'

'Do you think we shall ever stop missing him?'

'In time, I suppose, my dear,' he said, giving a weary sigh.

'Perhaps it will be easier for us with that dreadful wife of his gone from our lives forever,' she said, beginning to cry.

'Maybe, my dear,' he said. But he had a terrible suspicion that Clifford's 'dreadful wife' had not gone from their lives at all.

*　　*　　*

And as Amy walked home through the Broadway she was thinking much the same thing, though she was a little perplexed as to what her next move would be. There was no doubt in her mind that the shares belonged to her, but actually obtaining them was not going to be easy.

People were piling into the Hippodrome for the second house as she passed, and she was overwhelmed by sadness, for she and Clifford had shared so many happy times at music halls together. She stifled her tears. At least the battle with his parents had angered her out of self-pity.

The night was dry and scented with the aromas of the season: woodsmoke, mist, earthy dampness. It was fully dark and the bright lights in the Broadway emphasised her single status for they spoke of carefree socialising and happier times. The road was busy with motor vehicles and carriages, the pavements thronged with people, many of them couples on their way to some place of entertainment.

Some boys were shaking the trees for conkers on Ealing Green as she walked by, their youthful voices carried in the moist air. Reminded of her own childish conker-collecting in Victoria Park, she was imbued with nostalgia and a longing for her own people. She had written to Alfie about Clifford's death and he had visited her with his own and their parents' condolences. But no olive branch had been offered by the latter. Alfie blamed their father's pride.

Part of Amy, the grief-stricken young woman of a sensitive nature, wanted to leave Ealing and the Jacksons behind her forever. But the other part, the mother and hater of injustice, knew she must stay and fight for what she knew was right. When her sons were old enough, they could take or leave their place in the business, as they so wished. She would never force it on them or interfere in their lives as her father had in hers. But somehow, she *must* make sure that they had the choice.

Passing The Queen Victoria public house, she turned down a side road leading to Merrydene Avenue, a quiet street of modest detached houses lined with plane trees, currently gilded with the light from the street lamps. Loneliness consumed her as she walked up the front path and turned the key in the lock.

*   *   *

A few days later, Amy's afternoon was considerably brightened by a visit from Bernie Banks.

'Wotcha, Princess,' he said, as Violet showed him into the parlour where Amy was ensconced on the sofa with Dickie on her lap while Victor played on the floor with a clockwork motor car.

'Bernie,' she said, setting Dickie on the floor and going to her dear friend and hugging him, 'I'm so pleased to see you.'

Being a natural extrovert with a charm that drew a response from every generation, Bernie made an instant hit with the children. Squeals and chuckles abounded as he threw them in the air and piggy-backed them round the room. But as persistent cries for more echoed to the rafters, he spoke with surprising authority. 'That's enough for now, kids. You go and play while I talk to yer mum. There's good boys.'

As ever, Violet appeared at exactly the right moment and whisked them away.

'I can't tell you how good it is to see you, Bernie,'

202

she said, when they were alone, 'I've been feeling very low.'

His grin faded. 'I'm sorry about your 'usband. I 'eard about it from Alfie this morning, and came straight over.' He shook his head, drawing a long breath. 'It's a bad business.'

She ran a weary hand over her brow. 'I still can't believe it. It's all like some awful nightmare.' She paused as a lump gathered in her throat. Seeing one of her own people had made her feel very emotional. 'Thanks for coming over. I really do appreciate it. There's no one quite like old friends at a time like this, is there?'

With that she burst into tears, whereupon Bernie held her in his arms as he had so many times before.

'That's it, love,' he soothed. 'Let it all out. A good cry'll make yer feel better.'

Indeed, she did feel more relaxed afterwards, and more able to do justice to the tea which Violet served with her usual sense of good timing.

'A maid, eh?' remarked Bernie, whose shrewd eye had not been slow to notice the signs of affluence around him. 'You've certainly come a long way from Tucker Street.'

'Violet's more of a friend than a maid,' she explained. 'We sort of run things together.'

'You pay her wages, though.'

'Oh, yes, of course, but not for much longer,' she confided ruefully, biting her lip as the worries flooded back. 'Not unless I can get my affairs sorted out before my savings run out.'

His brows lifted in surprise. 'Blimey! I thought he'd 'ave left yer well provided for,' he said, 'him bein' a toff.'

Because Bernie was a very old friend and she

203

needed a sympathetic ear at that particular moment, she told him about her predicament. 'Do you think I'm entitled to Clifford's share of the business?' she asked.

'Not 'alf,' he said. 'But nothing comes easy to the likes of you and me. You're gonna 'ave to fight the Jacksons for it.'

'I know,' she agreed. 'And I've been trying to work out how. Not easy when you have no power or legal rights.'

He narrowed his eyes thoughtfully. 'Yer might not 'ave any legal rights but yer do have power,' he said.

'Oh? In what way?'

'You told me all about it that day in the park when you'd fallen out with yer dad, remember?'

'Oh, that.'

'Yes, that,' he said firmly. 'You give old man Jackson a reminder of 'is ill-spent past, and he'll be only too eager to give yer what's yours.'

'I couldn't,' she said. 'It wouldn't be fighting fair.'

'Are they bein' fair to you?' he asked hotly. 'You're the mother of their grandchildren and they're prepared to see you and the kids in the gutter. You call that fair?'

'Well, no, but...'

'It ain't as though they can't afford to do right by yer,' he reminded her.

'But even so, I draw the line at blackmail.'

He munched a digestive biscuit, observing her thoughtfully. 'It's an 'ard world out there, Ame,' he said wisely. 'I know, I'm in the thick of it every day of me life. It's dog eat dog. If you want what's right for yer kids, you'll 'ave to fight with everything you've got. And if all you've got is a little bit of naughty in the old man's past, you have to use it.'

204

'No, I don't think so, Bernie.'

'All right, so yer don't wanna do that,' he conceded. 'So, 'ow about me roughin' 'im up to make 'im see things more clearly?'

'No, no,' she said quickly. 'No violence.'

'You're too bloomin' good for yer own good,' he said lightly.

'Perhaps I am, by your standards,' she said. 'But this is something I must sort out in my own way.'

'Just as yer like,' he said. 'But if you change yer mind, or want any 'elp with 'em at all, you can contact me at work. They've got a phone there.'

'Thanks, Bernie.' She ran her eye over his well-tailored light grey suit edged with dark grey braiding, saw the gold watch-chain looped from his waistcoat pocket. 'Still working at the Empire?'

He nodded. 'I'm chief barman now.' He winked meaningfully. 'And you know me, I'm not short of sidelines.'

And some of them to the detriment of the bar takings, she couldn't help thinking, knowing him as she did. 'Things are still going well for you, then?'

'Never better, ducks,' he told her cheerfully. 'Never better.' He consulted his watch. 'I'll have to be orf now. I'll pop over again to see yer when I get time. In the meantime, don't hesitate to get in touch if yer need me. Even if yer just want a shoulder to cry on, give me a ring and I'll be 'ere as soon as I can.'

'Thanks, I'll remember that.' She fell into a thoughtful silence, then came to a sudden decision. 'Can you hang on for a minute while I pop upstairs? There's something I'd like you to have.'

'Yeah, sure, I'll wait.'

She hurried upstairs to her bedroom and returned with the birthday gift Clifford hadn't lived to see.

Having explained the history of the jewellery to Bernie, she said, 'I can't bring myself to sell it.' She paused, controlling a violent rush of emotion. 'And I don't want it to lie in my drawer for years never seeing the light of day till one of the boys is old enough to wear it. So, as my oldest friend, I'd like you to have it.'

Since he made no secret of his fondness for an easy acquisition, he made no attempt at false protests. 'Cor, they're beautiful!' he said, his eyes glistening with admiration of the stylish cuff links and tie-pin. 'I'll look a real gent wearin' those. Ta very much, Ame.'

'You're welcome,' she said, feeling stronger for having taken such a practical step, and going with him to the front door.

'Now don't forget what I said about those in-laws o' yours,' he said, as they stood in the porch. 'Don't let 'em do the dirty on yer, love. Yer don't deserve it.'

'Don't worry, I won't.'

Watching him swagger down the front path, his whole manner radiating confidence, she found herself smiling. He'd certainly cheered her up. In fact she hadn't been so pleased to see anyone in a long time.

CHAPTER ELEVEN

An atmosphere of suspense hung over the proceedings at a directors' meeting in Ralph's office that evening when Harold Cox decided it was time to broach a delicate subject.

'I realise this can't be easy for you, Ralph, old boy,'

206

he said, sniffing and emitting a nervous cough. 'But business must go on regardless of our personal feelings.' He cleared his throat. 'Painful though it is for all of us ... um ... er ...' Another cough. 'I think we ought to decide what we are going to do about a replacement for Clifford.'

A tense silence prevailed while they awaited his reaction. 'I can't argue with that,' Ralph said gruffly, drawing heavily on a cigar. 'So let's get on with it.'

There was a general feeling of relief that this matter had been brought out into the open. Although each of the two shops was separately managed, the business was run as a whole and decisions concerning either branch made collectively by the directors.

'Would it be best to replace him from outside, or promote Rawlings and take on someone new in the lower ranks, which would be cheaper?' Harold coughed again. 'Not that one can measure Clifford's worth in financial terms, of course, but since he has left a gap in the team at your shop ... er ... well, I mean ...'

'Don't fuss, Harold,' Ralph said irritably, 'I take your point.'

'While we're on the subject of the gap Clifford has left, what's happening as regards his widow?' asked Ned, unaware of the conflict already raging on this subject. 'Will she be taking his place as a director?'

Ralph stared at him aghast. 'Of course not. Why on earth should she?'

'Isn't it obvious?'

'Not to me, no.'

Up went Ned's brows. 'I presume Clifford's shares will automatically become hers.'

Shocked by this development, Ralph gaped at Ned. 'Of course not. Clifford died before the transfer had been made,' he announced sharply at last. 'I thought you knew that.'

'Well, yes, I do,' said Ned, frowning darkly. 'But as it was only a few hours before it was due to take place, I naturally assumed that the transfer would go ahead as planned. Morally the shares belong to Amy.' He paused, his gaze holding Ralph's. 'Surely?'

'There's no *surely* about it,' objected Ralph, his cheeks suffused angrily. 'The shares I was going to hand over to Clifford now remain with me.'

'But Amy is entitled to a part of the business,' insisted Ned, growing hot under the collar. Everyone knew about the Jacksons' vendetta against Amy, but this really was taking it too far.

'No, she isn't,' protested Ralph. 'The shares in question belong to me. What I choose to do with them is a personal matter and no concern of this meeting.'

Since Clifford's passing had been so untimely, Ned doubted if he'd made provision for Amy. And now it seemed certain that she was going to be left with nothing of her husband's birthright. 'But Amy has the children to raise alone, so she'll need an income,' he pointed out.

'That,' roared Ralph, 'is none of your business.'

'Ralph's right, Ned,' reproached his father. 'You're speaking out of turn.'

Ned felt almost irrationally upset on Amy's behalf. Whether or not she had used Clifford to better herself, he didn't consider it his place even to speculate. But whatever the truth, she *had* been his wife and as such deserved some consideration from the company.

'I don't think I am,' insisted Ned. 'As a friend and colleague of Clifford's, I consider it my duty to see to

208

it that his widow gets what she is owed from the firm.'

'How many more times must I say it?' snarled Ralph through gritted teeth. 'Clifford's proposed share in Jackson & Cox is a private matter and has nothing to do with the company.'

'That's true, Ned,' admonished Harold. 'Now let's hear no more about it.'

Forced to concede that the issue was personal between Amy and Ralph, he decided to try another tack. 'All right, maybe it isn't my place to comment on a family matter,' he said. 'But personally I think Amy would be an asset to the business. What she's done for us in the past is proof of that.'

'Rubbish,' said Ralph.

'So,' Ned persisted, 'if she's not going to be given a share in the business, then the least we can do is to offer her a job on the management.'

'Out of the question,' said Ralph.

'A woman on the management!' exclaimed Harold disapprovingly. 'Whatever next?'

'My thoughts exactly,' said Ralph with unveiled relief at having gained Harold's support. 'It's a recognised fact that women have no place in business.'

Violence wasn't in Ned's nature, but it was as much as he could do to stop himself from physically removing the complacency from Ralph Jackson's face.

*   *   *

Amy was surprised to receive a visit from Ned Cox that evening.

'Just thought I'd pop in to see how you are as I was in the area,' he said, perching uneasily on the sofa in

209

her parlour.

'How kind,' she said, smiling uncertainly at him. 'Would you like some tea or coffee? I'm afraid I can't run to anything stronger these days.'

'Nothing, thanks,' he said cordially. 'Molly will have a meal ready for me when I get home. I've come straight from a meeting at the Ealing shop.'

He looked uncomfortable, as though he had something to tell her and wasn't sure how to begin.

'Is anything the matter?'

Ned hesitated as he struggled with his conscience. As much as he wanted to, it wouldn't be ethical to take sides with Amy against one of his co-directors. But since her in-laws were obviously not going to help her, he felt compelled to offer some sort of support. She was, after all, the widow of one of his oldest friends. But she was a proud woman, he would have to tread carefully.

'Look ... er ... I've been thinking that it can't be easy for you, bringing up two children on your own,' he said at last.

'No, it isn't, but I'll manage.'

'I want you to know that you can call on Molly and me if you need help at any time.' He paused, then added meaningfully, 'Help of any sort, that is.'

She gave a half smile at his refined approach. 'Money, you mean,' she said candidly.

'I mean help of any sort,' he explained earnestly. 'But, yes, I'm sure we can help with that if necessary.'

Although she had never liked him, she found herself warming to him, realising that she had a friend in this sober, rather distant man. 'Thanks for offering, Ned,' she said. 'And I'll bear it in mind, but I'm all right at the moment, really.'

'Well, you know where we are if you need us,' he

said. 'Please don't hesitate...'

'I do appreciate it,' she said, cheered by this sincere offer even if she was too proud to accept it. 'And thank Molly too.'

He hadn't actually told Molly yet of this visit to Amy, but he and his wife were of one mind when it came to this sort of thing. She would have been angry if he hadn't offered their assistance. 'I will,' he said, and rose to leave.

*　　　*　　　*

'I do hope this visit isn't about the shares Clifford would have inherited,' said Ralph the next morning as Amy faced him across his desk. '*Would have* being the operative words.'

'It is, I'm afraid,' said Amy, who had been awake most of the night pondering on Bernie's advice.

'In that case, I must ask you to leave,' he informed her briskly, rising and striding towards the office door. He couldn't get rid of her quick enough. Just the fact that she was an Atkins made him nervous, even though his potentially incriminating link with them had ended. 'Had I known that was your purpose, I would not have agreed to see you. But I didn't think even *you* would be thick-skinned enough to pursue the matter, since both my wife and I have made the position clear.'

Feeling nauseous with tension, Amy clenched her hands together on her lap. She hated herself for what she was about to do, but the Jacksons had left her no alternative. 'I'm not leaving,' she said firmly, though her mouth was dry and her knees trembling. 'And I suggest that you come and sit down over here, because I doubt if you'll want to risk anyone outside

211

this office overhearing what I have to say.'

Eyes narrowed suspiciously, he returned to his seat. 'Well?'

Sensing his fear, Amy realised that he knew what she was going to say.

'Unless you agree to give me what is rightfully mine,' she said, 'I shall tell Florence that you are the father of my cousin Connie.'

His face was colourless against his dark mourning dress, and his chest heaved beneath his black waistcoat. 'I should have known, being an Atkins, you'd resort to gutter tactics,' he said, his deepset eyes almost disappearing with the force of his contempt.

'You've left me no choice.'

'Even your aunt didn't keep her word,' he said in a despairing voice. 'She promised not to name me as the father. I've kept my part of the bargain. I've sent her money regularly every month.'

'Aunt Clara hasn't broken her word to you. Connie is being told she's the daughter of a merchant seaman,' Amy explained. 'Only close family know the truth and it was obvious to all of us, since Clara didn't see other men.'

'You Atkins are riff-raff, every man jack of you,' he said, 'I wish to God I'd never set eyes on any of you.'

'As you sow, so shall you reap,' Amy said.

'And God knows I've paid dear for my affair with your aunt,' he said.

'And so has she. You broke her heart, even though she'd rather die than admit it.'

'Blackmailers, the lot of you,' he muttered, as though she hadn't spoken. 'I ought to call the police.'

'Blackmailers demand money to which they are

212

not entitled,' said Amy. 'I am only asking for what I truly believe to be morally mine. But call the police if you wish. I'm sure Florence would love to know why her husband is involved with them.'

'Don't you threaten me,' he said, reaching for the telephone.

She waited, watching him as he slowly replaced the receiver. 'So do we have a deal?' she asked.

'I'm making no deals with the likes of you,' he told her. 'You can tell Florence whatever you damned well like. It will be your word against mine, and you know as well as I do who she'll believe. And it's no use your trying to drag Clara into it to back up your story, because she would never do anything to harm my marriage.'

'You're right, she wouldn't,' Amy admitted, 'she's far too good for you. I've been forced down to your level by your unfair treatment.'

'Forced down to my level indeed,' he sneered. 'That's rich.'

'As for it being my word against yours,' said Amy, ignoring the insult in order to move things forward, 'you have never seen your daughter so you wouldn't know how much of a Jackson she is.'

For a fleeting moment she saw a hint of pleasure in his eyes. 'I don't believe you,' he said.

'That's up to you,' she said. 'She has her mother's eyes, it's true, but a definite look of Clifford about her in other features. And her hair is sandy-coloured, just like yours where it hasn't turned grey. If Florence needs convincing, I've only to bring Connie to see her. Aunt Clara would know nothing about it. I'd tell her I was having Connie over to be with her cousins.'

'You wouldn't!'

He was right, of course. She wouldn't dream of

213

dragging her cousin into such a shabby plan, but it didn't suit her to admit it. 'Try me,' she said determinedly.

'So if I want to protect my wife from pain, I have no option but to give in to you?'

As fraught as she was, Amy had to smile at that. 'Don't make me laugh,' she said. 'The only person you want to protect is yourself. You don't want Florence to know because it will make things difficult for you at home, not because you care about *her* feelings.'

'How dare you!'

'It's true,' she said. 'You're a very greedy man, Ralph. You had everything, but still you wanted more. You wanted my aunt because she did something Florence is incapable of doing—really loving you, for all your faults. She doesn't speak ill of you, even now.' She dabbed her perspiring brow with a handkerchief. 'Personally, if it wasn't for my sons, I wouldn't come within a mile of you, but you're not going to get off scot free. Oh, no.' She met his gaze. 'I want nothing for nothing, you know. I'll earn every penny.'

'I'm sure.'

'So what is your answer?'

'*No*.'

She rose in a dignified manner, her outward appearance betraying none of the uncertainty she was feeling inside. For this whole exercise was just a bluff and she had no idea what her next move would be if it failed. 'Very well. I shall call on Florence personally this very day.' She walked to the door knowing that if he didn't take the bait she was lost. She reached for the door handle and began to turn it.

'Amy.'

214

'Yes.' She waited without moving.

'You'd better come back and sit down.'

She turned, but there was no smile of victory on her face. She didn't like what she had been forced to do any more than he did.

*   *   *

The altercation Ralph had had with Ned at yesterday's meeting over Amy's right to the shares was inspirational to him later that day when he was faced with the task of telling Florence that Amy's demands were to be met.

'So when Ned raised the subject of Amy, it made me realise just how bad it looked, us cutting her off without a penny,' he lied smoothly. 'With us being the grandparents to her children. This way she'll receive a regular income from the business and we need have nothing to do with her or her children personally.'

'But you'll have to see her,' she said.

'Only now and again when she attends directors' meetings. I doubt it'll be often, probably only when her vote is needed on some major issue,' he said. 'She's asked for a meeting to be arranged to have her position formally announced, but we won't see much of her after that.'

'Mmm, I suppose you're right,' she said. 'But I don't like it. I want her out of our lives altogether.'

'So do I,' he agreed. 'But if she stays on in Ealing and makes it generally known that she was treated badly by us, it won't do our reputation any good.'

'Yes, I can see that, but even so . . .'

'Believe me, Florence,' he said, desperate to win her over, 'this is the most sensible way of dealing with

215

the matter. If Ned Cox is spending time thinking about it, so are other people. The wretched woman has caused us enough scandal already, we don't want more.'

'No, but...'

'It will be purely a business arrangement,' he assured her. 'You'll have no need to see her or the children at all.'

'Put like that, I suppose it's the best thing to do in the circumstances then, dear,' she said, too engrossed in her own feelings to notice her husband's sigh of relief.

*   *   *

The meeting Amy had requested was arranged for the following Tuesday evening. Ralph opened proceedings formally and introduced Amy in her new capacity as part of the firm, after which congratulations from the Coxes were offered.

'Welcome aboard,' said Ned, puzzled but pleased by Ralph's sudden volte-face. 'I'm sure you'll be a valuable asset to us.'

'Yes, I'm sure you will,' said Harold courteously, but with less conviction.

Ralph didn't like the sound of this at all. They both obviously needed educating as to Amy's function within the firm. 'I think you have misunderstood Amy's position,' he said, as though addressing a room of five year olds. 'She isn't actually going to take an active part in the business.' He threw Amy a withering look. 'Are you, my dear?'

'Of course I am,' said Amy, treating all three to one of her most winning smiles. 'Surely you didn't think I was going to sit back and take an income without

216

doing anything to earn it?'

'I would have been very surprised if you had,' said Ned. He didn't know how she had brought this off, but he certainly admired her spirit.

'You mean you'll be attending all our directors' meetings?' muttered Harold in bewilderment, for a female at these gatherings was quite unprecedented in this company.

'Yes, among other things,' said Amy brightly. 'I intend to make a real contribution to the company.'

'But what about your children?' Ralph asked miserably. 'Your place is with them at home.'

'My maid will look after them while I'm out working,' she said briskly. 'She's more than happy to stand in for me, and both the boys love her.'

'That's terrible,' objected Ralph. 'What kind of mother are you?'

She met his accusing stare with a challenging look. 'The kind that cares about her children,' she informed him crisply. 'Which is why I am going out to work. The share of the profits I would receive as a non-executive director won't be enough to support them, which is why I need a salary too.'

'Oh, really!' exclaimed Ralph with a cynical laugh. 'Why don't you just demand the job of managing director and have done with it?'

Ignoring his sarcasm, she looked at all three men. 'I'd like to propose that I replace Clifford, in an indirect way.'

'Good heavens!' exclaimed Harold.

'Now I've heard everything,' sneered Ralph.

'Let's at least hear what she has to say,' suggested Ned, frowning at the two other men.

'But Clifford was the overall manager of the Ealing branch,' Ralph said, ignoring Ned and looking at

217

Amy. 'Surely you're not suggesting that you have the experience to cope with such a position?'

'Of course not, not at the moment anyway,' she replied. 'I suggest that Mr Rawlings takes over as official manager. He's been doing the job for years anyway. The title was just window dressing for Clifford as the son of the family.'

'Really...'

'Job titles don't bother me,' she continued, ignoring Ralph's heated interruption, 'but obviously junior status would embarrass us all, including the staff, my having once been a member of the family. With Mr Rawlings being made official manager, he can spend more time on his paperwork while I make up the deficit at the counter as a senior assistant. I get on well with the customers, probably because I enjoy serving them. Obviously I shan't be able to be at the shop for such long hours as Clifford because I shall want to spend part of the day with the children.'

Thank God for small mercies, thought Ralph, but said, 'Which means the idea is not viable, because the position is a full-time one.'

'Clifford never worked a full day in his life,' she told her astonished colleagues, 'even though he was at the shop all day.'

'That's a terrible thing to say,' said Ralph.

'I'm only stating facts,' said Amy. 'I worked with him for five years, remember? I saw what went on.'

'Were you never taught that it is evil to speak ill of the dead?' asked Ralph with predictable indignation.

'Yes I was, and I'm not speaking ill of him,' she denied. 'Clifford would be the first to admit that he wasn't dedicated to his job. I'm not saying he was lazy, or bad, or anything. Just that he was preoccupied with the social side of life and spent

218

more time chatting to customers and staff than actually working.'

'She's talking nonsense,' blustered Ralph, looking sheepishly towards his colleagues.

Disregarding his comment, Amy continued, 'I'll get more work done in half a day than he did in a full day with overtime. Naturally, I shall expect a lower salary than him until the children are older and I can put in more time. So that will save the firm some money.'

Ralph stared at her incredulously. Harold frowned. Ned watched her performance with interest and admiration. 'That seems fair enough,' he said.

'It's ridiculous,' opined Ralph.

'Why exactly?' queried Ned sharply, 'It seems like the perfect solution to the problem of Clifford's replacement to me.'

'He does have a point you know, Ralph,' agreed Harold, stroking his chin thoughtfully.

'A woman's place is in the home,' Ralph blustered, waving his arms wildly as control of the meeting slipped from his grasp. 'That's something that will never change, and those who are foolish enough to try only bring trouble on themselves. The antics of the Pankhursts and their cronies are proof of that. Where are they now for all their fine talk? In prison, some of them, that's where.'

'Amy is proposing to do a job of work, Ralph,' Ned pointed out calmly. 'Not chain herself to the railings in Downing Street.'

Ralph could feel his influence draining away, leaving him vulnerable and afraid. It was bad enough that an Atkins could vote on company policy. Having one actually *involved* in the business on a day-to-day basis would be hellish. Every second she was around he would be on edge, wondering what she was plotting to do next with the information she had about him. He gave it one last shot. 'How can we rely on her? If one of the children is sick she'll not come in, and we'll be short staffed.'

This was something Amy and Violet had discussed at length. 'Violet is quite capable of dealing with any minor ailments in my absence,' she explained. 'But, obviously, if there's anything serious, I won't come in to work. The children come first, there's no point my denying it.'

'There you are,' said Ralph, facing Ned and Harold with this morsel of hope. 'Children are always getting ill with one thing or another. She'll be leaving us in the lurch every other week.'

'I think we should give her a chance,' said Ned.

Harold glanced at his longstanding partner rather shamefacedly. 'It does seem to be the cheapest and most sensible way of filling Clifford's position.'

Ralph knew he must seem to accept defeat like a gentleman or lose face with the Coxes. 'Since I am outnumbered,' he said briskly, 'the matter is settled. Now is there any other business?'

Outside the shop, after the meeting, Amy took Ned to one side before they went their separate ways. A fine, penetrating rain was falling and they sheltered in the shop doorway while Ralph and Harold were still inside. 'Thank you for standing up for me in there,' she said.

'No need to thank me. I think you'll be an asset to the business,' he said brusquely. 'That's why I did it.'

'Yes, of course.' She was surprised at his abrupt attitude. 'I appreciate your confidence in me, though.'

There was an awkward silence. It was almost as

though his friendliness of the other day hadn't happened. 'As co-directors, I doubt if we'll always be in agreement on matters of company policy.'

'Of course not,' agreed Amy, realising that she was being given some sort of a warning. 'But your support was most welcome today.' She gave him an uncertain smile, before opening her umbrella and preparing to brave the elements. 'Anyway, I must go. Violet and the children will be waiting. Goodnight, Ned. Give my love to Molly.'

'Will do. Good night, Amy.'

The wet pavements in the Broadway gleamed like oil as Amy walked home, the lights hazed with mist, carriages and motor-buses spraying out muddy water as they splashed through puddles. She was too preoccupied to pay much attention to the weather though, smarting from Ned's sudden return to his old aloofness. She admonished herself, knowing she must toughen up now that she was entering the world of business, and not be affected by the changing moods of a colleague. But she still felt oddly depressed as she made her way home in the rain.

* * *

Ned stood in the rain with his father waiting for a tram back to Shepherds Bush, since they had not yet succumbed to the convenience of the motor car, wondering if it had been necessary to be quite so sharp with Amy just now. In retrospect, he thought he must have been trying to establish a business-like relationship with her since she was now a colleague. It was important she was made aware of the harsh reality of commerce. That one must not allow one's business decisions to be affected by personal feelings.

221

And just because she was Clifford's widow and a friend of his wife, didn't mean he wouldn't battle with her on matters relating to the company, if necessary.

Yet for all this, he felt unaccountably miserable as he boarded the tram.

*   *   *

By the summer of the following year, Amy was firmly established in her role at the shop. Her previous experience in the trade served her well at the counter. But responsibility at director level was something that took some getting used to, especially when it involved making her own decisions during a crisis without being influenced, against her better judgement, by those more experienced than herself. Whether or not to guard their stock from smash-and-grab robbers, who were currently wreaking havoc on jewellers' shop windows in the West London area, was one such example.

'If we decide to take steps to protect ourselves, we can either put strong screens in front of the stock in the windows after trading hours,' said Ralph, who was chairing the meeting, 'or remove the goods from the window at night. Either of those two options is advised by the police.'

'That's all very well from their point of view because it will prevent the raids and save them work,' argued Ned. 'But our windows are our best advertisement and we pay high rates and taxes for a High Street position which will use this to its full advantage.'

'Too true,' said Harold.

'And after all,' continued Ned, 'our window displays bring in business, whether we are open or not. People enjoy window shopping when they are out of an evening.'

'I agree,' said Ralph.

'Me too,' said Harold. 'We contribute to the maintenance of the police force, so we've a right to expect protection for our shop fronts.'

'Our insurance rates are bound to be increased unless the police arrest these criminals,' said Ralph gloomily.

'Not if we take sensible precautions,' suggested Amy. 'Surely prevention is better than cure, in this instance? The police are obviously doing their best to catch the thieves. But until they do, it makes sense for us to do what we can to protect ourselves.'

'And lose our best advertisement,' said Ned disapprovingly.

'Just temporarily,' she suggested. 'I read in the local paper that the police know the robberies are the work of an organised gang who work in pairs. They'll catch them eventually and we can revert to normal.'

'Normal!' barked Ralph. 'What's normal as far as crime is concerned in the jewellery trade? We're magnets to thieves by the very nature of the goods we sell.'

'Yes, but just now it's exceptionally risky,' Amy pointed out. 'And a lot of the other jewellers are taking precautions by protecting their windows.'

'And that's the only bit of good to come out of the robberies,' said Ralph. 'Our displays will have more of an impact with the competition reduced. We'd be mad to lose the chance of picking up the extra business this could produce.'

'Is it worth paying higher insurance premiums and risking the misery of a burglary just for the sake of a few extra sales?' asked Amy.

223

'It could be,' said Ralph.

'I don't think so,' said Amy.

'Why should we be forced into losing our best advertisement by a bunch of crooks?' said Ned.

The matter was put to the vote. It was obvious that Amy was going to be outvoted, and her lack of experience could easily have led her to follow the opinion of the rest. But convinced that she was right, she stood her ground.

'I told you that we wouldn't always agree,' remarked Ned, as they gathered their papers together at the end of the meeting.

'Let's hope you don't regret your decision,' she said. 'But, frankly, I think you're asking for trouble.'

* * *

She said as much to Bernie, who was given the full story when he called to see her one afternoon later that week. 'It seems most irresponsible to me. What do you think?' she asked, for she found it useful to have an objective view of her business worries from someone outside the firm.

'It doesn't seem all that clever, I must admit,' he agreed. 'But I don't suppose they leave the best stuff in the window overnight, do they? Probably just rolled gold and imitation stones.'

'Oh, no, Ralph wouldn't put rolled gold on show,' she said. 'We're far too classy for that. Bond Street standards, no less.'

He whistled, shaking his head sagely. 'Phew, they are taking a chance then.'

'I know.'

'Still, you've done yer best, love, yer can't do more,' he said. 'I should forget all about it now if I

224

were you.'

'You're probably right.'

She changed the subject by asking him if he'd seen any of her folks recently.

'I saw Alfie the other day,' he said. 'He's doin' all right for 'imself in the fight game.'

'So I gather from Aunt Clara,' she said. 'I had a letter from her. I don't get to see her and the baby nearly often enough now that I'm working. I never seem to get time to do anything much outside of work and home.'

'Well ... you know what they say about all work and no play,' he reproached lightly. 'You need a night out. What do yer say we go to the Hippodrome or the Cinematograph on my next night off?'

'I'd like that, but it would look bad,' she said, frowning. 'Clifford's not been dead a year yet.'

'You don't care what people say, surely?'

'Not for myself, no, but I don't want the boys to be subject to gossip.'

'But you and me are mates,' he said. 'There'd be nothin' like *that*.'

'We both know that,' she said. 'But you can bet other people will read more into it.'

'Why don't you and Vi go to the pictures one night then, and I'll look after the kids?' he suggested cheerfully.

'That's an idea,' she said. 'I might take you up on it.'

Bernie's friendship had been more valuable to her than ever since Clifford's death. He visited her regularly, teased the boys, tormented Violet, and generally brought a breath of fresh air into the house. The children enjoyed his company enormously because he did something their father never had—he

225

played with them.

'I 'ope yer do, 'cos I think it'll do yer good,' he said. 'Just give me a few days' notice and me and the kids'll have a boys' night in.'

'You're a real tonic, Bernie,' she laughed, the pressures of business eased by his lighthearted company.

* * *

The following Sunday, around midday, Bernie strolled along Club Row in London's East End towards The Pink Parrot. Outside the pub there was a crowd of men selling caged birds and animals. A dubious assortment of livestock, ranging from canaries and kittens to hens and hamsters, was on sale here. Pushing his way through the gathering he entered the bar, dark and dismal after the sunshine outside and packed with men as always at this time on a Sunday. The walls were dismally patterned in dark red and cream, the wooden tables stained and scratched on the sawdust floor, and placed around the room were notices prohibiting the sale of wild birds, for this area was at the centre of the bird fancying business and rare birds often changed hands illegally in the bar.

Observing that the reason for his being here was waiting for him at a corner table, he made his way over. 'Wotcha, Cruncher. What yer having, mate?' he asked.

The man, who was made up of sixteen stone of solid muscle and had a jaw like a housebrick, said he wouldn't say no to a drop o' gin. He was employed as a minder to a local small-time crook and was well connected in the underworld around here.

Having attended to the drinks, Bernie joined him at the table whereupon Cruncher opened proceedings without further ado. 'I understand you've somethin' that might interest my guvnor?'

Bernie nodded. 'Have you 'eard about the smash and grab raids over in West London?'

'Yeah, course I 'ave.' He took a swig of his gin. 'They ain't down to us though.'

'I guessed that. They're a bunch of amateurs compared to you lot,' lied Bernie to gain favour with the man in the interest of business. 'But if your guvnor is interested in a one-off job, I know of a shop that's just asking to be done. Unprotected windows full o' top class stuff.' He swallowed his whisky. 'No rubbish. No rolled gold or paste stones. Not too risky for yer either, cos the cops'll put it down to this other mob, as long as yer use their style—a quick haul and away on foot, less noticeable than having get away transport waiting.'

'Where?' asked Cruncher.

Bernie put his glass down on the table and grinned meaningfully. 'Come on, mate, yer don't think I'd be daft enough to tell yer that at this stage, do yer? You find out from your guvnor what the information is worth and we'll talk some more.'

Cruncher nodded.

'I'll meet yer in here, same time tomorrow,' said Bernie.

'Righto, mate.'

Bernie finished his drink and left, feeling pleased with himself. The tip should be worth a few quid. And it wasn't as though Amy personally would lose by it. He wouldn't have entered into the deal if there was any chance of that because she meant a lot to him. She always had. But her firm was insured, she'd said so. And if those colleagues of hers were daft enough to put temptation in people's way, they deserved to be robbed.

His idea of honesty was somewhat distorted, having encountered so little of it in his life. Satisfied that Amy would not actually come to harm as a result of his business dealings, it didn't occur to him that in using information he had gained as her trusted friend, he had betrayed her. His mind didn't work like that. He deemed it proper to profit from any chance opportunity. It was the only way forward for someone like him who had dragged himself out of the gutter. In fact, he was quite proud of the way he had progressed from the straightforward thieving that had been his living as a boy. Nowadays he liked to think of himself as a businessman, a trader, dealing in anything of a lucrative nature whether it be goods or information. He enjoyed the thrill of a deal, the heart-stopping uncertainty, the revitalising sense of power when it succeeded.

Not a bad morning's work, he thought, as he hopped on to a homeward bound tram.

*   *   *

The following week Amy decided to take advantage of Bernie's baby-sitting offer, mainly because Violet was keen to see the film they were showing at the Cinematograph and she felt her friend deserved a well-earned break from the house.

'You go and enjoy yourselves, girls,' said Bernie. 'The kids'll be fine with me.'

It was, indeed, very relaxing sitting in the dark watching a romantic drama, their pleasure enhanced by a pianist setting the mood of the scenes with dramatic vigour. They were so engrossed in the story, they barely noticed the spots and flickers on the screen as the heroine survived one hair-raising incident after another before finally sinking into the arms of her hero to a rousing crescendo from the piano.

'Lovely, wannit?' said Violet, looking moist-eyed as they made their way past the commissionaire into the street. 'Takes yer right out of yerself.'

'It certainly does,' agreed Amy.

It was a warm August night with clear skies and a light breeze, the shop windows shining invitingly all along the Broadway.

'Shall we do a spot of window shopping before we go 'ome?' suggested Violet. 'I need a new 'at and I'd like to see what's around.'

'Good idea,' said Amy. 'The boys will be all right with Bernie.'

'They'll be 'aving a whale of a time, I bet,' said Violet. 'He's a real caution, is Bernie.'

'Yes, he's a good friend to us.'

'It does the kids good to 'ave a man about the place now and again.'

'Mmm, I'm sure it does.'

'Now where would they 'ave some nice 'ats, I wonder?' said Violet.

'They've some lovely ones in a shop near ours,' said Amy.

'Be a nice price ticket on 'em an' all,' said Violet. 'The shops in Danby Walk ain't for the likes o' me.'

'We may as well take a look, though,' said Amy. 'Just to give you an idea of styles.'

They strolled through the Broadway, glancing idly in the windows and chatting companionably. The high-class shops in Danby Walk looked smart and

229

elegant, the leaves on the trees bleached to a pale green by the street lights. There were fewer people about on this exclusive promenade than in the centre of the Broadway, most of the Cinematograph crowd having hopped on to trams, headed for the station, or disappeared into sidestreets. And the punters had yet to emerge from the pubs and the Hippodrome.

Approaching the hat shop near Jackson & Cox, Amy noticed two men standing under a tree on the other side of the road looking across to Danby Walk. They seemed to be taking a particular interest in the jeweller's shop, though they quickly averted their eyes and stared down the street as though looking for a tram when they perceived her observation of them. She had the distinct impression that they were waiting for her and Violet to move on.

Telling herself she was letting her imagination run wild, she said nothing to her friend and dutifully studied the milliner's window, forcing an interest despite her palpitating heart. Eventually having decided that there was nothing to suit Violet, the two women began to walk back towards the Broadway.

But Amy was still ill-at-ease. Giving the men time to make a move, she turned around. They had crossed the road and were standing outside Jackson & Cox. Breathless with horror, she watched one of them hurl a brick through the shop window.

CHAPTER TWELVE

Events moved swiftly after that. In the time it took for Amy to gather her wits sufficiently to move, the thieves had made a grab for the window and disappeared into an alley that was used as a shortcut to the station. 'You chase after them, Vi,' she gasped to her bewildered companion. 'I'll go the other way and head them off at the other end of the alley.'

With pounding heart she tore along the main road and turned at The Feathers, hindered by the second-house crowds from the Hippodrome who were moving in a steady throng towards the station. Knowing the robbers would be lost to her forever in the dim light and the crowds if she didn't catch them when they emerged from the alley, she struggled through the bustle to the row of shops beyond the station entrance where the footpath came out. Just before she got there, two hurrying figures darted out and rushed across the road to the cab rank.

'Stop, thief!' she shouted, dodging through the traffic after them. 'Stop those men ... thieves ... thieves!'

Confusion ensued as the criminals, startled by this development, decided against a cab for their getaway and ran into the shadows of Haven Green with Amy and a gang of cabbies after them. A passing policeman, blowing furiously on his whistle, joined in the chase, followed by a breathless Violet.

Had the thieves not been hampered by their ill-gotten gains they might have escaped. But the weight of their spoils upset the balance of the man who was carrying the bag, and he stumbled and fell and was immediately set upon by a burly cab driver. The robber's accomplice made the mistake of stopping to look behind him, thus narrowing his lead, and was soon caught.

'So you've 'ad more excitement than the characters in the film,' grinned Bernie, when they finally arrived home, full of their adventures.

231

'We did an' all,' said Violet, who had secretly found the incident a rather exhilarating diversion from her humdrum life.

'The police are bound to catch the rest of the gang now they've got two of them,' said Amy, quite naturally misunderstanding the situation. 'Don't you think so, Bern?'

'Yeah, o' course,' he fibbed not in the least upset by the failure of the raid, since he had already been paid for his small part in it. If Cruncher's friends were careless enough to be foiled by a couple of women, they didn't deserve to stay in business.

*   *   *

In all due credit to Amy's colleagues, they did admit to having made the wrong decision, and agreed to take the necessary precautions when, to everyone's except Bernie's surprise, the robberies continued.

Greed and over-confidence finally brought about the downfall of the real gang who lingered too long in pursuit of a larger haul at a shop in Hammersmith, and were caught red handed by the owners of the shop who lived over the top.

Time passed and the drama was forgotten. In the first year of the new decade the nation mourned the death of King Edward VII who was succeeded by King George V. There had been some changes in society since Queen Victoria's death nine years ago, Amy reflected. New inventions had made the pace of life faster. Travel was easier now as the railways improved and cars became cheaper and more reliable. Not much use to the poor, of course, but at least the Liberals had introduced a few social reforms and an old age pension was now available for people

232

over seventy who had an income of less than ten shillings a week and no criminal record.

Now aged twenty-three, Amy was competent in her work, having gained good all-round experience of the jewellery trade. But being so heavily involved in the retail side of the business, her talent for design was neglected.

'It's about time you gave me something interesting to make, young lady,' said Mr Burridge lightly one day when she was in the workroom delivering some repairs to him.

'I just haven't been inspired,' she said ruefully, for in the whole of the two years since she had re-joined the company as a director, she had designed nothing. 'I suppose I've been too busy with other things.'

'You know what they say about inspiration,' he said, peering at her sagely over the top of his spectacles. 'It only comes with conscious effort.'

A round-faced man of middle years with a ruddy complexion and mid-brown hair combed smoothly to the side, he was neatly dressed in a stiff-collared white shirt with a dark tie and waistcoat, over which he wore a white apron. A variety of tools lay on his workbench: a hammer and saw; tongs; a drawplate for stretching gold and silver wire to required widths. On a metal stand beside him containing equipment for heating metal, was a gas and air blowpipe which produced a small flame with which he had just annealed the gold ring he was in the process of altering. He was currently correcting the size of the ring on a tapering iron rod Amy had come to know as a triblet.

Although a very diligent worker, Mr Burridge was never too busy for a chat with Amy, for even as a young girl she had shown an interest in what went on in the workshop. As a general rule, he was unimpressed by the attempts at design of those who were unqualified in the craft of jewellery making because their ideas often showed total ignorance of the limitations of tools and materials. But since Amy had taken the trouble to learn a few basics, she was unlikely to present him with an idea which would be either impractical to produce or with nothing to recommend it but novelty value.

'How about you making the effort to get inspired yourself then, Mr Burridge?' she teased gently.

'I'm trained to make and mend jewellery,' he said in his usual unassuming manner. 'The designing I leave to those with a gift for it, like you.'

'Point taken,' she grinned.

After some inconsequential chatter, he returned his attention to the task in hand, and Amy made her way back across the workshop to the door of the showrooms.

Seated at benches around the room were several other craftsmen, some busy on repairs, others making jewellery almost identical to mass-produced lines but made exclusive by some minor modification. Each bench was strongly constructed of wood and had a wedge-shaped wooden jutting peg screwed to the edge, on which sawing and filing was done. In the centre of the room a man was using a hand-operated machine to press a piece of gold to a particular thickness while another was working at a lathe. The shelves attached to the stone walls were filled with glass bottles and jars containing chemicals and acids for cleaning and polishing, evidence of which filled the room with a pungent aroma. Standing on a worktable in a corner was a pair of scales with penny weights.

Underfoot was thick rubber, grille-style matting used to protect the gold and silver dust which fell from the workbenches and accumulated on the floor, from where it was collected every so often and sold to bullion dealers to be treated and re-used.

Back in the shop, Amy mulled over Mr Burridge's comments which had made her feel as though she was letting the firm down by wasting her small talent for design. Unable to dispel such doubts, she did some sketching in her limited spare time, usually just before she fell asleep at night. The result was a gold butterfly brooch set with diamond studded wings, which found a buyer soon after appearing in the window.

Since ladies of the jewellery-owning classes were not usually blessed with restraint, they made excellent advertisements. A series of commissions followed the butterfly brooch, each generating more custom for Jackson & Cox as their reputation for exclusive pieces grew. Amy worked closely with Mr Burridge on these orders, discussing the customer's requirements thoroughly with him before making a first sketch.

In using her creative ability in this way, Amy felt she had struck a good balance. For the commissions came in in a spasmodic trickle rather than a steady flow, which meant they didn't demand too much of her time, thus leaving space for her other work and her family. And that was exactly how she wanted it.

*   *   *

The capital was sweltering in a record-breaking heat-wave. Milk turned sour, food went bad and sickness prevailed as a soaring death rate made London the second most unhealthy city in the world.

Mopping the perspiration from her brow, Clara shuffled breathlessly across her sitting room and peered out of the window. Down in the street her daughter was playing with a group of children. While two little girls turned a rope, Connie was skipping, the whole gang of them chanting in loud delight. Where they found the energy for such games in this weather Clara couldn't imagine.

Even the pavement weeds had turned brown in the heat; cobblestones lay parched and dusty, and the sour smell of bad drains clung to everything. A large horse lumbered wearily by, dragging a greengrocer's cart behind it, flies and wasps blackening the rotting fruit and vegetables.

Satisfied that Connie was safe and did not need her attention for the moment, Clara shook her head against some bluebottles buzzing around her hair and sank gratefully into a chair by the open window, her heart palpitating uncomfortably. The hot weather didn't agree with her at all. It made her feel sick and short of breath and gave her pains in her chest. And the extra weight she carried nowadays made everything such an effort in this bloomin' heat.

The curvaceous figure that had once drawn the crowds to the music halls had disappeared along with her career. But she didn't lose sleep on either count. Being at home with her daughter was a damned sight more enjoyable than treading the boards three times nightly. Especially as Ralph, for all his faults, continued to provide the means for them to live comfortably.

A bit too comfortably as far as her figure was concerned, Clara thought wryly. She'd never reverted to her normal shape after Connie's birth.

And since she was no longer reliant on her looks to earn a living, she'd got into the habit of having an extra muffin or portion of mutton stew, and leaving her corsets off whenever she was alone. She'd known enough hunger in her life to have a healthy appreciation of self-indulgence. Anyway, it was more fashionable to be plump than have the skinny proportions of the poverty-stricken.

Glancing at the walnut clock on the mantelpiece, she realised that it was time to prepare tea for herself and Connie. Humming to the tune of 'Alexander's Ragtime Band', she heaved her gargantuan body out of the chair, only to flop back down again with the force of a sudden sharp pain across her chest. Damned nuisance, she cursed, feeling even hotter as sweat suffused her face and neck, dampening her hair. This freak weather wasn't doing anyone any good. In fact people were dying because of it, according to the papers, a lot of them kiddies too. They developed breathing problems, poor mites. And all sorts of diseases were spreading like wildfire in the unnatural temperatures.

Feeling uncomfortable but unafraid of her own pain, which she had experienced quite often lately and knew to be short-lived, she dwelled gloomily on the recent rise in the death rate among children. Connie had become her life, and just the thought of losing her crushed her with agony. This last four years had been the happiest Clara had known. Connie was everything anyone could want in a child. She was lively, loving, intelligent and already showing signs of having inherited her mother's extrovert personality. She had a mind of her own too, even at this early stage, and needed a firm hand at times. But not a day passed when Clara didn't thank

237

God for her. Ralph had missed so much by shutting her out of his life.

The pain in her chest lessened, so she dragged herself up and went into the kitchen. She sliced and buttered some bread and took some of the small rock cakes she'd made that morning from the larder and arranged them on a plate. Then she made a pot of tea for herself and poured a glass of ginger beer from a stone bottle for Connie. Having set the table in the living room, she plodded towards the window to call her daughter.

But she stopped midway, clutching her chest as the pain returned stronger than before, squeezing ... squeezing...

'Connie, love,' she called, staggering to the window. 'Connie...' She clutched at the sideboard, her hands wet and slippery as she tried to hold on. The pain increased, pulling tighter till she thought she would choke. The scene outside the window became dazzlingly bright then swam before her eyes. 'Connie, love,' she called again, but although her mouth opened, no sound came.

* * *

'I'm goin' in to see if me tea's ready,' said Connie, her face flushed from the heat, sandy hair damp around the edges, 'I'm too 'ot and thirsty to play any more. Be out again later. Tata.'

She skipped across to the house and scampered upstairs to their flat, happily anticipating a drink of ginger beer and one of the little cakes she'd seen her mother making earlier. The door was left on the latch for her and as she pushed it open, she automatically listened for the familiar sound of her mother singing.

238

Connie liked to hear it, it gave her a warm, safe kind of feeling. The silence was perceived with disappointment.

'Is tea ready, Mum?' she called, as she entered the living room. 'Mum . . . are you asleep?' That was odd. Why was Mummy lying on the floor? 'Wake up, Mum, it's tea-time.'

Frowning, the child gave her mother's arm a gentle shake, then a more vigorous one. 'Why won't you answer me, Mum? Please?'

Quite soon, uncertainty turned to fear and the child rushed from the house and headed for Tucker Street and the safety of her Aunt Gladys.

*   *   *

News of her aunt's death reached Amy through Bernie who called at her house that evening.

'Yer mum rang me at work and asked me to come over and tell yer,' he explained, having broken the news. 'Yer dad's very cut up about it, apparently, 'im being so close to 'is sister. Alfie's away boxing, or he'd have come to tell yer.'

'I can't believe it,' she exclaimed, trembling with shock and taking comfort in the shelter of his welcoming arms. 'I mean, she's not even been ill. Not that we know of, anyway.'

''eart attack, they think,' he said. 'Caused by the hot weather.'

'Poor Connie,' she said, biting her lip anxiously. 'Such a shock for the little mite.'

'Terrible, but she'll be all right,' he said soothingly. 'Kids are tougher than yer think.'

'I'd better leave Violet in charge here and go over to Bethnal Green first thing in the morning,' she said.

'Good idea.' He was thoughtful. 'I can stay with yer for a while now, if yer like. I should think you'll be glad of a friend.'

'Thanks, but I expect you've things to do.'

'Nothing that can't wait.'

'Shouldn't you be at work?'

'Yeah, but you need me more than the music hall punters tonight,' he said gently. 'I'll get the last train back.'

A rush of affection for him brought tears to her eyes. He had helped her over her last bereavement, and looked set to do the same with this one. 'You're such a comfort,' she said. 'I don't know what I'd do without you at times like this.'

'I'm glad to 'elp,' he said.

*　　　*　　　*

'Am I pleased to see you, love,' greeted Amy's mother the next day, her arms opening to her daughter immediately she entered the room.

'I came as soon as I could,' said Amy, hugging her tight.

'Thank Gawd yer did,' Gladys said emotionally. 'But I wouldn't 'ave blamed you if yer hadn't after being banned from the house for so long.'

'I couldn't stay away after what's happened.'

'And we wouldn't want yer to. Poor Clara popping off like that makes yer realise the pointlessness of clinging on to old grudges, dunnit?' Glady said, moving back and looking at her daughter. ''Ow smart you look, love, I've missed yer somethin' shocking.'

'Where's Dad?'

'Round at Clara's flat,' her mother explained.

240

'There's a lot to do with the funeral to arrange and everythin'. And it's gotta be quick, or she'll go off in this 'ot weather.' This produced a gush of tears. 'Ain't it awful, what we all come to in the end? Nothing more than something in a butcher's window.'

'Do you think he'll want to see me?' asked Amy.

'I'm sure 'e will, but it might not be easy for 'im to admit it.'

'I think I'll go round there to see him,' she said. 'Rather than wait for him to come home.'

'Good idea,' her mother said. 'He needs you now, but yer know yer dad—he's a proud and stubborn man.'

Moving further into the room, Amy saw a pale-faced little girl sitting on the sofa between Bobby and Pete, the boisterous brothers unusually subdued by the occasion. The gravity of Connie's circumstances registered sharply with Amy. Decisions were going to have to be made about her future. But before Amy did anything else, she must go to see her father.

*　　　　*　　　　*

She found him sitting beside the coffin staring into it. Bracing herself against the dread of looking upon death, Amy approached him from behind and followed his gaze. Thanks to the expertise of whoever had laid her out, Clara looked quite presentable, her plump face powdered and rouged, her fair hair fluffed out around it.

'Hello, Dad,' Amy said warily, standing behind him.

He didn't reply, or look around.

At that moment there was room in Amy's heart

241

only for grief for her aunt, who had still had so much left to give. 'She looks beautiful,' she said, tears filling her eyes.

'Always was a goodlookin' woman, my sister,' he said in a shaky voice.

'Mmm, that's a fact.'

'Since Connie arrived she's bin 'appier than I've ever seen 'er.'

'I know.'

'Then this had to 'appen,' he said, sniffing. 'Makes yer wonder what it's all about, dunnit?'

'At least her last years were happy,' Amy said, in an attempt to cheer him.

'Thirty-six, that's all she was. It doesn't make sense.'

'No.'

Amy could see his body quivering in front of her. She put her hands on his shoulders in a gesture of sympathy, prepared to be rejected. He did not respond but his pent-up emotion was a palpable force in the room, electrifying the atmosphere. She bent closer to him, putting her face against his hair, smelling the sooty, sweaty scent of him, her heart overbeating with tension. He began to tremble violently but still struggled for control. Then suddenly his whole body crumpled and heaved with sobs. He turned and put his arms around her.

'Thanks for coming, love,' he mumbled, almost inaudible in his anguish. 'Life's too short for old quarrels, ain't it? It's taken somethin' like this to make me realise that. I should 'ave put an end to it years ago ... but I'm a proud old bugger. I've bin a fool.'

'So have I for going on at you when you thought you were doing the best for me,' she said.

Together they sobbed, father and daughter reunited by tragedy. 'Aunt Clara would have been tickled pink to know she brought us together again,' Amy said.

'She would an' all.' And George managed a watery smile.

*   *   *

A week or so after the funeral, Amy went to see Ralph, who had heard of her bereavement through talk in the shop.

'I thought it only polite to tell you,' she said, standing before his desk at which he remained seated, 'that my parents and I have decided that the best thing for Connie will be for her to come and live with me and the boys.'

'Oh?' He looked bewildered.

'My parents are quite willing to have her to live with them,' she explained, 'but I don't think it's fair to expect them to take on another child at their age when there is a sensible alternative. So I have applied to be her legal guardian.'

'Oh, I see,' he said, in an unusually subdued tone.

'I have more room than them, and it will be good for Connie to have other young children around,' she continued. 'I'm sure it's what my aunt would want for her.'

'You're probably right,' he said dully, looking down at his desk.

Perceiving an air of profound sadness about him, she wondered if perhaps he had been affected by the death of his one-time mistress. It wasn't easy to imagine him being touched by anything beyond his own selfish considerations, but he was only human

243

and had once been close to Clara.

'I know you've supported Connie financially up until now,' she resumed briskly. 'But I intend to take over.'

He looked up in surprise. 'Oh, really? Why is that?'

'Because I don't like the idea of her being raised on conscience money, when I can afford to support her,' Amy explained candidly.

'But I'm quite willing to pay you for everything she needs in the same way as I used to pay Clara,' he said, 'provided I can be assured of absolute secrecy.'

'No thanks,' she said firmly, his final comment strengthening her resolve. 'I don't want my little cousin growing up with shamefaced handouts taking place behind her back. Clara had to accept money from you because she had no option. I'm rather more fortunate in that respect.'

'But I would be willing . . .' He paused and lowered his voice to a whisper. 'I mean, she is my daughter after all.'

'I'm surprised to hear you admit it, even if it is only in a whisper.' she said with a dry laugh. 'I thought that was something you preferred to keep safely swept under the carpet.'

At least he had the grace to look sheepish, she noticed.

'Obviously I can't make the fact that I'm her father public,' he hissed irritably, 'but I've never once missed a payment to Clara.'

'Yes, I'll grant you that much, but it's easy for someone with your resources to ease your guilt with cash.' She paused thoughtfully. 'But even so, it must be a relief to you to find yourself suddenly free from the burden.'

'I never objected to supporting Clara and the

child,' he said, affronted.

'Maybe not, but you must be pleased the payments are over.'

'Well, no. I . . .'

He seemed completely lost for words, she thought, a rare occurrence indeed.

'Naturally I shall honour my aunt's wishes and perpetuate the myth that Connie is the daughter of a sailor,' she resumed briskly. 'So you've no need to worry on that score either.'

'You seem keen to take on the responsibility,' he said. 'I'd have thought you had enough to do.'

'Someone has to give her a start in life, and since I'm her first cousin, I feel a certain responsibility towards her,' she explained. 'Anyway, I'm very fond of her.'

'I see.'

Detecting a hint of regret below the surface of his indifference, she deemed it wise to make certain things clear. 'As far as I'm concerned you have no claim on Connie whatever, either now or in the future, having disowned her for so long. I have told you of my plans only out of courtesy.'

Much to Amy's surprise, his tone was mellow when he replied. 'Yes, I realise that. Thank you.'

*   *   *

After Amy had left, Ralph propped his head on his hands and stared gloomily into space. Loath as he was to admit it, Clara's death had devastated him. Although he hadn't seen her for some years, she had never been far from his thoughts. In his daydreams he had planned, somehow, to return to her one day. And these obscure intentions had lightened his existence which had been dull without her as a part of it. Now it was too late and life seemed gloomy indeed.

Not a man normally burdened by compunction, it was annoying to find himself plagued with thoughts of how he had deserted her and their child in all ways but financial. Dammit, what else could he have done? A man in his position could hardly admit to having a mistress and an illegitimate child. It would have ruined his marriage and reputation in the community. It could even have affected his business and brought hardship on them all. Finer feelings were all very well, but one had to be realistic.

But he did feel bad, for all that. He comforted himself with the thought that it was all out of his hands now and it was pointless to feel guilty. Clara had known from the start that she could never be anything more than a mistress to him. But in his heart she had been, he could deny it no longer. Imbued with regret for her, he felt unexpectedly compelled to make contact with the only bond he had with her now: their daughter. In a moment of impulse he wanted to throw caution to the winds and become a part of her life as she grew up. The idea was banished almost as it came. Such sentimental notions were dangerous, he admonished himself. Pull yourself together, man, and face the truth. Clara is dead and the only daughter you have is Gwen.

*　　　*　　　*

Three months after Connie moved in with Amy, the latter was at her wits' end. The dear little girl who had been such a charmer when her mother was alive, had become a wild, spiteful monster, who wouldn't eat the food she was given, deliberately broke her own

246

and her cousins' toys, disobeyed Violet and Amy and fought with Dickie and Victor with the ferocity of a street urchin.

'I don't know what to do with her,' Amy confessed to Bernie one Sunday afternoon in November. 'I've tried to be as patient as I can, but she's simply beyond the pale. Allowances must be made for the fact that she's missing her mother, but it isn't fair to the boys to let her get away with it all the time. She's turning poor Violet's hair white.'

'She'll settle down eventually,' he said, his dark eyes warm and sympathetic.

'Will she though? I'm beginning to wonder if, perhaps, she'd be happier living with my parents,' she said, 'she's more used to them than she is me, having always lived so close to them.'

'I ain't no expert,' he admitted, his thick brows meeting in a frown, 'but in the long term she's gotta be better off livin' with you.' He glanced around the comfortably furnished room. 'This lot is proof o' that, innit?'

'There's more to a happy childhood than having a decent sofa to sit on and regular meals,' Amy pointed out.

'Such as?' he challenged. 'I wouldn't 'ave said no to either when I was a nipper. Who in their right mind would wanna grow up in a couple o' rooms in Bethnal Green when they can live somewhere like this?'

'Love and a feeling of security are essential to a child's happiness, in my opinion,' said Amy.

'And she won't lack for either from you,' he pointed out. 'So if she can have those things and a bit of material comfort too, she's on to a winner, ain't she?'

'My parents aren't so badly off now,' she reminded him, 'Alfie and I both help them out. With our assistance they could even move from Tucker Street into something better.'

'But even so,' he argued, 'Connie will still be better off 'ere, once she's settled down.'

Amy threw him a shrewd look. 'Do you measure everything in terms of money?' she asked.

'Usually, yeah,' he said breezily, and apparently without compunction, 'I've 'ad to, all me life. Somehow the so-called finer things don't seem to matter when you're starvin' 'ungry and your folks are relying on yer to get them somethin' to eat. But I don't have to tell you about hunger, do I?'

'I've had my share of it, yes, but it hasn't made me as single-minded as you about the importance of money.'

He gave a nonchalant shrug. 'P'raps not as much was expected of you when you were little as it was of me.'

'Maybe not,' she agreed. 'But it's all in the past for both of us. You're doing well now. Surely you can afford to soften your attitude?'

'Not on your life,' he told her, shaking his head vigorously to emphasise the point. 'Once I start softening up, I'll soon be skint again. I ain't fallen on me feet like you. I ain't got shares in a good business and money in the bank. Sure, I can afford to eat decent grub and wear good togs, but I've gotta keep me wits about me, 'cos they're the only skills I've got. I don't mix with gentlemen jewellers like you do, Amy. Mine is a world of hard men and villains.'

His attitude bothered her. 'I hope you don't think I married Clifford for his money?'

'I wouldn't blame yer if yer did.'

248

'But I didn't,' she said crossly, 'I loved him, and I'd have married him if he'd not had a brass farthing to his name.'

'More fool you,' he said, grinning broadly. 'But it was a bit o' luck that he had a damned sight more than a farthing, wannit?'

'You're saying you don't believe me.'

'No, I'm not saying that,' he explained, throwing her a sharp look. 'What I *am* saying is that it's easy to claim you didn't care about his money since you'll never have to prove it, even to yourself.'

'That's a terrible thing to say.'

'Why is it?' he asked, genuinely surprised at her offence. 'I'm not criticising you, love. I'm just statin' facts. We're all only human.'

'You shouldn't judge everyone by your own standards,' she warned.

''Uman nature is 'uman nature, I don't care what yer say,' he persisted. 'And there's nothing wrong with making the most of yer chances. Gawd knows, people from the East End like us don't 'ave any other choice.'

'Of course they do.'

'Face up to it, Amy, no one is ever going to give the likes of us anythin' for nothin'.'

Forced to accept the fact that their opinions differed on this issue, she said lightly, 'You're a hard man, Bernie.'

'I've 'ad to be for so long I suppose it's become a habit,' he said.

The sound of a commotion in the kitchen ended the conversation. 'Now what's going on?' asked Amy, as Connie's shrieks rang through the house followed by the thunder of running feet. All three children burst into the room followed by Violet,

249

red-faced and apologetic for letting them get out of hand.

'Connie's taken my toy soldiers,' said a flushed Dickie, staring at his sobbing second cousin with pure hatred.

'There was no need to hit her,' defended the gentle Victor. 'She *is* a girl, remember.'

'She's more like a wild animal than a girl,' wailed Dickie, deliberately pushing against his cousin, whereupon she flung herself at him and the two fell to the floor in a wrestling heap.

'Eh, eh, you two,' said Bernie, separating them and holding them apart. 'Now what's all this about?'

'She keeps taking our things and breaking them,' complained Dickie.

'Is that right, Connie?' asked Bernie, whilst Amy and Violet watched with approval at the capable way he was dealing with the situation.

Connie hung her head, snivelling and saying nothing. Had her face not been a blotchy mass of tears and snot, she would have looked a picture in her blue velvet frock with white lace collar and cuffs. As it was, she resembled a gutter ruffian, her face almost matching the mass of untidy red curls that had been carefully brushed and combed five minutes before.

'Why do you keep taking their things, Connie?' asked Bernie firmly. 'Haven't you got lots of things of your own?'

'No.'

'Oh, Connie,' admonished Amy, on her haunches in front of her engaged in a mopping up operation. 'You know that isn't true. You've lots of things—all your toys from home, and new ones too.'

'Don't wan' 'em,' she said.

'You ungrateful little beast!' snapped poor Violet.

250

'Why don't you want 'em?' asked Bernie, somehow managing to remain strict without losing all sympathy for her.

''Cos they don't belong 'ere,' she said, in a small voice.

'Of course they do, love,' said Amy kindly.

'No, they don't and nor do I,' she said. 'I 'ate it 'ere. I wanna go 'ome to me mum.'

There was an awkward silence. Amy stayed kneeling in front of her, looking into her face. 'But your mummy isn't there, darling,' she said, gulping back the tears. 'She's in heaven like I told you.'

'Why can't I go there too?' asked Connie.

'How about goin' to the park instead?' came a timely intervention from Bernie. 'Let's all go.'

'Yeah,' chorused the boys, their attention temporarily diverted.

'Would you like that, Connie?' asked Amy patiently.

Her indifference was registered with a shrug.

'Dobbin would like to go out, I'm sure,' said Amy, referring to the child's favourite toy, a pull-along wooden horse she'd brought with her from Bethnal Green.

'All right,' she conceded, without interest.

'Good, that's settled then.' Amy stood up. 'We'll have to wrap up well though, because it's very cold out.' She turned to Violet. 'Are you coming, Vi, or do you want a break from this noisy lot?'

'I'll stay 'ome and have a bit of peace and quiet, if yer don't mind,' she said, looking from Amy to Bernie with a knowing grin which appeared to be lost on them both. It seemed obvious to her that Amy and Bernie should get together properly, as a couple. All this talk about them being friends was plain stupid.

251

They were meant for each other and it was about time they realised it. Without her tagging along, perhaps they might just do that.

Violet ran an admiring eye over her friend. Amy was a good-looking woman of means. Someone was bound to come courting her soon, for it was three years since she'd lost Clifford. Violet would rather it was Bernie than any of the posh types she met in the course of her work. No one who knew Bernie would be fool enough to leave their money or valuables unguarded while he was around, it was true, but he was easy-going and good fun. He treated Violet like an equal and made her laugh. So what if he was a bit of a villain? Everyone had their faults. And there was a lot to be said for having a cheerful man about the house.

CHAPTER THIRTEEN

The party left the house swathed in mufflers and heavy coats over their Sunday best, the boys rolling their hoops with the aid of a stick, Connie trailing the barrel-shaped horse behind her.

'It was a good idea of yours to bring them out,' said Amy, as they trooped into Walpole Park.

'I thought some fresh air might stop them killing each other,' he laughed.

'You're very good with children, aren't you?' she remarked, thinking how odd it was that someone who was so hard and ruthless in some ways, could be so caring in others.

'I've 'ad enough experience, bein' the eldest of seven,' he reminded her.

252

'You should get married and have some of your own,' she said lightly.

'I dunno about that,' he grinned.

The day was cold and still with barely a stirring through the trees or a rustle in the lingering autumn leaves scattered on the grass. Not the sort of weather for standing about so they walked briskly behind the children, the soft-hearted Victor hanging back from his brother and trying, unsuccessfully, to hold Connie's hand.

'She's quite a character,' commented Bernie.

'She's a holy terror.'

'You can't help liking her though, can you?' he said. 'She certainly has a mind of her own.'

'She takes after her mother in that way,' said Amy. 'Aunt Clara was always a law unto herself. It's a pity her sunny nature is noticeably absent in Connie at the moment.'

'She'll settle down, you'll see,' he said, turning and smiling at her.

Looking into his eyes, so full of tenderness, she finally admitted to herself that their friendship had gradually turned to love over the years since Clifford had died. She raised her lips to his as though it was the most natural thing in the world. They were in a secluded spot beneath some trees, a hazy sunshine filtering through the leafless branches. The children were playing on the grass nearby, totally engrossed in their games. There were a few other people around, dog walkers, ball players and so on. But they went unnoticed by the embracing couple.

'Well, well,' she said breathlessly, drawing back and looking at him. 'After all these years, you and me.'

'I've always loved you,' he said. 'Even when we

253

were kids you were the only girl for me.'

'What a lovely thing to say,' she said. 'I didn't know you were a romantic.'

'Oh, I didn't realise my feelings at the time,' he admitted ruefully, 'I was always too busy tryin' to make me fortune to bother with girls when me mates started courtin'. You moved away and got married, but you were always there.' He pointed to the area of his heart. 'In there. I ain't wanted to rush yer since yer 'usband died. I thought I'd let things take their natural course. But I must admit, I've bin 'opin'.'

It seemed strange to hear down-to-earth Bernie uttering such sentiments, but it felt very good. 'You've become very dear to me, these last few years,' she said truthfully.

'I'm glad,' he said, taking her into his arms.

Their caresses were interrupted by the return of the boys, flushed and breathless, Connie trailing behind.

'Can we go to the lake?' asked Victor. 'There might be people sailing their boats.'

'I doubt it, on a cold day like this,' she said.

'Can we go and have a look though.'

'Go on then, but be careful you don't fall in.'

'We will.'

'No pranks now, Dickie,' Amy warned her mischievous son.

'All right, Mum.'

'Bernie and I are right behind you,' she said, but the boys were already galloping away across the grass.

With her horse rattling noisily behind her, Connie tore after her cousins.

'Victor, Dickie,' yelled Amy. 'Connie is coming after you. Wait for her and look after her.'

Dickie ignored the summons but Victor turned

and waited for her. Two such opposites, their mother thought. Victor was so sensitive and gentle while his sanguine brother was too full of adventure to show much concern for others.

Amy and Bernie walked towards the lake arm in arm, enjoying this new stage in their relationship. They had almost reached their destination when Victor hurtled towards them, ashen-faced and tearful. 'Come quick, Connie's fallen in the water,' he screamed.

Even as Amy reached the water's edge, Bernie was in the lake up to his knees fishing the child out. The fact that the lake area was devoid of adults on this cold day, emphasised the danger of the situation to Amy, filling her with remorse. It wasn't deep here, but there was enough water to drown a mite like Connie. Bernie lifted the shivering child, who was crying silently, on to his shoulders and they headed for home.

'You shouldn't have let her go near the edge,' Amy admonished her sons as they hurried through the streets. 'I let you alone for a few minutes and this is what happens.'

'Sorry, Mum, but you can't stop Connie when she wants to do something,' said Victor, 'I told her she shouldn't try to copy Dickie.'

'And what was Dickie doing?' asked Amy suspiciously.

'Lying on his tummy looking over the edge searching for tiddlers,' explained Victor.

'Oh, Dickie, you naughty boy,' she rebuked, but blamed herself for being preoccupied with personal matters and letting the children go on ahead.

Back home, Violet, alarmed by all the commotion, appeared on the scene and made herself useful. She

255

peeled off Connie's wet clothes and prepared a hot bath for her, while Amy searched for something for Bernie to put on since his trousers were soaked and needed to be dried by the fire. Clifford's clothes had long since been disposed of, so he had to make do with a towel draped round his waist while his trousers steamed on a guard in front of the parlour fire. 'I'll understand if you want to take back what you said in the park,' she laughed. 'Having three children around doesn't exactly make for a peaceful romance.'

'I wouldn't have it any other way,' he said, pulling her on to his lap.

She leapt up hurriedly as her sons clattered into the room and made a beeline for Bernie.

'Will you play with us, Uncle Bernie?' asked Victor.

'With the train set,' said Dickie.

'Or Meccano,' said Victor.

'Well, I . . .'

'Oh, do say you will . . . please?'

'Go on, be a sport.'

Bernie and Amy exchanged glances. 'See what I mean,' she laughed.

*   *   *

A few days later when Amy got home from work, she found Violet in a state of agitation about Connie. 'She's so poorly I've put her to bed,' she explained.

'She seemed a bit off colour yesterday,' said Amy. 'But I thought it was just a cold coming on.'

'I think she must have caught a thorough chill from her soaking on Sunday,' said Violet, as the two women went upstairs to the little girl's bedroom.

256

'Hello, Connie,' said Amy kindly, leaning over the child's bed. 'I hear you're not very well. Can you tell me what you feel like?'

'I hurts all over,' she said feebly, her lips dry and two unhealthy red patches staining her cheeks 'And I feel sick.'

Alarmed by the sound of her breathing, Amy called the doctor in which proved to be a wise move because by the time he arrived, Connie was in a high fever and delirious.

'Pneumonia,' he announced gravely.

'Oh, no, not that!' Amy cried.

'It will be touch and go,' he said, anticipating her question. 'But she seems like a tough little thing. Give her plenty of liquids and sponge her with tepid water to keep her temperature down. I'll come back later.'

Under no illusions about the possible outcome of this killer disease, she telephoned Bernie at the music hall. He dropped everything and came over.

'Thanks for letting me know,' he said, joining her at the bedside.

'I guessed you'd want to see her, just in case...'

'She'll pull through,' he said cheerfully. 'She won't dare not to, now that I'm here.'

His resolute optimism, which she knew must be an effort even for him, was very comforting. 'I'm glad you're here,' she said, squeezing his hand.

The doctor came and went several times during the night and the next few days as the fever continued to rage.

'She just *has* to get better, Bernie,' Amy said emotionally. 'I can't bear to lose her as well as her mother.'

'We won't lose 'er,' he said. 'She's too much of a fighter to let go.'

257

For several days Amy and Bernie were together at her bedside, supported by Violet who kept the household ticking over and relieved them at the sickbed while they tried to sleep. When the crisis came, they were as one person in their hopes and prayers for her. Amy could hardly bear to watch as Connie writhed and squirmed, demented in her utterings. When she fell into a deep sleep, Amy thought her own heart would stop.

'She'll be all right now,' said the doctor who had been present as the fever reached its peak.

Never had Amy felt closer to anyone than she felt to Bernie at that moment. They wept tears of relief together.

'There yer are,' he said, sniffing, and reverting to his lighthearted manner now that the danger had passed. 'I told yer she'd come through it all right.'

'Oh, Bernie,' she said, hugging him tight. 'You're wonderful. I don't know what I'd have done without you.'

'You'd have managed,' he said.

Amy took time off from work in the early days of Connie's convalescence, 'She looks so frail,' she explained to Violet, 'I'm afraid to leave her even though I know you'll take good care of her.'

Connie was indeed a shadow of her former self, emaciated and pale, her greenish-brown eyes protruding in a face so thin it seemed as though her cheekbones might actually break the skin. Violet plied her with beef tea and broth, Amy read stories to her, and the boys came to the sickroom to keep her up to date with all the news from the outside world.

As her strength returned, Amy expected the rebellion to do the same. But it didn't. Nature had found a way to settle her to life with her new family.

Being so reliant on them in her weakened state had forced her to accept them. Amy intended to keep her mother's memory alive for her, but as a thing of happiness and pride, not sadness and regret. To Amy, Connie was the daughter she didn't have and she cherished her.

*　　*　　*

In February of the following year Londoners found themselves in the grip of a big freeze. Ponds and rivers froze over as temperatures dropped to astonishing levels. Cruel winds whipped across the capital, hardening earlier snowfalls and turning anything that dripped into icicles. People hugged their firesides or went to bed fully dressed to keep the cold at bay. Some grew sick and died.

Being a resourceful sort of a fellow, not given to dwelling on the morbid side of life, Bernie was quick to spot the advantages of the inclement weather to a courting man wishing to find favour with his lady. And one Sunday morning, having made a purchase from a mate who was currently doing a roaring trade in skates, he arrived at Amy's house with a pair for them all, including Violet. 'The Serpentine's frozen solid,' he announced cheerfully, 'so let's go skating.'

He received no opposition, and thick scarves, woollen stockings and gloves were quickly donned in addition to their warmest coats.

The snow-covered plains of Hyde Park were crowded with people eager to try out the new natural ice rink. Amy and her gang trooped on to the ice, slipping and sliding then falling into a giggling heap. Connie looked as though she might burst into tears as she fell on to her bottom, but even as Amy slithered

259

to her aid, the child was up, clinging to Violet's hand, her cheeks pink with excitement. There were many more tumbles to come but Connie was the first to get the hang of it. While the rest of them continued to stagger and stumble drunkenly on the fringes of the ice, she was off among the crowds gliding as gracefully as a dancer.

'It's a treat to watch her,' said Amy to Bernie, as the little girl soared past looking like a miniature Santa Claus in her red coat and hat trimmed with white fur, her scarf flying out behind her.

Screams of delight filled the air as people skated and slipped; some were even being towed by friends on bicycles. The street traders were quick to capitalise on this heaven-sent opportunity and set up their stalls around the lake, selling hot potatoes, roast chestnuts and gingerbread.

By midday they were all beginning to get better at keeping their balance, and were warm and glowing as they sat on a bench blowing on the hot potatoes Bernie had bought them. The children were impatient to get back to this tremendous new sport. Violet went with them while Amy and Bernie watched.

'Does your heart good to see them enjoying themselves, doesn't it?' she said.

'It does an' all,' he agreed.

'Connie looks so well you'd never think she was at death's door just a few months ago. I must be careful she doesn't stay out too long and get cold though.'

'Yeah, we'll have to watch that.'

A heatless sun shone from a steel blue sky, glinting on the frozen snow and seeming to warm the atmosphere. The scene before them was gay and colourful, with the bright blues, reds and greens of the skaters' clothes looking even more striking against the glaring white of the snow.

The wind cut through to the bone, though, and Amy shivered as the heat generated by her exertion began to wear off. 'Ooh, it's cold when you sit still,' she said, hugging herself. 'We'd better get back on the move.'

They rejoined the fun, skating sometimes together and sometimes holding hands with the others in a chain. Amy hadn't enjoyed herself so much in ages.

It was late afternoon when they got home, and they all sat round the parlour fire talking about the day and roasting potatoes which they ate with cheese and pickles, until it was time for the children to go to bed. Violet also retired to her room saying she was 'Fair worn out from all that bloomin' exercise.'

Alone at last, Amy and Bernie sat together in the firelight glow. 'It's been a perfect day, hasn't it?' she said contentedly.

'Not 'alf,' he agreed.

They sat in companionable silence until Bernie finally managed to say what had been on his mind for some time. 'Will you marry me, Amy love?' he asked.

'I thought you'd never ask,' she said, smiling into his eyes, 'but are you sure you want a wife with a ready made family?'

'I want you, and if they come too that's fine with me,' he said.

'In that case, yes, I'd be honoured.'

*   *   *

They were married at Ealing registry office at Easter-time, and the ensuing months were blissfully happy for Amy. Bernie was everything Clifford hadn't been:

strong-minded, masterful, and good fun with the children. Since they were from a similar background, things were easier than they had been with Clifford as far as her parents were concerned too. They visited regularly and because they knew Bernie so well, there was always a good atmosphere.

'Well, Bernie,' Amy said, raising her glass to him on the occasion of their first anniversary, 'thank you for a wonderful year.'

'Thank *you*,' he said, chinking her glass and observing her tenderly over the rim.

Sitting beside him on the sofa in the parlour, the children and Violet having gone to bed, Amy cast her mind back over the last year. A lot had happened since their wedding, she thought. There had been the terrible loss of life when the *Titanic* had sunk. Oh dear, it still made her blood run cold to think about it. And more recently Emmeline Pankhurst had been in court on bomb charges after an explosion wrecked Lloyd George's golf villa in Surrey.

Closer to home, there had been scandal in the Jackson family when Gwen's husband had left her penniless for another woman. Poor Gwen had been forced, in the absence of any alternative, to return to live with her parents. Amy suspected that the latter aspect had been the worst part of the whole miserable experience for Gwen.

Nothing very dramatic had happened to Amy personally, though it had been an eventful year for Bernie. He had bought a Ford motor car which had meant plenty of family outings, especially as he now had more spare time since he'd resigned from his job at the music hall. It was a decision she had favoured because the unsocial hours of the job had meant they saw so little of each other. He was still out on business of an evening sometimes, but not every night as before. These days he earned a living trading through contacts he had in the East and West End, apparently, but she never asked too many questions. Bernie liked to keep his business and personal life separate, and she respected his right to that. Summing up their first year of marriage, she could honestly say it had been very good.

'Here's to many more happy years together,' she said.

'I second that,' he said.

*　　*　　*

Six months later Amy stared at her bank manager in disbelief. 'Overdrawn?' she exclaimed. 'But that can't be right.'

'I can assure you it is, Mrs Banks,' he informed her smoothly, 'but as you have such good standing with the bank, I wanted to have a chat with you before I stopped honouring cheques.'

'You're going to bounce my cheques?' she objected hotly.

'Well, yes, that is the standard procedure if there are insufficient funds to meet the payments.'

She shook her head. 'But there are funds,' she said impatiently.

His brows lifted. 'Do you not check your bank statements?'

'Of course I do ... well, my husband usually does that, actually,' she said crossly. 'I'm always so tied up with business and the family and everything. He helps me out with little things like that.'

'Perhaps you'd better take a look at this then,' he said, handing her a copy of her statement.

'What is this cash withdrawal of two hundred pounds?' she asked, having studied the document. 'I haven't drawn that amount.'

'The cheque with which it was drawn is signed by you,' he said, handing it to her. 'Here, take a look.'

The man across the desk was showing none of the misery she felt as the grim implications of the evidence in front of her registered. 'Yes, I can see that's it's my signature. I had quite forgotten that particular transaction.' She gave him a polite smile. 'I'm terribly sorry about this. My deposit account is very well funded. I'll transfer sufficient from there to cover the amount overdrawn.'

'That will be quite in order,' he said, in a business-like manner, 'I guessed it was just a simple mistake.'

Amy completed the interview calmly and left the room in a dignified manner. Outside the door, though, she was shaking so much she thought her legs would give in.

*   *   *

'You forged my signature to get money from my bank account, didn't you?' she said to Bernie that night after the children and Violet had gone to bed.

More than anything in the world, she wanted him to give her some plausible explanation.

'I don't know what yer talkin' about,' he said, his sudden pallor indicating otherwise.

'Please don't lie to me,' she said. 'You've hurt me enough already, don't make it worse. You've been milking my account and you've put it in the red.'

He was standing with his back to the fire, staring at his feet, guilt written all over him.

'How did you get the signature to look exactly like

264

mine?' she asked, deeply disappointed in him.

'I practised, using a letter with your signature on it that I found in the bureau.'

'And I suppose you forged a letter from me authorising you to collect the money on my behalf?' she said. 'The bank would have insisted on that for such a large amount.'

'Yeah, that's right.'

Amy was sickened by the sly, premeditated nature of the crime. A crime against her, the woman he was supposed to love. 'Why did you do it?' she asked.

'Isn't it obvious?' he said, aggressive in his guilt. 'I needed some dough to do business with, and you've got plenty.'

'But why cheat me, Bernie?' she asked, her voice breaking with emotion. 'If you'd asked me I'd have given you what you wanted. Surely you know that?'

'Exactly. So what does it matter?' he said. 'What's yours is mine and vice versa, ain't that how it is when you're married?'

'It matters a whole lot to me,' she said. 'You deceived me. And I thought you loved me.'

'And I do love you,' he said with feeling, as though one was not related to the other. 'What's that got to do with it?'

'You really don't know?' she asked in astonishment.

'No, I don't,' he said. 'So, I took some dough off yer. So what? It ain't gonna cause you any problem.'

'That isn't the point. And anyway it already has,' she said. 'I've been called in to see the bank manager like an irresponsible fool. It was humiliating.'

'If that's the worse problem you'll ever 'ave, then you're bloomin' lucky.'

'Isn't it about time you got rid of that chip on your

265

shoulder?' she fumed. 'It's becoming boring.'

He didn't reply, but went to the sideboard and poured himself a gin.

'Why didn't you ask me for the money?' she asked again.

'Because I didn't want to,' he said bluntly. 'It was simpler this way.'

'Oh, I see, you're too much of a big man to ask a woman for money, is that it?'

'Nothing as complicated as that,' he explained, taking a swallow of gin. 'All my life I've obtained money by whatever means is at hand when I need it, and I needed it then.'

'But you must have known it was only a matter of time before I found out,' she said.

'Not really.' He gave a careless shrug. 'You'd never 'ave known if I'd not let the account go over the top, since I look after yer bank statements.'

Bernie liked to deal in ready cash, so he didn't have a bank account of his own. He was always keen to pay his share and contributed regularly to the basic housekeeping, though Amy insisted on clothing the children herself, considering them to be her sole responsibility.

'I had no idea you had financial problems,' she said. 'And I'm your wife. How do you think that makes me feel?'

'I don't 'ave financial problems, as such,' he said. 'I merely wanted somethin' to tide me over. Some geezers owe me money, and I couldn't wait for them to pay up. If I've got no dough, I can't buy. And if I can't buy, I can't sell.'

'But why didn't you tell me about it?' she entreated. 'We could have sorted it out together.'

This made him very angry. 'I am what I am,' he

266

told her, white with temper. 'I've always looked out for myself, living from day to day, earnin' a living as best as I can. You knew that when you married me. I'm a small trader. I deal in cash. I've never 'ad a bank account in my life. We're on different financial planes, you and me.'

'But to steal from your own wife,' she said accusingly.

'It was simply business as far as I was concerned,' he shouted. 'Can't you understand that? It had nothing to do with my feelings for you.'

She sank down in a chair feeling emotionally drained. 'No, I can't understand how you could have done such a thing.'

Finishing his drink he banged the glass down on an occasional table. 'All this bleedin' fuss about money,' he roared. 'I didn't realise you cared so much about it.'

'I couldn't give a damn about the money,' she yelled, frustrated at not being able to make him understand how she felt. 'It's you cheating me that's tearing me apart. You don't lie and cheat on people you love, it just isn't on.'

He came and stood by her chair, looking down at her. 'I wouldn't harm an 'air of yer 'ead,' he said. 'Or the kids', and I'd kill anyone who tried. That's because I love yer, all of yer. And what's 'appened doesn't change that.'

'You don't have to beat someone up physically to hurt them, Bernie.'

'Oh, well, if you choose to be upset by somethin' like this, more fool you,' he barked. 'I'd have thought a girl with a background like yours would have understood this sort of thing.'

'My parents were never dishonest,' she pointed

267

out. 'No matter how poor they were.'

'Grow up, Amy,' he said. 'Everyone fiddles if they get 'alf a chance.'

'I don't,' she said. 'And I don't like having people around me who do. Quite apart from anything else it's a bad example to the children.'

'Meaning what?'

'Meaning that I can no longer trust you,' she said. 'Do you realise that you have committed fraud?'

'Oh, do leave orf, Amy. How can something like that between 'usband and wife be fraud?' he said.

'It is, even if a woman can't testify against her husband. Morally it's fraud. You stole money from me.' She shook her head. 'I still can't believe it. I've always known you fly close to the wind. But not with me. I'm your pal as well as your wife. You don't cheat on a pal. It hurts, Bernie. It really hurts.'

'All this bleedin' drama,' he snapped. 'Anyone would think I'd bin with another woman.'

'You don't think what you did is just as bad then?' she asked.

'O' course not,' he said emphatically. 'It's only money, Amy, *only money*. I never look at other women, you know that.'

She had thought she could trust him in that way, it was true. But how could she have faith in anything he said now? If he cheated her in one way, he could do so in another.

'Maybe not,' she sighed.

He pulled her into a standing position, slipping his arms around her. His anger seemed to have abated. 'I'm sorry if I've hurt yer, love. I honestly didn't think it mattered that much. It is only money, after all.'

'All right, Bernie,' she said dismally, forced to accept the fact that they did not share the same values. 'But if anything like this ever happens again, we're finished.'

'You're bein' dramatic again,' he said.

'I mean it,' she said, looking into his face. 'I can't take dishonesty between us. If there is a next time, there'll be no more us.'

'There won't be, I promise you,' he said, kissing her affectionately. 'Now let's forget all about it and go to bed.'

'You go on up,' she said. 'I'll follow you in a minute.'

'Don't be too long now,' he said meaningfully.

*   *   *

Alone in the room, Amy leaned back in the chair and closed her eyes. This time yesterday she wouldn't have wanted to waste a precious minute of the night away from him. But he had sullied something in their marriage and she needed time to think. This had nothing to do with money. He was welcome to everything she had. But it went much deeper than that. It was all about trust and loyalty, without which she didn't see how true love between two people could survive. And the worst part of all was the fact that she couldn't communicate with Bernie about it. His apparent lack of compunction could be a front for a guilty conscience, of course, but she had a terrible suspicion it wasn't.

Snippets from the past came into her mind. 'He'd sell his grannie if he could get a good enough price for her,' her father used to say. She had known he had no scruples as far as money was concerned when she had married him, so why be so upset now that he had run true to form? The answer came quickly. Having

269

fallen victim to his indiscriminate dishonesty, she could no longer close her mind to it, as she now realised she had been doing ever since she had allowed herself to become romantically involved with him. As his pal she could ignore the devious side of his nature; as his partner in life she could not. His ways weren't hers, and that was all there was to it.

But she had married him for better or worse, and she wouldn't give up on him now. He'd promised not to do it again and she must take what he said on trust, as difficult as that now was. As she made her way upstairs to bed, she knew that something irretrievable was lost to their relationship, and she felt sad.

*   *   *

Bernie lay in bed waiting for Amy with increasing irritation. It was quite beyond him why she had taken on so about a miserable two hundred pounds. It wasn't as though she was short of cash, and she was welcome to everything he owned. Admittedly, his finances had been in poor shape recently but that wasn't the point. If he had money she could have every penny, and willingly. So why wasn't it the same for her? All right, so perhaps he had been a bit naughty about it, but that was just the way he operated. A bit of trickery meant nothing to him. Why she had chosen to think it altered his feelings for her, he couldn't imagine. Oh, he loved her, there was no doubt in his mind about that. All right, perhaps the fact that she had money had made her even more of an attractive proposition as a wife, but that didn't mean he wouldn't have married her anyway.

His mistake had been in taking too much from her

account. But funds had been difficult ever since he'd been sacked from the Empire. What with that and a couple of deals going sour on him, things had been very dodgy indeed, because he had to have money to pay his way with Amy. He couldn't have her think he was sponging.

Losing his job at the music hall had been a real blow because he'd been operating a very lucrative scheme there for years. He'd been lifting full bottles of spirits from stock, selling them on the street and pocketing the money, making up the deficit in the bar takings by watering down the drinks he served across the bar. Foolishly, he'd overdone it. Customers had complained. 'I've known about your fiddling for some time,' his boss had told him. 'And I turned a blind eye because you're so good at the job and you bring in the custom. You've a way with you that goes down well with the punters. Some of 'em come to see you more than the artistes. But you got greedy, and that I won't tolerate.'

At least there had been no problem with Amy about it, because she had been only too happy for him to 'give up his job' at the music hall to be at home more in the evenings. He missed the work though. The company as well as the money. Still, he'd get by somehow. He always had. A couple of good deals would soon put him back on top.

He frowned at the thought of the current situation with Amy. She would come round in time, he was sure. She was far too goodhearted to bear a grudge. But he'd have to be more careful in future as regards that sort of thing because he hated to be on bad terms with her. They had so much in common, he and Amy, it was a pity she couldn't understand the way he operated. For, despite what he'd done, she really did mean everything to him.

CHAPTER FOURTEEN

'Ned and I have something to tell you,' said Molly Cox, smiling rather coyly at her guests.

'Ooh, something nice, I hope,' said Amy.

'Let's 'ear it then,' grinned Bernie. 'Don't keep us in suspense.'

'I expect you can guess...'

'Oh, Molly, are you...'

'Yes,' she squealed joyfully. 'The baby is due in the autumn.'

'That's the best news I've heard in ages,' said Amy, hugging her friend, her own problems resolutely concealed beneath the cheery façade she had almost perfected, 'Isn't that wonderful news, eh, Bernie?'

'Not 'alf.' He planted a kiss on Molly's cheek. 'I'm very 'appy for yer, ducks.' He shook hands with Ned. 'Congratulations, mate.'

Amy offered her hand to Ned a little warily, for she was still more at ease with him at business meetings than social gatherings. But such were his high spirits, he opened his arms to her unreservedly. 'Congratulations,' she said, embracing him, albeit rather formally.

It was April 1914, a Sunday afternoon. Amy and her family had had luncheon with Molly and Ned at their home in Ravenscourt Park, a large, rambling house with a walled back garden where flower beds and shrubberies thrived in well-ordered abundance beneath the branches of some lovely old trees. Lustrous from a recent shower, the cherry tree was fluffy with blossom, the lilac just coming into bud, and the lawns bordered with yellow daffodils. Sunshine and showers were alternating and the children were taking advantage of a sunny spell by playing outside while the adults lingered over coffee in the drawing room, having enjoyed roast beef served with all the trimmings.

'Thank you, Amy,' Ned said, grinning broadly.

It was plain to see that his marriage to Molly was a happy one. And now, at last, they were to have the child they had wanted for so long. It was hard to imagine anyone ever coming between this devoted couple. Yet even now when Amy saw Ned and Gwen together, occasionally at work or at gatherings like this, his affection for her could not be mistaken. It was strange...

The port was produced and a toast made to the delighted couple.

'Are we the first to know?' asked Amy.

'Yes.'

'I'm flattered.'

'Yeah, me an' all,' agreed Bernie.

While the two women lapsed into baby talk, the men discussed the prospect of war which was becoming increasingly grim as the powerful nations of Europe built up their defences, and the arms race threatened to run out of control.

'We've gotta make sure we can defend ourselves,' said Bernie, whose knowledge of world affairs came mainly from pub talk.

'Admittedly,' agreed Ned, who was an avid reader of newspapers. 'But they're taking it too far. All this money being poured into defence is bound to create a hostile atmosphere.'

'But if the other countries are doing it, so must we.'

273

'And have men die!'

'There's always bin wars.'

'That doesn't mean there always has to be,' said Ned hotly.

Sensing a disagreement, Molly steered the conversation to the less emotive subject of Bernard Shaw's new play, *Pygmalion*, which had just opened in the West End.

'They say it's very good. Mrs Patrick Campbell plays a cockney flower girl who's taught to speak like a lady,' she said. 'Apparently, one of her lines includes a swearword which she delivers with great aplomb. The audience loved it.'

'It sounds very daring,' said Amy.

'Times are changing,' said Molly. 'I mean, who would have thought a woman would ever show her ankles in public? Yet these shorter skirts are getting to be quite commonplace.'

The sound of raised voices outside drew their attention to the window through which they could see Victor in the role of peacemaker between Dickie and Connie. Frowning, Amy gave an admonitory tap on the glass.

'I'm trying to stop her climbing the apple tree,' came Dickie's shouted explanation.

Connie turned towards the window, cheeks flushed and smudged with dirt. 'He's been up there, so why can't I?'

'Because you're a girl,' he told her. 'You'll only fall and hurt yourself, you silly thing.'

Annoyed to have a contretemps occur whilst enjoying someone else's hospitality, Amy pushed the window up and poked her head out. 'None of you is to climb that tree, or any other tree, or wall, or fence, or anything at all. Is that clear?'

'Why?' asked the irrepressible Connie.

'Because I said so,' stated Amy.

'But, Mum...' pleaded Dickie.

'No climbing, and I don't want to hear another word about it,' bellowed Amy, drawing her head in and closing the window.

United against the inexplicable workings of the adult mind, the trio outside went into a huddle.

'They're up to something,' said Bernie. 'I think I'd better go and sort 'em out.'

'I'll go,' offered Amy.

'It's all right, I don't mind,' he said, smiling warmly at her. 'You stay 'ere and take it easy.'

'If you insist,' said Amy, stifling her feelings towards him and returning to her armchair, her face set into a smile.

'He's very good with the children, isn't he?' remarked Molly, as they watched him taking charge of the youngsters outside. 'Hardly the archetypal cruel stepfather one hears about.'

'Far from it,' agreed Amy.

'The children seem very fond of him.'

'They are.' She paused thoughtfully. 'But who isn't susceptible to Bernie's charm?'

Molly smiled. 'Not many, I shouldn't think. He's a very likeable sort of a chap.'

Indeed, her husband's popularity seemed even to transcend class differences, Amy thought, for he was equally at home with Violet as with their current hosts, who obviously enjoyed his blunt cockney humour. Even the starchy, well-to-do residents of Merrydene Avenue, who had been shocked by the appearance of this flashily dressed rough diamond in their midst initially, were now devotees of his entertaining company. To the male of the species he was a man's man, a comic spinner of yarns. To women he was an agreeable wag, with his saucy manner that made them giggle and blush.

What these people didn't know was that Bernie was a thief. An unprincipled crook who violated the laws of decency without a moment's compunction. After the devastating incident last year, things had been all right between them for a while. Amy had put the matter behind her and behaved as though it had never happened, suppressing the urge to keep everything under lock and key because she didn't feel that that was the way forward for their marriage. Her chequebook was kept in an unlocked drawer and she took his word for it that her bank statements were in order.

There were no further summons from the bank manager, but cash began to go missing. Mostly money she kept in the house to pay tradespeople. A sixpence here, a shilling there, a pound taken from her purse. Sly, petty thieving that seemed to mock her good nature. She had not yet confronted him with it because when she did it would mean the end of their marriage, and she dreaded that. But trust between husband and wife was of the essence, in her opinion, and Bernie had betrayed hers in him for a second time. Now, she feared it was gone irretrievably.

Apart from her own personal anguish, she was worried about his influence on the children. Stealing was as natural as breathing to him, and he had a powerful personality. What if his evil ways rubbed off on them? It could happen even without his realising it.

'Yes,' she said, in reply to Molly. 'He's always been popular, even when we were children. Everyone in Bethnal Green liked Bernie Banks.'

Watching Amy observe her husband through the window, Ned sensed a deep unhappiness about her. Having been a colleague of hers for some years, he had come to know her quite well. She was strong-minded and independent, with a good head for business. She had even shown artistic talent. But she was not a convincing actress. And he could see right through that cheerful, happy families act she was putting on.

He also sensed something more sinister beneath Bernie's congenial manner. He was, indeed, amusing company, with his sharp wit and sense of humour. But Ned had a horrible suspicion he was the sort of man who would steal the rings from his sick mother's fingers without a second thought. There was something about him that just didn't ring true.

Feeling compassionate towards Amy, Ned wanted to help her in some way. She had had more than enough trouble in her life already. He didn't want to see her hurt again. But what could he do? He certainly couldn't interfere between man and wife, especially as he only had his intuition to go on. Maybe I'm wrong about them, he thought. And hoped he was.

*   *   *

Amy finally came to terms with what must be done two months later, after a great deal of soul searching.

'You've been stealing money from me again, Bernie,' she said quietly, in the privacy of their bedroom one night. 'And because of that I must ask you to leave my house.'

'Leave?' he exclaimed in astonishment. 'What the 'ell are you talkin' about?'

'Don't insult my intelligence by pretending to be innocent,' she said. 'I warned you we were finished if it happened again. It has, so you'll have to go.'

'Have you gone barmy or somethin'?' he said. 'I ain't bin nicking yer dough.'

'I'd like to know who has then,' she said.

'It must 'ave bin one of the kids.'

She took a sharp breath, amazed and disgusted that he could put the blame on the innocent children he claimed to love. Any lingering doubts about her decision were finally laid to rest. The part of him that could steal from his own, was just as ruthless in trying to clear himself. He'd been living this way for so long, he simply couldn't help it.

'I want you and your things out of this house when I get home from work tomorrow,' she said.

'You'll be lucky,' he said scornfully, 'I ain't going anywhere. This is my 'ome.'

'Please don't make it harder than it already is,' she said briskly. 'We had something good between us and you destroyed it.'

'I'm sorry, Amy,' he said, with a sudden change of mood, 'but it was all so easy. You shouldn't 'ave left the money about.'

'I must be able to leave money around with confidence in my own house,' she said. 'It's something called trust. But you wouldn't know much about that, would you?'

'Don't let this break us up,' he pleaded. 'It's only money.'

'This *isn't* about money,' she said. 'This is about disloyalty.'

'I love you,' he said. 'Surely that counts for

278

something?'

She stared at him sadly. 'I love you too, Bernie,' she said wearily. 'But I don't like what you are. I can't live with a man I can't trust.'

'You know me,' he said, giving a wry grin, 'I'm a bit of a rascal but I don't mean any 'arm.'

'Stop making excuses for yourself,' she snapped. 'You're a villain through and through. All right, so it's just the way you are, and I think you're even proud of it. But it isn't my way. I won't have my children growing up under that sort of influence. Pack your bags and go in the morning. I shall sleep in the spare room tonight.'

'But Amy . . .'

'It's over, Bernie,' she said decisively, before turning away and marching from the room.

*　　　*　　　*

Thoroughly upset by this turn of events, Bernie lay in bed mulling things over. All right, so perhaps he shouldn't have taken her money, but he still didn't think it warranted all this fuss. People cheated him out of dough all the time and he didn't lose sleep over it. Amy, more than anyone, ought to know how someone like him lived. After all, she hadn't always languished in the respectable avenues of Ealing.

The way things had turned out made him wish he'd resisted the temptation, though. It wasn't as if he had really needed the money now that he was making a few good deals again. But a spot of easy dibs was irresistible, no matter who it belonged to. And the habit wasn't easy to break.

And now it had lost him the woman he loved. But he *wouldn't* let her go. Somehow he had to persuade

279

her not to do this terrible thing. One more chance was all he needed. If it meant so much to her, he'd change, he'd become a reformed character. He swore, on his mother's life, he'd make it up to her. In all his sincere intentions, the fact that his mother had died some years ago conveniently slipped his mind.

*　　　*　　　*

He was sitting in the parlour reading the newspaper the next day when Amy got home from the shop. 'More trouble abroad,' he said, looking up at her as though nothing untoward had happened between them. 'Some Austrian Archduke and his missus 'ave bin assassinated. Shot in their car, just like that. Him the heir to the throne an' all.'

'Why are you still here?' she asked, trembling at the knees. This whole wretched business had made her feel thoroughly ill. It was bad enough having to face up to the fact that her marriage had been a mistake. But to have the parting prolonged was agony. For all their sakes she dare not allow him to persuade her to change her mind.

'I couldn't go without seeing you, and leave things so bad between us,' he said.

'Just go, Bernie.' She blinded herself to those appealing dark eyes that could make even the darkest day seem sunny. 'I want you out of here before the children get home from school.'

His newspaper fell to the floor in his eagerness to get to her. 'Don't do this, Amy,' he said, putting his hand on her arm.

'Please go.'

'You know you don't want me to, not really.' He tried to force her to meet his gaze. 'You and me go

280

back a long way. We're right for each other. Just give me one more chance, I promise I won't let you down.'

Inwardly shaking, Amy moved back, brushing his hand from her arm. He was right, she didn't want him to go. Life was going to be bleak without him. She wanted to feel his love around her and his cheerfulness filling the house. Forcing herself to be hard, she said, 'What's the matter? Are you afraid you won't find another woman with such a healthy bank balance?'

'Now that isn't fair,' he said. 'Money was *not* my reason for marrying you.'

Oddly enough she believed him about that. He'd have stolen from her if she had had the income of a shopgirl. 'Wasn't it?'

'No, it wasn't. Whatever I've done, and whatever I am, I *do* love you.'

She believed him about that too, as far as he was able to love any woman. If she weakened now she must be prepared for a lifetime of mistrust because he would never change, *could* never change. As he moved towards her again, she shrank back, frightened of the effect his proximity would have on her. 'It's no good, Bernie. It won't work now that the trust has gone between us.'

'It'll come back.'

'Don't make it any worse for me by staying around. Nothing you can say or do will make me change my mind.'

He searched her face thoroughly, finally accepting that she meant what she said. 'All right,' he said miserably, 'I'll go. Don't worry, I'll be gone before the kids get 'ome.'

'Thank you.'

'I'll miss 'em though.'

'They'll miss you.'

He turned at the door. 'I'm sorry I tried to blame 'em for my thievin'. I said the first thing that came into my 'ead.'

'I know.'

Half an hour later she stood at the window watching him saunter down the path with his suitcase, a sad victim of his own personality. Even now though, in defeat, there was a jauntiness about him. He would miss her, she knew that, but not to the extent that she would miss him, simply because his feelings didn't go that deep.

She turned away from the window as he shut the gate and marched away down the street, leaving her to readjust to single status for the second time. Oddly enough, this seemed even harder to cope with than Clifford's passing. Death was beyond her control. This break-up left her with a sense of failure as well as sorrow. And worst of all was the pain of having lost a friend. A part of her would always be Bernie's. Her mistake had been in marrying him.

*　　　*　　　*

'And so we come to the last item on the agenda,' said Ralph, a week later at a directors' meeting. 'The question of whether or not to invest in some new fittings for our shop windows.' He pushed forward a brochure from a company in Hatton Garden. 'There are some display stands in there that are well worth considering. They are very well made with bevelled glass shelves and lacquered brass fittings.'

The literature was passed around and studied briefly. 'Mmm, I like the one that adapts to a "staircase",' said Harold, pointing to an illustration of a single-frame display stand which easily adapted for use with the glass panels rising in steps.

'Yes, I like that one too,' said Ralph. 'Personally I think anything we spend on our window display is money well invested.'

Ned flicked through the brochure. 'Yes, I'll go along with that.'

'That just leaves you, Amy,' said Ralph, turning to find her staring vacantly into space. 'Amy...'

She came to with a start. She had drifted off some time ago, in the middle of the review of their charges for repairs and cleaning.

'Yes?'

'Are you in favour of the firm spending some money on new fittings for the window?'

At that particular moment, Amy really couldn't have cared less if they had spent the firm's money on a job-lot of headless teddy bears. Such disinterest was most unusual for her, but weighed against the problems she had at home in the aftermath of Bernie's departure, shop fittings really were low on her list of priorities.

Not only was she finding it difficult to pacify the children because their pal Uncle Bernie had left, and cope with the guilt of being the cause of his departure, but she was missing him dreadfully too. The house seemed gloomy and lifeless without him.

Violet, who was usually such a comfort at times like this, was no help at all. Her energies were all flowing in the direction of a delicatessen shop assistant from Acton called Karl. All she seemed to care about these days was getting time off to meet him.

However, knowing that Ralph wouldn't hesitate to use her current lapse in concentration as an excuse to criticise her, she hurriedly collected her thoughts and applied herself to the matter under discussion.

'Yes, I think it would be an excellent idea,' she said. 'Why don't we all gather some information about what's available, and pool our ideas at the next meeting.'

'Good idea,' said Ned.

The other two agreed and the meeting finally closed, much to Amy's relief. Until things had settled down at home, it was impossible to keep her mind on her work.

'Anything wrong?' asked Ned, as they made their way downstairs together. 'You seem worried.'

'Heavens, is it that obvious?'

'To me, yes,' he said. 'It's most unusual for a meeting not to hold your attention.'

She heaved a sigh of resignation. 'Oh, well, everyone is going to have to know sooner or later,' she said wearily. 'So you might as well be the first. Bernie and I have split up. He's left.'

'Oh, Amy, I am sorry,' said Ned.

'So am I.'

'I sensed something was wrong when you were together at our place.'

'Yes, things haven't been right between us for some time.' She ran a tired hand over her brow. 'Oh God, it's been awful.'

He studied her pale face, noting the dark shadows under her eyes, the lines of tension around her mouth. She looked badly in need of a friend. 'Look, how about a cup of something and a chat in the ABC? Or do you have to go straight home?'

Looking into the eyes that had once seemed so cold and unfeeling, she saw only kindness and concern. 'I really should go home,' she said. 'But it would be
284

such a relief to talk to someone and half an hour won't make much difference.'

The Aerated Bread Company teashop served good plain meals and beverages. Amy and Ned sat at one of the marble-topped tables with cast iron legs, while the neatly uniformed waitress served them with coffee.

'Well,' he said, as she concluded her story, 'personally I think you did the right thing in telling him to leave. The man is an absolute bounder.'

'Even that wouldn't have been so bad if he hadn't actually stolen from me,' she said. 'It was the betrayal of trust by my own husband I couldn't take.'

'I doubt if many people could.'

'I feel so empty, though,' she admitted ruefully. 'For all his faults I miss him dreadfully. Can you understand that?'

'Oh, yes,' he said, sipping his coffee. 'I'd be completely lost without Molly if she wasn't around.'

'Which reminds me, how is she?' Amy asked. 'I haven't seen her for a while. This business with Bernie has tended to dominate me rather.'

He frowned. 'Not too good actually.'

'Oh?'

'She's been sent to bed. Doctor's orders.'

'Oh dear,' she exclaimed anxiously. 'What's the trouble?'

'Nothing too serious, I hope,' he said, adding in a softer tone, with typical male reserve, 'A woman's problem. The doctor said she must rest.'

'Why didn't she let me know?'

'She didn't want you to worry.'

'I'll pop over and see her as soon as I can,' said Amy.

His expression brightened. 'Oh, Amy, I'd be

terribly grateful if you would. Being laid up gives her time to worry. You know how much this baby means to her. I'm afraid she'll work herself up into a state.'

'Is the baby at risk then?' she asked worriedly.

'The doctor seems to think everything will be all right as long as she takes things easy,' he said. 'But she'll tell you all about it when she sees you. A visit from you will do her the world of good. You've had babies, you know what it's like.'

'Well, yes . . .'

'Try to stop her worrying, if you can.'

It was all very mysterious but Amy knew she would get no more details from Ned on such a delicate matter. To him, like most men, female biology was a taboo subject. But she could see how worried he was. Such devotion accentuated Amy's own loneliness. She knew that neither of the men she had loved had been capable of caring for her in such a way. Molly was a lucky woman.

'I'll do my best,' she promised. 'I'll call and see her tomorrow straight from work.'

'Thanks, Amy, you're a real sport,' he said, covering her hand with his on the table for a moment in a gesture of friendliness.

He was so genuinely dependable and warmhearted, she thought. How on earth could she have ever found him to be otherwise?

* * *

Molly had had a show of blood, which was the cause of the concern. 'It gave me quite a scare, I can tell you,' she confided to Amy the following day.

'Yes, I can imagine.'

'I was convinced I was going to lose the baby. But
286

everything seems to have settled down again now, thank goodness, though I might have to rest until the birth.'

'How long to go?'

'Two months.'

'Oh, poor you, that's a long time to be laid up,' said Amy.

'I'll put up with anything so long as the baby is all right,' she said, her soft brown eyes full of anxiety. She was propped up with pillows, her hair worn simply, with a side parting and loose curls.

'The baby will be just fine, I'm sure,' said Amy reassuringly.

'Oh, Amy, I do hope so,' said Molly. 'We've waited so long. Poor Ned is so worried. I'd hate to let him down after coming this far with the pregnancy.'

'He's more worried about you than the baby, you know,' said Amy.

'Yes, I think you're probably right,' she said, a sudden warmth brightening her eyes. 'I suppose it's because we've been on our own for so long with no children to claim our attention, that we've become so close.'

'I think it's wonderful,' said Amy.

'Be a dear and make sure he doesn't worry too much.'

'He told me to do the same with you,' Amy laughed. 'But don't fret, I'll do what I can.'

Molly became contrite. 'All this talk about Ned and me, when you've problems of your own. Ned told me about you and Bernie. I'm so sorry.'

'Thinking about someone besides myself and my family is just what I need right now.'

And, indeed, over the next few weeks Amy found solace in her involvement with the Coxes, and her

287

friendship with both of them strengthened. She visited Molly every day, either in the evenings or after finishing work at the shop, depending on whether or not Violet was going out for the evening.

'Looks as though I'll be losing Violet to this man of hers,' she said to Molly one day in July. 'I expect she'll be leaving to get married and set up in a home of her own.'

'A German fellow, isn't he?' asked Molly with interest. The highlight of her days was Amy's visit and she enjoyed keeping up to date with all the gossip.

'Yes, that's right.' She paused and sipped her tea. 'I'll miss her terribly if she goes, of course. But I'd like to see her married. She's a good sort, and she deserves some happiness.'

'To a German though,' said Molly doubtfully. 'Our relations with them are not very good at the moment, are they?'

'No, but what do politics matter when you're in love?'

'Not a jot,' agreed Molly. 'But it will be difficult for them if war breaks out.'

'There have been rumours about that for ages and it hasn't happened yet,' said Amy.

'Ned seems to think that things are very volatile in Europe now, with Austria blaming Serbia for the murder of Archduke Ferdinand,' said Molly. 'If they attack, it could escalate into a war, he says.'

'Umm, I saw something about it in the paper. Let's hope nothing comes of it.'

* * *

Amy received a telephone call from Ned on the

Tuesday night after August Bank Holiday Monday, just as she was about to go to bed. 'I'm sorry to call you so late, but Molly's gone into labour and there are complications.'

'Oh, Ned!'

'I was wondering if you could come over? She's asking for you.'

'Of course, I'll come right away,' said Amy, breathless with fear because the baby still wasn't due for another few weeks.

Having arranged with Violet to hold the fort at home, she took a cab to Ravenscourt Park.

Ned was in the drawing room, grey with worry, when Amy arrived. The midwife had called the doctor who was upstairs with Molly, Ned having been banished from the proceedings.

'I wish I could be with her,' he said, as Molly's cries filled the house. 'I feel so helpless waiting down here while she's in such pain.'

'Giving birth is a woman's business,' Amy reminded him. 'It'll soon be over and you'll be able to tell her how clever she is.'

The doctor appeared at the drawing-room door, looking grave. He beckoned to Ned. The two spoke in ominous undertones before Ned returned to Amy with the alarming news that an ambulance was to be called for Molly.

'The birth isn't progressing properly,' he said grimly.

'The hospital is the best place for her then,' she said, feeling totally inadequate for it was obvious that Molly's condition must be serious for such drastic action to be taken.

Seeing her into the ambulance, with Ned who was to accompany her, Amy said, 'Good luck, Molly, you'll be in good hands.'

'Will you wait here till Ned gets back, Amy?' Molly asked, her face drained of colour, her skin and hair wet with perspiration.

'Well . . .' began Amy, unsure as to the reason for such a request.

'Please . . . I'd like there to be someone here for him to come home to.'

Amy was horrified at what she saw in her friend's eyes. *She doesn't think she's going to come through this birth.* 'Of course I will, if that's what you want,' she said, forcing a bright note, 'I'll be longing to know whether it's a boy or a girl.'

'Help Ned to cope if anything happens to me,' she gasped, clutching Amy's hand.

'Now what sort of talk is that? You're going to be fine.'

'You will though . . .?'

''Course I will,' said Amy, choking back the tears. 'Don't you worry about Ned. You just concentrate on yourself and getting that baby born.'

*   *   *

It was almost dawn when she heard his key in the lock. The slow thud of his footsteps down the hall was not the sound of a man bearing good news. With a heavy heart, she went to the drawing-room door to meet him.

'Oh, Ned,' she said, observing his grim expression. 'Is it . . .'

'It was a boy. He didn't survive the birth.'

'Oh dear, I'm so sorry,' she said, swallowing hard. 'Molly . . . she must be heartbroken?'

'The baby just wouldn't come. It went on too long.

290

Her heart couldn't take it,' he said, through dry lips. 'They tried to save her, but in the end there was nothing they could do.'

Amy couldn't move. She felt as though the breath had been physically beaten from her. She had prepared herself for the loss of the baby, but not Molly too. Molly had known, though. She'd known she wasn't coming back. With her friend's words ringing in her ears, Amy forced herself to look at Ned. He looked dazed, his eyes oddly vacant. But the thing that struck her most was the greyness about him, almost as though a fine layer of ash suffused his skin.

'I don't know how to help you, Ned,' she said. 'I can hardly take it in myself. But tell me what to do and I'll do it. Anything at all to ease your pain.'

He looked at her as though surprised to see her, as though the sound of her voice had brought him back from some other place. 'I feel so peculiar,' he said. 'So detached. I'm numb. I can't feel anything. Isn't that terrible?'

'That will be the shock, I expect.' Her lips felt dry and stiff, her own voice echoing in her head. She was so tired she could hardly stand, yet too tense even to sit down.

'I suppose it must be.'

'I'll make some tea.'

'Thank you.'

She made a pot of tea and they drank it in silence, each lost in their own thoughts, as the pale light of dawn crept through the curtains.

'Won't you be needed at home?' he asked. 'The children . . .'

'They'll be all right with Violet.'

'There'll be things for me to do,' he said. 'Funeral

291

arrangements, that sort of thing.'

'Not now though,' she said. 'There'll be plenty of time for that later.'

'Perhaps once I start being practical,' he said, 'it might begin to seem real.'

He got up and drew back the curtains to reveal the garden glistening with dew. The familiar beauty of it seemed odd, as though it should be tarnished somehow in respect for the sorrow that had fallen upon the house. Amy recalled that Sunday in the spring when she and Bernie had lunched here and she had been preoccupied with her own marital problems. How insignificant they seemed against the terrible burden Ned now had to bear.

Ned pulled the curtains across. 'I'll leave them closed out of respect.'

'Yes, of course.'

'Not a custom I've ever been fond of ... too damned gloomy. But still...'

'You ought to get some sleep,' she said, for his eyes were red and shadowed.

'I couldn't, not just yet.'

'No, I didn't really think so.

'I was thinking about that Sunday when Bernie and I came to lunch,' she continued. 'And Molly told us she was pregnant...'

'Those were happy days.'

'We mustn't be afraid to talk about her.'

'No.'

He turned away suddenly and she knew from his trembling shoulders that he was crying. This was the trigger to release her own grief, and with tears streaming down her face, she went to him. 'Let it out, Ned,' she said gently, slipping her arms around him. 'Don't try to hold back.'

292

Clinging to her, his body became convulsed with weeping. 'I'm so ashamed,' he muttered thickly. 'A grown man crying. You must think me very weak.'

'Nonsense,' she said. 'There's no shame in a man showing his feelings.'

They wept as one, holding each other for comfort until they were exhausted but calmer, their mutual grief seeming to bind them together against the rest of the world.

'You must try to sleep now,' she said.

'Yes, I think I might be able to now,' he said. 'And you too, Amy, you must be worn out.'

'Yes, I'd better go home to bed,' she said. 'I'll go in to the shop later.'

'You've been so kind,' he said. 'Thank you.'

'I haven't done anything.'

'You've been here, and it's helped.'

'It's helped me too,' she said, 'Molly was a dear friend.'

*   *   *

Sitting in the cab on the way home, Amy was imbued with a plethora of confused emotions. She was aware of having undergone some kind of turning point in her life, though quite what it was or how it had happened she wasn't sure. Her empathy with Ned over Molly's death was stronger than she had thought possible. This, added to her own grief and lingering regret at her failed marriage, seemed to have culminated in a feeling of profound love for him. Compassion not love, she told herself. It was all too easy to misread one's feelings at a sensitive time like this.

As the taxi rolled past Ealing Common, richly

293

verdant in the early sun, and into the crowded Broadway, she became aware of an unusual amount of activity on the streets. People were moving with a kind of urgency about them, gathering in groups on the pavement and chattering excitedly. Everyone seemed to be holding a newspaper. Something important must have happened.

A glance at a newsstand headline told her what it was. BRITAIN AT WAR was written across it in capital letters. She could hardly be surprised since everyone had been talking about it for so long. And already in a state of shock from her own personal tragedy, she accepted the grave news as inevitable.

CHAPTER FIFTEEN

Absorbed in his grief, Ned found himself somewhat detached from the patriotic fervour that swept through the populace after the declaration of war. The crowds of eager young men queueing outside the recruiting offices left him unmoved, as did the other manifestations of 'war fever' that seemed to be affecting everyone else. People waved Union Jacks and held parties to celebrate the fact that the Hun were to be given a good thrashing. Brass bands blasted out patriotic songs in the parks and streets.

Horrific anti-German stories filled the newspapers, producing a wave of hatred for anyone even remotely connected with that race, and inspiring men to join up in their thousands. Every day the recruiting offices were forced to turn volunteers away simply because the staff couldn't cope with such large numbers. Many parents and girlfriends, confident they would

294

be home again by Christmas, urged their men to enlist, and openly doubted their courage if they refused.

And still, as memories of Molly's funeral receded into the past, Ned could feel nothing much beyond his own sorrow. Chaos prevailed at the shop as staff numbers were depleted by young men leaving to take their King's shilling, to much cheering and flag waving from their ineligible workmates. But none of it seemed to touch Ned. He employed older men to replace those he had lost and struggled on automatically from day to day. Even the knowledge that trade would be severely affected if the war continued and produced shortages of materials as well as manpower did not stir him from his apathy, unlike his father who was forever fretting about how they would be forced out of business altogether if fighting went on for too long.

'You need a night out, Ned,' said Amy, one evening in the autumn when she paid him a friendly visit at his house.

'I'm still in mourning,' he reminded her, grateful for the excuse.

'Ignore it for a few hours,' she suggested. 'I'm sure Molly wouldn't want you to mope around the house.'

'I don't feel like going out,' he said, disinterestedly.

'Something cheerful to take you out of yourself,' persisted Amy. 'A music hall would be just the thing. I'll go with you to keep you company, if you like.'

'Thanks, but I'm not in the mood.'

'You'll soon brighten up once we get there. There's nothing like a spot of lively entertainment to lift the spirits.'

'I'd rather not, *really.*'

She tried another tack. 'How old are you, Ned?'

295

'Thirty-two.'

'Mmm, well, maybe you are past the first flush of youth,' she said lightly. 'But you've a long way to go before I'll let you sit back and become an old man. You're mooning about like a disembodied spirit.'

'Leave me be, please, Amy.'

'I can't do that, I'm afraid,' she informed him brightly, 'I promised Molly I'd do what I could to help you cope, and I'd be letting her down if I left you to sink deeper into yourself. Lord above, I'm only suggesting an evening out, not a complete change of lifestyle.'

He sighed heavily. 'Oh, all right, if you insist.'

'I do.'

They went to the New Middlesex Theatre of Varieties in Drury Lane which was packed to the doors. Infected by the warmhearted ebullience throbbing through the auditorium as they settled into their seats, Amy began to unwind a little. For although she went to pains to hide it from Ned, she was actually in a state of trauma herself, for various reasons...

Firstly, she missed Molly terribly. Added to this was her concern about Ned who seemed more depressed every time she saw him. She had tried to be supportive to him, visiting him regularly in the hope that some cheerful company might perk him up. Matters had been complicated by the increasing sense of being in love with him that had begun the night Molly had died, a feeling she constantly strived to squash since it was neither decent nor reciprocated.

Finding herself with such impulses so soon after parting from Bernie, caused her to question her own volatile emotions. Logically, it must be the

296

circumstances that had produced this romantic illusion. She'd been drawn to Ned by their mutual grief whilst still emotionally unstable from her own broken marriage. There was no more to it than that. But none of this down-to-earth reasoning made any difference to the way she felt.

And as if all this was not enough, she was also very concerned about Violet. Keeping company with someone of German origins was a dangerous thing at the moment while feelings were running so high. As well as being verbally insulted by people in the street, Violet was isolated from the friends she had made among the other servants in Merrydene Avenue who wanted nothing to do with a 'Hun Lover'. The effects of her controversial romance were beginning to be felt by the rest of Amy's household too. Only the other day they had been alarmed by the arrival of a brick crashing through the sitting-room window. Amy had told Violet she considered the relationship to be unwise, but had refrained from insisting that she stop seeing him, since the poor fellow's only crime seemed to be his nationality.

But now the curtain was going up and she settled back to enjoy the show. The first half contained the usual run of jugglers, contortionists and performing animals, ending on an emotional note with a glamorous female singer, swathed in a Union Jack, giving a rousing rendition of 'Rule Britannia', her eyes shining with tears. Promising a kiss to any young man who would enlist at a desk behind the stage at any time during the show, she strutted into the wings to deafening applause. There was no shortage of response. Men poured on to the stage to loud cheers from the rest of the audience.

In the interval Amy and Ned went to the bar for a

drink.

'Well,' she said, 'did I do right to drag you from your armchair?'

He seemed preoccupied, but managed a smile. 'Yes, I'm quite enjoying it actually.'

'Thank goodness for that,' she laughed. 'My name would have been mud if you weren't.'

'You're a good sort, Amy.' He looked into her face. 'Thanks for bothering.'

'It's my pleasure,' she assured him.

* * *

As the second half of the show drew to a close with the artistes and audience joining together to sing 'Land of Hope and Glory', Ned's conscience, which had stirred during 'Rule Britannia', was now fully awakened. He was ashamed of the self-pity which had allowed him to neglect what he had been taught to consider as every fit man's duty. Without a word to Amy, he rose and joined the men queueing in the aisle to sign on. At least the army would give him a purpose in life.

* * *

'You gave me quite a shock,' said Amy, on the way home in the taxi.

'I surprised myself.'

'Was it wise to join up on impulse?'

'What other way is there?' he asked. 'It isn't exactly anyone's lifetime ambition, is it?'

'No, of course not.'

'You don't sound very pleased,' he remarked. 'I thought all you women were keen for us men to join up.'

'Not necessarily. I can see that you might feel compelled to do your duty to your country with there being such strong emphasis on recruitment,' she explained quickly, 'but why not leave it to the younger men?'

'And have a white feather pinned to my lapel?' he said. 'No thanks. I've no dependants now. And, as you have already pointed out, I'm not quite past it yet.'

Amy was imbued with dread. Only last week her brother Alfie had joined up. Now Ned. But she must do her part and send them off willingly and with praise for their courage. 'In that case I can only admire your spirit and wish you well.'

'Thank you.'

'I'll miss you.'

'That's nice to know.' His mood was noticeably brighter now that the decision had been made. 'I shall miss you too.' He smiled into her face in the dim light. 'You're a real pal.'

'Likewise,' she said, turning away and looking out of the window into the lit streets, the heavy West End traffic thinning out slightly beyond Marble Arch.

'Will you write to me?'

'I certainly will,' she said.

Neither of them said very much for the rest of the journey as they hovered on the brink of yet another watershed.

*   *   *

Bernie's decision to join up came more as a way of escaping from his problems than from any great urge to do his duty as an Englishman. His marriage was over, his business had taken another dive and he was in debt all over East London. Lord Kitchener had been staring accusingly at him from posters all over town for weeks, pointing a finger and telling him to 'Join Your Country's Army'. So why not? He'd always been partial to a spot of excitement, and at least as a soldier he'd get regular pay and his keep all found. And there was the added attraction of having everyone treat you like a hero the minute you donned a uniform. And it wasn't as though it would be for long. It was a recognised fact that it would be all over by Christmas. When he came back his creditors wouldn't have the heart to bother him, not when he'd been away doing his bit for his country.

Eager to get this new adventure underway, he went to the recruiting office at the town hall and queued up with all the rest. A few well-told jokes soon made him the centre of attraction among this exuberant bunch, and he enjoyed the camaraderie. Things became more serious inside the office where he found the procedure to be quicker and more final than he'd expected. He gave his details to a polite, uniformed man behind a counter who dealt with his application with quiet efficiency. Within a very short time Bernie was leaving, complete with a copy of his army form and his King's shilling. That was all there was to it. He'd taken that irreversible step. They would be in touch with him soon, the officer informed him, as calmly as if he'd done nothing more daring than pay a visit to the pawnbroker.

As he stepped out into the sunshine, he was besieged by second thoughts. 'Well, you've bin and gone and done it now, mate,' he muttered to himself, then headed for the nearest pub for a drop of something to soften the blow.

300

*   *   *

Violet stepped lightly from the tram in Acton High Street one chilly afternoon in October and walked briskly towards the cooked meats shop where her boyfriend worked for his uncle. Heavy grey clouds rolled ominously across the sky, and specks of rain were carried in the wind. Looking smart in her best red coat and deep-brimmed hat which she wore jauntily to one side, she was in good spirits. Not so long ago, she hadn't known what to do with her spare time. But Karl had changed all that.

They had first met in Grover's Drapery Store in Ealing Broadway, at the haberdashery counter. She had been buying some hair-ribbon for Connie, he was on an errand for his aunt who particularly liked Grover's range of embroidery silks. Violet had accidentally dropped her change on the floor; he had recovered it for her. And nothing had been the same again.

They had strolled together in Walpole Park that first day, chatting easily and exchanging details. He'd come to England after leaving school, eighteen years ago, and lived with his uncle and aunt in the flat above their shop. He was a thin, long-limbed man with fair hair and earnest blue eyes. She'd liked his serious manner, and had trusted him instinctively. He was almost entirely Anglicised after all this time, his slight accent only noticeable when he was nervous or upset. The last thing Violet had expected was to find love for the second time. But it had happened despite the disapproval of all and sundry, and she didn't regret a moment of it.

Things had been difficult for them, of course, particularly since the outbreak of war. And now,

301

with all the talk of the police rounding up German citizens for internment, she lived on a knife's edge, dreading that each meeting might be their last.

Because his family were doubtful about his relationship with her, she didn't go as far as the shop but waited at a pre-arranged spot in a nearby sidestreet. When he didn't appear at the appointed time, she became uneasy. She was usually the one who was late, they had often laughed about it being a woman's prerogative. So where was he? The possibility that he might have stood her up didn't even occur to her because he simply wasn't the type.

After half an hour or so, she walked up to the main road and began to make her way towards the shopping parade. A smile of relief lit her face as she saw him hurrying towards her, smiling and waving. Quickening her step to close the gap between them, she was alarmed by the sudden appearance of two men who grabbed him and dragged him out of sight into an alley.

Rushing to investigate, she found him on the receiving end of a brutal attack. Dressed in dirty overcoats and heavy boots, the ruffians worked as a team. One held Karl still while the other aimed blows at his stomach and chest, spitting at him and calling him a 'Hun bastard' with guttural venom. Their faces were contorted with hatred. Pale with fear, Karl was squirming and struggling to free himself, wincing and groaning with the impact of the blows.

In a blind fury at such monstrous injustice, Violet marched fearlessly towards the affray and swung her handbag across the shoulders of the man who was hitting Karl with enough force to send him staggering back. Caught offguard by the interruption, the other man released his grip on Karl just before receiving

302

the full weight of Violet's bag across the back of his head.

'Cowards!' she shrieked, bringing the bag down again and again on them. 'Two against one ain't fair. You're a pair o' rotten cowards. Stinkin' rotten cowards!'

After aiming a stream of abuse at Karl, and telling Violet she was a filthy slut who needed hanging, they slouched away, leaving the sour smell of unwashed clothes behind them.

'You poor thing,' sympathised Violet, dabbing Karl's grazed face gently with her handkerchief. 'Let's go an' 'ave a cuppa tea somewhere. Tea's supposed to be good for shock.'

The ABC teashop was warm and reassuring with its pleasant aroma of coffee and toast. They ordered tea and sticky buns, but Karl had no appetite. Violet could see he was still shaken up. 'Those lousy hooligans, I could kill 'em for what they did to yer,' she said vehemently. 'They make me so ashamed.'

'I've been in this country a long time,' he said forlornly. 'I've never been in any trouble. I've always got on vell vith the people. Now they call me names and punch my guts.'

'Only some of 'em,' she said tenderly, putting her hand over his on the table and looking into his eyes. 'Yer don't wanna let a few roughnecks who don't know any better upset yer.'

'But I am causing you much trouble too,' he said.

'Oh, lor, don't trouble yerself about me,' she said cheerfully, her teeth catching over her bottom lip as she smiled. 'I've got a skin like a rhino.'

Noticing he still seemed troubled, she said, 'Is there anything else wrong, Karl, apart from the beatin' you've just taken?'

303

He frowned. 'I think this vill be our last meeting,' he said sadly.

'I see.' Tears filled her eyes. It was perfectly understandable that the malevolence he was receiving would begin to flow in the other direction. But not towards her personally, please. 'Why?'

'Isn't it obvious?' he said miserably.

'We can carry on seeing each other,' she said enthusiastically, 'war or no war.'

He shook his head gravely. 'No, it is no good, Violet. Ve must face up to it.'

'But Karl...'

'Have you not read the papers?' he said. 'Tomorrow, the next day, who knows when...'

'Internment?'

'That's right. I'm not naturalised British.'

'But you can hide until the war is over,' she said, desperately clutching at straws.

'And spend my time looking behind me, afraid to go out?' he said. 'No, that isn't the vay.'

'We'll keep in touch,' she said, 'and when it's all over...'

'There's so much hate between our countries now,' he said, shaking his head wearily, 'I think the burden vill be too great for both of us.'

As painful as it was for her to admit it, she knew he was right. Patriotism was a powerful force. She had sympathised with him just now, but she could never side with him against her own country to any real degree. 'All right, Karl,' she said, in a tone of sad resignation. 'But do one thing for me before you disappear from my life.'

'Of course, if I can.'

*   *   *

304

'I've a favour to ask of you, Amy,' said Violet, when she arrived back home.

'Ask away.'

'Can Karl stay with me in my room tonight?'

Frowning, Amy recalled the brick through the window, and the disgusting slogans chalked on her front wall.

'Please, Amy,' entreated Violet. 'Just one night is all I ask. I won't be seein' 'im again.'

Amy ran a shrewd eye over her friend, a woman whose warm and loving heart was about to be broken for the second time if she wasn't very much mistaken. 'It's your room, Violet,' she said. 'And when have I ever imposed rules about visitors?'

'Thanks, Amy,' said Violet, hugging her.

'I'll make sure the children don't bother you.'

'You're a real pal.'

'Hadn't you better fetch him in before the poor bloke freezes to death outside?'

*   *   *

The fervent love of country that urged so many to give up their jobs and go to war was not exclusive to the male of the species. Many women were eager to do their bit by getting out of the home and taking over the jobs the fighting men had left behind. Women of all classes became taxi drivers, bus conductresses, chimney sweeps, or even undertakers. Many worked in munitions factories, making shells and bullets. Some even joined the armed forces, though they were not actually sent to the front line. The nickname given to upper-class women, 'the lilac and sun-bonnet brigade', soon disappeared when people saw how hard they worked.

Gwen Jackson, who had returned to her old job in the accounts department of Jackson & Cox after her marriage had broken up, was one of those who decided on a change of direction, though not to a masculine occupation.

'I've decided to leave the firm and train as a nurse,' she told Amy, one day just before Christmas when the latter happened to be in the accounts office with a query.

'Well, well, that's a surprise,' said Amy. 'But good for you.'

'They're desperately in need of people to look after the wounded soldiers,' explained Gwen. 'And I think I might be rather good at it.'

'I'm sure you will,' said Amy. 'We'll miss you around here though. You've always been so good at the job.'

Although Amy liked Gwen, she had never managed to get close to her even when they had been related. She was still a very private person, not cold exactly but distant. Now in her late-twenties, she was quite attractive but seemed intent upon disguising the fact. Since her marriage had ended she had dispensed with elaborate clothes in favour of drab browns and greys, taking full advantage of the plainer, easier-fitting clothes that many women were wearing now.

'Yes, I don't suppose my father will be too pleased, having lost so many of the staff already to the war.'

'You can bet he won't!'

'But it's something I feel I must do, regardless of any opposition,' Gwen explained. 'I want to be involved in the war effort. I mean, the jewellery trade can hardly be called essential at the present time, can it?'

'I suppose not,' said Amy with a wry grin.

'It's different for you,' Gwen continued, 'you've the children to look after, so you can't take on anything new that will demand all your time and energy. I've no ties. I can really commit myself to something like nursing.'

'So when are you leaving?' Amy asked.

'I'll stay until a replacement can be found for me.'

'Am I the first to know?'

She nodded. 'Though I've written to Ned about it, of course.'

'Yes, I suppose you would have,' said Amy thoughtfully, 'since you're such close friends.'

'That's right,' said Gwen, in a tone that did not invite enquiry.

'How is Ned?' asked Amy conversationally. 'In the last letter I had from him he was training down in Hampshire.'

'He's expecting to go to France quite soon, I think.'

'Oh God,' said Amy, her stomach turning over.

'My sentiments exactly,' said Gwen. 'All these reports of casualties . . . it makes you want to weep.'

'It does indeed.'

Seeing her own fears for Ned reflected in the other's eyes, Amy wondered again about the special bond that existed between Gwen and Ned. Might they get together as a couple after the war, now that they were both on their own?

'I wish you the best of luck with the nursing,' said Amy. 'I admire you enormously. I've not the stomach for it myself.'

'I won't know if I have until I start,' Gwen said, making a face. 'I hope I don't pass out at the first sight of blood.'

'You'll be all right once you get used to it.'

Private Bernie Banks was used to the sight of blood. He'd seen plenty of it since he'd been in France. In fact, many horrors that would have been inconceivable to him a few months ago were now taken for granted every day—such personal discomforts as sleeping in a muddy dugout in the side of a trench and being woken by rats nibbling his person, or playing host to lice who lived in his hair, on his body and in every crease of his clothing. Then there was the misery of having constantly wet feet; and the cacophony of shelling and gunfire punishing the ears for hour after hour; and always the fear of being hit. He must have been mad to get mixed up in this lot. If he'd known what it was going to be like, he wouldn't have gone within a mile of that blooming recruiting office. But the posters hadn't mentioned anything about trench foot and dysentery, or the permanent stench of excrement, urine, and the rotting flesh of dead men and horses. Or the agonising tension of long days in the trench waiting until it was time to go over the top into no man's land.

First light had come on this bitter cold February morning in a trench a few miles from Ypres. The sentries relaxed as the threat of a night raid from the enemy passed. Tired and stiff from staring into the daybreak, Bernie moved along the trench to collect some frozen snow to melt and use for a shave. Water, which was brought to the front in petrol cans, was always in short supply, especially for washing and shaving.

'Oh, bloody 'ell,' he cursed, finding the ice beneath the frozen snow blood-tinted and containing the stiff hand of a corpse, as he chipped a piece off.

'Whassa matta, Banksy?' asked Private Ginger Smith, peeling off a filthy wet sock to reveal a foot wrinkled from constant wetness.

'There's a bleedin' body in the ice over 'ere.'

'Poor bugger,' said Ginger. 'I wonder 'ow long he's been there?'

'Gawd knows,' said Bernie. 'It doesn't matter to 'im, does it? He ain't got no worries now.'

'Ugh! Better make sure the water for our tea don't come from that bit of ice,' said another soldier waggishly.

'Don't be so squeamish,' laughed Bernie. 'A dead tommy in yer tea'll do yer the world of good.'

Such obscene humour wasn't considered offensive in this uncouth male atmosphere where any reverence for death was destroyed by its sheer abundance. A few of the men laughed, those who could manage it, given that they were frozen to the bone. You either let the war drive you mad or you joked about it. Bernie's ability to remain comical under even the most atrocious circumstances made him popular with the other men. He couldn't let the lads know that the 'hard man' from the East End was shit-scared most of the time. They were a nice bunch of blokes, especially young Ginger, a thin eighteen year old from Tottenham. A bit too strait-laced for Bernie's civilian taste—he went to church of a Sunday, and all that sort of stuff—but he was a good mate for all that.

Having chipped through the ice to get the dead soldier's identity disc and handed it over to the sergeant, Bernie shovelled some topsoil over him until the ground softened sufficiently to bury him properly. Basic ablutions primitively completed, tea was brewed all along the trenches on little fires made up from scraps of wood collected from local ruins. The men breakfasted on bread and jam.

'Tickler's plum and apple jam. Well, strike me dead if that ain't a surprise,' said Bernie sarcastically, since that was the only flavour the men ever saw.

'At least it ain't cheese again,' said Ginger.

'That'll be on the menu later, Ginge, don't you worry.'

It was rumoured among the men that it was the tendency of cheese to cause constipation that made it such a regular feature of their diet, a deliberate ploy to ease the problem of trench latrines.

When they had finished eating there was the daily medical check, during which Bernie always hoped some disease would show itself and necessitate his immediate return to Blighty. As ever, this didn't happen and by mid-morning he was hard at work with the rest of his platoon, repairing damaged sections of the trench, filling sandbags, cleaning weapons and running errands up and down the trenches. These were deep enough for a man to walk without his head being seen and wide enough for soldiers to rest while others passed by. The soil dug out of the trench was piled in front to form a parapet as extra protection from enemy bullets. A man showing his head even for a second in daylight could be killed by snipers.

After a midday meal of tinned meat and bread, the men sat around smoking, playing cards or writing letters home. Then came the regular afternoon bombardment when the enemy attacked British trenches with shells and machine-guns. The earth shook and the air was thick with the din of explosions, the relentless crack of gunfire, the whining of shells and splinters whizzing by. Human moans and screams could be heard during lulls in the deafening commotion.

Pausing for a moment in his counter-fire with the machine-gun, Bernie felt the ground beneath him shudder from a distant dull thud which seemed to come from behind enemy lines. A mortar-gun being fired, he thought, and looking skywards saw a drum-shaped missile sailing through the air with a lighted fuse trailing behind it. His heart stopped and sweat poured down his back as he watched it heading directly towards them. There was no time to stop it or move out of its path. Shouting a warning to his mates, he dived to the duckboard floor of the trench.

The bomb crunched to the ground with an earth-shattering explosion, throwing Bernie some distance and knocking him out. When he came to he was lying against the inner wall of the trench with the other side collapsed around him. Men who had been his mates just a few minutes earlier now lay dead among the debris, staring sightlessly at him through the mud. Ginger was one of them. Bernie had thought he was immune to the sorrow of death. Wiping his eyes with his sleeve, he found he wasn't.

Gathering his wits, he used his hands as a shovel to scoop away the earth that was covering his legs. He'd had enough of this bloody lot and that was a fact. He'd work a Blighty somehow even if he had to shoot himself in the foot. Sitting there surrounded by carnage, with bombs smacking the ground all around him, he cheered himself with thoughts of home. He was glad he'd written to Amy. Letters as such were not allowed to go out from the front line troops but he'd sent one of the standard postcards to tell her he was well. He'd been thrilled to receive a reply. She hadn't actually said all was forgiven, but the mere fact that she'd answered was hopeful, he thought.

*   *   *

One evening in spring, at another part of the front, Lieutenant Ned Cox was in the officers' dug-out, stretched out on an iron bedframe that had been found among the ruins of a village, reading a letter from Amy. The small, cramped room, which was deeper in the ground than the main trench, was lit by a single candle-flame, undulating eerily over the mud walls and the wooden planks held up by timber posts which served as a roof. A pool of slimy water lay beneath the duckboard floor, and the smell of stagnation was suffocating. The officers with whom he shared these quarters were up the trench somewhere, so he was quite alone.

His eyes were so sore from lack of sleep he could hardly read the words in the dim, flickering light. He had barely slept for days and when he did drop into an exhausted coma it was usually disturbed by nightmares about the recent attack on Neuve-Chapelle when they had sustained heavy losses. The offensive had been a success, they had broken through German lines, then everything had stopped. Orders had failed to get through; field telephones didn't work. The Germans had had time to move some machine guns into position and stop the British advancing any further. There were no shells left with which to destroy the machine guns. Thousands of men were killed and injured. As an officer, Ned felt the heavy burden of responsibility, something that had befallen him as a result of his public school education.

'We are all quite well here,' Amy wrote. 'In fact life

312

goes on pretty much as normal despite various restrictions and staff shortages. I want to introduce some war work into the business, but I'd better not go into detail or this letter might not get through to you. I think Ralph is feeling his age. He seems tired and doesn't come into the shop so often. I run the Ealing branch when he isn't here. Bernie and my brother Alfie are in France somewhere. Gwen is training as a nurse in a London hospital so I don't see much of her. But she'll have written and told you all about that. The children are growing like weeds...'

His reading was interrupted by the appearance of Sergeant Parry through the rubberised gas curtain that served as a door.

'A spot o' trouble above, sir,' he said. 'It's Private Biggs.'

Instantly alert despite his fatigue, Ned stuffed the letter into his pocket and followed the sergeant up the steps past the sentry and into the main trench, towards the unmistakable sounds of a disturbance.

Private Peter Biggs was nineteen years old and a good soldier, popular with the men and not normally one to shirk his duty. Until just recently. Now he was crouched in his dug-out with his head in his arms, weeping.

'He's due to go on sentry duty, sir,' explained the sergeant.

'He's turned yeller,' said one of the other men, and there was a ripple of angry agreement.

Ned had seen this sort of behaviour before after a run of long periods of heavy shelling. Personally he thought it was a medical condition, but it wasn't recognised as such by the army who considered it to be mere cowardice.

'Come on now, Biggs,' said Ned sternly. 'You're

313

upsetting your mates.'

'I can't stand any more, I can't,' sobbed the poor, demented man, shivering violently.

'On your feet, man,' said Ned.

He didn't respond.

'You know what the army does to men who fail in their duty,' said Ned, hating himself for carrying out orders.

'Please help me, sir,' snivelled the soldier, holding his head. 'In God's name, somebody help me.'

'I can't do anything for you while you stay huddled in that hole.'

'Come out, coward,' jeered one of the other battle-weary men.

Biggs crawled out of the hole. His whole body was trembling as though he was about to have an epileptic fit. Ned wished he would. Then he could declare him unfit and have him sent for treatment.

But he seemed to calm down suddenly. He stood up straight, brushed himself off and made his way towards his position on watch. Considering the immediate crisis to be over, Ned turned and headed back to his dug-out, for his legs were threatening to cave in with weariness. As he began to walk away he heard a scuffle and swung round to see Private Biggs scrambling up the trench wall. The young soldier stood at the top in full view of the enemy. Within seconds he slithered back in a lifeless heap, an obvious victim of suicide.

There was a stunned silence among the men. Well, at least the poor soul is at peace now, Ned thought as he went towards the corpse. But he doubted if that would be of much consolation to the young soldier's mother. With the necessary duties performed, Ned returned to the dug-out and continued reading his

314

letter.

Quite a lot of chit-chat about the children. Then: 'We have the easy part here at home, it's you boys I feel sorry for. It's probably my fault that you're out there, Ned. If I hadn't dragged you to the music hall that night . . . Anyway, let's hope you'll soon be safely home. I'm thinking of you, and looking forward to seeing you again.'

He was unexpectedly stirred by the letter. Affection for Amy washed over him in a poignant tide. He wanted to write her a proper letter telling her what was really going on in France. He wanted to bare his soul to her about poor Biggs and the thousands of brave young men who were eliminated like vermin every day. But even if that was permitted, he knew he would want to spare her from knowledge of the carnage that would have been unimaginable to him before the war. Somehow he knew these horrors would stay locked inside him, even if he did have the good fortune to get back to Blighty.

During the long days at the front, thoughts of Molly's death had filled his mind till he nearly went crazy. Lately they had lessened. Now he was thinking of Amy, and wanting to see her again. He wondered if he ever would. Home seemed an impossible dream when there was a very strong possibility you wouldn't live through the next day. She mentioned Bernie, so they were obviously in touch. Perhaps they'd get back together again after the war. The possibility depressed him.

Disturbed by recollections of the incident with Private Biggs, he put the letter aside. Perhaps if he had handled the situation differently, the poor boy would be alive now? But what else could he have done? Choice was limited when you were acting under orders. And it had all happened so fast.

Reaction to having a letter from home and the horror of the Biggs affair culminated in a flood of uncontrollable emotion. Shamefully, he turned to the wall to hide the tears that rolled down his cheeks. Perhaps they should shoot me for the crime of compassion? he thought, as he drifted into an exhausted sleep, unaware of a fat grey rat scampering over him.

*　　*　　*

A public outcry followed the sinking of the transatlantic liner *Lusitania* which was torpedoed by the Germans in a deliberate attempt to cut Britain off. Over a thousand people were drowned, many of them women and children. Anti-German feeling was renewed, bringing a fresh wave of violence to the streets of London.

'A mob over Stepney way dragged a German-born baker from 'is shop and set fire to it,' reported Gladys one Sunday afternoon in May when Amy and the children were visiting.

'Why, that's dreadful,' declared Amy hotly. 'None of us can help where we were born. It's all just an accident of nature.'

'We can stay put where we belong, though,' said her father aggressively.

'That sort of talk only helps to fuel the violence,' countered Amy.

'You wanna watch what yer sayin', my girl,' snapped her father, whipping himself up into a fever of prejudice. 'Specially since yer brother is out in France fighting the Hun.'

'Blame the politicians for the war, Dad, not some

316

poor baker in Stepney,' said Amy. 'Ordinary German people don't want war any more than we do.'

'You'd better not let the people round 'ere 'ear you talk like that,' warned her mother. 'A lot of 'em 'ave sons at the front.'

The neighbourhood to which her mother was referring was no longer Tucker Street, for Gladys and George had gone up in the world. Encouraged and financially assisted by Amy and Alfie, they had moved to a pleasant flat with a proper kitchen and bathroom in a block on the outskirts of Bethnal Green, towards Bow. Amy still subsidised them but it was no longer as vital as it had once been because the war had brought a general improvement to their finances. For the first time in his life George was earning regular money, on war-work in a factory, as were Bobby and Pete, who were now in their teens. Gladys did her bit for her country by working in a factory canteen.

'Don't worry, I won't cause trouble for you with your neighbours,' she assured them. 'Even though what I say is true.'

'Maybe it is, but we *are* at war with the Germans when all is said and done.' Gladys was thoughtful for a moment. 'O' course, that maid of yours was goin' out with a German, wasn't she? What happened to 'im?'

'I've no idea, that was all over ages ago.'

'Good job an' all,' said George.

'Does she still talk about him?' asked Gladys.

'Never mentions him,' said Amy.

'Well, fancy that,' said Gladys.

Amy had been surprised by the suddenness with which Violet had put the matter behind her. After

317

spending that one night with Karl, she had behaved as though the affair had not happened, never once even mentioning his name. Obviously her way of coping, Amy assumed.

'Where are Bobby and Pete?' asked Amy.

'Out somewhere with their mates,' said Gladys.

How times had changed since she had left home, Amy thought. No screaming babies, no chaos, no filthy smells and disgusting conditions. Even her own children had gone to Victoria Park and left the adults to chatter in peace. She glanced round the living room, cluttered but cosy, with easy-chairs and rugs and a comfortable sofa.

There was a knock at the door. 'That will be the children back from the park,' said Amy, leaving the room to let them in.

'Oh!' She froze at the sight of a young messenger boy waving an envelope towards her. She took it with a shaking hand, her legs turning to jelly. 'Just a minute, son.' She went, trance-like, into the living room to get a penny with which to pay him.

Her mother turned very pale when she saw the envelope. She snatched it from Amy and flicked it at George as though it was burning her fingers. They all knew what was inside. When Amy came back from paying the messenger, both parents were staring at the contents of the envelope in silence. Grey-faced and trembling, her father handed it to Amy.

'... my painful duty to inform you ... Private Alfred George Atkins killed in action...'

Newspaper reports of mass slaughter across the Channel should have prepared them. But nothing could. There wasn't a breath or a rustle in the room as all three of them stood in shocked silence trying to take it in. Eventually Gladys muttered something about making tea and walked woodenly towards the kitchen.

Her movement seemed to be the catalyst to send George into action and he turned on Amy in a ferocious rage. 'Not so keen to stick up for the Germans now they've killed yer brother, eh, Amy?'

'Dad, please,' she said, going to him. 'Don't upset yourself even more.'

'Hun bastards,' he growled, barely seeming to notice her arms going around him.

'Now, Dad, that sort of talk won't bring him back,' said Amy, trying to soothe him. 'It'll only make you feel worse.'

But his suffering blinded him to reason. 'Bleedin' Germans,' he growled viciously. 'Don't you dare to defend them in my 'ouse, I won't 'ave it, do you understand?'

'I wasn't . . .'

'They killed my boy,' he ranted.

'Come on, George,' said Gladys, reappearing with a tray of tea. 'It's no use passin' blame.' She placed the tray on the table and poured the tea with slow heavy movements. ''Ere, drink this.' She handed both her husband and Amy a cup of tea, then sat down on the sofa and began to sob quietly and helplessly, talking through her tears. ''E was always a good boy, my Alfie, never got into no trouble, always kind to 'is mother.' She blew her nose. 'My boy died for 'is country and I'm proud of 'im.'

Seeming calmed by his wife's outburst, George sat down beside her, slipping a comforting arm around her shoulders, tears running down his own leathery cheeks.

Gladys looked up at Amy, who was standing over them crying openly. 'We shan't 'alf miss 'im.'

'I know.'

''Ow are we ever gonna get used to it, Amy?'

'I don't know, Mum,' sobbed Amy. 'But we've got each other.'

A loud knocking at the front door, accompanied by the sound of childish laughter, indicated that Connie and the boys had returned from the park. In this grief-stricken atmosphere it was a welcome sound indeed, a reminder of life and hope for the future. At the door, Amy gathered them into her arms and thanked God for them.

'Not too much noise,' she whispered. 'Granny and Grandad are upset, we've had some bad news...'

Before she could finish the sentence her mother appeared in the hall on her way to the kitchen. 'Wotcha, kids,' she said, her voice still thick but composed now. 'You 'ad a good time down the park?'

'Yes thanks, Gran.'

'You'll be wantin' some tea.'

'Yeah, we're starvin',' said Dickie.

'Have we got winkles?' asked Connie.

'No, jellied eels today, ducks,' said Gladys. 'And a nice bit of seed cake for after.'

'I'll get the tea ready, Mum,' offered Amy kindly. 'You go and sit down.'

'Sittin' about ain't my way,' said Gladys. 'Not when me grandchildren 'ave come to visit me, anyway.'

'But, Mum...'

'Stop fussin', Amy, and go and lay the table,' said Gladys, her strength already returning. 'And you kids go and see yer grandad. He needs cheerin' up and you're just the people to do it.'

Amy didn't argue. The children would be told

320

about Alfie all in good time. Right now she watched her mother resolutely set about the task of coming to terms with her loss.

CHAPTER SIXTEEN

The war dragged on and the slaughter continued. Trainloads of casualties poured into London every day, overcrowding the hospitals and forcing the government to appropriate other buildings to accommodate the injured men. As the real cost of the war began to become apparent, men were less keen to join up. It became clear to the government that the heavy British losses could not be replaced by volunteers alone.

'As if we haven't lost enough men to the war,' fumed Ralph one day early in 1916 at a directors' meeting, 'now they're going to take them whether they want to go or not. Conscription. Bah!'

'Count yourself lucky you're too old to be called up,' said Amy. 'Our problems are nothing to what the boys out there are having to put up with.'

'I know that,' he said. 'But it doesn't alter the fact that we do have to try to stay in business.'

Despite her attempts to keep a sense of proportion, Amy could anticipate the devastating effect this new legislation would have on the jewellery trade, which had been plagued by various government restrictions since early in the war. Not only were gold and other metals severely rationed, but all stocks of platinum had been ordered to be returned for use in munitions. A ban on the importation of unset diamonds caused problems too but it was only one of many.

It was clear to Amy that if they did not diversify in some way they would be forced to close. No one could pretend that jewellery was an essential commodity in these terrible times. So why not turn the business over in part to something that was, until things got better? And help the national effort in the process. Many of their contemporaries had gone out of business. Amy was determined that was not going to happen to Jackson & Cox, and having taken the trouble to keep up to date with what was happening in the trade, could see no reason why it should—not with a little innovation on their part. They had one big asset, Mr Burridge, who was over conscription age and therefore around to teach the untrained staff they now employed in the workshop.

'And to make sure that we do,' said Amy in reply to Ralph, 'I suggest we make a few changes.'

'Huh, we've done nothing else since the war started,' he said.

'Too true,' agreed Harold.

'Mmm, well, now I think it's time for something a bit more drastic.'

'Go on,' sighed Ralph wearily.

'To help solve the problem of staff, I suggest we use women and disabled soldiers in the workshop. Some of the wounded men discharged from the army are in need of a new occupation. Ours is light work and Mr Burridge is a good teacher.'

Ralph and Harold looked doubtful. 'And what will we give them to do if we can't get sufficient materials either to carry out repairs or make jewellery?' asked Harold.

'We turn the workshop over to the war effort.'

The two men stared at her in baffled silence.

'The Ministry of Munitions is looking for people

to make gauges for guns,' she announced. 'The machinery jewellers use can easily be adapted for this. Indeed some jewellery firms are already using their workshops for it. With a few minor alterations to our equipment, there is no reason why we shouldn't join them.'

'Yes, I heard something about that,' said Ralph, stroking his chin thoughtfully, 'but it's too complicated. Burridge is a jewellery craftsman, not a gun maker.'

'I'm sure he'll be only too happy to adapt,' she said. 'There *is* a war on, after all.'

'But he doesn't know how to make gauges,' Harold pointed out.

'The Ministry will show him, and he can teach the others.'

Both men were dubious. 'Are you suggesting we close down the jewellery side altogether, until after the war?' asked Harold.

'No,' she explained. 'We keep going in the same reduced way we have since the restrictions began, but we turn a large section of our workshop over to munitions.'

The two older men were still not convinced. They were of an age to find change difficult whereas Amy, who was still not yet thirty, saw it only as a stimulating challenge.

'I'll get it all organised,' she said. 'But obviously I won't make a move without your agreement.'

Ralph and Harold exchanged uncertain glances.

'It's the only sensible thing to do,' she said.

'We'd better get started on it then, I suppose,' said Ralph, rather reluctantly.

'Yes,' agreed Harold.

Preparations for the big push had been going on for months. Bernie had been sent home on leave to rest, and on his return had spent some time well back behind the lines where he and the other troops had been fully briefed. Now, during the night, he marched with his platoon towards the front. Although burdened by sticky mud underfoot and the weight of their packs, the men kept up a smart pace, singing 'It's a Long Way to Tipperary' accompanied by someone in the line playing a mouth organ.

Looking into the distance ahead of him, Bernie could see tongues of flame from the explosions of British shells piercing the blackness. Staff cars containing officers rolled past, overtaken by despatch riders on their motor bikes. From far away the rumble of the preliminary bombardment could be heard. Boom ... boom ... thud ... crunch. The lengthily planned offensive on the Western Front was about to begin in the valley of the River Somme in Picardy, and men were gathering in their thousands.

Winding in single file through the communication trench towards the front, Bernie felt the onset of the usual pre-combat stomach gripes. He calmed himself by remembering how simple the officers had made this attack seem. All he had to do, at the appointed time, was to climb over the trench parapet and advance at walking pace across no man's land towards the Germans, with about another thousand men formed into a line. His wave was to be just one of many that would advance towards the enemy in this way.

According to the platoon officer the Germans and

their trenches would have been thoroughly blasted by the bombardment and their barbed wire destroyed, leaving the way clear for the troops. The job sounded like a piece of cake to Bernie.

The morning dawned bright and sunny. 'Nice day for it, lads,' he said to his mates as the first wave of men went over and Bernie's platoon moved forward. 'Who needs a day out at Brighton, when you can 'ave a picnic by the river in the sun?'

There was a ripple of nervous laughter. Some of the boys were just over from England, fresh-faced and eager. Some of them didn't even look old enough to shave. The sky was clear and in the post-bombardment silence he heard the cheep and twitter of the birds flying above the trenches. In civvy street the nearest Bernie ever came to feeling close to nature was when he fed the pigeons in Trafalgar Square. Now, with his nerves stretched to breaking point, the sound pierced his senses with bittersweet clarity. It brought to mind the birdsong in Victoria Park, reminding him that beyond this life of misery and terror, a normal world still existed. The sour pains in his stomach turned to bowel-watering fear as they took the final steps towards no man's land. Each carrying equipment weighing almost seventy pounds, the men waited for the order to go over the top.

In the dread of the moment, Bernie found himself wishing he'd had the courage to put a bullet through his foot. He'd have been shot if they'd proved he'd done it on purpose, of course, but at least he'd have been out of this bloody lot. He was sick and tired of being cold, wet, muddy and afraid. In the absence of any alternative, however, when his turn came he scrambled over the parapet with the rest.

Even the most battle-hardened soldier would have been shocked by the horror that greeted them as they trudged across the war-torn wasteland towards enemy lines. What was left of the men who had gone before littered the ground; thousands of blood-stained khaki bundles. Those still alive groaned and screamed with the agony of their wounds. Bernie saw limbs and heads blown off, and could feel nothing, his senses deadened by the carnage around him. And all he could do was obey orders and walk on through the smoke-filled valley towards the guns.

The barbed wire was littered with dead soldiers, some strewn across it, others heaped alongside like piles of old clothes. Countless numbers of them. There's been a cock-up somewhere along the line, he thought, just before a sharp pain pricked at his leg somewhere around the knee.

Feeling strangely off balance, he looked down and was bemused to see a bullet hole in his trouser leg through which blood was gushing. 'Gor blimey, they've got me bleedin' knee,' he muttered, before he fell to the ground, writhing in agony and eventually blacking out.

What Bernie and the rest of the British Army hadn't known was that their 'secret' plans had been known to the Germans for some time, and so they had been expecting them...

*   *   *

Life was hectic for Amy as the gauge manufacture got underway. About three-quarters of the workshop was used for this and the remainder kept for repairs, mostly of clocks, watches and barometers. Jewellery stock was in short supply but they kept the retail side going with what they could get from the wholesalers and operating with much less staff than in pre-war days. The workforce throughout the shop and workshop consisted of women, men who had come out of retirement, and a couple of disabled soldiers.

Amy was forced to spend more time at the shop to cope with the heavy workload. Between this and the children, every second of her day was accounted for and she fell into bed at night exhausted. It was during this frantic period, one day in August, that she received a letter from Bernie who was in a hospital near Barking in Essex. Her initial alarm was tempered by the tone of the letter which was cheerful and bore no reference to any serious injury. Thinking he must be suffering from some sort of battle fatigue, she decided to visit him the following Sunday; the very least she could do for someone who had been away fighting for his country, she thought.

*   *   *

The military hospital was actually the converted recreation hall of a soap factory, a wooden pavilion set in spacious grounds with lawns and flowerbeds. It was a light, airy-looking building with plenty of windows, and a verandah along the front which was crowded with beds and wheelchairs in which patients were taking advantage of the sunshine.

London was full of wounded soldiers so Amy was used to seeing them struggling about on crutches, bandaged and disfigured. But she was completely unprepared for the shock of seeing so much suffering at close range. Everywhere there were broken bodies; minds destroyed by shell shock; missing limbs; eyes peering blindly through bandages; men with scarred tissue replacing part of a face. Young men in the prime of life were being fed like geriatrics because they had no hands with which to do the job themselves.

The wooden floor of the reception area was highly polished but the smell of carbolic overpowered the scent of wax. To Amy's shame her knees began to shake and she had a powerful urge to leave without even seeing Bernie. Her skin felt damp and clammy as a feeling of faintness engulfed her. Oh God, don't let me disgrace myself, she prayed silently, nausea tightening her jaws. The squeak of rubber soles and the swish of starched skirts heralded the appearance of a nurse who was asked with a degree of urgency as to the location of a ladies' cloakroom, to which Amy speedily departed and was violently sick.

'Feeling better?' she asked when Amy re-emerged looking slightly less grey-faced.

'Yes, thank you. I'm sorry,' she said. 'I'm so ashamed.'

'There's no need, my dear,' the nurse assured her briskly. 'None of us can help the way nature takes us. I've known strong men faint clean away the minute they step inside a hospital.'

Amy introduced herself.

'Ah, yes,' said the nurse who informed Amy that she was a ward sister. 'Has Bernie told you the nature of his injury, Mrs Banks?'

'Injury?' She felt alarmed. 'I assumed there was nothing seriously wrong in as much as he didn't say so ... he'd have mentioned it if there was anything awful ... wouldn't he?'

'Probably couldn't bring himself to mention it in a letter. Some accept their disablement quicker than others.'

'Disablement?'

'His left leg was so badly damaged from a bullet wound, we had to amputate,' the nurse explained calmly. 'Just above the knee.'

'Oh God!' The shock and the mental image this information evoked made her feel queasy again. 'Poor Bernie.'

'You'll need to be patient with him when he comes home, my dear,' said the ward sister. 'These men have been through an awful lot. You'll probably find he won't be the man you knew at all, for a while at least.'

'Bernie doesn't live with me,' she explained. 'We're separated.'

'Oh, I see,' said the nurse with undisguised concern. 'Well, let's take you to see him. He's out in the sunshine at the back.'

Bracing herself, Amy followed her down a corridor, through a ward and out on to a paved terrace where Bernie, dressed in the blue hospital uniform, was sitting in a wheelchair. He was staring vacantly across the garden which was dotted with wounded soldiers and their visitors, some being pushed in their chairs, others with limbs intact taking a stroll.

He was so deeply engrossed in thought, he didn't notice her approaching so she was able to study him for a moment, unobserved. To her relief he looked quite well. He was much thinner than before the war, but she was prepared for that because he'd been very skinny when he'd paid her a visit when he was home on leave. His cheekbones protruded slightly with the loss of weight, but he was tanned from sitting in the sun and his dark hair was combed neatly into place.

The thing that struck her most was the fact that he was sitting alone, even though there were several other soldiers nearby chatting and laughing in groups. That wasn't like him at all.

'Hello, Bernie,' she said, bending down and kissing his cheek.

'Wotcha, Amy,' he said, looking up and grinning, though his eyes remained dull. 'Thanks for comin', love.'

'It's good to see you,' she said.

Having said she would arrange for some tea to be brought to them, the sister made a diplomatic exit.

'Take a pew,' he said, pointing to a chair nearby.

She handed him a bag of fruit and some cigarettes.

'Ta very much,' he said, putting them down on a table beside him.

'I'm sorry about your leg,' she said.

'Oh, that.'

'Why didn't you mention it in your letter?'

'Dunno. P'rhaps I didn't wanna put you off comin'.'

'As if it would.'

He looked down at his left trouser leg, hanging loose and empty. 'I won't be a complete cripple,' he said. They're gonna give me an artificial one.'

'You'll be running circles around us all then,' she teased.

'Me mates'll be envious,' he said in an attempt at humour. 'Those who ain't dead.'

'Envious?'

'At me copping a Blighty,' he explained. 'I wished for one often enough.' He gave a wry grin. 'It ain't quite 'ow I imagined it, but at least I won't 'ave to go back.'

'It's an ill wind then.'

In all the years Amy had known Bernie, she had never felt awkward in his company. Angry perhaps,

330

preoccupied maybe, or even bored occasionally. But *never* awkward. Now, for the first time, she simply didn't know what to say.

A pretty young nurse appeared with a tray of tea and cakes. 'This is Maisie,' he said, with resolute brightness. 'Ain't she a sight for sore eyes?'

Amy smiled uncertainly.

'We're gonna run off together when I get me new leg, ain't that right, ducks?'

'Go on with you,' the nurse said, blushing. 'You men are all talk. You'd run a mile if I took you up on it.'

'I'd have a job, wouldn't I?' he said with an empty laugh.

Superficially the same waggishness was there but all the old spark had gone. Losing a leg was sure to have a psychological effect, but Amy sensed something else . . .

The nurse trotted away, and Amy poured the tea. Bernie's cup rattled in the saucer as he held it, his shakiness seeming incongruous in someone who had always been so confident. Amy ached with compassion for him. He asked after the children and the business, and they indulged in polite, stilted conversation which Amy found exhausting. She longed to get away but didn't want to hurt his feelings by leaving too soon. Unfortunately, because most of the men were a long way from home, there didn't seem to be any time limit for visitors. Eventually she said, 'Well, I'd better be making tracks. It's quite a long journey back to Ealing.'

'Yeah, o' course,' he said, 'I'm really glad yer came. Seein' yer 'as been a real treat.'

And guessing what he wanted to hear, she said, 'I'll come again next Sunday, if you like.'

331

'Ta, Amy, I'd love that,' he said.

She visited regularly after that, and hoped he didn't mistake kindness for encouragement. For, although he hadn't said as much, she suspected he still wanted a reconciliation. She was fond of him, for all his faults, and felt a sense of responsibility towards him in his vulnerable state which would never allow her to desert him. But the last thing she wanted was to try again with something that was doomed to failure. The only reason she hadn't done anything about a divorce was because it was so difficult. A woman couldn't even divorce her husband for adultery, so she doubted if the courts would consider theft sufficient grounds.

A few weeks later, her fears were confirmed. 'They say I can leave 'ere soon,' he said. 'How about my coming back to your place? I don't fancy the idea of bein' on me own, even if I did 'ave anywhere to go.'

Amy knew she must be honest rather than hurt him later on. 'You want to give our marriage another try, is that what you mean?' she asked.

'Well...' he said hopefully.

'It wouldn't work, Bernie,' she said firmly. 'Too much has happened.'

'If we both tried hard...'

'No, it's over, we can't bring it back,' she stated categorically.

'Oh, I see. Well, 'ow about letting me stay for a while anyway? I'd sleep in the spare room.' He gave a small dry laugh. 'I wouldn't bother you. Me leg ain't the only thing that's bin buggered. Shrapnel splinters ... yer know.'

'Oh God, Bernie,' she cried, her eyes moistening with pity. 'I would never refuse you a home, you know that, but anything more...'

'I just want somewhere to go till I get on me feet again.'

Feeling cornered, she told herself that she owed him nothing after the way he had behaved. But she knew it wasn't true. She couldn't turn away from a friend of such long standing.

His dark eyes looked beseechingly into hers. 'I need you, Amy.'

'All right, you can come back,' she said gently. 'And welcome.'

*   *   *

To give Bernie his due, he made no demands on her beyond companionship, but his presence in the house was a strain. He was a changed man. Not self-pitying exactly, but preoccupied and jumpy. All the old swagger had been stripped away, leaving a quiet, nervous person. Even when he could confidently get about with his artificial leg, he didn't seem to want to go far from the house. Sometimes his stump was too sore for him to bear the false limb against it and he had to revert to crutches. He made jokes about it, and laughingly referred to himself as a Pegleg, but he was very sensitive about the contraption itself. One Sunday, when he had not been home long, Amy had gone into his room not realising he was there. The leg with its harness and strapping was lying on the floor beside the bed where he was taking an afternoon nap. He had flown into a rage and told her never to come into his room without knocking first.

He was keen to pay his way, which he did with his army disability pension. In the mornings he sometimes limped down to the Broadway with his stick for cigarettes and a newspaper, and the rest of his day was spent sitting around smoking, reading the paper or lying on his bed. The children soon sensed that his heart wasn't in any attempts to have fun with them, and his status became more one of a distant uncle than the pal he had once been to them.

Time passed and the war went on. The numbers of casualties from the front continued to rise. On the home front too there were civilian deaths from air raids. German submarines made the importing of food difficult and as the reserve supplies began to run out, food queues appeared. The grain shortage led to the introduction of 'standard bread' which was made from flour mixed with powdered potatoes or beans, and was grey in colour.

And still Bernie showed no signs of reverting back to his old self.

'Why don't you go and see your mates in the East End?' Amy would frequently suggest, in an effort to perk him up.

'Those who ain't dead are away fightin',' was his reply. Or, 'I ain't in the mood.'

The restrictive nature of his presence in her life really came home to her one day in the summer of 1917 when Ned Cox called to see her whilst home on leave, and she realised for certain that her feelings for him had not just been a passing fancy. She wondered if he might have grown to love her if things had worked out differently.

'Sorry about the leg,' said Ned, as the three of them drank tea in the parlour.

Bernie shrugged. 'There's a lot worse off than me, mate.'

'How are you managing with the false one?'

'Mustn't grumble. Me stump aches and burns a bit sometimes, but I manage. I ain't got no choice, 'ave

I?'

'Not really, no.'

'When you going back?' asked Bernie.

'In a couple of days.'

'I suppose this leave means you'll be on something big when you go back.'

'Yes, that's right.'

Amy thought Ned looked terrible. He was thin and grey and his eyes had the same hollow look as Bernie's. The two men behaved as though they were close friends, yet they had never been particularly friendly before the war. Drawn together by shared experience, she thought. Horrific experience too, by all accounts. And the authorities could no longer pretend otherwise now that the wounded were back to tell the truth.

Not that she ever learned anything about the front from Bernie. He clammed up the minute the subject was mentioned. And Ned wasn't exactly painting a picture.

The conversation became general. They discussed the business. Amy mentioned Gwen's new career.

'Taken to nursing like a duck to water,' said Ned. 'I think she's found her true vocation. Gwen has a lot to give.'

When it was time for him to leave, Amy showed him to the door. 'You've patched things up with Bernie then?' he said.

'I couldn't refuse him a home when he came back disabled,' she said.

'No, of course not.'

She didn't feel able to tell him the truth about her celibate relationship with Bernie without being disloyal. Nor could she tell him the truth about her feelings for himself without embarrassing him, so she

335

just said, 'He's not the man he used to be, by any means.'

'He'll improve with time, perhaps.'

'I hope so. We'll just have to see how it goes.'

'Goodbye, Amy.'

'Goodbye, Ned,' she said, reaching up and kissing his cheek. 'And good luck.'

He took long strides down her front path, a lean, upright figure, his uniform looking well on him. He seemed so terribly alone, somehow. Amy wanted to run after him and kiss away that haunted, lost look. But she waited until he had turned the corner and then went back inside, stopping before rejoining Bernie to brush the tears from her eyes.

* * *

About the only thing Amy could persuade Bernie to leave Ealing for these days was to pay a duty visit to his father in Bethnal Green. They usually made a day of it. Amy and the children would spend the time with her parents while Bernie went to see Mr Banks Senior. Bernie would join her for tea with Gladys and George and they would catch a train home quite late in the evening.

One Sunday in the autumn their routine was alarmingly disturbed.

They were just getting their coats on to go home when the thud, thud, thud of the maroons sounded. They were all used to air raids, especially Gladys and George who had bombs fall much closer to home than their visitors, being nearer to the docks. So no one flew into a panic. In fact the children were quite excited at the prospect of being closer to the action than they were at home and rushed to the window,

336

thrilled to have a third-floor view. The adults turned off the lights and gathered with them, looking out over the town rooftops, silver in the moonlight which was very bright tonight.

'Cor, look at that,' said Dickie, impressed by the pencil-slim beams of the searchlights traversing the navy blue sky above a red glow on the horizon from enemy fires.

'Ooh, look at the fireworks,' said Connie innocently, as sparks and flames from exploding bombs shot upwards.

Thuds and bangs shook the building. Gunfire cracked reassuringly around them.

'If it seems like a bad one, we'll go downstairs to Mrs Daly on the ground floor,' said Gladys.

'Can we go now, Gran?' asked Victor, looking pale.

'Scaredy cat,' taunted the fearless Dickie.

'That's enough of that,' rebuked Amy, slipping a comforting arm around the shivering Victor. 'And, yes, I think it would be safer downstairs.'

'Oh, let's stay and watch, Mum,' begged Dickie. 'We won't be able to see anything from down there.'

The entertainment value of the raid ended abruptly as a cigar-shaped aircraft loomed over them in the sky. There was no time for action before a harsh whistling sound preceded an explosion so violent it shook the house and rattled the windows. Amy pushed the children on to the floor and flung herself down on top of them. Several other explosions followed as the Zeppelin shed its lethal load, probably meant for the docks.

In the silence that followed no one moved. Then Amy heard the slow, uneven plod and tap of Bernie walking across the room with his stick.

337

'Come on, on your feet and downstairs, the lot of you,' he said in an aggressive tone.

'We'll all be killed,' said Victor, sobbing with fear.

'Don't talk daft, boy,' said Bernie commandingly, ushering everyone ahead of him to the door. 'Get downstairs and don't 'ang about.'

Amy saw them all out of the flat and turned at the door to wait for Bernie. 'Don't wait for me, yer daft cow,' he said. 'You know 'ow slow I am on the stairs with this bleedin' leg.'

'I can't leave you here...'

'Go with your children, woman,' he yelled, afraid for her safety. 'Go on, I'll see yer down there.'

But he didn't appear, and when Amy went looking for him, during a lull, she found him sitting in a chair by the fire as though nothing more threatening than a shower of rain was happening outside.

'Why didn't you come down, Bernie?' she asked. 'I've been worried.'

'I'd rather stay 'ere. If the bombs get me they do,' he said. 'I've done enough dodgin' the Hun. I ain't doin' no more.'

He couldn't tell Amy that the close proximity of the explosions and gunfire put him back on the battlefields so vividly he could feel the fear and smell the death. It tore his nerves to such an extent he feared he would lose control. Better he was alone when he felt like this, just in case. He'd seen men snap at the front, and he wouldn't want Amy and the children to see him like that.

'You don't mind being on your own?'

'Course not.'

'I'll have to go ... the kids.'

'Yeah, get downstairs with 'em sharpish.'

Alone again, he stared into the fire. He knew

338

people were saying he'd changed, that he didn't make them laugh any more. They were right. Everything had seemed different when he'd come home after the Somme. He'd felt quiet and peculiar inside. Nothing had seemed important since then; nothing had seemed funny. He supposed something must have happened to his nervous system.

When the explosions finally petered out and the gunfire stopped in the early hours, they all trooped back upstairs. The children were put to sleep in Gladys and George's bed because they were too tired to make the journey home. Gladys made tea and the adults drank it, staring wearily out of the window where fires still burned on the skyline.

'Well, we're all still 'ere,' said Gladys, yawning and flopping into an armchair, 'I thought we'd 'ad our lot at one point.'

'Some poor buggers have caught it, though, that's for sure,' said George.

*　　　*　　　*

Indeed they had. And one of those 'poor buggers' was Harold Cox. The news came through the next day, casting a cloud over the Ealing shop.

'His house took a direct hit, apparently,' Ralph told Amy gravely, having heard about it from the manager of the Shepherds Bush branch. 'The whole place is in ruins. They say he wouldn't have felt a thing, so I suppose that's one blessing.'

'Poor Harold,' said Amy.

'Indeed.'

'And poor Ned.'

'Yes, Ned will have to be told,' said Ralph, scratching his head worriedly. 'Can't have him coming home on his next leave to such a shock. I'll ask Gwen to write to him, she's closer to him than anyone.'

CHAPTER SEVENTEEN

It was another filthy night. The wind and rain lashed across the muddy swamplands of Flanders, beating against the troops as they huddled in their flooded shell holes. Soaked and sick with cold, many were suffering with feverish chills and coughs. Ned himself had a sore throat and streaming nose. He had been at the front for three years, on and off, and had thought he was immune to misery and degradation. But here on the battlefields near Passchendaele, human endurance was pushed to incredible extremes.

Relentless rainstorms and constant bombardments had turned the ground into a crater-filled bog. Soldiers fell into the mire and were sucked out of sight. Horses and guns disappeared in this honeycomb of ponds and deep chasms filled with slimy mud. There were only about fifteen of his company left. Of the others, those who hadn't fallen victim to the Germans had drowned in the slime. The survivors were in this water-logged hollow with him, or shivering on the banks of nearby cavities. Somehow, they seemed to have become isolated from the main battle. Exactly what his position was at this moment Ned wasn't sure, just that they were a few miles from the lower slopes of Passchendaele Ridge. He'd seen the outline of the outcrop in the distance before dark.

In his pocket was a letter from Gwen informing

him of the death of his father. It had been there since they last had any mail through, about a week ago, and still Ned was unaffected by the news. It was as though he had no capacity left with which to care about anything beyond this death-ridden swamp littered with bloated, decomposing bodies. Personal discomfort had become the norm. He couldn't remember the last time he had been warm or dry. His bones ached and his eyes smarted from fatigue and gunsmoke.

He and the men were resting here for the night, before pushing on tomorrow towards the Ridge. Their captain hadn't been seen for days. Ned assumed he was dead. They hadn't had any rations up for ages so were managing with hard biscuits and Oxo cubes dissolved in cold water. One of the men was waging a personal war against nature by trying to light a fire with some damp brushwood to heat some rainwater for tea. Some were smoking silently, others talking in low voices.

Snippets from Gwen's letter ran through his mind. 'It's fallen to me to tell you, Ned dear . . . I'm so very sorry.' It was odd really, he thought, that although he and his father had never been close, he knew more about him than the other man had ever realised. Now that he was gone, only two other people knew the truth, and Gwen was one of them. Dear Gwen, how sensitive she was to his feelings. Her concern for him had leapt off the page.

Vaguely he wondered who would run the Shepherds Bush shop in place of his father. But it was hard to take an interest in something which seemed trivial in comparison to the more pressing matter of how to keep his men's spirits up through another freezing wet night, and alive during a battle-filled day

341

tomorrow. Working on the law of averages, he knew that his own chances of survival in the daily slaughter were not good. He had reached a state of mind where he assumed, almost calmly, that it was only a matter of time before enemy fire or the mud got him. Though, naturally, he didn't let the men know this.

A triumph over the elements had been accomplished and Sergeant Parry squelched over to him with a mug of tea. It was lukewarm and tasted muddy but at least it moistened his sore throat.

The sergeant glanced skywards, rivers of water running off his steel helmet. 'The rain seems never ending, doesn't it, sir?'

'It does indeed.'

'Shocking battle conditions.'

'Not the best,' he admitted, 'but we'll beat the buggers, don't you worry.'

'I'm sure we will, sir.'

Actually, Ned thought it was inhuman of the army to insist that the troops continue to fight under circumstances that could bring little gain. But the word down the line was that General Haig wanted them to struggle on. Apparently there was no limit to the demands to be made on the heroism of these men. But it wouldn't be good for their morale to know that their commanding officer questioned the judgement of those of superior rank.

The wind rose and at daybreak the rain was torrential. After breakfasting on tea and hard biscuits, they gathered their equipment and waded onwards through the treacle-like mud towards the ridge. In daylight the scene was just as bleak, not a blade of grass or a living tree in sight. Just mud, slime, and thick, dark water.

They came across a driver with two horses pulling

a water-cart. One of the animals had slipped off the brushwood track and was sinking fast in the morass along with the cart and water-drum which had toppled to one side and was almost completely submerged. The driver, sitting astride the other horse, was leaning over frantically trying to cut it free from the shaft with his army knife while at the same time struggling to keep it on the track as the descending weight pulled them both towards the edge.

It was obvious to them all that it would be physically impossible to drag such a weight from the mire. So Ned cut the steady horse free from the cart, took his revolver from his holster and braced himself to commit the kinder act with respect to the other. Having been unable to save all that badly needed fresh water from going down with the horse and cart, the driver and the surviving horse continued wearily on their way.

And still the rain came and the fields were a quagmire with duckboards acting as bridges. Approaching a small hillock they were suddenly attacked by some stray enemy gunfire. A British grenade was aimed and all was silent after the explosion. Keeping to the planks, they progressed cautiously through an area of dead trees as bare as bean poles, and widely flooded areas.

A sudden scream from behind alerted Ned to the fact that Sergeant Parry had slipped off the planking into a hole and was up to his thighs in rising mud. The more he struggled to get out, the further he strayed from the wooden path.

'All right, Sergeant,' Ned shouted. 'We'll soon have you out of there.'

The men collected brushwood while Ned stayed

343

close to the sergeant.

'Shoot me, sir,' the man begged, as the mud rose around him, 'it'll be better than suffocating in this lot.'

Ignoring his panicky pleas, Ned piled bits of dead trees on to the surface to make a platform.

'I think I've hit the bottom, sir,' said the sergeant more cheerfully.

A burst of gunfire nearby interrupted the rescue attempt. Ned ordered the men to take cover while he stayed with the sergeant. He was now confident that the risk of drowning was over but it would take some time for the man to drag himself out of the mud. Stuck there without cover, he was a sitting target to the enemy.

Closing his mind to the danger he was in from German bullets, Ned threw the rest of the dead wood the men had collected on to the pile and gingerly tested it with his foot. Judging it to be quite firm, he picked up a tree branch and inched slowly towards the trapped man.

'Here, pull yourself towards me with this,' he said, offering the end of the branch to the sergeant. 'I'll give you a hand up when you get nearer. It's quite firm on the brushwood.'

Very slowly the sergeant waded forward until he was near enough to be helped. Using every bit of strength he could muster, Ned took Sergeant Parry's hand and heaved as the man began to haul himself up. But the sergeant was not a lightweight and Ned began to slide forward.

'Let go, sir,' urged the sergeant. 'It isn't gonna work.'

But Ned wouldn't be defeated. He gripped the man's hand even tighter and gave one tremendous tug. At last the sergeant's shoulders slipped on to the brushwood, followed by the slime-covered rest of him. Relieved, Ned straightened up from his crouching position. But fresh mud had come up with the sergeant. Ned's foot slipped on some of it, and he slithered uncontrollably off the brushwood into the mire.

'Sod it!' He was looking up towards the mud-covered sergeant, who was struggling to get to his feet, when he saw a German soldier aiming his gun at them from behind a nearby hillock...

*   *   *

In the absence of a viable alternative, Ralph took over as manager at the Shepherds Bush shop after Harold's death, leaving Amy in sole charge of the Ealing branch. Naturally it was necessary for them to communicate about business, but Amy didn't see so much of him which was no hardship to her. In all fairness, though, he had changed a lot these last few years. Age seemed to have mellowed him. He was often preoccupied; sometimes even seemed glad to leave the decisions to her. And since responsibility suited her, she didn't complain.

Because of the changed nature of the business and the fact that they were permanently short-staffed, she usually found herself in the role of general dogsbody, despite the fact that she was now deputy managing director. Workshop assistant, gauge packer, shop assistant, clerk, and even sometimes shop cleaner were all within the sphere of her duties.

She was dealing with a particularly difficult customer at the counter when Gwen called at the shop one day in the summer of 1918.

345

'I'm very sorry, madam,' Amy was saying, 'but I just can't spare anyone to come to your house to repair your barometer.'

'Oh, so how am I supposed to get it fixed then?'

'If you bring it to the shop, I'll get someone to take a look at it,' Amy suggested, adding with concern, 'but I can't promise it will be right away. Our people are rushed off their feet in the workshop.'

The woman, a formidable matron of broad girth who was outlandishly dressed in a frilly pink dress and rose-trimmed toque, redolent of pre-war opulence, glared at Amy. 'Well, really,' she huffed. 'That simply isn't good enough.'

Amy bit her lip. She hated to upset customers. 'It's the best I can do, I'm afraid.'

'I don't know what this country is coming to,' tutted the woman, whose little dark eyes peered superciliously from her fat countenance, 'I mean to say, what's happened to service? There's precious little of it around these days.'

'The war happened,' Amy informed her with polite briskness, irritated now by her unreasonable attitude. 'We had to stop doing personal visits for clock and barometer repairs when we went over to war work. With so many people away we just can't get enough staff, and I need every assistant I have here at the shop.'

'And how do you expect me to get my barometer here?' the woman asked. 'It is not a small item.'

'Perhaps your husband could bring it?' suggested Amy patiently.

'Certainly not. He's far too busy,' she tutted. 'The time was when shopkeepers cared about their customers.'

'They still do, but there's a war on . . .'

346

'That's no excuse to lower standards.'

'It can't be helped under the present circumstances.'

'And as for food rationing,' she ranted as though Amy hadn't spoken, 'well ... my butcher doesn't even bother to open his shop some days. I really don't know where it will all end.'

Amy struggled to keep her temper. It was obvious from the woman's appearance that she didn't go short. The black market thrived from the patronage of people like her. 'You can blame German submarines for the food shortages,' Amy pointed out, 'for blowing up the ships carrying our supplies from abroad.'

'The cause of food rationing is not the subject under discussion here,' the woman said crossly. 'The repair to my barometer is.'

'In that case I suggest you get yourself a barrow and wheel the barometer here, if it is too heavy to carry,' said Amy, stifling a giggle at the images this evoked.

'If that's all you can suggest, I'll bid you good morning. And I shall take my custom elsewhere in future.'

And, with suitable hauteur, the customer swept out.

'Good riddance, eh?' said Gwen, who had been patiently waiting to speak to Amy.

'I'll say,' she agreed. 'Honestly, the public at large are enough to drive you to murder at times.'

'I can see that.'

Amy continued in more serious vein, 'I don't like not being able to give pre-war service but it just isn't possible at the moment.' She calmed herself and smiled. 'Anyway, enough of my problems. It's been ages since I've seen you. How are things on the wards?'

'Damned hard work mostly but for the first time in my life I feel really useful,' said Gwen. 'And they're a grand bunch of lads on the whole. You get the odd difficult patient, but mostly they're lovely.'

'Sounds as though our accounts department has lost you forever,' said Amy.

'I think you're right. I'd like to stay in the profession after the war.'

Having served a man with some cuff links and a woman with a brooch, Amy asked one of her staff to hold the fort while she took Gwen into the office and made her a cup of tea. 'No sugar, I'm afraid,' she said. 'All our ration has gone. Grim, isn't it?'

'I've got used to doing without it.'

As they drank their tea, Gwen came to the point of her visit. 'I was wondering if you'd heard from Ned, lately,' she said. 'I know you've been writing to him.'

Amy's heart lurched as Gwen raised the subject that had been worrying her for months. 'I was about to ask you the same thing,' she said. 'I haven't heard from him in ages.'

Gwen's face was creased with worry. 'Oh dear, it doesn't seem too hopeful, does it? And if there has been bad news it would have gone to his father and been returned when they couldn't deliver it.'

'Is there any way we can find out?' Amy asked.

'No, details like that are only given to relatives, and there was only Ned and his dad.'

'How awful not to know,' said Amy.

'That sort of news sometimes comes years old,' Gwen informed her. 'One of the nurses I work with was saying that her mother got official notification that her brother was missing presumed dead eighteen

348

months after the date he was first reported missing. There are so many thousands of casualties and so much chaos out there, I suppose it's impossible to get the news back efficiently.'

'Perhaps he's just not had a chance to write,' suggested Amy hopefully since it was obvious how worried Gwen was. 'I doubt if conditions make it easy to write letters.'

'Let's hope that's all it is.' Gwen looked at Amy gravely. 'Some of the stories I've heard from men back from the front are enough to make your hair curl. They don't tell me, of course, but I hear them talking to each other. And they say things in their sleep.'

'I gather it's pretty awful.'

'All we can do is keep hoping,' said Gwen. 'Let me know if you hear anything, and I'll do the same.'

'I certainly will.'

*   *   *

Peace came at last in November. Victory Day began quietly under dismal grey skies. People went to work as usual, uncertain if the Armistice would be signed today. Then at eleven o'clock it came—the sound hitherto used as an air raid warning—giant maroons being fired all over the country, this time to mark the end of the war. People poured on to the streets, cheering, waving flags and hoisting servicemen shoulder-high. Church bells pealed; boy scouts cycled through the town sounding the 'all clear' for the last time on bugles and sirens.

Amy closed the shop for the day. 'Let's take the kids up West,' she suggested excitedly to Violet and Bernie.

349

Violet and the children didn't need any persuasion but Bernie declined, saying his leg would be too much of a hindrance in the crowds. Knowing how reserved he was these days, Amy didn't press him.

Even the rain didn't lower the spirits of the West End crowds who bobbed and swayed noisily in a welter of patriotic fervour. By the time Big Ben struck one o'clock, after four years of silence, the whole of central London was ablaze with flags of every Allied nation flying from the rooftops. The tops of omnibuses were loaded with excited passengers arriving to join in the celebrations. Revellers sang and shouted and danced in the streets. Amy and company even managed to catch a glimpse of the King and Queen as they drove to Hyde Park.

Darkness brought no let-up in the festivities. Blackout curtains were torn down, and the rigid war-time licensing laws were ignored as people flocked into pubs and proceeded to drink them dry. Street lamps were uncovered and the porches of several theatres were ablaze with light. Long queues of people waiting at music hall doors for the evening performance sang popular songs and cheered at the end of every chorus. Merrymakers let off fireworks and cakewalked in the squares, oblivious to the persistent drizzle and the muddy roads.

Amy's party were exhausted but happy as they piled into a cab to go home. Amy herself fell silent as thoughts of Ned came to mind. It seemed unlikely that he was still alive, but she preferred not to give up hope.

'So, back to normal now, eh?' said Violet, yawning as they rolled homewards through streets still filled with partying throngs.

'Yes indeed,' said Amy, but it was hard to imagine

350

that life could ever be the same.

* * *

One good thing to come out of the war was the progress of the women's cause. Their contribution to the war effort earned them more recognition than the violent pre-war methods to which they had been forced to resort. In the general election of December, some women were allowed to vote for the first time. Amy was thrilled to be eligible, but she still found the new law somewhat lacking.

'By the time you're grown-up, Connie,' she said, 'let's hope all women will qualify, not just those over thirty who own some property.'

She gave a lot of thought to her first vote and finally favoured Lloyd George's coalition government. To have the Liberals and Conservatives working together in Parliament seemed to her to be the most sensible way of getting the country back on its feet again.

But that much vaunted state of being 'back to normal' didn't happen. Instead, the populace was thrown into more hardship. Shortages of food and fuel were grave, unemployment and homelessness rife, as servicemen flocked home looking for jobs and somewhere to live. Being cold and undernourished, people had no resistance to disease.

February of the new year brought an epidemic of influenza so virulent it caused many deaths. Such large numbers of people fell ill, some shops were forced to close from lack of staff and public transport was thrown into confusion. Those suffering from the disease were advised to go to bed and take aspirin. But many people were so sick the doctor had to be called in—if they could find one who hadn't taken to his own bed.

When Ralph Jackson went down with it, Amy found herself with real problems at work for there was no one on the staff competent to do his job. The firm had reverted to being jewellers again since the end of the war, and were fully staffed. But at least half of them were off sick. Sales of precious jewellery might not have returned to their pre-war level but the shops were frantically busy with the craze for patriotic accessories.

Having no other choice, she put the most senior assistant at Shepherds Bush in charge, with strict instructions to telephone her with any queries. It was ironic really, she thought, that having fought so hard for her place as one of four directors, she now found herself with no one with whom to share the load.

In the midst of this chaos, she received the terrible news that her father had died.

* * *

An emaciated Ned arrived home to an empty house one afternoon in late February, having spent the last year of the war as a prisoner. No one was more surprised than he that he was still alive, for he had literally waited for death as he had stood thigh deep in the mud with a rifle pointing at him. But the Germans, seeing the utter helpnessness of himself and Sergeant Parry, had decided to spare them.

Dumping his kit in the hall, he went on a tour of the house, finding it undamaged but musty and damp from standing empty for so long. It was clean though and everything was as he'd left it. He guessed that Gwen had kept her promise and called in to give it a

352

once-over every so often.

He felt completely out of touch with the world and all the people that had been in his little part of it. It seemed so long since he had heard from anyone. When mail failed to arrive for him at the prison camp he guessed the authorities didn't know he was there. And he suspected that letters home never got past the camp censor. No one knew he was back. He hadn't bothered to telephone anyone to inform them he had landed back in Blighty. It hadn't seemed important as there could be no welcome from Molly.

Gloomily, he mooched through the freezing rooms, shivering, his every movement seeming to echo in the silent, unwelcoming house which had once been a real home, alive with the warmth and comfort of Molly's presence. Then there had been flower-filled vases everywhere, fires in all the rooms; her gentle voice, her laughter, her footstep on the stair. He plucked a photograph of her from the dusty piano top and stared at it, moist-eyed. His life with her seemed distant, almost as if it had happened to someone else. Suddenly he realised that he missed her but no longer mourned for her. She was gone. Only now, in the misery of this final homecoming after the war, did he truly accept it.

In the drawing room he stared out of the window at the back garden in which weeds and grass grew waist-high. Even the trees looked taller and oddly unfamiliar. He ran his eye over the bare branches of the apple tree extending over the ivy-covered wall. He found himself smiling at the memory of the fuss there had been over Amy's children wanting to climb it that Sunday. Amy. How was she? Still settled with Bernie, he supposed.

Despite the fact that nature had run riot in his

garden, it seemed acutely beautiful. Leafless trees; weed-filled flower beds; wild grasses swaying in the wind. Here and there little patches of colour where crocuses flowered under the trees where the grass wasn't so high. Loneliness washed over him in a debilitating tide. He needed desperately to feel cared for at this moment. He left the house in search of the one person he knew who would do that unconditionally.

*   *   *

He was disappointed, on arriving at Floral House, to find that Gwen had moved into rooms near the hospital. So instead he had to listen to Florence's tale of woe about her husband's indisposition. She gave Ned a welcome of sorts, hugged him rather formally and had tea sent up, saying she'd thought she was seeing a ghost, for he was so thin and pale and they'd all thought him dead. She said she'd give him Gwen's address before he left.

Ned wanted to go at once, but it wasn't polite to leave too soon. And he couldn't very well go without seeing Ralph, who was still in bed recovering. After checking that her husband was awake and feeling up to a visitor, Florence showed Ned to Ralph's bedside. He was shocked by how much Ralph had changed. He looked elderly now. His remaining hair had turned white, and his face had hollowed out and was a greyish tone with red and blue broken veins standing out. His eyes were sunken and shadowed, his lips pale with a slight bluish tinge.

Propped up with pillows, he said, 'Well, well, the hero back from the dead.'

'I don't know about that.'

354

'No need for modesty, old boy,' said Ralph, with a watery smile. 'It's good to see you.'

'Likewise.'

'Does Gwen know you're back?'

'No, not yet,' he said. 'I thought she'd be here. I'll go and see her later.'

He brought Ralph up to date with where he had been this long time, and the older man told him what had been happening at home.

'I'm so sorry about your father, old chap, we were all devastated.'

'I'm sure.'

'I miss him terribly, you know. We'd been friends and partners for so long.' To Ned's astonishment, tears began to trickle down the older man's wrinkled cheeks. He mopped his face with a handkerchief, sniffing. 'Sorry. This damned 'flu has left me feeling very low. It's taken the stuffing right out of me.'

'Yes, I can see that,' said Ned with concern. 'I don't want to tire you. Perhaps I should go . . .'

'No, no, stay a while longer,' Ralph urged. 'I'll enjoy the company.' He blew his nose. 'I suppose you were very cut up about your father, especially getting the news out there?'

'It hasn't really hit me yet,' admitted Ned. 'With being away, I suppose.'

'You'll notice it now you're home.' He became more composed and thoughtful. 'I suppose you realise that you are the major shareholder in the firm now?'

'Yes, I suppose I would be,' said Ned, though he hadn't given the business much thought. He'd been far too war-weary to consider the future, and still lacked interest in it.

'Things have changed in the trade while you've

355

been away,' said Ralph.

'I expect things are getting back to normal after the war, aren't they?'

'Not really.'

'Oh? Why?'

'The market for fine jewellery is depressed,' Ralph explained despondently. 'People think it's unpatriotic and frivolous. Women would sooner have cheap costume jewellery.'

'Really?'

'Yes. Of all things, *Vogue* magazine recently featured tin and shrapnel jewellery made by wounded soldiers.'

'You can't criticise that, Ralph,' said Ned. 'It's a very good idea.'

'It's all very fine,' argued Ralph, 'but it's still competition for us who deal in precious jewellery, isn't it?'

'There's room for both kinds, surely?' said Ned. 'And it will even out again when people start to forget about the war.'

'Maybe, but I can't see things ever going back to how they were. Women have changed too much. Working outside the home has altered their outlook. They seem to want a more practical type of jewellery now to go with the general trend towards plainer clothes. But where's the dignity in calf-length dresses, short hair and cheap jewellery?'

Since the question was a rhetorical one, Ned just said, 'There'll always be a market for precious jewellery.'

'I suppose so.' Ralph seemed to brighten up. 'We're doing a roaring trade in aviator's wings and regimental badges.'

'Things aren't so bad then,' said Ned. 'The firm

356

will survive change, don't you worry.'

'If there's a firm left by the time I get back on my feet,' grunted Ralph, fiddling with the edge of the eiderdown.

'Oh? How do you mean?'

'Amy's been in sole charge while I've been ill.'

'She's very capable...'

'But her father died yesterday, so God knows what's going to happen now. She'll have to have time off to be with her mother, which means there will be no one in authority in either shop.' He sighed. 'Quite frankly, I feel too groggy to care.'

Ned was instantly concerned, but for Amy, not the firm. 'I'd better go and give her a hand, she must be rushed off her feet.'

'It would put my mind at rest, if you feel up to it,' said Ralph, leaning back and closing his eyes for a moment as the crippling exhaustion washed over him.

'You can relax.'

Since he had seen Ned in better shape, Ralph felt duty bound to make a token protest. 'Shouldn't you take time to recuperate before you start work again, old boy? You look a bit peaky.'

In actual fact Ned felt as frail as Ralph looked, and hadn't been officially demobbed yet. But he said, 'Don't you worry about me. The sooner I get back to work, the better. I'll only mope if I sit round the house on my own all day.'

As weak as Ralph was, he could never resist the chance to have a sly dig at Amy. 'That's a relief. Lord knows what sort of a mess that damn' woman is making of our business.'

'Now that isn't fair,' admonished Ned sharply. 'You know in your heart that she'll not make a mess

357

of anything. But I'll go and offer my support. It sounds as though she needs it.'

* * *

After Ned had left Ralph tried to sleep, mainly to escape from the depression that plagued him. He felt so feeble, so old, so very alone. Strange feelings for a man who had been married for a very long time to a good and loyal woman. But he'd never felt really close to, or at ease with Florence, not like he had with Clara. And as the years passed he missed the latter more rather than less.

Oddly enough the news of George Atkins' death hadn't given him the pleasure he had always imagined it would. After all, the man's very existence had been a threat to Ralph for the best part of twenty years. Amy knew too much, of course, but he didn't think he had anything to fear from her because he no longer had anything she needed. So he was free, and relief should be automatic.

Instead he was tormented by thoughts of his own mortality, for George had been a good bit younger than Ralph. Where had the years gone? How could he be sixty-four years old when he still felt twenty-one inside? Increasingly his imaginings drifted back to the time he had spent with Clara, and he was filled with a hopeless yearning for the past. Time was one thing that money could not buy, he thought, looking at the papery texture of his aging hands resting on the eiderdown.

And what had his life amounted to? A comfortable home, a long marriage, no financial worries. But no real warmth either; no fun or laughter. Not since he stopped seeing Clara. How deeply he regretted ending their affair. How many times had he cursed himself for not putting things right with her before she died. Even now, eight years after her death, he still found it hard to believe she wasn't around. People like Clara didn't do things like dying.

He'd caught a glimpse of her daughter, his daughter, one day recently when he'd been at the Ealing shop. Lustrous green eyes like her mother's and sand-coloured hair like his had once been. She must be about twelve now, he thought. She had been with Amy's sons waiting for their mother to finish work. All three had ignored him, the boys because he was the grandfather who had blatantly disregarded their existence, the girl in sympathy with her cousins, he presumed. All three had his blood, and all three treated him with disdain.

Because he was in a mood to be honest with himself, he could see that it was no more than he deserved. Connie didn't even know she was related to him, and he could hardly expect the boys to behave like grandsons towards him when he had made himself a stranger to them. The ease with which he had cut himself off from all three children astonished him now that they were no longer babies but young people with their own personalities. In middle age he had always felt too competitive towards the young to feel at ease with them. Now, the gap was too wide for that.

Since the complications were too great for him to become a part of Connie's life, he found himself mulling over the idea of himself as an active grandfather. He'd never had much of a rapport with Gwen or Clifford, but might he not have a better relationship with his grandchildren?

As the idea took shape, he began to feel quite

excited, imagining himself indulging them with treats and offering advice on matters they couldn't discuss with their mother. Grandchildren were renowned for that sort of thing. His cronies at the club were always going on about it.

So why didn't he make friends with his grandsons? Florence would disapprove, of course, but he'd probably be able to talk her round if he pointed out the advantages of having some young company around to take an interest in and give them both a new lease of life. After all, they *were* Clifford's sons and it wasn't as though she'd have to see their mother. Absorbed in this selfish flight of fancy, the feelings of others did not exist for Ralph. It seemed like the simplest thing in the world to him. He would get to work on Florence, then arrange to have the boys over to the house for a visit. Why, he felt stronger already, and elated with a new sense of purpose.

*   *   *

'I'd like to have a brooch made in the shape of aviator's wings,' said a lady customer across the counter to Amy. 'My husband was a pilot in the war, you see.'

'How brave,' said Amy, smiling.

'Yes, he was.'

'We'd be delighted to make one for you. If you can give me the details of the actual design you'd like, and which material you'd like it made in . . .'

The sound of the telephone ringing in the office set Amy's nerves on edge. It was probably someone from Bethnal Green, where she should be at this very moment. As none of the other counter staff was free

360

to take over from her with this customer, she said, 'Would you excuse me for a minute while I answer the phone?'

'Certainly.'

It wasn't one of her bereaved relatives, but Miss Carey, the assistant in charge at the other shop. She was finding the responsibility all a bit too much on account of an irate customer who was dissatisfied with a repair to his watch.

'Offer our sincere apologies and tell him we'll have it back in the workshop free of charge,' said Amy.

'But he's demanding to see someone from the management,' wailed Miss Carey. 'And he was most insulting when I told him there was no one available.' Incipient hysterics were noticeable in her voice. 'I'm not trained for this sort of thing.'

'I know, Miss Carey,' said Amy sympathetically, 'and I'm sorry you've been burdened with the job. But you're doing very well and I'm grateful to you for taking it on. Could you possibly bear with it for just a bit longer, until Mr Jackson gets back?'

'Well...'

'Your efforts will be reflected in your pay packet, of course.'

'Oh, I see. Well, all right then,' she agreed, though still with some reluctance.

As she replaced the receiver, Amy's head was spinning. She needed to go to Bethnal Green to be with her mother. Bobby and Pete were back from the war and dealing with the funeral arrangements, but it was her daughter Gladys wanted right now. Yesterday, after that devastating telephone call, Amy had dropped everything and rushed to her mother's side. But if she did that too often, with Ralph being away, there would be no business for

361

him to come back to. The only solution was to go to Bethnal Green after work this evening.

She still felt shaky from the news. It had been very sudden. Her father had caught influenza and complications had set in. He had been fifty-three years old. Amy's legs threatened to give way and she sank on to a chair, realising that she hadn't eaten anything all day.

There was a tap on the office door. 'Come in,' she said without looking up, assuming it would be one of the staff with another wretched query.

'Hello, Amy.'

She turned.

'Ned!' She was up and hugging him, tears streaming down her face. 'You're alive. Oh, Ned, how wonderful! How abso-blooming-lutely marvellous!'

'Well, that was quite a welcome,' he grinned breathlessly when she finally let him go.

'Oh, it's so good to see you,' she said exuberantly. 'What happened? Where've you been all this time . . . ?'

There was another knock on the office door and this time it was an assistant, a female junior. 'Sorry to interrupt you, Mrs Banks,' she said, 'but the customer you were seeing to about a wings brooch wants to know if you are ever coming back or shall she go elsewhere with her custom?'

Nothing could curb Amy's joy at this moment. 'Tell her I'll be with her in two ticks, please, dear,' she smiled.

The girl trotted away. Amy turned to Ned. 'Take a seat, I'll be back in a minute to make us some tea.'

'When you come back,' he said, feeling enormously cheered by the genuine warmth of her welcome, 'I'll take over and you can get yourself off to your mother's.'

She stared at him, bemused. 'How...'

'Ralph told me. I'm so sorry about your father.'

She swallowed on her tears as harsh reality flooded back. 'Thank you. It was such a shock. I didn't even know he was ill.'

'You'll want to be with your mother.'

'Of course, but I can't. Ralph's away, there's no one...'

'Go and see to the customer about the wings brooch,' he said. 'Then put me up to date with things and be on your way. I'll look after Jackson & Cox.'

'But you've only just got back.'

'And just in the nick of time, too, by the look of it,' he said. 'Now go and serve your customer before she goes somewhere else with her business.'

'Oh, Ned,' she said impulsively. 'It's so good to have you back.'

'It's good to be back,' he said, smiling into her eyes. She couldn't know just how happy he was to see her again. He was surprised himself.

*   *   *

Amy stared at Ralph in astonishment. 'I can't believe I'm hearing this,' she exploded one day in late-spring, having been summoned to his office. He was now restored to health and back at the Ealing shop, Ned having resumed his former position at the other branch. 'After ignoring the existence of my sons for the whole of their lives, are you now saying that you want to acknowledge them as grandsons?'

'Yes, that's right.'

'You're about thirteen years too late.'

'Better late than never.' He felt deflated. All through his convalescence this new idea had kept his spirits up. He might have known she would spoil everything.

'Better not at all than to have them as toys, just boosts to your ego,' she said. 'Feeling your age, eh, Ralph? Fancy having a couple of grandchildren around to make you feel immortal, even though you feel nothing for them at all?'

She was too close to the truth for his comfort.

'You're a hard woman,' he blustered. 'All I want is to make amends.'

'So when the fancy takes you, you want to make amends,' she said. 'Just like that.'

'And what's so terrible about that?'

'You really don't know?'

'I can't see what all the fuss is about, no,' he said.

'Oh, Ralph, you can't play around with people's lives as though they're some sort of commodity,' she said. 'And then drop them again when you get fed up with them.'

'I won't drop them, I really do want to make it up to them,' he said earnestly, his eagerness increased by her opposition.

'What does Florence have to say about it?' she asked. 'Surely she hasn't had a change of heart too?'

'She doesn't oppose the idea,' he said.

And she doesn't welcome it either if I know Florence, Amy thought, but said, 'I hope you're not planning to have a change of heart over Connie too.'

'No, I don't intend to do anything about her.'

Giving the matter thought, Amy believed him. The only amends he was prepared to make were the ones which required no suffering on his part. And if Florence found out about Connie's origins, he'd wish he'd never been born. 'I'm pleased to hear it,' she said, 'because I wouldn't want Clara's wishes to be disregarded. Connie is happy in the knowledge that her daddy was lost at sea. It could be devastating for her to find out otherwise at this stage.'

'She won't find out from me,' he assured her.

'Good.'

'I mean your sons no harm, you know.'

'There is more to hurting a child than physically harming it, you know, Ralph,' she said. 'Rejection is far more painful. They've grown up accepting that from you and Florence. They were too young when Clifford died to remember much about him, but obviously they know who you are. It must have been hard for them to understand that grandparents living in the same neighbourhood didn't want anything to do with them.'

'Surely you won't stop me from trying to make it up to them?'

The welfare of her sons was her only consideration in all this. The last thing she wanted to do was to deprive them of something they might value. 'No, I won't stop you. But I think the only fair thing to do is to let Victor and Dickie make up their own minds,' she said. 'They are thirteen and twelve, quite old enough to make a decision of this kind. I'll put it to them. If they want to come and see you, I'll co-operate in any way I can. If they don't, I shall not force them.'

'You'll not try to influence them against the idea?'

'Certainly not,' she said. 'I have never done anything to turn them against you. They know there was some sort of a rift between us, that's all. No, I will simply explain that you wish to make friends with them.'

'Thank you,' he said.

* * *

'The ghastly Jacksons want Victor and me to go and visit them at their house, Connie,' said Dickie, a few days later. 'What do you think about that? Isn't it the most incredible nerve?'

'I'll say it is,' agreed Connie, who had heard from the boys all about their hated paternal grandparents. 'What do they want to see you for, after all this time?'

'To make friends with us, apparently,' exploded Dickie, his blue eyes bright with rage. 'Just like that, after ignoring us for all these years.'

'Will you go?'

'Not likely. I wouldn't go within a mile of them if they offered me sackfuls of diamonds, after the way they've treated my mother,' he exclaimed, 'banishing her from their family after Father died just because they didn't think she was good enough for them.'

Amy had been speaking the truth to Ralph about not having given her sons a detailed account of the events of the past. She'd felt they were too young to understand. Later it might be different, but some sort of a family rift was all they needed to know for the moment. But Victor and Dickie had become curious, and unbeknown to their mother had got Violet talking one day...

'I don't blame you,' said Connie. 'They sound like rotten snobs to me. I think it's wicked to disown your own family.'

'So do I,' said Dickie. 'Granny Atkins is the only grandparent I want.'

'Yeah, I'm glad I'm not related to those awful Jacksons,' said Connie, who adored her cousins and

366

was fiercely loyal to them.

'You're lucky. I wish I wasn't,' said Dickie. 'Still, as long as I don't have anything to do with them I can pretend I'm not.'

They were in the drawing room. It was late afternoon and school was over for the the day. A beam of sunlight shone across the corner of the piano at which Connie was seated. Until Dickie had entered the room she had been trying to perfect her rendition of a popular song, accompanying herself on the piano. She had inherited her mother's gift for entertaining and had a pleasant singing voice. The weekly piano lessons Amy insisted she have had made her competent enough to play the songs she liked to sing. Most of her spare time was spent putting on shows around the house, roping in her friends, her cousins, anyone . . .

'What does Victor think about it?' she asked.

'You know Vic,' said Dickie a touch scornfully. 'He always tries to make excuses for even the most dreadful bounders, he's famous for it at school. But even *he* agreed it was a frightful cheek and would be disloyal to Mother for either of us to go near the Jacksons.'

His mother entered the room with Victor. 'Hello, you two,' she said breezily. 'Are you going to sing something for us, Connie?'

The girl beamed, always glad of the chance to perform to an audience. 'Certainly. What would you like?'

'What about that one Violet's always singing?' said Dickie. 'Something about bubbles.'

'"I'm forever blowing bubbles",' said Connie, her eyes shining. 'I like that one too. I don't have the music but I know how it goes.' She turned to the

367

keyboard and began to pick out the tune.

Dickie interrupted. 'Wait a minute, Connie.' He turned to his mother. 'Did you tell Grandpa Jackson that Vic and me wouldn't be seen dead anywhere near him?'

'I didn't put it quite like that, no.'

'Why not?' he queried. 'The pompous old duffer needs putting in his place.'

'Because it would have been rude and hurtful.'

'He deserves it.'

'Now then, I don't want to hear any more of that sort of talk, Dickie,' said Amy, who prided herself on having raised her sons to be fair and well mannered.

'Sorry, Mum,' he said, for both boys knew just how far they could go with her. She was warm and kind and gentle, but she was also a stickler about manners and being fair to people.

'I should think so too,' she said. 'Now be quiet and let Connie sing her song.'

As Connie launched into an enthusiastic version of the song that was currently on everyone's lips, Amy mulled over her meeting with Ralph earlier that day. He'd seemed genuinely disappointed and rather subdued by the boys' decision. Hard though it was to believe, he seemed to have expected it to be easy. He seemed to have the idea that gaining favour with his grandsons was just like going to the tobacconist to buy a packet of cigars. Perhaps this would teach him that money simply did not buy everything.

She hoped she'd been fair when she had put his suggestion to Victor and Dickie. She'd tried to remain neutral and had said a lot about not judging people too harshly. He was their only grandfather now, after all, and maybe a relationship might be of some benefit to them. She had tried to raise them not to have bitterness in their hearts against the Jacksons, even though she had never been able to shake hers off entirely. But they had minds of their own apparently.

Would Ralph let it end here though? she wondered, with a shiver of fear.

CHAPTER EIGHTEEN

Amy liked the clean-cut look of the Art Deco style of jewellery that was so popular in the new decade. Born from the mood of austerity immediately following the war, it continued to dominate the trade in the ensuing consumer boom. The simple geometric shapes of the new designs were very much in tune with the atmosphere of the time. Modern pieces were often based on images of speed and machines, such as the automobile and the aeroplane. She could see a contradiction in the style though. Whilst plain and streamlined, there was often a tendency towards ostentation. Only to be expected, perhaps, in an era of such rapid change and sharp contrasts, she thought.

New technologies and materials, developed during the war, had changed the nature of manufacturing. Thriving industry produced a mood of extravagance. People were buying precious jewels again despite the growing popularity of costume jewellery. Business boomed at Jackson & Cox in every department, from mail order right through to the workshops. But there were large numbers of unemployed people who couldn't afford to buy basics, let alone jewellery.

Whilst, by the very nature of her work, Amy was involved with society's higher echelons, the plight of those without jobs came sharply into focus every time she visited her mother. The East End was full of ex-servicemen looking for work. Some sold matches on the street to make a living; and all this in 'a land fit for heroes to live in' the politicians had promised. Amy's brothers had been two such victims until she had set them up in business selling clothes on a market stall. Having inherited their father's gift for survival they were doing very well.

Amy tried to persuade her mother to move to Ealing, to be closer to her.

'I like livin' in the East End,' Gladys explained. 'It's all very fine over your way for visitin', but I wouldn't be comfortable bein' there all the time. I know everybody round 'ere, yer see.'

But she did visit often, and sometimes stayed for a week or so now that she had no husband to rush back for. Not being the sort to stay idle while Amy was out at work, she usually helped Violet with the chores. Being of a similar type, plain-speaking and down-to-earth, the two became firm friends. Sometimes, on Violet's day off, they would go to the pictures together, or even on a day trip to Brighton if the weather was nice.

Amy's professional life was busier than ever as Ralph became semi-retired. Between them she and Ned managed the business with Ralph functioning more as a figurehead than a contributing member of the team. He liked to be involved with the firm and appeared at the shop quite often. He'd offer advice about stock buying, and take valued customers out to lunch. Sometimes he'd just stand about making his presence felt by keeping a supervisory eye on the staff and chatting to the clientele. But he no longer had set responsibilities within the firm.

Commissions still came in spasmodically. A man wishing to have a brooch made for his wife, and giving Amy carte blanche, offered her the opportunity to design something in contemporary style. The result was three intertwined circles in gold, coral and diamonds. Stunningly simple, but extremely elegant.

'Wouldn't you like to do more designing?' asked Ned, one day.

'Not really,' she said. 'It's fun now and then, but I enjoy being involved with the business as a whole. I like variety in my work.'

'You certainly get that when you're running a shop,' he laughed.

Parallel with the changes in the jewellery trade, the fashion industry was undergoing something of a revolution too. Having had their role changed by the war, modern women were no longer content to lead such restricted lives. They demanded casual, functional clothes in keeping with their new freedom. When Amy was a girl it had been prohibited to show an ankle. As the twenties progressed calves and even knees were displayed by young women who poured into dance halls and nightclubs to do the Shimmy Shake and the Black Bottom. Flat chests, straight clothes and bobbed hair became the height of fashion.

Being a working woman with a modern outlook, Amy approved of the emancipated clothes, though many older people thought the new fashions immoral, especially as women began to use make-up and smoke cigarettes in public.

'It's an exciting age in which to be young,' she remarked to Connie one day. 'Heaven knows how far skirts will have risen by the time you're old enough to follow fashion.'

'I can't wait to wear grown-up things,' sighed Connie wistfully.

'Don't fret. It'll come quick enough,' said Amy.

'I shall dress in style,' declared Connie lightheartedly. 'Stage people always do.'

'Only the successful ones can afford to,' said Amy, endeavouring to keep the girl's feet on the ground. 'You keep your theatrics as a hobby, love, it's safer.'

'I don't care about being safe.'

'No, I don't suppose you do.' Connie was just like her mother: cheerful, warm-hearted and extrovert. Since she so loved singing and dancing, Amy spared no expense to make it an enjoyable pastime for her. In addition to her music lessons, she now went to a local dancing school every Saturday morning. Since Amy thought of her as her own child, she supported her willingly and as a matter of course. 'So it's up to me to care about it for you.'

*   *   *

Bernie continued to show no sign of returning to his former self. Four years after the end of the war, he had still done nothing about finding a suitable occupation, and sat moodily around the house all day. He was not irritable so much as withdrawn and lacking in interest. When Amy tried to talk to him about it he said there was no employment for a one-legged man, and since he was paying his way with his army pension, what did it matter anyway? He couldn't seem to understand that Amy's only concern was for him to enjoy life again.

'I'd sooner he was stealing my money than behaving like some docile domestic pet, staying in the house day after day,' she confided to Ned one day after a directors' meeting.

'I don't think you would, you know,' he said. 'It was very traumatic for you last time.'

'Mmm, perhaps I don't mean it literally,' she agreed. 'But I certainly prefer the man Bernie used to be, for all his faults, to this watered down version. You know what he was like before the war— definitely not a homebird. He liked to be out and about, doing some deal or other. I know he hates what he's become but I just can't shake him out of it.'

'At least he's paying his way,' he said, for Amy had confided in him about that.

'Oh, yes,' she said, 'I've no complaints in that direction. It isn't that he's self-pitying or anything. But he's different. It just isn't Bernie sitting opposite me in the chair of an evening. It's as though he's undergone a complete personality change.'

'Perhaps it's better this way. At least you don't have to keep an eye on your valuables all the time now.' Ned was uneasy about Bernie's presence in Amy's life. He never quite trusted him to do the decent thing by her. Behind that quiet, almost humble manner lived Bernie Banks, inveterate crook. His trickery was only lying dormant, it wasn't dead. But Ned didn't consider it his place to voice these thoughts to Amy. Presumably she was in love with him or they wouldn't still be together.

And how could he think otherwise? As much as Amy valued Ned as a friend and confidant, she still felt that to tell him that she had taken Bernie back only out of pity, would be a betrayal. Bernie obviously drew some comfort from being seen as her husband rather than her lodger and the least she could do was to go along with him. After all, it

373

couldn't be easy for him, managing with such a disability. Quite apart from the inconvenience, his stump still gave him considerable pain at times.

'That isn't much consolation, I'm afraid.' She sighed. 'I get irritated with him then feel guilty, and so it goes on.'

'What does he find to do all day?'

'He sleeps in late, reads the paper and just potters about, I think, though I'm out at work a lot of the time,' explained Amy. 'I bought a wireless set to help amuse him. He listens to that a lot.'

'Perhaps you're making things too easy for him,' suggested Ned.

'Maybe,' she sighed. 'But I feel so sorry for him. He was always such a bright spark, for all his villainy.'

'And what about you in all this?' asked Ned. 'The worry must be a strain.'

'It is at times, but while he needs me I'll be there for him.'

'Yes, I know,' he said.

Their eyes met. Amy looked away. In that moment, she was on the verge of telling Ned how she really felt about him. But there was no point. Even if he did feel something more than friendship for her, she had nothing to offer him. For what she had said was true. While Bernie needed her, she would continue to be there for him.

*　　　*　　　*

Bernie's return to form was as unexpected to him as it was to Amy. And it all came about because of the wireless set she had given him.

Since the British Broadcasting Company had been formed, regular daily programmes were transmitted and everyone wanted to listen to the new broadcasts. Not everyone could afford the valve-and-battery receiver in a smart cabinet like his but the crystal set, which was tuned by 'tickling the cat's whisker' and could only be heard through headphones, cost only about seven shillings and sixpence. With a flash of his old-style inspiration, Bernie saw the commercial potential. If the shops were making money out of this new craze, so were the backstreet dealers of the kind he had once been. His adrenaline began to flow properly for the first time in years. It was time he got out and about. He'd been grounded for far too long.

'I'm going over to the East End,' he said to Amy.

'Oh,' she said, hardly daring to hope. 'For any particular reason?'

He gave a nonchalant shrug 'Not really. Just to see a few mates, have a couple of drinks...'

'Will you be able to manage the train on your own?' she asked.

'O' course I will,' he said, almost boastfully. 'This is Bernie Banks you're talkin' to.'

'Yes,' she said, seeing that old roguish gleam in his eye. 'Yes, it is, it really is.'

*   *   *

'Nightclubs are the thing to get into, mate,' said an old acquaintance of Bernie's called Danny Flint whom he met in a Bethnal Green pub a few days later. 'People just can't get enough of 'em. Every club in London is packed to the doors every night. They fight to get in, I ain't kidding.'

'I was thinking of getting in on the wireless trade myself, crystal sets, yer know,' said Bernie. 'But I've bin out of the trading game a long time, I'm a bit

375

short of contacts.'

'Now, I always 'ad you down as a bright boy, Bernie,' said Danny, sipping a whisky and observing his companion shrewdly. 'I thought you'd have moved on from small-time stuff by now.'

'Losing me leg in the war put me back a bit,' he explained defensively, not wishing to seem a failure to one of East London's most successful entrepreneurs. Danny had had several businesses when Bernie had last seen him, pubs, cafes, that sort of thing.

'Mmm, it must have been a bit of a blow,' said Danny, who had a deep, bronchial voice from chain smoking cigars. 'But now you're back in circulation, you mustn't let it cramp yer style.'

'As if I would,' said Bernie, affronted at such a suggestion.

'You wanna start aiming high, mate,' advised Danny. 'Get yourself into a legit business and finish with all this wheeler dealing.'

'Such as?'

'What about the nightclub game?' he suggested again. 'Someone with the gift of the gab like you would do very well.'

'Do yer think so?'

'Cor, not 'alf.' Danny was a large, flamboyant man in his thirties, dressed in a gaudy black and white checked suit. His unruly brown curly hair was oiled into place and worn with a centre parting above thick, chaotic eyebrows. His expression of constant amusement was derived from the fact that his waxed moustache curled upwards at the ends. Despite the symbols of wealth that glittered about his person, the gold watch and chain, the diamond studded cuff links, he still had a look of the gutter about him. 'You wouldn't 'ave to go out looking for customers then. They come looking for you. Business comes at you from all sides.'

'It's that good?'

'I'll say it is. Apart from the entrance money, there's the profits from the bar and the food. It's money for old rope, I tell yer, mate. All you gotta do is provide good food, a well-stocked bar, a dance band and some cabaret entertainment. Jazz music is all the rage with the punters at the moment.'

'You seem to know a lot about it,' said Bernie. 'You already dipped yer toe in?'

He nodded. 'I've got two clubs, and about to take on another.' He observed Bernie thoughtfully. 'I'm looking for a partner, as a matter of fact, for this latest one.'

'You got somewhere definite in mind?'

'Yeah, there's a place going just off the Edgware Road,' he said. 'An established business, name o' Bubbles. The owner's bin taken bad sudden, and can't keep it on. Dicky 'eart or somethin'. It'll be going cheap because they want a quick sale. How about you, mate? Do yer fancy the idea of coming in with me on it?'

Bernie's blood was positively bubbling. 'I might do. Depends 'ow much it's gonna cost me.'

'A grand.'

A thousand pounds. Bernie's spirits plummeted but he couldn't lose face by admitting that he was skint except for his army pension. 'It's an interestin' idea, I must say.'

'I'm looking for someone to run the place while I see to all my other business interests. So you'd take a salary out of the business as well as your share of the profits.'

377

The proposition was getting more attractive by the moment and Bernie's excitement grew, despite his lack of funds. 'Sounds fair enough,' he said, without betraying his eagerness.

'There's accommodation at the club if yer wanna stay there some nights, to save the bother of goin' home.' Danny paused, and knocked the ash off his cigar into the ashtray. 'Well, how about it?'

Embarrassed by his lack of resources, and in need of time to think, Bernie prevaricated. 'It's a tempting offer but I ain't got the experience to run a place of me own.'

'You used to run the bar down the Empire Music Hall. And managing a club is the same sort of thing. It's all a matter of keeping the punters 'appy.'

'I dunno...'

'You'd be working for yourself.'

'Mmm.'

'You're a natural for a nightclub with your personality.'

Flattered to have someone of Danny's status take an interest in him, and desperate not to let this golden opportunity pass him by, Bernie decided to forget his pride.

'Couldn't I just be yer manager, instead of partner?' he suggested.

'No, I need a partner to share the financial outlay. A lot of my cash is tied up in other things.'

'I ain't got the dough,' admitted Bernie at last.

'I'd be putting in a higher stake than you,' said Danny.

'It makes no difference,' said Bernie. 'I still ain't got a grand.'

Danny was thoughtful for a moment. 'I'm sure an enterprising bloke like you won't have any trouble raising it.'

Such confidence was inspiring. 'I suppose I could give it a try.'

'You and me would make a good team, I reckon,' said Danny. 'With my business experience and your personality.'

'Can you give me time to try and sort something out?' asked Bernie.

'Sure,' said Danny. 'But don't be too long about it. I wanna snap this place up before someone else does. And I won't have any trouble finding a partner if you ain't interested.'

'Just give me a couple of days.'

'Right. Meet me in here Saturday dinnertime,' Danny said. 'If yer don't show up, I'll offer it to someone else.'

'I'll be 'ere,' said Bernie, tingling with excitement just like in the old days before the war. It was so good to be back in the swing of things again, living on the edge of a deal. If he could somehow pull this off, it would put him into the big time. A club owner. Oh, yes, he liked the sound of that. And he'd be good at it, that much he was certain of.

The two men lapsed into thoughtful silence while they finished their drinks. 'There's just one thing I'd like to make clear before we go any further, though, mate,' said Danny.

Bernie looked up enquiringly.

'You've always had a reputation as a villain.'

'Maybe I 'ave but . . .'

'Don't worry, I ain't bothered about it,' Danny assured him swiftly, 'I ain't a saint meself. But if we go into business together, we don't cheat on each other.'

'Course not.'

'I don't care how much you con the rest of the world, but you don't turn me over.'

'There'll be nothing like that,' Bernie assured him.

Danny's sharp grey eyes hardened, his expression becoming grave. 'I want you in on this deal with me because I think you'll be good at it, but if I ever find out you've been linin' yer own pocket at my expense, I'll kill yer. Is that understood?'

'There ain't no call to be so dramatic,' said Bernie lightly.

'I mean it. There'll be no second chances.'

'All right, all right,' said Bernie, surprised at his vehemence. 'You have my word.'

'Good. Just as long as we understand each other,' said Danny, adding in a lighter vein, 'Now, how about another drink?'

*　　　*　　　*

'You want me to lend you the money to buy into a nightclub?' said Amy that evening.

'I'd pay it back with interest,' Bernie said persuasively. 'We can 'ave it all done legally, if yer like, and I'll pay back so much a month once I get started.'

'A legal agreement between husband and wife— don't be ridiculous,' she said. 'If I decide to let you have the money, it will be on trust, though God knows you don't deserve it.'

'I've changed, Amy,' he said. 'You know I've been straight for years.'

'Mmm, that's true.' She looked at him thoughtfully. He hadn't looked so alive in years. His dark eyes, so lacklustre for so long, now gleamed with enthusiasm and, she had to admit, wickedness.

380

His whole persona had regained its self-assurance. Once again he looked as though the universe was his to command, despite his wooden leg. It was a treat to see it. And she could think of no business for which he was more suited than a nightclub. She accepted the fact that she probably would never see her money again but it would be worth the loss to have him leading a normal life again. Normal by his standards anyway.

'So what do you say?' he asked earnestly. 'I need to know right away or he'll offer it to someone else.'

'Tell your friend you're in,' she said. 'I'll go to the bank tomorrow and arrange to withdraw the money.'

'You won't regret it,' he said, limping to her and giving her a hug. 'You're a real diamond, Amy.'

He was just like one of the children when they had won her over. All his old charm was back with the return of confidence. 'Go on with you, Bernie Banks,' she said playfully. 'You're all sweetness and light when you get your own way. But you're welcome to the cash. And good luck with the club.'

And silently she said, Well, Amy, it's time to lock up your valuables. Bernie's back on form.

*　　　*　　　*

As it happened she had no worries on that score because once the club deal was finalised he was hardly ever home. Having had no interest in anything for so long, he now went to the other extreme and made the club his life. Because he worked until the small hours, it made sense for him to stay in the flat at the club. And because there was always a lot of administrative work to do there, he never seemed to find the time to come home during the day. But because of their odd connubial circumstances, this peculiar arrangement worked very well.

'Hello, stranger,' she would say good-humouredly on the odd occasion when he did appear on the scene. 'I thought you'd left home for good.'

'You don't get rid of me that easily,' he'd laugh. 'I'll still turn up to torment you every now and again.'

Anyone could see he was happy in his work and Amy was delighted. He didn't discuss the club with her and, knowing he liked to keep his business affairs to himself, she didn't pry. They both benefitted from his new lease of life. He had found his niche in life, and Amy was relieved of the burden of having him constantly close at hand. She knew that if ever she needed him, he would come. He always had, married to her or not. Since their marriage had petered out so amicably, and neither had plans to remarry, the question of formally ending it never arose.

*　　*　　*

Seasons changed, time passed, and Amy's children grew up. It came as a shock to her, having worked so hard in the business for her sons' future, to find that neither of them wanted to go into it. Dear, intelligent Victor announced that he wanted to become a school-teacher, after matriculating, and went away to training college. Wild, adventurous Dickie decided that the jewellery trade was not nearly exciting enough for him, and joined the navy.

Whilst she was disappointed, Amy admired their spirit and didn't try to persuade them to change their minds. Remembering how bitter she had felt towards her father for interfering in her life, she wished them well and assured them that if they did feel differently, later on when they had seen something of life, there would always be a place for them in the firm.

By 1925 the household was entirely female except when the boys visited. Amy, Violet and Connie lived harmoniously together, though the latter was more often out of the house than at home. Wanting her to have secure employment when she left school, Amy had given her a job at the shop with the idea of training her for promotion, and later a more permanent position in the firm. But although the girl had tried to take a real interest, her heart hadn't been in it. Despite all Amy's commonsense lectures, she still wanted to go on the stage as a musical comedy performer.

Finally, Amy had decided that if she was determined on such an insecure path, she should at least have the advantage of being properly trained. Now eighteen, Connie was taking a course in stage training at a small academy in Kensington. She loved it, and enjoyed a hectic social life with the friends she had made there. Both Amy and Violet took vicarious pleasure in her girlish escapades. Her life was so much more lively and colourful than theirs had been at that age.

When she did happen to be at home, the house reverberated to the cheerful sound of her gramophone and the bump and shuffle of her feet as she practised the Charleston. She dressed fashionably in short skirts and shapeless dresses, but much to Amy's relief didn't join the craze for cigarette smoking that was so prevalent among young women. Though her abstinence was more from concern for her singing voice than anything else, Amy suspected.

'She's so much like her mother, and such fun to have around,' Amy said to Ned one evening in February after a business meeting. 'She makes Violet and me feel like girls again. Things were so dreary in our day in comparison.'

'Do you think she has sufficient talent to make a living on the stage?' he asked.

'Yes, I do,' she said, 'I was very impressed by her performance in a show the academy put on recently. Her singing voice is stronger than her mother's was, and I'm hoping the training will improve her chances. It isn't so easy to get started as it was for her mother, now that so many of the music halls have gone.'

'There's still the variety theatres.'

'Oh, yes, and there's a good chance for a girl with her talent in revues and musicals.'

'Does she realise that for every one that makes it on the stage, thousands of others don't?'

'Oh, yes, I've been through all that with her many times over the years, but there's no putting her off. Her mother would have been proud of her, and so am I.'

'I suppose she's like a daughter to you, isn't she?'

'Definitely. And I can't help admiring her determination.'

They had both had a particularly tiring working day which had concluded with a long directors' meeting during which they had discussed the latest spate of burglaries at jewellers' shops in the London area. Now they were unwinding with a cup of coffee in Amy's office, Ralph having declined an invitation to join them because he was tired. Now past seventy, he still attended directors' meetings and took a close interest in the firm, making regular visits to the Ealing shop despite a heart condition that had

384

slowed him down these last few years.

'It was lucky for her that you took her in,' Ned remarked conversationally, finishing his coffee and gathering his papers together.

'Lucky for me too,' said Amy. 'She's given me so much.'

'Her life didn't get off to a very good start though, did it, with her father drowning before she was even born and her mother dying so young,' he said chattily. 'The poor kid could have had a far less easy path if you hadn't stepped in.'

'Maybe.'

'You've made sure she didn't want for anything.'

'No one could replace her mother, of course,' she said, 'but I've done my best for her, and enjoyed every moment.'

'Are we off then?'

'Yes, I'll just pop these cups into the kitchen,' she said. 'Then we'll be on our way.'

*   *   *

Later that same evening, Ralph Jackson sat in his fireside chair absently watching Florence who was sitting with her head cocked towards the wireless set, listening intently. They had been the first people in the avenue to get a loudspeaker, which made listening in so much more convenient than having headphones clamped to the ears, he thought. There was a day when that triumph of one-upmanship would have given him pleasure. But these days he tended to make purchases for practical reasons rather than for show. Another burden of old age, he thought, one became so boringly ordinary.

The BBC was transmitting a programme of light

music which suited his mood perfectly. Firstly because it entertained Florence, thus relieving him of her conversational demands; secondly because it required no concentration on his part and left him free to mull over the conversation he had overheard between Ned and Amy earlier. 'So much like her mother ... such fun to have around ... lucky you took her in ... a far less easy path if you hadn't stepped in.'

He hadn't intended to eavesdrop. He'd popped into the gents' cloakroom after the meeting. Passing Amy's office on his way to the stairs afterwards, his attention had been attracted by references to his daughter, a young lady in whom he had become increasingly interested these last few years. As the past had become more important to him than the present, regret and conscience had begun to dominate his life. And overhearing his daughter's circumstances being discussed aggravated the situation even more.

When it had become clear to him that it was not going to be possible to forge any sort of relationship with his grandsons, his thoughts had turned to Connie. He'd begun to make a point of listening when Amy spoke of her to the staff in the shop. He often paid a visit to the shop at closing time in the hope of seeing her if she came to meet Amy. When this did happen he never spoke to her, but these glimpses gave him a perverse pleasure because, in looking at her, he was seeing her mother who, had she lived, would have made his old age tolerable. And he had treated her as of no more importance than his household bills. Regular payments ensured no further trouble.

He looked across at Florence, white-haired and

frail now, her ample proportions diminished with age, back humped, features sharper. She was nodding her head in time to the music, totally immersed in her own pleasure. Typical of their relationship, he thought, for they had never really shared anything beyond the material possessions he had acquired for them. They had never talked about life or love. He didn't even know what her favourite colour was, or what piece of music she liked in particular. All his fault, of course. He'd always been far too full of himself to make the effort to get to know his own wife. Often, in recent years, he had found himself on the point of telling her about Clara, to ease the burden and purge the guilt from his autumn years. But, somehow, the moment had never been right.

A sudden need to be alone overwhelmed him. 'I'm going out for a walk, dear,' he said, rising from his chair.

She turned to him, frowning, as though irritated at being interrupted in her musical enjoyment. 'A walk?' she said with puzzled disapproval. 'It's a bit late to turn out, isn't it?'

He took his watch out of his waistcoat pocket and consulted it. 'It's only just gone ten o'clock. And I'll sleep better after some exercise.'

'Make sure you wrap up well then,' she said, more from habit than any great concern. 'It is February remember.'

Warmly clad in his street clothes, a dark overcoat, bowler hat and gloves, he left the house and walked along Orchard Avenue towards the Broadway. It was a cold, dry night with a clear sky and a large disc of moon spreading a silvery light over the rooftops and privet hedges. There wasn't much activity in this back

387

road on a winter night: the odd motor car, a few people hurrying home. The lit windows looked cosy, the clarity of the night air making everything more sharply defined.

The Broadway had more of a bustle about it but being a winter week-night there were not many people on the streets. They were all snugly ensconced in the pubs or picture palaces.

Away from the cloistered atmosphere of the house, Ralph's spirits lifted, the fresh air revitalising him. He had no particular destination in mind, intending just to wander where the mood took him. But after passing The Feathers he found himself irresistibly drawn towards Danby Walk.

Having the shop keys on the key-ring in his pocket compelled him to call in. Being there alone, outside business hours, was always a source of great joy to him. It gave him the chance to survey his kingdom; the one he had created. These days he left others to run it, but it was still the empire he had built from nothing.

Deciding to go in by the rear entrance, because there were fewer bolts to manipulate on the back door, he made his way through the back-alley and into the small yard at the rear of the shop. The door led into the workshop, and he stepped carefully into the dark shadowy room. Hearing the clink of glass under his feet, he turned on the gaslight and looked above him to see that the skylight had been broken.

Fury rather than fear was Ralph's dominating emotion. How dare anyone break into *his* shop, the shop *he* had worked hard and long for? How dare they violate his privacy by entering his premises without permission. *How dare they!* In his eagerness to find out what was missing, it didn't occur to him that the burglars might still be there. It wasn't until he heard a movement in the showrooms that he realised this was the case.

'Come on out of there,' he called, outrage at someone trespassing on his domain obliterating any thought for his own safety. 'Come on, out of there, you varmints.'

Not a sound. He walked boldly into the shop and turned on the light, whereupon two rough-looking young men peered at him from beside one of the central glass showcases which had been smashed open.

'Orlright, Grandpa,' said one of them. 'Keep quiet and yer won't get 'urt.'

'Not a word,' said the other.

Never taking their eyes off him, they moved backwards through the showrooms towards the workshop, obviously intending to make their escape through the back door. One of them was clutching a sack which Ralph guessed contained items from stock. *His* stock.

'Give that bag to me,' said Ralph, still blinded to danger by rage.

'Do give over,' said the robber.

'Whatever you've got in there belongs to me.'

'Shut yer mouth, old man,' growled the man with the bag.

'Yeah, shut it,' said the other.

'I certainly will not,' puffed Ralph, making a grab for the bag but missing it as the men made a dash for the workshop.

Ralph tore after them, managing to clutch one of them by the arm as he made his way past the work-benches. The robber shook off his grip and swung round. 'Get away from me, you silly old fool!'

But Ralph was far too angry to be deterred, and grabbed his arm again, ignoring the fact that he was no match for the man's youthful strength. 'You don't scare me,' he gasped, breathless with exertion and anger.

'I told you to get away from me and I meant it,' said the sack carrier.

'Don't you tell me what to do,' wheezed Ralph. 'I own this shop.'

His assailant grabbed Ralph by the arms and pinned him against the wall, kicking him sharply on the shins. 'P'raps this'll make yer shut up.'

Ralph cried out in agony, but continued to struggle.

'Right, you've asked for it,' the man snarled, aiming harsh blows with his fists at Ralph's chest and stomach.

As he creased over, winded, both the men ran out through the back door, leaving him staggering dazedly across the room. As dizziness overwhelmed him, he slumped to the floor, banging his head on the corner of the pressing machine as he fell.

*   *   *

'How are you feeling now, Ralph dear?' asked Florence, a week later when her husband was recovering from the assault, having suffered concussion and severe bruising.

'How do you expect me to feel when scoundrels like that are allowed to get away with hundreds of pounds-worth of our stock?' he barked.

'You really must try to forget about it.'

'I mean to say, what do the police get paid for?' he raged, ignoring her advice. 'To sit around drinking tea all day or to protect us from criminals?'

'Calm down, Ralph,' Florence urged him. 'Remember what the doctor said about avoiding stress.'

'Easy for him to say it, he hasn't been robbed.'

She tutted. 'Fancy taking on those burglars single-handed when you have a weak heart. A man of your age, too. Why, you're lucky to be alive.'

'They wouldn't have got away with it if I'd been thirty years younger,' he said.

'But you're *not* thirty years younger, are you?' she pointed out.

'So what was I supposed to do? Just let them get on with it because I'm getting on a bit?'

'Yes. The business is insured against theft,' she reminded him firmly. 'You should have slipped away as soon as you realised what was happening.'

'Not likely,' he ranted, his cheeks stained with an unhealthy flush.

'I mean, what have you gained but some nasty bruises?'

'It's a bloody disgrace on the part of the police to let this sort of thing happen,' he said. 'They should have more men patrolling the Broadway at night. They'll never catch the bounders now.'

'I expect they'll do their best.' Florence sighed wearily for Ralph was not an easy patient.

'Huh! That's debatable.'

'Now, is there anything you want from downstairs? The wireless perhaps?'

'No, thank you,' he said, wincing as a sudden movement reminded him of his bruises. 'I just want to be left in peace.'

Alone in the room his fiery spirits calmed, leaving him deflated and gloomy. Another failure, he

391

thought, recalling his powerlessness against the thieves. Was he to meet his Maker not having got one thing right in the whole of his life? Florence's words lingered in his mind. 'A man of your age too. You're lucky to be alive.'

Yes, but for how much longer? A feeling of panic consumed him. Something that had been nagging at the back of his mind for a long time now came to the fore, increasing in importance with each passing second. When the maid brought his afternoon tea, he said, 'Will you ask my wife to come and see me, please?'

'Certainly, sir.'

Thinking a change of heart over the wireless set was the reason she had been summoned to his bedside, Florence was surprised when he asked her to arrange to have the family solicitor visit him as a matter of urgency.

'But Ned will see about the insurance claim for the burglary,' she said, misunderstanding the reason for the request. 'There's no need for you to worry about it.'

'I do not wish to see him about the burglary,' he said cryptically.

And Florence didn't change the habit of a lifetime by prying into his business affairs.

*   *   *

When his meeting with the solicitor was over, Ralph felt better than he had in ages. But the job was still incomplete. So he sent for Florence and told her exactly what he had done and why. Everything about the past was laid before her. There were no more secrets between them. Her pain and humiliation was

392

not something he enjoyed, but the knowledge that it was better for her to hear the truth from him rather than someone else if she survived him, made him feel justified in his actions. He had left her well provided for financially, so he could rest easy in that respect.

Having confessed his sins to his wife, he felt cleansed and complacent. Now he could die a happy man. Since Ralph was to sensitivity what the Pankhursts were to subservience, it didn't occur to him that perhaps it might have been kinder to have left the poor woman in ignorance.

Nor, in his selfish quest for absolution, did he consider the pain and bitterness his so-called act of charity might cause its recipient—which it did when his heart finally gave up on him a few months later.

CHAPTER NINETEEN

'But it doesn't make sense,' said Connie in bewilderment. 'Why would my cousins' grandfather leave all his share of his business to me and not them? I mean, he doesn't even know me?'

Bracing herself for what now must be done, Amy said, 'Because he was your father.'

The young woman stared at Amy, green eyes wide with disbelief. 'You're joking.'

'No joke.'

'Don't be silly, Amy, you know my father was lost at sea.'

Amy shook her head.

'*None* of it was true?'

'I'm afraid not.'

'Why?'

'It was your mother's invention to spare you from the truth.'

'The truth?'

'She and Ralph Jackson had been lovers for a very long time,' she said. 'But he ended it when she fell pregnant with you.'

Connie's face was bloodless, her eyes dull with pain. 'Oh God, poor Mum.'

'This legacy is his way of making amends, I suppose.'

It was a May afternoon and they were in Amy's parlour, having just arrived back from the solicitor's office to which Connie had been summoned by letter. Amy was glad the lawyer had been unable to offer Connie an explanation for her bequest. Since Ralph had made it impossible for her to continue in blissful ignorance, it was better she learn the truth from someone who loved her, rather than a stranger at an office desk. For, generous though the legacy was, learning of its origins could be an emotional disaster. How typical of Ralph to leave some ghastly melodrama behind him, Amy thought.

'I just can't believe it. I'm used to being illegitimate but this . . .'

Deeming it wise to highlight the positive aspects, Amy said, 'This means you'll be quite well off. You'll have a regular income, even if you don't take an active part in the firm.'

Connie stared silently into space, biting her lip anxiously. 'I suppose it was his idea for my mother to tell me a pack of lies,' she said eventually, ignoring Amy's last comment. 'To protect himself rather than me.'

'I should think his circumstances had a bearing on it, yes,' she was forced to agree.

'So my mother was just his bit on the side and he didn't give a damn about either of us.'

'That isn't quite true,' said Amy, keen to soften the blow. 'He supported both of you right up until she died, and I took over.'

'Charming,' Connie said in a thin high voice. 'He dumped his responsibilities on to you without so much as a second thought.'

'No, it wasn't like that at all,' Amy corrected emphatically. 'I *wanted* to support you once I became your guardian. And I could well afford it.' She searched for the right words to explain how all this had come about. 'I was very fond of your mother. She was more like an elder sister to me than an aunt. I hated Ralph for what he had done to her, and to me. He offered to continue to pay for your upkeep. But I wouldn't take his money.'

Realising how baffled Connie must be, Amy said, 'It was through your mother's relationship with him that I first became involved with the Jacksons. But I think I had better tell you the whole story.'

When Amy had finished, Connie was distraught. 'So my whole life has been based on a rotten lie. Why didn't you tell me who I really was when I was old enough to understand?'

'Because it wasn't what your mother would have wanted.'

'My mother isn't around to confirm that.'

'All right, so it was my decision. I didn't think it would serve any good purpose for you to know.'

Connie got up and began to pace the room, her slender body trembling with suppressed emotion. 'Don't you think I had the right to know that I am the daughter of a pig, that I have bad Jackson blood in me? Ugh! Just the thought of him makes my skin

395

crawl.'

'I didn't see any point to your knowing. You've been like a daughter to me,' said Amy. 'And that's how I always think of you.'

'But I'm not your daughter, am I?' She narrowed her eyes viciously. 'Let's see. What relation does this make me to Vic and Dickie? Now let's work this out ...if I'm their grandfather's daughter, then I am their father's sister, which makes me their aunt.'

'Technically, yes,' said Amy. 'But you're their second cousin on your mother's side. And most of all you're their friend, and that's all that matters.'

'No, it isn't,' the girl said coldly. 'This changes everything. I'm a Jackson. I'm part of the family that disowned you and your sons because you weren't good enough for them. I have the rotten blood of the man who used and deserted my mother.'

'At least he's done something to make it up to you,' said Amy, hoping to soothe her, though personally she thought this one of Ralph's cruellest actions, albeit he probably hadn't realised it.

'He's done nothing that required any effort or guts,' she said. 'He didn't even have the courage to come clean about it while he was still alive.'

Amy couldn't argue with that without insulting Connie's intelligence. 'Well, he's dead now, so just forget all about him and make the most of your inheritance.'

'Make the most of it!' she shrieked. 'I don't want his bloody shares.'

'Sell them then,' said Amy. 'They'll be worth a bit.'

Connie raised her hands theatrically, on the verge of tears. 'Don't you understand? I don't want anything to do with them. I won't accept them so they are not mine to sell. I want nothing of his. It makes me feel sick just to think that I'm part of him.'

And bursting into tears, she ran from the room.

Hearing the front door slam, Amy went after her, cursing Ralph Jackson for troubling her family even from beyond the grave. It was only natural that Connie would be upset. Amy wanted to try to help her to get the whole thing into perspective before it ran wild in her imagination.

Connie's red hair and yellow dress made her conspicuous as she marched along Merrydene Avenue towards the Broadway. Amy hurried after her, keeping her eyes fixed on that splash of colour. Unfortunately it had been swallowed up by the crowds when Amy turned into the Broadway.

The whole area was packed with people as the General Strike reached its sixth day. Passions were running high here. Strikers were angry that the government had called in troops, special constables and volunteers to keep essential services going. But there was an equally determined group of people who didn't want the country brought to a standstill. Representatives from both sides insulted and chivvied each other.

Amy's path was blocked by an angry mob of pro-strike demonstrators, crowding round a 'black leg' bus which had a soldier at the wheel with a special constable and a uniformed policeman riding with him for protection. Through a gap in the crowd, Amy could see barbed wire tied across the bonnet of the bus as a deterrent to the protestors. These were ugly times. The shouting she could hear further along the street proved to be caused by a wall of humanity trying to immobilise a tram with stones and crowd power.

Scuffles were breaking out between volunteers and

397

strikers, union men and special constables. The crowds were pushing this way and that. Amy was swept along with them. All hope of finding Connie was lost. The only thing she could do was go home and wait until the girl got back. It took a while to free herself from the multitudes, and when she got home Connie had beaten her to it.

'She's in her bedroom,' Violet said.

'Thank God for that.'

She found Connie sitting on the edge of her bed. 'Sorry I went off like that,' she said in a surprisingly calm tone.

'That's all right, love.'

'I just had to get out of the house for a while.'

'It's understandable that you're upset.' Amy sat down beside her, slipping a sympathetic arm around her shoulders. 'We need to talk this thing through.'

'I don't feel like talking right now,' she said, shrugging off Amy's embrace and standing up. 'Maybe I'll feel more like it tomorrow.'

'As you wish,' said Amy, relieved that she seemed less hysterical, but suspicious of her strange mood.

Connie didn't eat any dinner and was very quiet all evening, spending most of the time in her room. But there was no music; no thump of dancing feet. Amy thought it best to leave her alone until tomorrow. A night's sleep could make all the difference.

*　　*　　*

The next morning Amy was wakened by Violet with the alarming news that Connie had gone.

'Her bed was empty when I took her in a cup of tea,' she said anxiously. 'Most of her clothes have gone.' She handed Amy an envelope. 'It was on her

398

dressing table.'

With trembling fingers, Amy tore the letter open.

Dear Amy,

I've gone away because it's time I stopped sponging on you and stood on my own two feet. I suppose it should have occurred to me long ago, the burden I was placing on you. But I never gave it a thought. Probably because I always felt like one of the family. Now I don't feel as though I belong anywhere. A hanger-on, you might say. You should have told me the truth as soon as I was old enough to understand these things. At least then I would have been off your hands sooner. Now I feel humiliated and ashamed.

Because I came to you at such a young age, I took all you did for me for granted. Now I realise I must have been like a stray dog who was left with no one to look after it. How annoying it must have been for you to have an 'orphan' foisted on to you when its father was still alive and able to take responsibility. I'm sorry if I seemed to accept it all without a second thought, and so ashamed. I am very grateful to you for everything you've done for me, really, but now I shall find lodgings somewhere.

I haven't changed my mind about the shares my 'father' left me. I don't want them and can't even bear to think about them because I hate that man so much, even though he's dead. I grew up loathing him for what he did to you and the boys, never dreaming what he'd done to my mother. Perhaps you can tell the solicitor that I won't accept them and he'll do whatever has to be done in cases like this? Perhaps they can be transferred to the boys, though I doubt if they would want them either. I know nothing about this sort of thing, as you know.

Thanks for everything.

Love,

Connie

'Oh, Vi,' sighed Amy, lying weakly back against the pillows. 'That poor misguided girl.'

*   *   *

That same morning Bernie was at the desk in his office, meticulously altering the figures on a bill from a comedian who had entertained at Bubbles recently. Careful to use the same shade of ink, he changed the figure of two pounds to three. Satisfied that the alteration was indetectable, he placed the invoice into his out tray for the club secretary to collect and file later on. He then set to work similarly on an account from a firm of decorators who had recently done a small job for the club. Pleased with his efforts he took a cigar from a silver box and lit it, leaning back in his chair, enjoying his superior position.

The premises that throbbed with life by night were still and silent now, the smell of stale beer and cigarette smoke permeating everything, even here upstairs in the office. The charwomen had done their work and left. Soon he would have to make a call to the brewery to find out what was happening about his delivery with this bloomin' strike dragging on. Then he had a couple of acts to see, a waitress to interview, and a meeting with his chef to discuss tonight's menu. There was always plenty for him to do outside opening hours, and Bernie enjoyed every single

400

moment of his life as a nightclub proprietor. He loved the prestige of having staff working for him, and the glamour of mingling with the punters, dressed like a toff. He was a somebody for the first time in his life.

True to his word, Danny gave him a free hand with the running of the place, and was always too busy attending to his other interests on the London entertainment scene to do more than call in occasionally to see how things were going. The perfect arrangement for a compulsive thief like Bernie. Just as long as he remembered to cover the amount he pilfered from the takings by altering various invoices from artistes and casual contractors, there was no chance of discovery.

Bernie was doing so well with his ill-gotten gains, he was building up quite a nest egg, which was safely hidden away in his flat. His legitimate earnings were good, and his lifestyle economical. He spent a fair bit on stylish clothes, but he certainly didn't pay for his drinks and cigars across the bar, not in his own club where his work was also his social life. One of these days he might even surprise Amy by paying back the money she had lent him.

The telephone on his desk rang.

'Hello, Bernie, it's Amy.'

'Amy,' he said, delighted to hear from her. 'That's a coincidence, I was just thinking about you.'

'Nothing bad, I hope.'

'Course not.' He puffed on his cigar. ''Ow are yer, love? Yer sound a bit odd.'

'I'm feeling a bit fraught, to tell the truth,' she explained. 'Can you come home for a few hours? I need your moral support.'

'Are you ill?'

'No.'

'What *is* the matter then, only I've got a lot to do here ... I'm not sure I can get away.'

She told him about Connie, concluding with, 'I telephoned the academy. They said she has contacted them to say she won't be going any more.'

'Is that all?'

'Isn't it enough?' She was surprised and disappointed at his lack of interest.

'I thought something really serious 'ad 'appened.'

'This is serious. I have to find her, Bernie. This could affect her whole future.'

'How old is she now?'

'Nearly nineteen.'

'Old enough to look out for her own future, I'd say.'

'But, Bernie ...'

'You've brought 'er up and done yer best for 'er, now it's up to 'er.'

'So you won't come home to help me look for her?'

'You know if it was anything urgent, I'd be there like a shot.'

'It is urgent to me.'

'Get it into perspective, love,' he said. 'You're the girl's cousin, not 'er keeper. If she wants to go off, she's perfectly entitled. Chasing after 'er'll do no good.'

'But to go rushing off like this when she's had a shock and doesn't know what she's doing ... Who knows what sort of a state she'll get herself into?'

'If findin' out her old man was loaded and has seen 'er all right in his will is the worst she'll ever have to suffer, I envy her.'

'What a terrible way of looking at it.'

'It's the only sensible way to look at it,' he said. 'Anyway, there's no point in trying to bring her back if she doesn't want to come. She's a big girl now.'

'I wasn't going to try to bring her back,' explained Amy, 'I just think I should talk to her, try to make her feel better.'

'Gor Blimey, she gets part of a business left to 'er and she needs to be made to feel better,' he said. 'She ought to be singing for joy.'

'You just don't understand, do you?' she said, and the line went dead.

Bernie replaced the receiver feeling uneasy, though he didn't really know why he should. After all, it wasn't as though Amy herself was in trouble. He'd walk through fire for her if she had been, she knew that. She *had* sounded upset though, and she wasn't the sort to make a fuss unnecessarily. Maybe he ought to show willing and go home for a few hours? Yes, he'd do that. He reached for the telephone, intending to tell her he was on his way, but was deterred by the fact that it started ringing.

''ello, Bernie, it's Danny.'

'Wotcha, mate.'

'I think it's about time I called in to see you. It's bin a while since we got together.'

'Yeah, sure, when did you 'ave in mind?'

'I'll be with you in about an hour, all right?'

'That's fine, mate,' he said, Amy and her problems disappearing from his mind completely.

* * *

Amy wasn't so much angry as hurt by Bernie's attitude. She no longer expected loyalty from him as far as money was concerned. But this was the first time in the whole of their long association he had ever let her down at a time of personal crisis.

403

But, being realistic, nothing would be gained by rushing all over London trying to find Connie. And in the meantime life and business went on...

She had a miserable day at the shop. Added to her own private hell, the business routine was thrown into disarray by the strike. The chaos on public transport caused staff to be late or absent altogether, deliveries didn't arrive, and shop trade was abysmal because all but those shopping for essentials were avoiding the Broadway for fear of violence erupting among the angry crowds.

When Ned appeared at closing time with a package of much needed brooch pins, he said, 'What's the matter, Amy? You look as though you've lost a sixpence and found a farthing.'

'I've lost a cousin,' she said. 'And found a whole lot of trouble.'

'Oh dear, you are in a bad way,' he said with a wry grin. 'Why not tell me all about it over dinner?'

'It's nice of you to suggest it,' she said, warmed by his sympathetic attitude. 'But I'll be rotten company. I'm not really in the mood for a restaurant.'

'Let's eat in then, at my place,' he suggested. 'I get fed up with dining alone, so you'd be doing me a favour.'

'Well...'

'Go on,' he urged. 'You've no little ones waiting for you at home, and I've got the car outside.'

'If you're sure you don't mind having a misery guts at your table, I'd love to,' she agreed at last.

After his earlier prejudice against motorised transport, Ned had succumbed to the convenience a few years ago when motoring had become a practical way of getting about rather than just a hobby for the rich. Now, as Amy climbed into his Austin Seven, she

404

realised that nothing seemed quite so bad when he was around.

*   *   *

'I'd like you to meet David Wood, Mother,' said Gwen Jackson that same evening, ushering her friend into the drawing room at Floral House. 'David is a very good friend of mine.'

Florence glanced at him without interest. 'How do you do?' she said, cutting a formidable figure in her black mourning clothes, her thin white hair drawn back in a bun.

'I'm very pleased to meet you, Mrs Jackson,' said David, smiling bravely. 'Gwen has told me a lot about you.'

'Has she indeed?' said Florence, observing him coolly from her armchair by the window.

'May I offer you my sincere condolences?'

She acknowledged this with a nod.

'David is having dinner with us this evening, Mother,' said Gwen. 'I told you about it, remember?'

'We shouldn't be entertaining,' said Florence curtly. 'We're still in mourning.'

There was an embarrassed silence.

'We're not having a dinner party or anything, Mother,' said Gwen through clenched teeth. 'It will just be David.'

'Having visitors seems awfully like entertaining to me,' said Florence sarcastically.

'As I have come back home to live I must be able to have friends call on me.'

'Perhaps it would be better if I just slipped off and saw you another time, Gwen,' suggested David worriedly.

Stifling murderous impulses towards her mother, Gwen placed a reassuring hand on his arm. 'Please don't be offended. I'm sure Mother didn't mean to be rude.' She turned an admonitory stare on her mother. 'Did you, dear?'

'If you say so,' was the icy reply.

After her father's death, a month ago, Gwen had felt duty bound to return to the family home to live, having dwelled happily in a small flat near the hospital for several years. Having stayed on in nursing after the war and passed all the relevant exams she had now reached the rank of sister. She had found fulfilment and independence through her work, and learning to live within the restrictions of the parental household again was not easy.

Within her professional environment Gwen felt like a confident, successful woman with a useful role in life. In her mother's house her status was nil because she had failed to keep a man. But her mother was frail now. She needed someone besides the servants around her. Gwen's father's death and the scandal it had uncovered had put years on her. Indeed it had been a shock to Gwen to discover the truth about her father. All those years and his own daughter had been living in the same neighbourhood in Amy's care. Frankly, Gwen thought it was scandalous the way he had ignored his responsibilities. But she hadn't upset her mother more than she already was by saying so. If blaming the whole thing on to his mistress helped her to cope, so be it.

Fortunately they had managed to stop the scandal getting out. Ned had had to be told since Connie had become a part owner of his business but no one else besides the participants knew. Knowing what she did

406

about her mother's past, the latter's outrage was a little hard for Gwen to take. But being familiar with the way Florence's mind worked she guessed that having her husband's infidelity become public knowledge would have been far more painful to her than the actual acts of transgression. Even in her old age, she was still paranoid about the family reputation. Personally, Gwen didn't give a damn about it. Twelve years in the nursing profession had clarified her priorities and cured her of all pretensions.

But right now she was more concerned with the way her present domestic arrangements were interfering with her personal life. She was used to privacy and freedom. She liked having people drop in casually to share food and conversation with her without having to account to anyone else.

She had invited David to the house as a way of establishing her right to some independence and companions of her own. If she allowed her mother to have her way, she would lose the circle of friends she had built up over the years. And she really didn't want to lose David's friendship. At the age of forty, Gwen felt comfortable in the company of a manfriend for the first time in her life. David was an accountant, a widower with a kind heart and a gentle humour with which Gwen was in tune. He was forty-five and she had been seeing him for several months.

They had met when he had been a patient on her ward, having a minor operation, and had struck up an immediate rapport. When he had gone home she had missed him and had admonished herself for allowing herself to become personally involved with a patient. But much to her amazement he had appeared at the hospital a few weeks later. He had invited her to a concert at the Albert Hall, having lacked the courage to offer the invitation before he was discharged.

That first outing had been such a success, others had followed. More concerts; dinners in restaurants; walks in the park; drives out to the country. It was a quiet, pleasant friendship rather than a heady exciting romance and finding someone like David to share her spare time with at her age was an unexpected pleasure. She had given up hope of such things years ago. Not that anything had actually happened beyond a few light embraces. David was far too much of a gentleman, thank goodness.

She had not dared to think ahead to a time when the friendship might move to another stage, fearing from past experience that all would be lost if that happened. But for the moment she enjoyed feeling she mattered to someone. Though if she wasn't careful, Mother would sabotage the relationship altogether.

'Since you're here, you'd better sit down then,' Florence was saying.

'Thank you,' said David, perching uncertainly on the edge of the sofa. He was not a robust man, but small and mousy-looking with a pale complexion, straight brown hair and warm shandy-coloured eyes peering out behind owlish spectacles. Gwen had often teased him because he looked so typical of his profession.

'Would you like a drink before dinner?' she asked.

'Yes, please,' he said. 'A small sherry, perhaps.'

'Mother?' said Gwen.

'Yes, a sherry, please.'

Gwen went over to the decanter on a highly polished cabinet and began to pour.

408

'Why not ring for one of the servants to do that?' said Florence.

'I'm not going to bring someone all the way up here just to pour three drinks.' Gwen thought how different all this was to the entertaining she did in her little flat where the guests usually brought a bottle of something and poured while she cooked. Moving back to Orchard Avenue was like taking a giant leap backwards in time.

'They are paid to wait on us,' Florence pointed out.

'Yes, but we're quite capable of seeing to a little thing like this for ourselves.' She put the drinks on a tray and handed them around. 'I told Cook to make dinner for eight o'clock. I hope that suits you, David.'

'Perfectly,' he said politely.

There was a painful silence during which he gulped his drink and cleared his throat nervously several times. Gwen didn't blame the poor man for feeling edgy. Mother in this mood was enough to paralyse a herd of stampeding cattle.

The atmosphere became even more mortifying when Florence spoke. 'So, what exactly is your interest in my daughter, Mr Wood?'

'Do call me David, please.'

'As you wish,' she said impatiently. 'But what is your answer to my question?'

Gwen stared dumbfounded as poor David choked on his sherry and went into a coughing fit. 'Oh dear,' he managed at last, face scarlet, eyes watering, 'it seems to have gone down the wrong way, I'm so sorry.'

'There's no need to apologise,' said Gwen, wondering whether to gag her mother with the nearest anti-macassar or strangle her.

'Surely you don't have marriage in mind?' continued Florence.

'I . . .'

'She's far too old. Missed the boat completely as far as having children is concerned.'

'Mother!' reproached Gwen, feeling about twelve years old and completely stripped of all self-esteem. How could she be so cruel? *How could she?* Smarting with humiliation, she stared at her hands in her lap, unable to face looking at David on the sofa beside her.

To her amazement she heard him say, 'Gwen and I haven't discussed the future, Mrs Jackson,' his voice trembling slightly, 'and I don't even know if she wants to get married, but I'd be honoured if she'd agree to be my wife.'

Slowly Gwen turned to face him. He was looking very flushed, but he smiled and winked at her before continuing to address the stunned Florence. 'Gwen isn't too old for anything as far as I'm concerned. On the contrary, her stimulating company keeps me young. As for children, I have no particular wish to have a family, though I'm sure it's still possible for Gwen.'

'Well,' gasped Florence, her skinny hand shaking as she held her sherry glass, 'you've certainly got plenty to say for yourself.'

'David,' said Gwen, throwing him a grateful look, 'I just don't know what to say.'

'I hope I haven't embarrassed you. I'm afraid I got a bit carried away.'

Florence stood up, glowering at them. 'I am going to my room. Tell Daisy I shall have my meal up there.'

'Don't be silly, Mother.'

410

'Oh dear, it's all my fault,' said David, 'I'm sorry to have upset you, Mrs Jackson, but you were being so unkind to Gwen, I had to speak up.'

'Your generation has no respect for its elders,' she said, her ashen face looking healthier for an angry flush to the cheeks, 'God knows what's happened to standards since the war. What with people saying what they like, and women showing their legs and smoking cigarettes, manners and morality seem to be a thing of the past. My daughter is one of the worst offenders. Flaunting herself, and with her father not yet cold in his grave.'

Since Gwen was far too inhibited to flaunt herself even if her life depended on it, she looked down at her black mourning clothes and said, 'That really is uncalled for.'

'There's more to mourning the dead than wearing dark clothes,' Florence pointed out sharply. 'You should be at home with me, not out at work and bringing strangers home.'

Being so deeply embarrassed as to be almost past caring, Gwen said, 'I do have my living to earn, Mother.'

'Rubbish,' she said. 'Your father saw to it that you are well provided for.'

'And as for bringing strangers home,' Gwen said, ignoring the last comment, 'David is not a stranger, he is a dear friend who has come to offer us comfort at this sad time.'

'He's no friend of mine.'

'Look, I'm most terribly sorry,' David interjected. 'I seem to be causing so much trouble, perhaps it really would be best if I were to leave.'

Gwen decided that her mother had tried her patience quite far enough for one day. 'You stay right where you are, David.' She turned to Florence, her brown eyes simmering with rage. 'If you would feel happier eating in your room, you go on up. I'll tell them downstairs.'

'Yes, you do that,' snorted Florence and left the room, trembling with rage.

'I'd better go, Gwen dear,' said David in the tense aftermath of her departure. 'I seem to have ruined the evening for everyone.'

'Nonsense,' she said. 'My mother is the one guilty of that. I invited you to dinner, and dinner you shall have.' She paused and looked into his face. The last few minutes had proved he was a big man whatever his physical size. How sweet it was of him to pretend to want to marry her just to counteract her mother's cruel remarks. 'Unless you feel the need to escape after such an ordeal?'

'Not at all.'

'I'm only sorry you've been so horribly embarrassed.'

'Don't worry about me,' he said. 'I can take it, but what about your mother? She is getting on a bit. Perhaps I shouldn't have spoken out of turn.'

'She's the one who did that,' she said. 'It will do her good to have someone stand up to her for a change. Now let's forget all about her and have another drink before dinner.'

But as she poured the drinks she was still burning with shame. How could things ever be the same between her and David after this? Damn Mother. Damn her.

CHAPTER TWENTY

Amy and Ned were having coffee in the drawing room, after dining on mutton and caper sauce, beautifully cooked by Ned's housekeeper, but only picked at by Amy whose appetite was diminished by stress.

'I hope your Mrs Walker won't take umbrage,' she said.

'Of course not, she's far too sensible for such whims.'

'It wouldn't do to upset her though, would it?' she remarked, 'Good domestic staff aren't so easy so find now that fewer people are going into service.'

'True, but I'm lucky with mine.' For several years he had employed a resident married couple as housekeeper and gardener. 'Anyway, I'm more concerned about you than the problem of servants. This business with Connie seems really to have upset you.'

'Yes, it has,' she confessed. 'I'm so worried about her. Can you imagine how she must feel? I mean, to have her cosy idea of her father shattered by the knowledge that he is really a man she hates, *and* that he rejected her.'

'I can see it must be traumatic for her.'

'And just when she needs me more than ever, she's gone off.' She put her coffee cup on the table nearby and leaned back in her chair, staring absently through the open window. It was a dry night with a hazy moon, the dark outline of the rooftops just visible against the urban, orange-tinted sky. The tall, shadowy trees outside the window waved and rustled

413

in the spring breeze. 'I feel so helpless.' She raised her hands despairingly. 'Is my family never to be free from the indulgences of Ralph Jackson? The bloody man is still haunting us from the grave.' She sighed. 'I keep thinking of her out there somewhere, miserable and alone. She could ruin her chances of having a future on the stage by giving up her training. It's such a waste of talent.'

'Do you think she might have gone to your mother's?' he suggested.

'I doubt it. I reckon she'll avoid relatives like the plague because they know the truth,' Amy declared. 'Connie is trying to run away from who she is and that means avoiding anyone who might remind her.' She looked across at Ned who was seated in a leather armchair on the other side of the unlit fireplace in which stood an embroidered fire-screen with a highly polished wooden stand. 'Bernie thinks I should just leave her to get on with it.'

'Does he really?' He sounded surprised.

'Mainly, I suspect, because he doesn't want to get involved,' she said. 'He's far too wrapped up in his night-club at the moment to care very much about anything else.'

'Oh dear, are things not going too well on the marital front?'

'There isn't a "marital front" to go well or otherwise between Bernie and me,' she explained, seeing no reason to hide the truth any longer. 'There never was much of one. I married him on the rebound from Clifford's death and I took him back out of pity and a sense of duty. What else could I do when he came back from the war disabled and homeless?'

'I can see it must have been difficult.'

'Now he's finding real success as a businessman he

414

can't even spare the time to come home when I need him.' She looked into Ned's warm brown eyes. 'And that hurts. That really hurts. Not from the point of view of a wife, but a friend. It's the first time he's ever let me down over something like this and I feel more betrayed than I did when he stole money from me. It's as though he's destroyed the only bond we ever had, that of friendship. I didn't want him to do anything for me or to stay long, just be there, for a while.'

And to her horror, the tension of the last forty-eight hours, coupled with her analysis of her thoughts about Bernie, culminated in a flood of tears. 'I'm so sorry, Ned,' she spluttered into her handkerchief, her head bowed, her whole body convulsed, 'I'm so very sorry.'

He was at her side instantly, sitting on the arm of her chair. 'Don't be sorry,' he said, slipping a strong, comforting arm around her shoulders. 'I'm here, and if you'll have me, I'll be here for you all the time.'

Drying her eyes, she turned slowly around and looked up at him, smiling but still uncertain. 'Ned?' she said quizzically. 'Do you mean ...?'

'Yes, I love you, Amy, even though it took me so long to realise it. I've kept quiet about it these last few years because I thought you and Bernie had sorted your marriage out.' He moved his arm away, wondering if he had spoken out of turn. 'But perhaps it was presumptuous of me.'

She blew her nose and stood up, opening her arms to him. 'Oh, Ned,' she said, chuckling shakily, 'I thought I'd never hear you say it. I started falling in love with you the night Molly died, I'm ashamed to say.'

'As long ago as that,' he said, kissing her joyfully.

'And in all those years you never said a word.'

'Well, friendship was all you seemed to want from me,' she said. 'Then, when I took Bernie back, there didn't seem to be any point in my making any sort of approach. Even though we didn't have a marriage as such, I wasn't free. I'm still not.'

'We'll sort everything out later,' he said tenderly. 'Connie, Bernie, the whole damned caboodle. But not now.' He looked meaningfully into her eyes. 'Not now.'

*   *   *

Gwen and David were at the coffee stage of their meal. 'I hope you didn't think all that talk about marriage was too cheeky of me.'

'Of course I didn't,' she assured him. 'I thought it was very kind of you to embark on such a pretence after Mother's crushing attack.'

'But I wasn't pretending, Gwen dear,' he said, reaching across the table and taking her hand. 'I meant every word. I know I'm not much of a catch for someone as rich as you, but I do have a steady job and a house of my own. I could afford to support you in reasonable comfort.' He looked earnestly into her face. 'You've come to mean so much to me.'

Her instinctive joy was followed by a feeling of panic and inadequacy. She couldn't go through all that again, the excuses, the fear, the whole damned trauma. Oh, why couldn't things have stayed as they were between them? Comfortable, pleasant and uncomplicated. If Mother hadn't been so rude, the idea might not have occurred to him, not for a while anyway. One fact remained. Despite all this turmoil. She loved David and wanted to share her life with

416

him. But what sort of a life would he have with a freak like her?

'Have I upset you?' he asked, frowning. 'You don't look very pleased.'

'Oh, David, I am, I am,' she said, gripping his hand even tighter, 'I've grown to love you too, but marriage ... I'm not sure.'

'Is it because your first marriage ended in divorce?' he said. 'And you're afraid to take the chance again?'

'No.'

'Is it because of your job then?'

'Not that.'

'Your mother then?' he said. 'You wouldn't want to leave her to get married.'

'Mother would be a problem,' she said, latching on to that as an excuse because she couldn't tell him the real reason.

'I see.'

'I'm all she's got now that Daddy's gone.'

'Surely we can work something out.'

'It won't be easy.'

'Perhaps we could have her to live with us, or if she wouldn't like that we could take a house nearby,' he suggested. 'I'd be prepared to sell my house and move nearer.'

'You'd do that for me?' she said.

'Certainly.'

'You're a dear sweet man, David,' she said. 'But I need a little time to think about it.'

'I see.'

He looked so downhearted, she went to him and slipped her arms around him. Whereupon he leapt up from his seat and swept her into his arms, kissing her thoroughly and passionately in a quite unprecedented manner. Gwen was so taken aback she didn't even tense. In fact she rather enjoyed it. But a kiss was one thing, the complications of its ultimate conclusion was quite another. Just thinking about it made her tremble.

*   *   *

When Amy woke the next morning in Ned's bed, she felt blissfully happy and relaxed, a feeling that was immediately superseded by a knot of tension in her stomach when she remembered the situation with Connie. But after consulting the clock on the bedside table to see that it was eight-fifteen, her immediate concern was getting to work on time. She was about to leap out of bed when Ned appeared fully dressed in his business clothes. He was carrying a breakfast tray.

'I thought I'd spare you the embarrassment of having Mrs Walker bring your tray up,' he said, 'though you've no need to worry, she's the soul of tact.'

'Has she had much practice with women she's found in your bed then?' she teased, calmed by his presence.

'Oh, yes, a different one every night of the week,' he laughed, setting the tray down on the bed-table and placing it in front of her.

'Breakfast in bed, eh?' she said, yawning. 'I *am* being spoiled.'

'You're worth it,' he said, planting a kiss on the top of her head and perching on the edge of the bed. 'I hope you're hungrier than you were last night though.'

'I'm ravenous.'

'That's what love does for you.'

418

'It may have escaped your notice,' she said, 'but I'm a working woman, and I'm already late.'

'As joint managing director, you're not expected to get there the minute they open the doors.'

'That's true.' She ran her eyes over him. 'But you're all ready to leave.'

'I want to get in early to sort a few things out because I am going to take the day off.'

'Oh?'

'Yes, I'm going to find Connie.'

'Really? But how?'

'Just leave it to me.'

'But why should you?' she asked. 'She's not your responsibility.'

'I think it's best if I find her rather than you,' he explained. 'She might be more receptive to me because I'm not involved. You can talk to her after I've had a go.'

'It's very good of you, Ned.'

'Nonsense. Your problems are mine from now on.'

Moist-eyed, she leaned over and kissed him. 'You're a good man, Ned. The only one for me.'

'And while we're on the subject,' he said, drawing back, 'you're going to have to get a divorce from Bernie, so that we can get married. I'm not keen on all this hole-and-corner stuff.'

'Nor am I,' she said. 'I shouldn't think Bernie will be difficult about it. He doesn't need me now he's back to his old self. We hardly see each other anyway, and he's very happy with his life at the club.'

'Have a word with him on the phone about it later on, if you get a chance,' he suggested. 'We need to get things underway as soon as possible. Divorce is a long drawn out process.'

'Yes, I'll give him a call later on.'

The news that Amy wanted a divorce brought Bernie rushing home, having been unable to talk her out of it on the phone. He was waiting for her in the sitting room when she got in from work that evening. 'I just can't believe it,' he said, full of affront. 'You want to end our marriage, just like that?'

'There's no "just like that" about it,' she pointed out. 'We've not had a marriage for many years, and since you've had the club you've hardly been home, so you can't possibly have any objections.'

'No objections?' he exploded. 'My wife wants a divorce and I ain't supposed to object. Oh, come on, Amy, grow up.'

Amy was astonished by his attitude. 'I've never felt more grown up,' she said. 'The immature bit was when I married you. It was a mistake and you know it. We were great as friends, we should have left it at that.'

'How long 'ave yer been carryin' on with Ned, then?' he asked sulkily.

'Since last night,' she said.

'*Last night*. Blimey! It's a bit soon to start talkin' about divorce, ain't it?'

'It came out into the open last night,' she explained. 'But I've been in love with him for years.'

'Oh, that's nice, innit?' he complained. 'You fancying another bloke while you were married to me.'

'Afraid you might lose access to my purse strings, Bernie, is that it?'

'That's a rotten thing to say.'

'Why else could you object to us divorcing?' she asked. 'Since we lead separate lives anyway.'

420

'You've always bin the only woman for me, Amy,' he said.

An unexpected lump gathered in her throat. Despite everything he was, and the way he had betrayed her, she still felt something for him. 'Maybe I am, but not as a wife. You're not cut out for marriage to anyone. You're far too single-minded.'

'Thanks very much,' he snapped sarcastically.

'It's true and you know it,' she said, 'I've done my best for you over the years and you'll always be special to me, but you and me are not meant to be man and wife. So give me what I want without a fuss, eh, Bern? Don't let's have any bad feeling. We've known each other too long to fall out now.'

'I ain't agreeing to a divorce,' he said, dark eyes black with anger.

'But, Bernie...'

'Nothing doin', darlin',' he said firmly. 'So you can go and tell that to yer fancy man.' He threw her a shrewd look. 'And I've never bin with another woman in all the years I've bin married to you so you'll find no grounds to divorce me, even if it is legal for women to do that now.'

'Don't you think you're being unreasonable?'

'No.'

'Think about it, Bernie,' she entreated. 'What I say makes sense.'

'There ain't nothing to think about. I ain't letting yer go and that's all there is to it.'

'But...'

'Now I must get back to the club,' he said, hobbling to the door on his stick. 'I do have a business to take care of.'

She rushed to the door and leaned against it, blocking his way. 'Oh, yes, you're a big man now,

421

aren't you?' she said bitterly. 'Far too busy to come home when I need you. So why not let me go and legally shed the responsibility that you don't want anyway?'

'Because I don't choose to,' he insisted. 'You're me wife and I ain't letting you go. Whatever you think of me, I love yer, in me own way.'

'So why not let me be happy?' she urged, 'You won't miss me because we hardly ever see each other.'

'We see enough of each other for you not to get me on grounds of desertion.'

'I must say I'm surprised at your attitude,' she said coldly, as she showed him to the door, 'I didn't know you could be so hateful.'

'Just goes to show how lackin' in common sense you are then, dunnit?' he said, limping through the front door and down the path.

*   *   *

The meeting with Bernie left Amy feeling depressed and not in the mood for company. So, when she received a telephone call from Gwen Jackson asking if she could pop over for a chat, she was tempted to put her off. She suspected it might be about Connie having inherited the shares Gwen perhaps considered should have stayed in her family. But deciding it was pointless to avoid the issue, she told her to come on over, and was surprised to find she was entirely wrong about the purpose of the visit.

'I just had to talk to someone about it,' she said, having explained to Amy about David's marriage proposal and her doubts about accepting it. 'I mean, who can a woman turn to for advice about intimate matters, since the subject is completely taboo?'

'It's difficult,' agreed Amy.

'I've been racking my brains all day, then suddenly it came to me. If anyone knows about that side of marriage, I thought, it's Amy with the experience of two children and two marriages.'

Amy laughed. 'I'd have thought you were more of an expert than me, being a nurse.'

'About the physical side, maybe,' she said. 'But mine are psychological problems.'

'Well, I'm not sure that I can help,' said Amy. 'But I'll certainly try. What's worrying you exactly?'

'It's all a bit embarrassing really,' Gwen whispered furtively as though they were not alone. 'I just can't bear the sexual side of things. I hate the whole wretched business.'

'Oh dear. Well, I'm sure you're not the only woman to feel like that if the truth were told,' said Amy. 'Was your husband very rough with you?'

'No, he wasn't, none of it was his fault,' she explained. 'I just used to go rigid. It got so bad I couldn't even bear him to touch me. I used to become almost hysterical when he tried to make love to me. Naturally he wasn't best pleased. Eventually he gave up trying and found someone else.'

'Did you love him?'

'Not really. I married him so that I could stop feeling like one of society's outcasts. I was under a lot of pressure from Mother. Having a spinster in the house was not good for the family image.' She gave Amy a sad look. 'I've been a big disappointment to her, what with being divorced and not producing any children.'

'I should think that was the trouble,' suggested Amy. 'Your not loving him.'

'Possibly. Though I always hated anything

423

physical with earlier boyfriends.'

'And you didn't love any of those either.'

'I was always too worried about the intimate side to allow any sort of feeling to develop.'

'Have you never been able to talk to your mother about it?' asked Amy.

'Good God, no,' exclaimed Gwen. 'She's the last person, with her Victorian attitude towards anything like that. She was preaching the evils of sex to me long before I was old enough to understand what she was talking about. She used to hammer on and on about it.' She paused thoughtfully and added almost to herself, 'Ludicrous, really.'

'Is it?'

'Yes, it is.' Gwen looked uncertainly at Amy. 'There's one thing that might have some bearing on my problem, something that happened when I was thirteen. An incident that changed my life. I realised later that it was probably the reason my mother came on so strong about sexual morality.'

'I'm willing to listen if you feel like talking about it.'

'Well ... I don't know if I should,' she confessed. 'Ned and I vowed never to tell anyone.'

'Ned?' said Amy, frowning. 'What's he got to do with it?'

'I'm not sure if I should say anything.'

Amy looked at her gravely. 'I think you ought to know that Ned and I will be getting married as soon as I can get a divorce from Bernie,' she said, 'so if it's something important, perhaps I should know about it.'

'You and Ned,' said Gwen, managing a smile despite her own problems. 'I've always had a feeling you two would get together in the end.'

'And I've always been curious about you and him,' said Amy. 'You've always seemed so close, yet you never teamed up as a couple.'

Gwen's expression was solemn. 'I think it's time you knew the truth.'

CHAPTER TWENTY-ONE

Ned finally got to talk to Connie that evening. He had begun his search with a visit to the academy where the principal was most co-operative and introduced him to Connie's particular friends among the pupils. They were not so helpful and denied all knowledge of her whereabouts. However, her special friend Lil proved less stubborn after a good lunch and several glasses of wine. Connie was apparently staying with her in her Paddington flat, but had gone to the West End to look for work in one of the stores and wouldn't be back until this evening.

Connie was decidedly hostile when he called on her, Lil having made a diplomatic exit.

'I'll kill that Lil for telling you where I am,' she said, having offered him a seat in a small, untidy living room.

'It wasn't her fault,' he explained, 'I plied her with wine at luncheon.'

'You're wasting your time anyway,' she said. 'I'm not coming back.'

'I haven't come to try to persuade you,' he said. 'I just want to talk to you.'

'What is there to talk about?' she said. 'My wonderful lineage?'

'At least go back and finish your stage training,' he

425

said. 'It will break Amy's heart if you don't.'

'No.'

'Why throw away something that means so much to you just because of Ralph Jackson?'

'I can't afford it,' she said. 'I'm not living off Amy any more.'

'But you've independent means now.'

'I'd sooner starve than touch anything of my father's,' she said hotly. 'I've got an interview tomorrow for a job as a shop assistant at Selfridge's.'

'It's wrong to waste talent.'

'Maybe it is, but I'm not going to sponge on Amy anymore.'

'But you've not long to go at stage school now, have you?'

'No, but the stage is too insecure as a career anyway. Amy's told me that often enough,' she said. 'I need a steady wage now that I'm on my own.'

'But why does your relationship with Amy have to change just because you have discovered who your father really is?' he asked. 'Amy is still your cousin. She still wants to look after you until you can afford to support yourself.'

'I can't let her, everything is different now.'

'No, it isn't,' he said. 'Your being Ralph's daughter is nothing new. All that's happened is that you know about it now. What does it matter anyway? The man's dead. Forget about him.'

'I want to make a new start,' she said evasively, 'away from people who know about it.'

'You can't run away from it forever,' he said, 'it will always be there inside of you.'

'I know that,' she snapped. 'I don't need you to remind me.'

'There is a way to be free,' he said.

426

'And what's that?' she said cynically.

'Stay and face up to it among people who love you,' he said. 'If you do that, eventually it will cease to matter. If you run away, you'll always be looking over your shoulder.'

She was so pale the freckles on her nose stood out like flecks of dirt. He watched her eyes brighten momentarily before becoming dull again, 'No, there's no going back. I'd rather make my own way from now on. I'm old enough to look out for myself.'

'Why does the idea of Amy helping you offend you so much now?' he asked.

'Because I know who I really am,' she said, 'and I feel dirty and poisonous. For all I know I might have inherited his mean nature.'

Ned couldn't help laughing.

'What's so funny?'

'If you had you certainly wouldn't be behaving like this,' he explained. 'You'd have grabbed your inheritance and made as much money as you could out of it without caring where it came from. And you certainly wouldn't be worrying about being a burden to Amy.'

'Dratted inheritance,' she said. 'If he'd not left me the shares, I'd have been none the wiser.'

'The shares,' he said, snapping his fingers triumphantly. 'Of course, that's the answer.'

'What is?'

'You can free yourself from the guilt you've seen fit to burden yourself with over Amy having supported you all these years.'

'Can I?'

'Yes. Pay her back by giving her the shares,' he said. 'If you can persuade her to take them.'

Connie's interest was aroused despite herself.

'Would she want them, do you think?'

'She'd probably refuse to take them at first, because of their financial value to you,' he said, 'but once she realises how important it has become to you to pay your way, I think she'd be delighted. It would make her the majority shareholder in the business.'

'Oh, how is that?'

'Ralph put more money in than my father when they originally set up in business together, so he had more shares to make him the senior partner,' he explained. 'I have my own shares and those I inherited from my father. Amy would have a few more than me if she were to have those that were originally Ralph's as well as her own.'

'And you don't mind?'

'Good God, no.'

'Maybe I'll think about it then,' she said, managing to smile for the first time since he'd been there.

* * *

'It all came to light the Christmas that I was thirteen,' Gwen was saying to Amy. 'As you know, my family and the Coxes were very friendly and Clifford and I were bought up like cousins to Ned.'

'Yes, I know that,' said Amy.

'Well, this particular Christmas, Ned and his father and a lot of other people were at our house on Christmas night for a party. There were several other youngsters there and we left the adults drinking and chatting and went off to play a game of sardines. Ned and I always got on well together and we usually stuck together in these sort of games. Anyway, we went and hid upstairs in my parents' enormous wardrobe. We were huddled inside as quiet as mice when we heard someone come in, naturally assuming it was the other participants in the game looking for us. But it wasn't. It was my mother and Ned's father. Both a bit tiddly. It *was* Christmas night, remember. We hardly dared to breathe in there. Our parents' bedroom was strictly off limits to us and there would have been a terrible row if we were caught.

'Anyway, we could hear odd sounds, and much to our astonishment realised they were kissing or something. Then Mother started telling Harold Cox to stop, and he began to come on strong, presumably influenced by the fact that he was slightly drunk. He began to talk about an affair they had once had and how good things had been between them then and how he wanted it to be like that again. Mother told him it was all over long ago, and had only happened because they were both lonely at the time, he because his wife had died, she because her husband was out of the house a lot and very preoccupied with his work.

'Harold started to get really stroppy then and said he could make real trouble for Mother if he was to tell the truth to Ralph—that he, Harold, was actually the father of his daughter.'

It took a minute for the significance of this to register with Amy. 'So you and Ned are brother and sister?' she exclaimed at last.

'That's right,' Gwen confirmed. 'And there we were in the wardrobe, hardly able to contain ourselves. We were both thrilled to bits, but afraid to make a sound.'

'So what happened then?' asked Amy. 'Did they discover you?'

'No, Harold seemed to calm down and they went off,' she said. 'Ned and I knew the trouble we would cause if we said anything to anyone, so we didn't even

429

tell Clifford. You're the first person to be told in all these years.'

'Amazing.'

'It made such a difference to our lives. Having always been such good friends anyway, it was lovely to know we were actually related. And, of course, he being an only child had always longed for a brother or sister. My mother gave me the most precious gift in making Ned my brother, and she doesn't even realise it.'

'Why not tell her that you know?'

'No, it would upset her terribly, you know how she is about seeming to be the very epitome of respectability,' Gwen said. 'I think, after all this time, she's managed to convince herself that her affair with Harold never happened. So it's probably best to let sleeping dogs lie.'

'I expect you're right.'

'Ned and I are very close but I've never felt able to talk to him about my personal problem. It's embarrassing enough discussing it with a woman, let alone a man.'

'I can understand that.'

'Anyway, that was obviously why Mother had always been so heavy with me about sex. She was afraid I might succumb to temptation as she had and land myself in trouble before I was safely married. Hard to imagine, isn't it? My mother getting carried away by anything so vulgar as passion.'

Amy grinned. 'But all of this could lie at the root of your trouble, couldn't it?' she said. 'You could have become so subconsciously afraid to give in to your feelings as a young girl, it became an obsession.'

'I was very ashamed of my impulses when I was growing up,' Gwen said. 'Thought I was wicked to have them at all.'

'Do you feel better for having talked about it, at last?'

'Yes, I feel slightly less alone now. But I'm still afraid of not being a complete wife to David.'

'Why not talk to him about it?' Amy suggested. 'He sounds a decent type and very fond of you. I'm sure you can work through it together.'

'I don't know if I can. It seems awfully indelicate.'

'Come on, Gwen,' said Amy. 'You're a nurse, you see life in the raw every day. And both you and David are mature, intelligent people.'

'It doesn't seem to help at a time like this, though.'

'You've nothing to lose but your pride if you do tell him,' Amy pointed out. 'And everything to lose if you turn him down or marry him and have it fail because of your problem. Tell him about it. If he's as nice as he sounds, he'll see you through it. And if he doesn't want to take you, complexities and all, he isn't worth marrying anyway.'

'Put like that, I don't have a choice, do I?' said Gwen.

CHAPTER TWENTY-TWO

Having derived so much pleasure from having Connie as part of her family, Amy was shocked to hear that the girl considered herself to be in her debt. But after much persuasion from Ned, who made her see that it would boost Connie's self-esteem and help her to come to terms with her new circumstances if the shares were accepted as a gift, Amy finally agreed.

So, Connie came home and life carried on

431

outwardly much as before, though there were changes. One major change was in Amy's relationship with Connie. It altered from the authoritative maternal kind to a more balanced sort of sisterly friendship. The trauma had matured Connie. She no longer took everything for granted, and having had her eyes opened to life's harsh realities, her attitudes became more adult. Amy felt more able to converse with her at a woman-to-woman level, thus adding a whole new dimension to her life.

Another improvement was the fact that she was no longer alone. She now shared her life with Ned even though Bernie refused to give her a divorce. In the interests of her reputation as a respected businesswoman of the town, they didn't actually move in together but it was not unknown for them to appear at the same breakfast table from time to time. It was not an ideal arrangement but to defy convention altogether could affect business by diminishing her standing in the community.

Her life was also enriched by her friendship with Gwen which blossomed after their tête-à-tête. Since Gwen and Ned were so close, it made things cosy, especially as Ned and David got along well too. Gwen married David in the autumn and they moved into Floral House with Florence because of her deteriorating health. But the death of her husband had robbed the old lady of the will to live, and when she became a fatal victim of the influenza epidemic early in 1927, Gwen put the house up for sale and moved into David's home in Chiswick.

Amy was surprised. 'I thought you'd want to keep Floral House in the family?'

'Not likely,' said Gwen. 'There are too many bad

432

memories in that house. I want a new start. No point in clinging to the past now that I have such a wonderful future to look forward to.'

It would have been impossible for Amy not to feel a twinge of envy, for although life was good, it would be even better if she and Ned could be together properly.

In the spring Connie got a part in a musical comedy, and went away on tour.

'So, there's just you and me to rattle about in the house now then, Vi,' said Amy, when they had waved Connie off in a taxi with her suitcase. 'We've certainly seen some changes.'

'I'll say.'

'Forty years old now, the both of us.'

'Don't remind me,' said Violet, now plump and matronly, her brown hair streaked with grey.

Amy studied the woman who had been her friend for so many years. 'Do you ever get fed up with keeping house for me, and feel you want more from life, Vi?' she asked chattily.

'Not now,' she replied, 'I gave up all those sort of ideas long ago ... after Karl.'

'It was a pity that didn't work out.'

'That's life, innit? Some things just ain't meant to be.'

'Don't you sometimes have a yen to do a different kind of work?'

'Domestic work is all I know.'

'There must be something you've always fancied doing though,' said Amy conversationally.

'I've got me dreams, same as everyone else,' Violet said, a touch pensively.

'Really? Do tell.'

'I'd like me own little seaside boarding 'ouse,' she

433

said. 'I'd really enjoy doin' somethin' like that.'

'You'd be good at it too.'

'Mmm, I would an' all,' she agreed wistfully. 'Ah, well, there ain't no 'arm in dreamin'.'

Amy smiled affectionately. She just couldn't imagine life without Violet.

*　　*　　*

Danny Flint didn't have much time for relaxation. What little leisure he did manage to take was usually spent in entertainment establishments that didn't belong to him. Somewhere he could have a bit of a chat and a few drinks knowing that he would not be called upon to solve some crisis or other. He needed time off to recharge his batteries but he wasn't comfortable too far from his own patch.

One summer evening he was sitting at the bar of the Peacock Club watching the cabaret, when he found himself particularly impressed by a male singer. He said as much to the man sitting next to him.

'He's a talented boy,' said the man. 'I'm his manager as a matter of fact.'

'Cor, what a coincidence,' Danny said. 'I was just thinking what a good idea it would be to book 'im to sing in my clubs. He could do a night at each of 'em.' He introduced himself and gave a brief account of his business empire. 'He'd pull in the punters, right enough.'

'Did you say Bubbles is one of yours?' asked the man.

'Yeah, that's right,' said Danny proudly.

'I know it. My boy's worked there a few times.'

'Has he really?' said Danny. 'I hope my partner has booked him for the future.'

434

'I wouldn't let him work there again,' said the man.

'No?' Danny frowned. 'Why not?'

'I don't see why he should work for Bernie Banks' prices,' he explained. 'Not now he's established and in demand.'

Danny was puzzled by this because he'd never found Bernie's figures for entertainment particularly low. Quite the opposite, in fact, on thinking about it.

'Oh, well, if you will charge the earth,' said Danny, slowly sipping a cocktail.

'Huh, that's a joke!' said the man with a cynical laugh. 'I realise you club proprietors cut your costs to meet your overheads, but Bernie Banks wants top-class performers at beginner's fees.'

'Does he now?'

'He certainly does. I went along with him for a while because my boy needed the work. But then I took a stand. We don't have to put up with that sort of exploitation any more.'

'I'll have a word with Bernie about it,' said Danny. 'And see what can be done.'

The man handed Danny his card. 'I'm always willing to talk business.'

'I'll be in touch,' said Danny, and left without finishing his drink.

*　　　*　　　*

Danny found Bernie sitting at the bar of Bubbles holding court to a group of spellbound punters, for Bernie on form could match any professional entertainer.

'Anyway, there's this bloke, yer see, and he goes to the doctor's and he says to 'im...'

Waiting until the tale was complete, Danny said,

435

'I'd like a word in private, mate.'

'Sure.' Bernie took him upstairs to the office and offered him a seat. 'So, what can I do for yer?'

'I need your books for last year, if you've got 'em handy.' As the accounts for all the clubs were looked after by the same accountant, Danny didn't think the request would cause undue suspicion.

'Why are they wanted?' asked Bernie calmly, though inwardly quaking at the possible complications for him in this development.

'The accountant wants 'em,' Danny lied smoothly. 'As I was passing through the area I said I'd collect 'em, save him sending someone over 'specially.'

'Is there a problem then?' asked Bernie, going over to the filing cabinet and opening a drawer.

'No, just some routine query or other, I think,' Danny said with contrived casualness. 'I dunno what it is, though. But then, who does know what goes on in the minds of accountants?'

The strain on Bernie's nervous system eased. This sudden interest in the books was obviously nothing to worry about. How could it be anyway? There was no way Danny could have found out about his little bit of perks. It was odd that the accountant wanted books that were finished and done with, though. 'Here yer go,' he said, gathering the file that was filled with all the relevant papers.

'Ta, mate, I'll bring 'em back to you as soon as he's finished with 'em.'

'Any time,' said Bernie. 'Now, are yer gonna have a drink with me?'

'Sure,' said Danny, because he didn't want to arouse Bernie's suspicions and put him on his guard. 'Just lead me to the bar.'

After Danny left, Bernie was feeling relaxed and happy, partly due to some good malt whisky but mostly because he felt safe again, after an uneasy period when Danny had first mentioned the books. His partner's visit had turned out to be quite pleasant, after all. They had had a few drinks together and a lot of laughs. Danny had been in a good mood and obviously didn't suspect a thing.

Feeling his usual sociable self, Bernie sat at the bar chatting to customers then took a wander among the tables near the dance floor, making sure everyone was happy. Later, in his office in sentimental mood, he felt a sudden urge to speak to Amy about this divorce she wanted. It had occurred to him just lately that perhaps his wisest course would be to give her her freedom and win back her friendship. He missed having contact with her, and she had made it obvious that there would be no sort of association at all between them while he insisted on staying legally married to her.

Why he had been so unco-operative, he didn't know. After all, she was right when she said he didn't want the ties of marriage. He could only put his stubbornness down to the fact that he did actually love the woman. Sometimes he even wished he could change his ways. The part of him that wanted Amy occasionally felt the urge to be the honest, upright family man. The other, realistic bit knew he couldn't live without the thrill of villainy.

He looked at his watch. It was turned one o'clock. Early for a small hours person like himself, but late for someone like Amy who lived a more conventional life. Given the importance of what he had to say to

437

her, he dialled her number.

*　　　*　　　*

Danny arrived home in his West End flat, poured himself a scotch and sat down on the sofa with the Bubbles accounts on his lap. He'd been in business a long time. He knew when something didn't smell right. He took a long swallow from his glass, set it down on the occasional table and opened the file. He didn't know exactly what he was looking for, but he knew he would recognise it when he saw it.

He leafed through various receipts and invoices for money spent in the line of business. Stationery; typewriter ribbons; laundry of tablecloths; monthly accounts from the butcher, the baker, the greengrocer. After scrutinising all these to find them to be in order, he passed on. What was this? A carpenter's bill for repairs to the foyer doors—eight pounds. It seemed a bit steep for a minor repair. Deciding on a closer look, he took a magnifying glass from his bureau drawer and held it over the figure. As he suspected, the eight had been altered from something else, indistinguishable under the new ink. The difference from the other figures was barely discernible. But it was there. And doubtless covered a lesser amount.

Working his way through the file, he found plenty more altered bills. None from regular suppliers because that would have been too easily checked, but all for casual labour and entertainers. So Bernie had been systematically milking the business and robbing his partner blind. A little bit of perks now and then might have been forgiveable, but this was downright greed. He'd obviously made a fortune over the years.

And all off my back, thought Danny furiously. Well, he's a fool if he thinks he can get away with it. I warned him what would happen. He picked up the phone and dialled the number of his henchman, a professional heavy called Big Joe.

'Get yourself over here right away,' he said.

And because Danny was one of the best payers in town, the man said, 'Righto, guv.'

Danny went to a drawer in his bureau and took out a gun.

*　　*　　*

'Hello,' said Amy sleepily, having staggered downstairs to the hall to answer the telephone.

''Ello, Amy, it's Bernie.'

'You?' she said crossly. 'Fancy phoning me at this hour.'

'Sorry.'

'It had better be something important to warrant waking me up in the middle of the night,' she said, yawning heavily.

'It is.'

'Out with it then so I can go back to bed.'

'I've decided to go along with you on this divorce idea,' he said.

'You have?'

'Yeah, I'll do whatever you want.'

'Oh, Bernie, that is good news,' she said with a sudden change of mood. 'Under those circumstances, you're forgiven for waking me up.'

'P'raps we can be friends again now?' he said chirpily.

'I hope so, though divorce proceedings can get very ugly, so I've heard. It can turn friends into enemies.'

'Yeah, well, if we're prepared for that, it might not be so bad.'

'Thanks for seeing it my way.'

'I'm sorry I've been so awkward about it.'

'Forget it.'

'There's never been anyone else but you, you know.'

'I know that, and we'll always be friends.' She steered the conversation to a less emotive topic, 'How are things at the club?'

'Sweet as a nut.'

'Good.'

There was a silence. 'Bernie, are you still there?'

'Yeah, but I'll 'ave to go, some people have just turned up.'

'I'll talk to you again soon,' she said, but the line was already dead.

*   *   *

'Danny,' said Bernie brightly, trying to hide the crippling fear that engulfed him on seeing his partner's black expression. 'Back already?'

'That's right.'

'Did you forget something?'

'Not me, mate,' he said coldly. 'I think you're the one with the bad memory.'

'I am?' Bernie said innocently. ''Ow do yer make that out?'

'You've conveniently forgotten to tell me about all the money you've been taking out of the business, ain't yer?' he said, moving towards Bernie at the desk with his henchman at his side.

'I dunno what you're on about,' blustered Bernie shakily.

440

Danny didn't reply but turned to Big Joe and nodded. Bernie's eyes widened in horror as the man pulled a revolver from his pocket and pointed it at him.

'All right, where is it?' demanded Danny.

'Where's what?'

'The dough you've been nicking, what else?'

'Dough?'

'You couldn't 'ave spent it because you never go anywhere. And you wouldn't have bin fool enough to go near a bank with it.' He paused. 'You've split up with yer missus, so the money has gotta be here on these premises somewhere.'

'Money?' He could hardly utter the word, he was trembling so much.

'Don't upset me even more by acting the innocent,' Danny rasped. 'Come on, hand it over.'

Bernie was paralysed with terror. A cold sweat suffused his skin and he couldn't breathe properly. The only thing in the room seemed to be the barrel of the gun pointing at him. 'All right, I'll get it,' he managed at last.

Plodding along in his ungainly way, he led them into his living quarters, feeling the hard point of the gun nudging into his back. He walked through a small, cluttered living room into the kitchen, clean and tidy and rarely used by Bernie whose meals usually came from the club kitchens.

'I 'ope you ain't thinking of pulling any tricks,' said Danny, glancing around this scene of domestic bliss.

'No tricks,' said the terrified Bernie, opening the larder door. He took out an enamel bread bin and set it down on the wooden table. Removing a false tin panel at the back, he produced a roll of bank notes and handed them to Danny. 'It's all there, give or

441

take a pound or two.'

Danny's eyes narrowed quizzically. 'Why did you do it? You were making a good living, you didn't need to rob me.'

Bernie shrugged. 'Because it was so easy, I s'pose,' he said, through parched lips.

The other man stuffed the money into his jacket pocket without counting it. 'You just can't keep your fingers out of the till, can you?'

'Come on, Danny, you're a man o' the world, you know that everyone's at it.'

'Not the people I choose to work with. You're a fool. You had good money, and a comfortable life, but still you weren't satisfied. I warned you what would 'appen if you cheated on me. Con your grannie if you must, but not your business partner. Not if 'is name happens to be Danny Flint.'

'I've bin stupid, I admit...'

'It's a bit late in the day to realise it.'

'Tell your man to put the gun away, for Gawdsake,' said Bernie, mopping his brow with a handkerchief. 'He's making me nervous.'

'You and me could 'ave gone from strength to strength if you'd played it straight,' continued Danny as though Bernie hadn't spoken. 'You could 'ave built this place up and we'd both 'ave been able to take more from it. The trade is all there, more than enough for everyone, and you're a natural for the job. But playing things straight just ain't your style, is it, Bernie? You just can't control that greed of yours.'

'You've got most of the money back now,' said Bernie shakily. 'And I'll not do anything like it again, I promise you that.'

'I know you won't,' said Danny ominously.

Bernie stared at the barrel of the gun. 'Tell 'im to

put that bloody thing away, Danny,' he said again.
'You've made your point.'

'Not quite, Bernie,' he said. 'Not quite.'

Danny turned to Big Joe and nodded. The
henchman took aim.

'Now stop playin' games, Danny,' said Bernie.
'You've got me sweatin', I admit it. Now you've 'ad
yer fun, tell 'im to stop flashin' the shooter about.'

The silencer on the gun rendered the shot almost
noiseless.

'Come on, let's get out of 'ere, Joe,' said Danny.

And the two men left the club quietly through the
back door.

*　　*　　*

The police came to Amy's house early the next
morning. Bernie had been found dead in his kitchen
by one of the cleaners, they told her. Murdered, they
said. She couldn't believe it.

As his next-of-kin she was needed to identify the
body formally. Violet went with her to the mortuary.
Stunned, Amy forced herself through this terrible
duty. 'Yes, that's my husband,' she said, when they
lifted the sheet.

*　　*　　*

A sea of dark umbrellas covered a large area of
Bethnal Green cemetery that wet August day when
they buried him. The rain poured down relentlessly
from angry grey skies, making the ground muddy
underfoot. It trickled off the edges of Amy's umbrella
on to her clothes as she stood at the graveside with
Ned, Violet and her mother, all respectfully attired in

443

black. Victor had come down from the North, where he had been assigned to his first teaching post, and stood nearby with Connie. Dickie was away at sea and unable to be present.

Shocked disbelief prevailed among the mourners. Admittedly, Bernie had been a petty crook, but never violent and always good to his mum and dad. The locals didn't like the idea of one of their own coming to such a tragic end, even if he was a villain. There were those, of course, who said he had had it coming to him, but they weren't at the funeral.

Amy couldn't explain to anyone how sad and regretful she felt at this time. Although it did not detract from her love for Ned, she felt as though she had suffered a major loss. It was as though part of her was being buried along with Bernie.

Why couldn't he have settled for an ordinary life like the rest of us? she asked herself. Why was he so attracted to crime? She looked across at his elderly father, darkly clad beneath his dripping umbrella, his head tilted mournfully towards the coffin as they lowered it into the ground. Maybe if he hadn't sent Bernie out thieving when he was only eight years old, things might have been different.

But passing blame wouldn't bring him back. It was strongly rumoured that his partner had murdered him for cheating him out of money, though the police hadn't made an arrest. Lack of evidence, apparently. Friends of Danny Flint swore he had been with them at the time of the murder. There was no doubt in Amy's mind that Bernie's dishonesty had brought about his untimely end, whoever had actually pulled the trigger. The truth would probably never come out. It was common knowledge that gangsters protected each other in situations like this.

After putting in a duty appearance at the funeral tea at Bernie's father's place, Amy gathered her sad little party together and left, feeling very much older somehow.

CHAPTER TWENTY-THREE

One day in the early summer of 1928, Amy stood on the platform at Victoria station seeing Violet off to a new life by the sea. Amy and Ned had moved Amy's mother down last week, but Violet had stayed on in London to help the newlyweds move house. Amy and Ned had married last month and sold both their houses and bought a property near Ealing Common in which to make a fresh start.

With the money left over from the sale, Amy had supplied the cash for Violet and her mother to purchase a small boarding house in Brighton which they were to run together.

'I'll miss you like mad,' said Amy to Violet who was hanging out of the carriage window.

'And I won't 'alf miss you, an' all,' said Violet, eyes moist but cheeks flushed with excitement.

'You will write?'

'Course I will. And we'll see yer when you come down to stay.' She sniffed into her handkerchief. 'Yer will come, won't yer?'

'Try and keep us away,' she said, 'but it won't be the same as having you around all the time.'

'No, course not, but things can't stay the same forever.'

'That's true.'

'Thanks for giving me the chance to do something

of me own.'

'It's the least I can do after all the years of service you've given me.'

Violet clutched Amy's hand. 'So much 'as happened since I've known you. It's a different world now to when we first met.'

Indeed it was, thought Amy, glancing around at the other women on the platform with their bobbed hair and cloche hats and low-waisted functional clothes. When she thought of those floor-length dresses they used to drag around in whilst trapped in the confines of whalebone! In the spring of this year the campaign of the suffragettes had finally come to an end when the vote was given to all women of twenty-one and over. And only the other day, America's Amelia Earhart had become the first woman to fly the Atlantic. It hardly seemed possible that when she'd first met Violet even the ubiquitous motor car had been a rarity.

But some things never change, she thought, seeing some ragged street urchins begging on the other side of the barrier from well-dressed people like herself.

The whistle blew. The guard shouted for people to mind the doors. Violet gave Amy one last hug and was still waving as the train drew slowly away from the steam-shrouded platform.

Amy stood where she was for a few moments after Violet had disappeared from sight, gulping back the tears. The movement of the train seemed to symbolise the passing of time. For twenty-eight years Violet had been a part of her life, yet in some ways it seemed as though just twenty-eight minutes had passed. What did the next thirty years have in store? she wondered. Would Connie become famous? Would they ever bring Bernie's murderer to justice?

446

Shrugging off thoughts of the past, she walked back along the platform towards the booking office to buy a ticket for a District line train to Ealing and her new life with Ned.